THE
FALLEN
4

THE
FALLEN
4

FORSAKEN

Thomas E. Sniegoski

Simon Pulse

New York London Toronto Sydney New Delhi

SIMON PULSE

An imprint of Simon & Schuster Children's Publishing Division
1230 Avenue of the Americas, New York, NY 10020
First Simon Pulse paperback edition August 2012
Copyright © 2012 by Thomas E. Sniegoski
All rights reserved, including the right of reproduction in whole or in part in any form.
SIMON PULSE and colophon are registered trademarks of Simon & Schuster, Inc.
For information about special discounts for bulk purchases, please contact
Simon & Schuster Special Sales at 1-866-506-1949 or business@simonandschuster.com.
The Simon & Schuster Speakers Bureau can bring authors to your live event. For more
information or to book an event contact the Simon & Schuster Speakers Bureau at
1-866-248-3049 or visit our website at www.simonspeakers.com.
Designed by Karina Granda
The text of this book was set in Adobe Garamond.
Manufactured in the United States of America
2 4 6 8 10 9 7 5 3
The Library of Congress Cataloging-in-Publication Data
Sniegoski, Tom.
Forsaken / Thomas E. Sniegoski. — 1st Simon Pulse pbk. ed.
p. cm. — (The fallen ; 4)
Summary: As the war between Heaven and Hell rages on, half angel and half human
Aaron and the other Nephilim are determined to protect humanity, but when casualties
mount around them, Aaron and his beloved Vilma's loyalty and faith will be tested.
ISBN 978-1-4424-4699-1
[1. Angels—Fiction. 2. Good and evil—Fiction. 3. Love—Fiction.
4. Supernatural—Fiction.] I. Title.
PZ7.S68033Fo 2012
[Fic]—dc23
2012012489
ISBN 978-1-4424-4700-4 (eBook)

For John Fogg—fighting the good fight

Thank you to my wife, LeeAnne, who deserves so much for all that she does. And to Kirby for allowing me the pleasure of his company.

And always to Mulder.

Big thanks also go out to Chris Golden, Annette Pollert, Liesa Abrams and James Mignogna, Erek Vaehne, Mom and Dad Sniegoski, Kate Schafer Testerman, Mom and Dad Fogg, Pete Donaldson, Dave and Kathy Kraus, Paul Deane, and Timothy Cole and the Abominations of Desolation down at Cole's Comics in the City of Sin.

I bid you good day.

—Tom

PROLOGUE

J eremy Fox thought he might be sick.

Not the kind of sick where his head hurt and his insides might shoot up his throat, but the kind of sick that he thought might be the end of him.

He thought he might be about to die.

He could still feel the effects of the wormy thing that had been inside his head, setting up house, taking control of his body and making him fight his friends.

Jeremy remembered fighting Aaron. Part of him had struggled not to hurt the leader of the Nephilim, but another part—not so much.

'Cause if Aaron were dead, Vilma would be mine.

He quickly stamped on the thought, ashamed that his fevered mind had even gone there. Instead he blamed that crazy idea on the foul creature that had tried to control him.

Yeah, that's right. It was all the worm's fault.

He'd hated to leave his Nephilim brothers and sisters, but he'd been compelled to do so. His mother's psychic cry had been like a hook inside his brain, pulling him from the old Saint Athanasius School to where she wanted him to be.

Jeremy opened his wings as he appeared in his mother's room at the Steward Psychiatric Facility. As they furled upon his back, he fell forward, as though the life had been taken from his body. Lying there on the cold linoleum floor, he became aware that it was not only his physical form that felt like it was dying, but his spiritual one as well.

Though his body had been seriously hurt in his battle with Aaron and because of his attempts at purging the wormlike monster that had possessed his actions, the Nephilim side of his nature sensed that the world around him had been savagely injured too.

Something horrible had happened to the world.

His body was suddenly racked with painful spasms, and he curled into a tight ball. "Mum," he managed through tightly clenched teeth.

"There, son," he heard her say. She knelt beside him, pulling his shaking form into her spindly arms. "Put these on now. It'll help with the cold."

Jeremy suddenly realized that he was still naked after his struggle to purge the evil creature that had taken up residence inside his skull. Gabriel's touch had healed his body, but it hadn't given him new clothes.

It took nearly everything he had left to uncurl from the fetal position and take the blue scrubs his mother offered him.

"That's a boy," she cooed as he pulled the short-sleeved top over his head and then awkwardly got to his feet to slip on the drawstring pants.

"Something awful has happened," he said to his mother, who was no longer in the hospital gown he'd last seen her wearing but was now in her coat. She looked as if she were ready to leave. He helped her up from where she still knelt on the floor.

"It's too late to do anything about that," she said, walking away from him to retrieve her purse, which rested on her chest of drawers in the corner of the room.

Slinging the purse over her arm, she turned to him and smiled.

"Ah, look at you," she said, head tilting wistfully to one side. "If only the fates had chosen the physician's path for you."

For a moment he hadn't any idea what she was getting on about. Then he realized she was talking about the scrubs he wore.

"Sorry to be a disappointment," he said. "Where'd you get these anyway?" he asked as he slipped a pair of black shoes onto his bare feet.

"I saw that you'd be needing something when I called out to you, so I helped myself to a poke about the nurses' station while they were otherwise occupied," she said. She hurried toward the door and peeked out through its window, careful to not be seen. "The hallway's clear now. If we move quickly we can—"

His mother had started to open the door, but he'd reached across and slammed it closed again.

"We're not going anywhere until you tell me what's going on," Jeremy said. His mother had been in and out of psychiatric hospitals for most of his childhood, and even though she seemed relatively rational at the moment, he wasn't about to blindly follow her anywhere.

"We don't have time for this, luv," she told him.

"Mum, you need to tell me," Jeremy said. "When you reached out, you said something about helping a child."

She looked him hard in the eyes, and Jeremy saw his mother as he hadn't seen her in a very long time. She seemed sane, and he was stricken by the intensity of her stare.

"I haven't the time to explain." She lay her hand upon his cheek. "The longer we wait, the bigger the chance that they'll find him."

"Find who?" Jeremy questioned.

She abruptly turned away and opened the door before he could stop her. "Every second we spend talking brings them that much closer to him," she whispered urgently.

Jeremy followed his mother down the hallway, scouting for hospital staff, and finding the corridor strangely empty. He could hear the droning of a telly broadcast off in the distance, and figured everyone was likely watching BBC One announcing the impending end of the world.

His body still ached from fighting his friends back in America, and his skin was still sensitive where it had blistered and burned away, but Jeremy ignored the pain. He hustled after his mother as she disappeared through another door at the end of the corridor. He had no idea where she was leading him, but he couldn't take the risk of her hurting herself as she wandered around the old hospital.

They ran down another hall and then an old stone staircase, the fluorescent lights above flickering eerily as they descended.

"Quickly, Jeremy," she urged, one hand clutching the railing for safety, the other her large purse.

His mother stopped before a metal door.

"It's locked," she said.

"Yeah, and what do you want me to do about it?" he asked. He gave the handle a twist just to be sure.

"You need to open it," she told him matter-of-factly.

"Well, I've left my bloody lock picks at home," Jeremy said, growing more frustrated and impatient with the situation.

"Is that any way to talk to your mother?"

Jeremy immediately felt ashamed. "I can't see myself kicking down a metal door," he said tritely.

"Think, luv." She tapped the side of her head with a skinny finger. "Use what God has given you."

He had no idea what she was getting on about, and she must have seen this in his befuddled expression.

"Your fire. Does this look like an obstacle that could withstand the fires of Heaven?"

Jeremy felt like a bloody idiot as he called forth a weapon of fire. Picturing the weapon in his mind, he watched it take shape in his hand. It wasn't his favorite battle-ax—that seemed a bit extreme. Instead it was a sword.

"What a marvelous gift," his mother said, smiling proudly.

"Isn't it, though," he agreed. He clutched the hilt of the blade and thrust it forward. The sword melted through the door with barely a hiss, leaving a puddle of molten metal on the concrete floor as he cut away the lock.

His mother started forward, but Jeremy held out a hand to stop her.

"Careful now," he instructed. "It's still hot."

Jeremy carefully pulled the heavy door open, and allowed his mother to pass into another darkened corridor. There was a strange feeling in the air. Jeremy considered keeping the blade alight, but thought perhaps a sword of fire might give them away. Instead he allowed his hand to surge with fire so that it would throw off just enough light to see by.

"Next best thing to a torch," he said. "So there's a child somewhere down here?" The concrete hall seemed to go on forever.

"There is," his mother said. "A very special child, one that must leave with us if he's going to live up to his promise."

Jeremy stopped, reaching for his mother's sleeve with his non-burning hand.

"Leave with us?" he questioned. "Are you saying that—"

"Ah, here we are," she said as she reached another door. This one appeared quite old, and was made out of heavy, dark wood. His mother daintily knocked.

There was no response, so Jeremy summoned his ax of fire. It looked as if something a little heavier might be required to open this door. He was just about to tell his mother to stand back, when the sound of a metal latch sliding back was followed by a click as the door was unlocked. It began to open.

"You can put that thing away," she said, moving to greet whoever was on the other side.

His mother let out a sharp cry as the barrel of a pistol was placed against her forehead.

"How did you get down here?" a man asked as he stepped out from behind the door. He was an older man, dressed in a doctor's lab coat, his shock of white hair looking as though it hadn't been brushed in quite some time.

Jeremy didn't recognize the man at first, in the dim light of the tunnel, but then realized that he was one of his mother's doctors.

"Dr. Troughton, it's me," his mother said carefully. "Irene."

The doctor looked at her strangely. "Miss Fox?" he asked. "Miss Fox, what are you doing down here? It's not at all safe. You should be in bed." He chastised her, but he did not lower the pistol.

"I'm supposed to be here, Doctor," she told him. "We've come for the child."

Troughton looked as though he'd been slapped. "Child? I—I don't have any idea what you're talking about," he sputtered, stepping back to close the door. "Go back to your room at once, and tell the nurse that—"

"We've come for the child." Jeremy's mother reached out to hold the door. "My son and I." She glanced back at Jeremy with a smile.

"Your son," Dr. Troughton repeated, taking a look for himself.

Jeremy still held his burning ax and did nothing to hide it.

"We're supposed to have him," his mother said. "Let us in before it's too late."

The doctor seemed confused, his mouth quivering, unable to release the words he wanted to say. He pointed the gun at Jeremy.

Instinct kicked in then. Jeremy's wings of smoky gray suddenly manifested and in one powerful push sent him hurtling through the air, as he brought the blade of the battle-ax down.

His mother screamed as Troughton stumbled back, holding the remains of his firearm. Jeremy's cut had been precise, slicing the barrel but sparing the doctor's fingers.

"I don't care for guns," Jeremy snarled as his wings furled closed.

Troughton dropped the remains of the gun to the floor.

"Oh, m-my," the doctor stammered, running a tremulous

hand across his brow, which was shiny with sweat. "We were told to expect someone . . . but I never would have imagined it would be you," he said to Jeremy's mother.

She smiled. "Can we see the boy?"

"The boy?" Jeremy interjected.

"Yes, it's a baby boy," his mother said, turning her attention back to Troughton.

"Of course you can see him," the doctor said, motioning them into the passage. "Quickly now. We haven't much time."

The doctor pulled the heavy door closed behind them and slid the dead bolt home.

Without another word he walked them along another stone hallway, which pitched downward, traveling even deeper below the psychiatric hospital.

Jeremy's curiosity was getting the better of him. He was about to ask the doctor where the passage led, when they passed through another doorway into an even larger chamber that looked as though it might once have been the hospital's laundry. A small medical staff awaited them.

"Dr. Troughton?" asked a younger doctor of Pakistani descent.

"It's all right, Rajat," the doctor said. "These are the ones we've been waiting for."

Jeremy's mother waved. "Hello!" she called out, her display causing Rajat and the others to look at each other with concern.

"Where's the child?" Troughton asked.

"Bea has taken him to be cleaned up," a woman in nurse's attire said.

"And the mother?" Troughton strode to a curtained-off area and pulled the drape back.

"She expired less than five minutes ago," Rajat said.

Dr. Troughton walked away from the bed, and Jeremy caught sight of the body of a young girl—she couldn't have been any older than sixteen—lying there, as pale as a ghost. He didn't know why, but he felt drawn to her, even though he would have preferred to look away.

"Who was she?" he asked. *She was pretty,* he thought. *Even in death she's pretty.*

Nobody answered him, so Jeremy asked a little bit louder, and a little more forcefully.

"I asked, who was she?"

The nurse looked to Troughton and Rajat. "We don't know," she answered, walking to the bed and covering the corpse with a blanket.

"What do you mean you don't know?" Jeremy asked. "There's a dead girl lying here, and you haven't a clue as to who she was?"

"She was the vessel for the child," Troughton said. "That's all we know . . . all we're supposed to know."

Right then a newborn squalled, and a woman in scrubs emerged from the back of the chamber, carrying an infant swaddled in a green hospital blanket.

"Oh, there's the little tinker," Jeremy's mother said as she headed for the baby, her arms outstretched.

The nurse looked to Troughton, terrified. The doctor nodded, and begrudgingly the nurse handed her the babe.

"Aren't you darling," Jeremy's mother said, bouncing the fussing child until he began to quiet. She carried the baby over to Jeremy, pulling down the blanket for him to see.

"Look at him," she said, enraptured by the newborn. "Have you ever seen anything so perfect?"

Jeremy hadn't been around babies much, and they made him very nervous with all that crying.

"Now what?" he asked his mother.

"We take him somewhere safe."

Jeremy couldn't stand it anymore. "Mum, it's a *baby*," he said. "Why are we the ones to have him? You're gonna have to give me something more."

The baby began to cry again, and his mother gently shushed the child until he quieted down.

"He's supposed to be with us," she told Jeremy. "That's all you really need to know right now."

Jeremy wasn't used to such resolution—such sanity—from his mother. "Mum, it's—" he began.

"We are to protect him with our lives," she interrupted. "Or what we see in the world now . . . what you're feeling now? It will all be so much worse."

Jeremy was about to question her more, when he noticed

the others' activity. They hurried about, attending to several clocklike devices throughout the room.

"Hold on here," Jeremy bellowed.

Rajat squatted near one of the devices on an old, wooden folding table, activated it, and moved on to the next.

"Those are bombs?" Jeremy asked.

"Yes," Rajat replied. "And they'll go off in a minute's time."

"Are you bloody insane?" Jeremy roared.

"The child's birth . . . ," Troughton started to explain, but he looked as though he were having a difficult time. "The child coming into this world—they're going to know about it."

"Who?" Jeremy demanded. "Who's going to know about it?"

"The Architects," Troughton said. "The Architects will come, but he'll be gone. Gone with you. No one will be alive to tell them anything."

"The Architects? Who are the bloody Architects?"

And then it hit him like a physical blow.

"Wait a second. Nobody here alive?" Jeremy asked aloud. "You're not planning on being here when the bombs—"

Rajat took a seat on the floor near one of the explosives. The nurses did the same.

"We're ready, Doctor," Rajat said with grim finality.

Troughton nodded, reaching into the pocket of his lab coat and removing a remote control.

"This is bloody madness!" Jeremy exclaimed. He looked

to his mother, who was still trying to calm the fussy newborn. "Mum, do you hear this?"

"We have to go, Jeremy," she replied.

A high-pitched beep sounded as the timers began their countdown.

"Godspeed," Troughton said. "Keep the child safe."

"From the Architects, whoever they are," Jeremy mumbled, going to his mother's side.

"From the Architects and the evil of the world at large," Troughton said as he lowered himself to the floor, leaning against the stone wall with a sigh.

"Jeremy!" his mother insisted.

There wasn't enough time to go out the way they'd come.

Jeremy called forth his wings and pictured where he wanted to go, away from the hospital. The timer was down to seconds as he wrapped his mother and the newborn within his wings' feathered embrace.

0:5

He took one last look at these people who had brought this supposedly special child into the world. *Who are you? Who told you to do this?*

0:3

Their mouths were moving as they sat there, waiting for their inevitable demise, each of them reciting what could only have been some sort of prayer.

0:1

A prayer for the dying.

0:0

Jeremy, his mother, and the baby appeared at the edge of a stretch of beautifully manicured lawn, which Jeremy remembered strolling across with his mother during one of their visits. They were farthest away from the older, more Gothic buildings of the hospital complex and directly behind the newer buildings that housed the patients.

They watched as, with a roar and the shattering of glass, one of the old buildings fell in upon itself. Fire and black smoke billowed out, as if Hell itself were forcing its way up from the bowels of the earth, clawing its way up into the world above.

"What are we doing, Mum?" Jeremy asked as clouds of smoke filled the sky and tongues of orange flame licked at the surrounding buildings.

"We need to get ourselves and Roger—"

"Roger?"

"That's his name," his mother said. "Until he can tell us otherwise. Why? Doesn't he look like Roger to you?"

"He looks like trouble to me," Jeremy said. "But that's beside the point."

"Don't you worry your head about a thing," Jeremy's mother said, cradling the sleeping child in her arms. "You just leave this up to your old mum."

Off in the distance Jeremy could hear alarm bells and wailing sirens. He knew that they had to leave this place before they were seen, or whoever . . . or whatever . . . came after the baby. After Roger. Jeremy called out his wings again.

"Where to?"

"Someplace with peace and quiet. Someplace by the sea? We always loved the sea, didn't we, son?"

It was the one thing that they could agree upon at the moment, and he closed his eyes, envisioning a very special place.

They always had loved the sea.

CHAPTER ONE

No matter how he looked at it, the Nephilim had failed. Troubled thoughts played through Aaron Corbet's mind, over and over again, day in and day out as he fought the forces of darkness that had risen because of the Nephilim's monumental defeat.

With the sound of fluttering wings and the rending of time and space, Aaron returned to the abandoned Saint Athanasius School and Orphanage, which had become the Nephilim's home. He smelled of the sweat of violence, and was covered in the blood of monsters. Even the small victories they managed were not enough to take away the true stink of their failure.

Aaron opened his wings in the former library that now served as their television room, to see that he wasn't the first to return. He could hear the chatter of one of the twenty-four-hour news channels they always had on now.

The Nephilim, the blending of humanity and the angelic in the perfect amalgam of God's most cherished creations, were supposed to keep the world from harm. They had fought hard against those who had considered them a blight in the eyes of God, and had won the honor of being the earth's protectors against the unnatural.

But then a heavenly threat had arisen. The Abomination of Desolation, an angel of destruction, had come to the world of man. He'd believed the earth was ripe with evil, and had attempted to destroy the planet.

The Nephilim had fought valiantly. Many had sacrificed their lives for what was only a partial victory. They had prevented the Abomination from ending the world, but they had not been able to stop it from severing the world's ties to God and Heaven.

And now humanity was suffering. Creatures that had hidden in shadow began to emerge to claim their stake in a world that seemed to have been abandoned by the Lord.

The first thing Aaron's eyes locked upon in the room was Vilma, and he was reminded of how beautiful his girlfriend was, and how much he loved her.

As if sensing his stare, Vilma turned to look at him. Behind her, Kraus, their resident healer, worked to clean up the newest injuries of the other two Nephilim who'd been out on their own missions. Melissa seemed to have injured her hand. It was bandaged, and she flexed and released it, testing her range of motion, as Kraus tended to a nasty-looking gash on Cameron's cheek.

"Are they all right?" Aaron asked Vilma as she came toward him.

Hearing his voice, Gabriel, who had been sleeping in a patch of sunshine, jumped to his feet with a loud bark and ran to his master.

"They're fine, but I should be asking you the same question," Vilma said, eyeing him.

Aaron looked down at himself. His clothes were caked with blood and the filth of violent death.

"You stink," Gabriel said, then sneezed violently.

"Sorry." Aaron shrugged.

Earlier he had seen a report on CNN that monsters had taken up residence under the Golden Gate Bridge, preventing any travel between San Francisco and Marin County. Local law enforcement, and even the National Guard, had been called in to deal with these creatures identified as a species of Asian troll called Oni—but the loss of life had been great.

People . . . civilians . . . were not meant to deal with creatures such as these, which was why he had stepped in. Normally Aaron wouldn't have gone alone, but there were other threats, other beasts emerging around the world, so they'd split up.

So many monsters out there now, and so few Nephilim.

"It's not my blood," Aaron replied. He flexed the muscles in his back, drawing his black wings beneath his flesh. He suddenly felt spasms of pain across his body, and stumbled slightly, dropping to one knee on the floor. "Well, not all of it anyway."

Vilma was by his side in an instant.

"Think the fight might have taken a little bit more out of me than I thought," Aaron said.

He'd flown to the Golden Gate and attacked before the little bit of sunlight had gone. Since the Abomination had cut off the world from heaven, the daylight hours were becoming shorter, the darkness falling earlier and earlier all around the world. Having confronted creatures like the Oni before, he knew that they disliked the daylight and would likely remain beneath the bridge while the sun was shining.

The trolls had been like sitting ducks, huddled together in a filthy group of fur and fang. Aaron remembered a time, not too long ago, when launching an attack on an unsuspecting enemy would have bothered him, would have made him think that he was somehow being unfair.

But that was before he'd started to bury his friends, and seen these nightmarish monsters feed upon the remains of the dead.

"Unmerciful" would probably be the best word to define him these days, and he found that very sad.

"Are you all right, Aaron?" Gabriel asked, coming in very close to sniff his face.

"I'm fine, boy." Aaron reached out to pet his dog's head. "Just a little tired."

"It's a wonder that you're still able to function at all,"

Vilma said, getting beneath one of his arms and helping Aaron to stand. "How much sleep have you had in the last few days? Be honest with me."

Vilma steered him over to where Kraus was finishing up with Cameron.

"Not much," he answered, wincing in pain as he sat in one of the old wooden chairs that had been left behind when the school had been abandoned.

Vilma stepped back, and Kraus went to work.

"Remove your shirt," he told Aaron in a no-nonsense tone.

Aaron tried, but he just couldn't seem to get the shirt up over his head.

"For Heaven's sake," Vilma said, rushing over to help him pull the bloody T-shirt from his body.

"No amount of washing is going to ever get this clean again," she said, tossing the filthy garment to the floor.

"Hey," Aaron said without much conviction. "That's one of my best shirts."

Gabriel sniffed at the filthy pile of cloth, and the hackles on his golden back rose like quills.

"Trolls," the Labrador said in the language of his breed. *"I don't like trolls at all."*

"The Oni aren't very likeable," Aaron confirmed as Kraus worked, cleaning up various bites and scratches.

Considering the level of combat he'd encountered, Aaron was surprised that he hadn't sustained more damage. He'd gone right at the Oni nest beneath the bridge, attacking with a sword of heavenly fire. The Oni hadn't cared for that in the least. Many had risked the pain of daylight to crawl from their hiding places and confront him.

He remembered the stink of their fur as they'd burned with the touch of his sword and the rays of the sun, and felt himself grow nauseous. The air had become saturated with the smell as he'd fought wave after wave of the snarling things. Beneath the suspension bridge Aaron had found the remains of people who had tried to cross, stored for later consumption in thick web-like cocoons created with Oni saliva. It was a horrible sight, and one that he doubted he would ever forget.

He'd used that memory, that horrible, disturbing memory, as he'd fought the trolls that had been responsible for such heinous acts against other living creatures, killing one after another until they were all dead.

Aaron leaned back against the chair now. His eyes were heavy with exhaustion, and he felt his head begin to nod, only to snap back up just as sleep was about to claim him.

"Is he all right, Kraus?" Vilma asked the healer as she reached out to steady Aaron.

"Unless there are internal injuries that I'm unaware of, he should be fine."

"Hear that? I'm fine," Aaron said, his eyes fluttering as he tried to stay awake. He glanced over to see Melissa and Cameron watching him, concern in their eyes.

"Are you two okay?" he asked them.

"Fine," Melissa said, holding up her bandaged hand. "I can feel it healing already."

"I'm okay too," Cameron said, touching the bandage on his cheek. "Besides, girls love scars; they add character." He laughed as Melissa punched him.

Aaron felt a pressure under his arm and looked up as Vilma pulled him up from the chair and began to lead him from the room.

"Where are we going?" he asked, trying to halt his progress.

"You need a shower, and some sleep," Vilma replied.

On the big-screen television behind him he heard the report of a city in Ukraine being besieged by what looked to be giant bats. He planted his feet to hear the rest of the news coverage.

"No," Vilma said firmly, pulling him around to face her.

"Melissa and Cameron are hurt. They aren't in any condition to go. I—" he started to explain.

"They're not going anywhere either," she interrupted, loud enough so they all could hear. "We're running ourselves ragged, and it's not going to do anybody any good at all if we're making mistakes. Mistakes could get us killed."

Gabriel stood beside her, his tail tucked and his head bowed in submission. *"She's right, Aaron."*

Aaron was going to argue, but deep down he knew that they *were* right.

"We all need to rest—to heal." Vilma looked around the

room again, certain to make eye contact with Cameron and Melissa.

"Okay," Aaron said, giving in. "We'll rest." Really, he was too damn tired to fight anyway. "Two hours. Then you wake me up. Deal?"

Vilma moved in close to him again, ushering him from the room.

"Shower first. You stink like death," she said. "Then two hours of uninterrupted sleep."

"You drive a hard bargain, Ms. Santiago." Aaron surrendered as the reports of even more horrors droned from the television in the other room.

Two hours. And then back to work.

Vilma waited until Aaron was finished with his shower, and then escorted him to bed.

He'd done exactly what she'd thought he would, telling her that he was feeling much better and much more awake, and that he could take care of those bats and be back for a rest in no time.

Vilma didn't even feel it necessary to respond. She and Gabriel escorted Aaron, wrapped in a towel, from the shower room to the bedroom they shared.

"Sleep," she commanded, pointing to the mattress.

He looked like he was about to argue, and then thought better of it. *Smart boy.*

Aaron stumbled across the room like the Corpse Riders they'd encountered not long ago. At least he now smelled better.

He fell onto the mattress, and barely had the sheet and comforter over him before he was asleep.

"Do you think he'll stay there if we leave?" Gabriel asked Vilma.

"You could stand guard if you want, but I think he's down for the count."

"And how about you?" the dog asked her.

"What about me?" she questioned, heading back to the TV room, where they'd left the others. She wanted to be sure that Melissa and Cameron were listening to her orders.

"You've taken on more responsibility as second in command, and you haven't been sleeping all that much either," Gabriel reminded her.

"I don't need that much sleep," she lied. "Never have. I was always the early riser in my family."

Which wasn't a lie, but it had had more to do with her studies in school. Those days seemed so very long ago now. She couldn't remember the last time she'd even looked at a book.

"You look tired," Gabriel said, looking up at her as they walked.

Vilma stopped, and squatted down to his level.

"I'm fine." She scratched him behind one of his golden yellow ears. "It's just that things are a little intense around here."

"I worry about you," Gabriel said, and licked her hand. *"I worry about all of you."*

She smiled, leaning forward to kiss the top of his head.

"Good ole Gabriel," she said. "It's nice to know that some-body is looking out for us."

She stood then, knees cracking as she did.

"That didn't sound good," Gabriel said.

"It felt even worse." Vilma laughed. "Must be getting old."

There was truth to what she said. Over the last few months she felt like she'd aged physically, and mentally.

She was sure that she wasn't supposed to feel this way at nineteen, but then again, most nineteen-year-olds weren't out killing beasts that seemed like they'd crawled out of Stephen King's worst nightmare.

"Or maybe you're just not taking care of yourself the way you should," the dog suggested as they walked down the hallway again. *"I'm just saying."*

"I'm not going to deny that there's some truth to what you're saying. Which is why I put Aaron to bed, and told the others to . . ." Vilma trailed off as they entered the TV room and saw Melissa's wings emerge from her back. Cameron's wings were out too, and he was about to cloak his body with them to disappear, off to who knows where.

"What the hell do you think you're doing?" Vilma asked, striding into the room.

Kraus stood silently nearby, putting away his creams and salves.

"We've had a breather," Cameron said. "There's something going on at the Great Wall of China, and an ocean liner is under attack off the coast of Africa. We thought we'd go and check things out before—"

"No," Vilma said.

Cameron gave her a quizzical smile. "What do you mean 'no'?"

"What part of 'everyone needs a rest' didn't you understand?" she asked sternly.

"I got it, but I thought you were just saying that to get Aaron to lie down for a while," Cameron explained. "We're fine," he said, looking at Melissa, who nodded in agreement. "We can handle a few more situations before we crash."

"And I said no," Vilma said with even more forcefulness.

Anger suddenly showed upon Cameron's face. "We can't just do nothing," the younger Nephilim said. "There are people dying all over the world in ways too horrible to even think about," he said, gesturing to the television screen that was reporting on some other bizarre and potentially fatal incident.

"We *can* do nothing," she said, snatching up the remote from one of the chairs and turning off the broadcast. "We *have* to do nothing," she stressed. "For a little while. Just until we've recharged."

"But people are dying," Melissa argued.

"Don't you think I know that?" Vilma snapped. "But I also know that we've been going nonstop, traveling all over the world, dealing with one emerging threat after another, saving lives, but we're killing ourselves."

Cameron was about to argue, but Vilma silenced him with a stare.

"As far as we know we're the only ones of our kind capable of dealing with these threats. And the last time I checked, there weren't all that many of us left."

"But we have to do something," Cameron insisted.

"And we are," Vilma answered him. "By resting we keep ourselves fresh and on the ball. We'll be less likely to make mistakes—and more likely to survive our battles."

Vilma paused, the realization of what she was about to say taking quite a bit from her.

"We can't save everybody," she said quietly. "And we're going to be able to help even fewer people if we go out there running on fumes."

She looked over at Kraus, who was trying to slip out of the room unnoticed.

"Back me up, Kraus?" she asked.

The healer of angels stopped, and slowly turned. "You're completely right, Miss Santiago," he said. "One's level of performance diminishes greatly while fighting the effects of mental and physical fatigue."

Vilma looked back to Cameron and Melissa. "So that's just how it's going to be."

"How long?" Cameron asked, his shoulders slumping, his wings sliding into his back.

"Go back to your rooms," Vilma said. "Rest . . . nap, do

whatever you need to do to recharge your batteries. We'll talk again in a couple 'a hours."

She could see that the Nephilim weren't happy, turning away in a huff to retreat to their rooms.

"Don't test me on this, guys," she warned, just in case they were thinking of going off against her wishes. "You wouldn't care for the repercussions."

The threat sounded good, even though she had no idea what the punishment would be. Maybe she'd make them hang out with Verchiel for an afternoon—and she wouldn't wish that on a goblin or rabid grackleflint.

Verchiel, she thought as she watched the two Nephilim leave the television room. He was the former leader of the Powers, the angelic host whose sole purpose had been to hunt down and slaughter all Nephilim. And he lived with the Nephilim now. After supposedly dying in battle, the murderous angel had been sent back to earth, for what purpose, nobody could really decipher.

One of the theories was that he'd been sent to make amends for the sins that he had committed as leader of the Powers. And what better way to make amends than by helping the Nephilim keep the world from plunging into total darkness?

She hadn't seen Verchiel in a few days and wondered if she should pay the nasty angel a visit. Maybe he would be able to impart some heavenly wisdom about what they could—or should—be doing in order to continue with their mission.

Vilma truly didn't expect much from Verchiel, but at this point she was willing to try just about anything that might help them.

Even talking with an angel who had tried to kill her.

The visions were killing him.

Dustin "Dusty" Handy lay on the mattress in the middle of the room the Nephilim had given him, and shook as if he were in the grip of a soaring fever.

His eyes were tightly closed, but he could see the images of all that was happening out there in the world—nightmares made reality.

The visions came at him in waves. It was as if every single television channel were being beamed onto one screen in his mind, all at once, and at the highest volume. He'd tried to fight the visions, to get them under control, but he just didn't think he was strong enough. And when they were at their worst, he knew that to be true.

Dying was starting to look better and better.

Sometimes Dusty would take a memory and try to focus on that, to drown out all the other images that cascaded through his mind. He would often think about the blind old man who had given him the responsibility of a special horn.

The responsibility of the Instrument.

The Instrument had belonged to the angel Gabriel, and it was to be given only to one strong enough to control its power.

The horn was to be blown only when all hope was lost and darkness was about to claim victory, when it was time for the world to die.

Dusty had tried to fight the urgings of the Instrument that had wanted him to play it, to call down an angel of destruction to end the world's pain, and he'd been doing really well until . . .

Until he wasn't. Overwhelmed, and unable to resist the Instrument any longer, he'd blown into it, then in the shape of a harmonica, sending the planet that much closer to extinction.

The Instrument had called down the monstrous angel—the Abomination of Desolation—and the Nephilim had done battle with the horrible result that Dusty had been responsible for summoning.

The Nephilim had managed to stop the Abomination from performing its sole duty, but not before it had transformed the Instrument into the mother of all swords and plunged it into the earth, severing the world's connection with Heaven.

The enormous sword was still there outside the Nephilim's haven, protruding from the ground like an antenna, broadcasting these visions inside Dusty's skull.

Driving him to the brink of madness.

When he wasn't thinking about how the world had become so screwed up, Dusty contemplated ending it all. But how he would kill himself was the question.

He wondered if Kraus had anything stronger than foul-smelling salves in that bag of his, something that could put him out of his misery quickly and painlessly.

But suicide would have to wait, as there came a knocking at Dusty's door. Before he could answer, the person on the other side opened the door.

"Rise and shine, handsome," Lorelei said as she limped into his room, the rubber tip at the end of her cane thumping on the wooden floor.

Dusty had just enough strength to lift his head. Since all the business with the Instrument and the visions, he'd been gradually losing his eyesight. Now he could only see blurred shapes and outlines. Soon he would have just the visions inside his head.

"Is it bad?" she asked.

Dusty must've looked as nasty as he felt. "Yeah," he managed, head falling back onto the pillow.

"Well, you're not doing yourself, or anybody else, any good lying here in the dark. Get your ass up, and we'll see if we can mix up something in the science lab to help you out."

Just the idea of standing was enough to send Dusty's body into fitful spasms, the visions intensifying to the point where he wanted to scream, but he was too weak to do so.

"Please," Dusty managed, wrapping his hands around his head to keep it from exploding. "I want to die."

He heard Lorelei grunt at this, and then felt her cane strike him hard in the groin. Dusty let out another painful cry, distracted suddenly from the torturous images inside his head.

"Get up," she commanded. "You only get to die when you've outlived your usefulness," Lorelei said cruelly. "And I see a whole lot of potential in you and that horror show going on inside your skull."

It was a spell that required strength Lorelei really could not spare, but she knew she had no choice. If she didn't do something to help Dusty, he wasn't going to be able to survive, and she needed him. The tiny mouse perched on her shoulder squeaked a warning into her ear, as if sensing what she was about to do.

"I know, I know," she muttered in response to the tiny rodent, who had been named Milton by his former owner—Lucifer Morningstar. Leaning heavily upon her cane, she knelt her magick-ravaged body on the floor with a minimum of discomfort. It was the getting up that would be a bitch.

"But there really isn't much of a choice."

She knew the spell well, having used it quite often over the last few weeks to give the Nephilim that extra power in order to accomplish their missions. Lorelei liked to think of it as the magickal equivalent of a Red Bull, only it was her supernaturally charged life force that gave her recipients the extra kick.

The spell she was going to use on Dusty was slightly different. It would boost his ability to focus, rather than his ability to wave a flaming sword around for a few extra hours.

She muttered the ancient Archon words beneath her breath, and felt herself grow weaker almost immediately. This side effect had heightened since the business with the Abomination of Desolation. Wielding the Archon spells now stole her life energy far faster than her body could replenish it.

But it's all for a good cause, she thought, bringing her tingling fingertips toward Dusty's sweaty face. The young man thrashed his head from side to side, as if in the grip of delirium.

"Hold still," she commanded as she placed her fingers upon his dampened brow, and let the power of the spell flow into him.

Dusty let out a cry, his body going rigid beneath the sheet as she momentarily entered his mind, strengthening his ability to hold at bay all that plagued him. At the same time she glimpsed a bit of what he was experiencing.

She'd helped Dusty before, each time understanding more about his strange gift related to having care of the Instrument. It was wild inside his head, and she honestly hadn't a clue how he had lasted this long, which was probably why he'd been chosen to receive this gift, this burden.

Dusty's mind was strong.

The potential she saw inside his brain was truly exciting. In Dusty, Lorelei hoped they'd found a way to track and hunt down the nightmarish threats that plagued the world. She also hoped he could eventually show them how to restore the world to some state of normalcy.

And perhaps even locate the missing Lucifer Morningstar in the process. Finding Lucifer was a priority. He'd been missing for close to a month, and no matter what sort of spell Lorelei attempted, she couldn't find a trace of him anywhere. It was as if Lucifer had vanished, or even worse, been eradicated. She didn't want to believe either of those options, so she kept on searching, even though each new spell shortened her life by minutes, hours, and sometimes even days.

She removed her fingertips from Dusty's brow, breaking their connection. She immediately felt dizzy. The spell had most definitely taken its toll. It took all the strength she had to rise to her feet again and make her way to lean against the wall.

"How's that?" she asked.

Dusty was sitting up now, his feverish look temporarily gone.

"It's good," he said, running a hand through his longish brown hair. His eyes seemed to focus on her then, taking her in. "But what about you?"

Lorelei pushed off from the wall, not wanting to show any weakness. Milton the mouse clung to her neck, his tiny whiskers tickling her ear as he told her in his simple mouse language that she should rest. But Lorelei wasn't listening.

"Don't you worry about me," she instructed. "Let's worry about getting you out of that bed and back to the lab with me."

Dusty crawled out from beneath the sheet, wearing only a pair of sweatpants. Lorelei turned around, giving him a little bit of privacy so that he could get dressed.

"How much longer can you keep this up?" Dusty asked. She could hear the jangle of his belt as he pulled on his pants.

"What? You mean helping you out?"

"All of it," Dusty said. Lorelei turned to face him as Dusty buttoned his shirt. "Helping me, finding new threats to the world, looking for Lucifer, giving up a part of your life energy so that—"

"I said not to worry," Lorelei said. "I signed up for this, and I'm in it for the long haul."

But she could sense that life would soon be coming to an end for her, and she didn't have the heart to tell Dusty that all of this responsibility would soon belong to him.

CHAPTER TWO

Lucifer knew he hadn't been destroyed, for the pain he felt was far too great.

He'd always wondered what death would be like, that final moment when it all came to an end.

But this wasn't it.

The darkness was all-encompassing, and the Morningstar could feel it gradually consuming him, like powerful digestive juices in the stomach of some giant beast.

Until he was no more.

This was how the monster Satan—the Darkstar, as he was now calling himself, mocking Lucifer's own title, Son of the Morning—planned to eliminate him.

Lucifer felt the blackness cajoling him to surrender and allow the sweet ebony caress of the void to take him.

Memories suddenly exploded in his mind like a newly

born sun, images so personal and painful to recall that they made him cry out. How could he even consider surrendering to the evil, when there was still so much he had to atone for?

When there was still so much penance to be done?

Lucifer cried out, pushing against the darkness, feeling it stretch. It tried to fight him, to lull him back into its comforting embrace, where he would slowly cease to be.

But the Morningstar was not ready to fade away. Lucifer tore at the fabric of shadow, ripping a hole in the shroud of gloom that had attempted to claim him. He pushed himself through the tear, exploding into the golden light of the day, to find himself standing on a battlefield.

The air around him stank of blood and burning flesh and feathers. There were bodies of fallen warriors as far as his eyes could see. Their wings, charred and broken, stuck up from the garden of corpses like vile plants.

Lucifer knew this place, and was sick that he was responsible for the destruction that lay before him. He had instigated this war, a war in Heaven, fought between brothers.

A war caused by Lucifer's own jealousy.

It took all he had to not crawl beneath the bodies and give himself over to oblivion, to give up the crushing despair that was his existence.

But that's exactly what you want me to do, Lucifer Morningstar thought as he gazed at those who had fallen while fighting for and against him during the Great War.

"You'll have to do better than this," Lucifer shrieked.

He knew the Devil had created this bizarre world somewhere deep within Lucifer's own subconscious to torture the Morningstar's soul, while the Darkstar continued to possess his body.

The landscape began to shift and fade as a thick, billowing fog rolled in, obscuring the carnage before him.

It was cold in this now blank, empty place. Lucifer pulled his cloak about him and began to walk.

To where, he had no idea. He only knew that if he wanted to live, this was what he must do.

The ancient evil called Satan seethed with the knowledge that the body he possessed was not yet entirely his.

He could still feel the Morningstar struggling inside him, like an itch that he couldn't scratch, somewhere inside a mind that should have belonged to him.

And only to him.

"Master, is something wrong?" a voice asked, distracting him from his annoyance.

Satan glanced up from his throne of ice to gaze at the red-skinned imp that he had made his attendant. "What is it, Scox?"

"I asked if there was something wrong, my lord," the squat, horned creature repeated. "For a moment the look upon your face . . ."

The Darkstar considered killing the imp right then and there, just to relieve some of his frustration, but he'd already killed all the other imp species. Poor Scox was the last.

There was a certain pleasure that Satan would take from the genocide of another species, but something stayed his hand. Perhaps this was what it was like to be a king, to be affected by whims of mercy. Perhaps he would get used to this feeling, or perhaps next time he would ignore it altogether.

"Nothing to concern yourself with, Scox," the Darkstar said, shifting his weight upon the seat.

He looked around the underground chamber that he'd made his home since first taking the Morningstar's body as his own. It had been one of the places where he had hidden while waiting to hatch his schemes for the world of man, concealed from the prying eyes of God and His angels.

Satan snarled, his handsome features reflected multiple times upon the slick ice walls, showing his seething hatred about how long he had been forced to wait until his glory could at last emerge.

"There it is again," Scox spoke up nervously. The scarlet-skinned demon rubbed his clawed hands together nervously.

Enormous wings as black as night exploded from Satan's back as he sprang up from his cold throne to advance upon his servant.

"He never suspected what I was up to," Satan snarled. "I doubt that He was even aware of my existence."

"Who wasn't aware, my lord?" Scox asked, backing away from the menacing advance of his master.

"But in the shadows I toiled, a nudge here, a tweak there, and my plans began to fall into place."

"They certainly did," Scox agreed as his back struck a wall of the underground cavern.

"And now this world, this breeding ground of humanity that He was so proud of, belongs to me."

Satan gazed about the cavern, his wings of night slowly fanning the air.

"Which reminds me," Scox said. "The leaders of the Community have requested an audience."

The Darkstar turned his unblinking gaze upon the imp.

"Some still do not recognize me as their lord," he said. "Even after all I have given them."

"The Community is an ancient fellowship," Scox attempted to explain. "To them you are young . . . unfamiliar."

"Young?" the Darkstar repeated with a snarl. "I have been since before the Lord God's pronouncement of light and the creation of the universe."

"But . . ."

"But?" Satan urged.

"But they do not know you," the imp finished, averting his eyes from his master.

If they did not know the Darkstar, he would show them who he was.

"Bring them to me," he ordered. "These lords of their monstrous communities."

He would show them the true countenance of a god.

And they would be wise to worship him as such.

Angels did not dream, although they did remember.

Kneeling before the deconsecrated altar within the Saint Athanasius School's church, Verchiel found himself in a sort of fugue state, his thoughts drifting back through the millennia.

The angel let it come, let the strange mental state take him where it would, for Verchiel sought answers.

Answers as to why he was here, amongst the Nephilim, when he had toiled so hard to end their existence.

His memories took him to a small, primitive village in an area of the world now called the Middle East. Verchiel did not recall ever knowing the name of the village, only that he had been drawn there by a prophecy.

At the time, he was not yet the leader of the Powers. That honor belonged to the great angel Camael. But Camael had heard the prophetic murmurings that were spreading across this land: It was said that the spawn of human and angel— the Nephilim—would be revered in Heaven, and would bring about an age of forgiveness in which the fallen angels of the Great War would be granted absolution, and be allowed to return home.

This was utter blasphemy. It had been the Powers' purpose

to hunt down those who had stood against God, and punish them for their sins.

The idea of the fallen angels' feet again touching the hallowed soil of the kingdom was enough to drive the Powers to silence the one who was prophesying this heresy.

Verchiel remembered how the Powers dropped from the sky, their shrieks of rage filling the night as they sought the one who spoke the poisonous words. He found it strange that the villagers attempted to thwart the Powers. Those humans who would normally bow down before their glory actually attempted to keep them from their task.

Camael and the others had held the village occupants at bay with weapons of fire as the citizenry attacked them with stones and farming implements.

Verchiel recalled how distasteful he'd found the whole affair, and was certain that if he had been in charge, any who'd attempted to lay hands upon their righteous personages would have met their fate far sooner.

But Camael had always had far more patience with the talking monkeys.

Focused on his task, Verchiel eventually found the prophet in a hut made of straw and mud, and in all his fiery countenance Verchiel demanded that the blind man explain his blasphemous lies.

Verchiel felt as if he were back there again as he relived this memory, feeling the rage as he'd experienced it.

"You," Verchiel had said, the burning sword that he clutched in his hand illuminating the darkened quarters of the hut.

The prophet just turned his milky white orbs toward him, and smiled his pathetic toothless grin from his seat cross-legged on the dirt floor.

Verchiel's fury was only intensified by the fact that the old man did not fear him.

"You will show me the proper respect," Verchiel demanded, bringing his sword of fire closer to the man's face.

Unfazed, the old man showed that he had a cup, and he shook the contents by his ear, listening to the rattle of what was contained within. He then emptied the cup, the yellow bones and teeth spilling out onto the dirt before him.

Verchiel was transfixed by the bones, and attempted to glean their meaning. But it was not for him to discern.

The prophet gazed down with unseeing eyes, somehow reading what the yellowed bones told him.

"The future diverges on many paths," the old man said, moving his hands in the air above the bones. "But one thing remains the same no matter how often the bones are thrown."

Verchiel knew what the man would say, and stepped closer.

"Even when your life hangs in the balance?" Verchiel asked, smiling cruelly at the man, even though the prophet could not see.

"My life has already ended," the prophet informed him, reaching down in a single swipe to pick up the bones again and place them back inside the cup. "The bones told me as much, just as they foretold your coming."

"So you knew Heaven would come for you . . . for the blasphemy that you spread."

"Heaven has not come for me," the prophet said, rattling his cup again and letting the bones fall. "This is how Heaven speaks to me."

Verchiel laughed cruelly. "Heaven . . . speaks to you?"

Squatting down, the Powers angel looked more closely at the yellowed remains of human and animal bones and asked, "And what does Heaven tell you now?"

"It tells me that a Chosen One, a savior of the Nephilim, will bring absolution to the fallen, no matter how hard you try to destroy them."

Verchiel then stood, his wings spreading out from his armored body in a threatening stance. He reached out, grabbed the neck of the old man, and hauled him from the floor, scattering his special bones.

"And what other messages have the bones delivered to you?" he demanded with a savage snarl.

In Verchiel's grip the old man struggled to speak. Still, the words came. "That this Chosen One will bring about the end of you and yours."

Verchiel was repulsed by the prophetic words, and savagely hurled the body of the old man to the ground, where he lay momentarily stunned.

It was then that Verchiel enacted his sentence upon the man—and the entire village that would harbor and protect such a pestilence upon the world—calling forth the power of Heaven that lived inside him, allowing his body to burn brighter and brighter until it burned like the sun.

That was where Verchiel wished the memory would end.

But there was more.

Through the fire, Verchiel witnessed the old man gazing at the bones he had thrown. As the prophet burned, he turned to point at a large slab of rock that the hungry fire had unearthed.

There were images painted on that flat piece of stone. And those images told the story of the Nephilim, and how there would be a Chosen One amongst them.

A Redeemer.

And through the fire, Verchiel watched the old man, his body aflame, pick up his brushes and continue to paint his visions.

The prophecy that he foretold continuing on even longer than Verchiel remembered.

Verchiel emerged from his memory and was surrounded by fire.

In his ruminations he had unknowingly called upon the divine power of Heaven, and had set the chapel altar ablaze. But what concerned Verchiel was not the fire that ate at the ancient wood and plaster of what had once been a place of worship.

It was the vision that haunted him.

How is this possible?

"What's going on?" screamed a female voice, and Verchiel turned from the burning altar to see the Nephilim Vilma Santiago, accompanied by the dog, charging down the aisle toward him.

"Verchiel!" she screamed. "What in the name of God are you doing?"

He couldn't explain, and didn't want to. That was all he needed, for her to know of his sudden lapse in memory.

Or would it be considered an addendum?

Vilma did not wait for him to respond, darting to a far corner of the church to grab a tarp that had once covered a leaking portion of the church's roof. She dragged it to the altar, where she threw the heavy cloth upon some of the flames, suffocating them. She stamped upon the smoldering cloth before picking the tarp up again, and was preparing to attack another section, when he'd seen enough.

Verchiel held out a hand.

"I'll handle this," he said, turning his attention to the wall behind the altar where the flames had seared the ancient paint and set the plaster alight.

He summoned his wings and began to beat the air. The sudden rush of wind temporarily fed the blaze. Then, hand extended, Verchiel called the fire of Heaven back into his body. It did not want to listen at first, preferring to feed upon the aged wooden structure, but Verchiel was not to be ignored, and the fire had no choice but to comply.

The fire leaped at him from the walls and burning debris, swirling around him in one last moment of freedom before it was absorbed back into his divine form.

"That is that," he said, turning his attention back to the girl as the last of the flame swirled on the tip of his finger, and then was gone.

In a rush of anger Vilma threw the tarp at him.

"What is wrong with you?" she bellowed, and the dog barked its own language of displeasure.

Verchiel ignited a sword of flame, and the tarp fell before the musty fabric could touch him.

"Do not test me, girl," he warned.

"Test you?" she screeched. "You almost set this place on fire, and you're telling me not to test you? How would you have explained what we're doing here to the fire department when they showed up? Tell me that."

"I wouldn't have," he said, wishing away the burning blade. "I do not talk to their kind. I may have fallen, but I am still far above the likes of them."

"Aaron was completely right about you," she said, turning to leave. "C'mon, Gabriel."

"And what did your precious Aaron . . . your Nephilim savior have to say this time?" Inside Verchiel's mind he saw the painting and the story that seemed to go on and on.

Vilma turned back to the angel, hands upon her hips defiantly.

"That you're still an asshole," she stated. "Even though you've most likely been sent here to help us . . . to redeem yourself . . . you're still a total jerk."

Then she and the dog strode away.

"And is that why you came in here? To tell me that?"

Verchiel remembered this girl before the angelic essence inside her had awakened. She'd been a timid bird who he thought might die from fright after learning about his kind, but now, since becoming Nephilim . . .

He hated to admit it, but she was a spectacular specimen.

Vilma stopped, considering how she would proceed.

"No," she replied. "I actually came to ask for your advice."

"My advice?" Verchiel said with a laugh. "Oh, how the mighty have fallen."

"Things are bad out there," she said, pointing to the church wall and beyond it. "And they're getting worse. We're dealing with things the best we can . . . the only way we know how."

"Yes?"

"Well, maybe there's a better way," she proposed. "We're new at this and really don't know about fighting an enemy that seems to grow in strength and number every day."

"So you're seeking my expertise," Verchiel declared. He stepped down from the altar and walked toward the girl.

"If I didn't have to speak to you, I wouldn't," she said with defiance. "Your voice makes my skin crawl—knowing what you and your Powers did to innocent people for a very long time."

"They weren't people, and they certainly weren't innocent."

"Whatever," Vilma said dismissively. "But even though I find you repulsive, I respect the fact that you're a warrior of Heaven, that this was what you were created to do . . . to fight."

Verchiel glared at the girl, stunned by her audacity. In another time he would have severed her pretty head from her neck.

"And since you're here with us, living with us, I thought you might share your expertise."

He considered what she was saying, and could not help but laugh.

"You're asking for my help?" he asked, trying to muffle his unexpected explosion of mirth.

He could see her look of absolute disgust as she again turned to leave.

"Never mind," she said. "I knew it was a stupid idea."

She was almost to the door, and he was about to let her go, when he decided to speak.

"You do what you have to do."

"Excuse me?" Vilma asked.

"He said, 'You do what you have to do,'" Gabriel repeated.

"I heard what he said. I just don't understand what it means."

"What do you think it means?" Verchiel asked. "You come in here, to speak to me—your mortal enemy—asking how to win the war you're fighting."

She crossed her arms, listening.

Verchiel began to pace before the charred altar.

"And I tell you the secret, which is no secret," the angel stated flatly. "Your enemy is out there. An enemy that wishes to kill you and everything you hold dear. To deal with that you must do anything that you have to do in order to be victorious." Verchiel paused, making sure that his words were sinking in. "Or you, and all that you know and love, will die."

Vilma thought for a moment before opening her mouth.

"That's it?" she asked. "Fight or die? Is that what you're saying?"

"Could it be any simpler?" Verchiel asked before turning his back and walking to the dark shadows within the abandoned church.

He was done talking to the female Nephilim.

For now.

CHAPTER THREE

Aaron had fallen so far into sleep that he didn't know he was dreaming.

He imagined a world where he'd graduated from high school, attended college, and gotten a good job. A world where he and Vilma were engaged to be married, and that his adoptive parents—Tom and Lori—had given them a substantial down payment for a house as an engagement gift. Life was better than he could ever have hoped.

But then something happened.

One evening darkness came earlier than it should have, and the sun never rose again. That perfect world began to fade away. No matter how hard Aaron tried to hold on to it—no matter how he screamed and raged and begged—nothing could stop the shadows from taking it all away from him.

The dream was replaced by a nightmare.

But the nightmare was a reality.

Aaron opened his eyes to find his vision blurred by tears.

Gabriel lay beside him on the mattress, the dog's dark brown, soulful eyes staring at him. *"You were crying,"* he said.

"Yeah," Aaron agreed, pulling his hand from beneath the covers to wipe away the residual tears.

"Sad dreams?" Gabriel asked.

Aaron rolled onto his side to face his dog.

"I dreamed of stuff that could have been if . . ." He paused for a moment, remembering how real it felt. "I went to college, Vilma and I were getting a house, Tom and Lori . . ."

"Were Tom and Lori still alive?" Gabriel asked. His tail suddenly sprang to life, thumping upon the bed.

"They were," Aaron said, smiling with their memory. "And Stevie."

"And me?" Gabriel asked. *"I was there too, right?"*

"Of course you were," Aaron assured him. "What kind of a perfect life would it be without you in it?"

"True," Gabriel agreed.

Aaron laughed. "Everything felt so perfect. It was all I could ever have asked for."

"But it wasn't real," Gabriel said softly, resting his muzzle on the pillow beside his master.

"No, it wasn't," Aaron said sadly.

"Reality is mean."

"Yeah, it can be." Aaron flopped onto his back, throwing his arm across his eyes, feeling sadder than he had in quite some time.

"I can help you," Gabriel said after a few moments.

Aaron lifted his arm to look at his dog.

"I can help you," he said again, scooting closer and nudging his blocky head beneath Aaron's hand.

Aaron hesitated, but then stroked the fine yellow fur atop the Labrador's head. Slowly Aaron realized that this was exactly what he had to do—what he *needed* to do.

For petting Gabriel would take away the lingering pain of his dreams.

Melissa tried to rest but couldn't.

She lay in her bed, eyes closed, trying to will herself to sleep. But it just wasn't happening.

Rather than stare at the cracked plaster ceiling, she got up to go for a walk, and found herself at the back of the school, where the remains of a greenhouse stood near the makeshift graves of her friends.

Melissa seemed to be the only one of them who felt compelled to visit the dead. But it had been some time since even she had come. The wildflowers she'd left on the graves had either withered or blown away.

"Hey, guys," she said, doing her best to remember each of the fallen Nephilim.

She wasn't sure if all of them would have considered her a friend or not, but she liked to think of them that way because of the experiences that they had shared.

Janice's grave was first. Melissa remembered the quiet black-haired girl with fondness, how they'd bonded over a love for really bad horror movies.

"Hey, you," Melissa said, kneeling in the dirt, imagining her friend's cheerful face. "How's it going?" She picked up some dried flowers and tossed them aside. "Things have been pretty nuts here, as you can imagine, but we're doing okay."

She paused, eyes wandering to the other graves.

"I'm still alive anyway."

Melissa didn't want to exclude the others, so she stood to address them all. "We really miss you guys," she said, remembering Kirk, William, Samantha, and Russell, and how brave they'd been when their end had come. "We could really use your help now."

She felt stupid for a moment, certain that her friends would rather be above the ground. Then she remembered the world in which she now lived, and seriously wondered who had the best deal.

From inside the pocket of her hooded sweatshirt, Melissa removed a handful of pretty colored rocks that she'd found on a remote beach in New Zealand. She and Vilma had dispatched a nest of sea serpents there that had been preying on local fishermen. Having grown up in Kansas, the stones were unlike anything Melissa had ever seen before. She'd kept them as a keepsake. She knew the graves of her friends needed to remain unmarked, just in case anybody in the outside community should stumble upon the property.

But these stones could be their markers.

Melissa looked through the colorful rocks, polished shiny and smooth by the ocean waves, and selected one for each grave, the colors she chose representing something she remembered about each of her friends.

Yellow for Kirk because it was the color of his hair. Blue for William because of his piercing stare. Black for Janice because of her nail polish . . .

When she was done, Melissa stood back to admire her work.

"Much nicer than dried-up old flowers," she told them, and wondered what color stone would be placed upon her grave when she was gone. She figured she would be lucky to even have a grave, guessing that she'd likely end up in the belly of some sort of monster.

She'd thought of it as a joke, but suddenly realized that there might be some truth there. The reality of their situation, and the world in which they now lived, weighed heavily upon her.

A tingle ran down her spine, and Melissa felt as though she were being watched. She turned to see that she was right. Cameron stood behind her, his wings out, sword of fire clutched tightly in his hand.

He was dressed for battle.

*   *   *

Cameron thought he might find Melissa in the makeshift grave-yard. He doubted that she could sleep any more than he could.

He'd honestly tried to settle down, but just the thought of those things out there . . . Images of the walking nightmares he had slain in his time as a Nephilim raced through his mind and kept him from being able to close his eyes.

Melissa left where their friends had been buried to approach him.

"What are you doing like that?" she asked. "Something going on?"

"I'm going out," he told her.

"Against Vilma's wishes?" Melissa asked. "Are you crazy? She's going to be royally pissed."

"I don't care," he said. "Besides, she's so wrapped up with Aaron that I'll be back before she even knows that I've gone."

"What if I tell her?"

"I guess that answers my question." He avoided her eyes.

"What question?" Melissa asked.

"If you're going with me or not."

"Look," the girl said. "I understand where you're coming from, I really do, but there has to be some chain of command. We can't just fly off to do battle whenever we feel like it."

"Why not? It's what we were created to do."

Melissa folded her arms. "I just don't think it's very smart.

We should wait until Aaron wakes up, and then—"

"And how many people will die during that time?" Cameron interrupted.

"Don't pull that on me," Melissa warned.

"I'm not pulling anything on you," he said. "It's a serious question, one I've been wrestling with since Vilma told us to stand down."

"You know why she asked us to stop," Melissa said. "We can't keep going the way we're going. We're going to get tired. Sloppy. Make mistakes. Then how many people will die because of us?"

Cameron shook his head, refusing to acknowledge the girl's point. "I'm not going to make mistakes," he told her. "Not when lives are at stake."

"Like you have control over that?"

"I'm going." Cameron spread his wings, preparing to wrap himself in their embrace.

"Cameron, please," Melissa begged.

"Will you cover for me?" he asked as his wings closed around him and he remembered the last place from the news broadcast.

Where he was needed.

Melissa didn't answer, but he saw a look in her eyes as he closed his wings, a look that said that she wished she were brave enough to disobey and join him in battle.

* * *

Walking home from the market, Jeremy glanced down the narrow, sloping side streets that would take him to the main street, which ran through the village of Southwold, on the edge of the vast, churning gray ocean.

He remembered when he and his mother had vacationed here, how important those times had been in his childhood. Other than those times, there had been mostly misery. Tempted to walk down to the shore, Jeremy reminded himself that there was a hungry mouth, other than his mother's, waiting for his return.

The baby formula was ridiculously expensive, and he had seriously considered slipping a can or two beneath his shirt on his way out the door, but had thought better of it. Best to keep a low profile, and being nicked by the local constabulary didn't quite fit into those plans.

Using what little his mother had had in a savings account, they had traveled to Southwold. It was the off-season, so they'd managed to get a decent enough cottage for a reasonable monthly price. The vacation cottage wasn't too far from the one that his mother had rented for them long ago.

Holding the bag of groceries in one hand, Jeremy fished the key from his pocket, and was just about to slip it inside the lock, when the door opened. His mother held the crying infant, whom she insisted on calling Roger.

"It's about time," she said, bouncing the squealing red-faced child on her hip.

"I went as quick as I could," Jeremy said, shutting the door behind him with a flip of his leg.

"The poor thing is starving," his mother said, kissing the top of the wailing child's head.

"How many times a day does the bugger eat, anyway?" he asked, emptying the contents of the paper sack onto the tiny kitchen table.

"He's a growing boy," his mother said, and the child grew louder.

"But it doesn't seem right. He's always squealing to be fed." Jeremy turned from the fridge, and his mother suddenly thrust the screeching creature into his arms.

"Take him while I mix his formula."

Jeremy had no choice but to accept the rather unpleasant gift. It was either that or let the infant drop to the floor, which would have just led to even more noise.

"Bounce him on your hip like I did," his mother said as she went about making the child's meal.

Jeremy tried to do as his mother suggested, not wanting to hurt the shrieking blighter.

"And walk around," she added. "He likes it when you walk around."

Jeremy bounced the crying babe, and walked into the sitting room, where the television was on BBC One. A news program reported on the state of the world.

And it was nothing pleasant.

He moved from foot to foot as the reporters discussed the increasing darkness and the strange new life-forms that were appearing across the planet.

Jeremy felt bad for the newsreaders. They were doing everything in their power not to call these emerging life-forms what they actually were.

Monsters. The world is overrun with monsters.

Jeremy again had to wrestle with the fact that he was here, with his mother and the mysterious Baby Roger, and not with his fellow Nephilim in the States. His mother swore that this was where he was supposed to be. And for some strange reason Jeremy believed her.

It was then that Jeremy noticed Roger had ceased his squalling. He was about to note that his mother had been right about the bouncing and walking too, when he noticed that the child's huge, unblinking eyes were staring at the telly.

As if listening to every word.

CHAPTER FOUR

Most of the time, Mallus did not miss the ability to fly.

Throughout the millennia he'd lived in the world of man, he'd found that humanity was constantly improving how they traveled from here to there. Horseback became horse-drawn cart and carriages; sailing ships evolved into steamships, locomotives, then automobiles, and finally taking to the sky with airplanes.

He was always fascinated by what these humans came up with, though at one time, he could have wrapped himself in his wings and been anywhere in the world in a matter of seconds.

The twin scars upon his shoulder blades grew warm and began to itch. Today of all days Mallus wondered what it was that made him think of his feathery appendages. Could it have been the escalating crowds in the New York subway station?

The squeeze of impatient bodies on the platform as they waited for a delayed train?

Or was it the changes that he felt in the world around him? Changes he had feared for a very long time. Changes that he tried to ignore, which yipped at him like dogs desperate for attention.

Mallus leaned against the wall at the far end of the subway station, rubbing his back across the tiles in an attempt to alleviate his discomfort. The scars had not bothered him for centuries, and he found it disconcerting that they would act up now.

More of the city's occupants poured down into the crowded station. From where he stood, Mallus could see umbrellas and coats dripping with moisture. It must have started raining, which explained the volume in the station, but not why it had been so long since a train had run through.

All he could do was wait, surrounded by the creatures he had grown to love, even at their most foul.

"Where's the damn train?" a large man dressed in a black suit and sporting a thick white beard grumbled under his breath. "The whole damn world is going to Hell."

Mallus didn't have the heart to tell the man he was right.

The signs were there for anyone with the knowledge to read them. They had been for quite some time. And during the last month these signs had become blatantly obvious. A part of Mallus wished that he was as painfully oblivious as humanity.

He wished he didn't know what the Architects were planning.

The crowd in the subway station grew so that there wasn't any more space on the platform, but Mallus didn't mind. He allowed their emotions to wash over him, anger, impatience, and annoyance. He breathed in the aroma of their human funk.

For he would miss it when they were gone.

The last report Cameron had heard before Vilma had shut off the television had been about a disturbance in the New York City subway system.

It was in an area he knew well from when he'd lived in the city. The picture of the tunnel formed inside his head, growing more and more detailed—more and more specific as his angelic ability zeroed in on where he wanted—*needed*—to be.

The damp stink of the underground passage, along with something else that he couldn't quite identify, assailed his sense of smell as his wings unfolded deep within the subway tunnel. He was immediately at the ready, a sword of fire igniting in his hand as his eyes adjusted to the dim light.

Cameron used the burning blade as a torch, lighting the pockets of shadow in his search for a possible threat. Finding nothing out of the ordinary, he started down the tracks, eyes darting here and there, searching for a sign of what had brought him there.

Around the bend he found a darkened train.

Part of him—his angelic nature—wanted to leap into action, sword flashing. But his calmer, human side wanted to be sure that such a reaction was necessary. He was certain that this wasn't the first set of subway cars to ever lose power, and they were probably waiting either to be pushed into the next station or for some minor repairs to get them moving again.

He moved closer to the back of the last car, trying to see inside the vehicle, but he could only make out the shapes of heads and bodies of people in the dimness of the emergency lighting. Tempted to go on ahead of the stranded car, to check out the tunnel in front or ahead in the next station, Cameron remembered Aaron words during training with his fellow Nephilim.

"Be thorough," their leader had said. *"Because evil has the nasty habit of sneaking up and biting you in the ass."*

Cameron actually turned around then, to be sure that nothing was following him. The tunnel appeared clear, and he again directed his attention to the train in front of him.

Wanting to be thorough, the Nephilim wished away his sword and hauled himself up onto the car. Then he pushed open the rear emergency door.

He thought about what he might say to the passengers, maybe that he worked for the MTA and that they were fixing the problem. Maybe he wouldn't say anything at all.

Cameron stepped into the car and immediately felt the disturbing sensation of webbing brush across his face. His hand shot up, wiping at what he figured were stray strands of spiderweb, but his entire hand became enmeshed in a curtain of webbing.

His brain barely had the time to register the oddness of the situation as disgust and near panic set in. He attempted to pull the sticky threads from his hands and clothes.

Cameron hated spiderwebs, and even more so the things that spun them. He guessed that it had something to do with some long-hidden childhood trauma. Maybe he'd been bitten by a spider, or one on the ceiling of his room had scared him as a baby; he couldn't remember.

All he knew was that spiders gave him the creeps, and that was pretty much that.

Cameron half expected the train occupants to be busting a gut over his squeamish reaction, but the train remained eerily silent. Not a single person in the train car looked in his direction.

In fact, they all appeared to be asleep.

It was more reflex than anything else, and he hoped that he wouldn't regret the act, but a sword ignited in his hand, illuminating more than the dim emergency lights could.

What he saw made him want to gag.

There was no doubt that the passengers were dead.

Their bodies were wrapped from head to toe in the thick webbing. What little of them that Cameron could see appeared withered—dried—as if mummified.

He had to restrain the part of him that wanted to run from the train in total panic. Blade out before him to light his way, Cameron slowly advanced down the aisle to investigate. The bodies were anchored to the plastic benches and metal poles with thick strands of webbing that covered the ceilings, walls, and floor.

But the answer to the most obvious and frightening question still eluded Cameron.

Where are the spiders?

The divine light of the sword cut through every deep, dark patch of the train, but there wasn't an arachnid to be found. Cameron eyed the ceiling vents, thinking that maybe they had gotten in and then climbed back out from there, but he just wasn't sure. Moving toward the opposite end of the car to cross into the next train car, he saw a similar scenario. A cold chill ran down his spine.

He'd hoped he wasn't too late to save these people, but much to his disappointment, he was. A spark of anger surged as he walked forward to the adjoining subway car. This was what he'd been trying to explain to Vilma. How many of these passengers would still be alive if he'd come here when he'd first seen—

An older woman sitting on a bench moved.

Cameron froze, staring. He wanted to be sure that he'd seen what he thought he'd seen. Again the body moved, rocking ever so slightly from side to side.

Maybe they weren't all dead, Cameron considered, heading toward the woman. Despite his unease he wished away his blade, not wanting to burn the woman, and prepared to rip open her cocoon.

"Ma'am," he said, sinking his fingers into the thick, sticky fibers. "Can you hear me? I'm going to try to help you."

Cameron suppressed his revulsion as he grabbed the web-bing with both hands and tore it away from the woman's body. He watched for signs of movement again.

"Hello?" he said. He wiped his hands on the legs of his jeans and tentatively reached out to touch her arm.

Cameron gasped as her skin gave way beneath his finger-tips. The woman's arm crumbled like ancient paper. He yanked back his hand. How was it that he'd seen her move? His mind raced with questions. There was no way that she could have been alive at all.

And then he saw it again, a movement beneath the woman's lime-green blouse.

The angelic nature inside Cameron stirred to life.

His sword reappeared in his hand as the first of the spiders emerged from beneath the blouse. It was big, about the size of city rat, and unlike any other spider he'd ever seen. Its body was covered in thick, black hair, and a hooked claw came at the end of each of its eight limbs.

The most nightmarish thing about the spider was that it had a humanoid face: eyes, nose, and mouth.

It was the mouth that freaked him out the most, for it was open, showing off rows of razor-sharp teeth. And it screamed.

Those screams were answered by other screams, and from the periphery of his vision, Cameron saw that all the bodies around him were moving.

Or at least the creatures inside them were.

While Cameron was momentarily distracted, the spider closest to him sprang at him with a hiss. The stink of its breath made Cameron recall the aroma that he'd experienced in the tunnel when he'd first arrived.

Cameron's blade sliced through the spider, cutting it in half before it could land upon him. Crawling out from their cocoons of desiccated flesh, the other spiders saw what Cameron had done and began to scream.

Sword at the ready, Cameron waited for the next attack. But it didn't come. The spiders in the subway car just screamed and screamed.

Mournful wails from the cars beyond joined in, and Cameron grew more nervous. *Why aren't they attacking? Maybe they are more afraid of me than I am of them?* he thought. He stood poised, sword at the ready, waiting for a sign.

Then he shuddered. Maybe they're calling for reinforcements.

Cameron would have liked to slap the part of his brain that had come up with that idea, but he was too busy swearing beneath his breath and trying to keep his balance as the subway car began to shake.

The spiders' shrieks were louder now, and that nasty thought about reinforcements was starting to look true. Something incredibly heavy was moving across the roof of the car, the impressions of its tremendous weight bending the ceiling panels above his head.

In their escalating excitement, some of the arachnids sprang from the bodies from which they had fed, seemingly no longer afraid of him. The sword of fire sizzled as it sliced through the grotesque creatures, but three managed to avoid his blade and clung to his body, tearing and biting at his shirt eager to get at his soft flesh beneath.

Cameron dropped to the floor in a roll, attempting to crush the spider on his back, while ripping off the one that was crawling toward his face. He kicked off the one eating its way through the leg of his jeans. Cameron was on his feet again in an instant, first stabbing one of the spiders and then slicing off the front limbs of another, and dismembering the third, which was trying to scuttle away beneath the plastic seats.

He was ready for just about anything, awaiting the next wave of attack, when he heard the sound of tearing metal above his head. The Nephilim warrior jumped backward with the help of his wings as the ceiling of the train car was torn away. Giant, clawed, and hair-covered limbs reached down to snatch at him.

Cameron couldn't believe his eyes. The spiders that he'd been fighting were the largest he had ever seen, but this was the super-size equivalent. And now that he'd seen it, he knew he'd never stop having nightmares about it.

The mammoth spider shoved its front portion down into the subway car, its too human face searching for him.

"Where, oh where, have you gone, angel-meat?" it asked in

a distinctly female voice. The other, smaller spiders scrabbled from the bodies of their victims to climb up the limbs of the giant's body.

"I'm right here," Cameron found himself responding, waving the sword of fire to attract the monster's attention. If he could get it into the train, the close quarters would work in his favor. "Why don't you come and say hi."

The thing looked at him with venomous hate, and almost lunged for him, before drawing back.

"Tricky, tricky, angel-meat," the giant spider spoke.

"Come on. I'll show you how tricky I can be," Cameron taunted.

"Uttu can be tricky as well," the monster said with a horrible chuckle, and then suddenly withdrew from the hole in the train's ceiling.

Cameron swore beneath his breath, charging across the car and spreading his wings to fly up through the ceiling in pursuit of Uttu, the giant spider. Thick strands of webbing suddenly shot through the hole, wrapping around his body as if they were somehow alive. The more he fought, the tighter they seemed to bind him, and even when Cameron managed to cut himself away from the cords that held him, more of the sticky stuff whipped after him.

"Tricky, tricky," he heard Uttu say from somewhere above. Then it started to laugh, along with its children. It was one of the most horrible sounds Cameron had ever heard.

The webbing grew tighter around his torso, and Cameron could feel a tug from above as the giant spider tried to extract him from the subway car. He was about to summon another blade of fire, when he remembered that the point of his mission was to kill whatever beast was threatening the subway.

He wasn't about to kill much of anything hiding down with the corpses.

Cameron let himself be drawn up through the opening, Uttu waiting to pounce just as he emerged from the subway car. But Cameron was ready, reigniting his sword of fire to cut away the webbing that bound his hands. As he flexed the muscles in his back, causing his wings to explode, he tore the rest of the fibers away.

The huge spider wasn't expecting that, and screamed in anger as it spun more webbing to capture him. Cameron had to move quickly, flying above the sticky cords that sought him out as he glided toward his adversary.

His skin crawled with the sight of Uttu's back, covered with the writhing bodies of its screaming babies, and he lashed out, the divine blade cutting a burning swath across the creature's crowded back.

Raging in pain and anger, the giant spider spun around, directing another barrage of webbing from its mouth in an attempt to pull him from the air.

Cameron angled his body so that the sticky spew missed him and connected to the tunnel wall. Sensing an opportunity, the Nephilim reached out with his fiery weapon and ignited the spider monster's webbing with the tip of his sword.

Just as he'd suspected, the heavenly flame began to consume the demonic fibers, racing down their length toward where they had originated.

To the still open mouth of Uttu.

There was a flash of divine fire, followed by the most horrific of screams, and Cameron could not help but feel satisfaction. Uttu's head was engulfed in yellow flames as the giant spider raced atop the subway cars, spreading the fire.

Cameron flew above Uttu and then dropped down to deliver what he expected to be a killing blow, but just as he drew back his blade, the spider showed that it still had some fight left.

One of its clawed limbs lashed out with blinding speed, trying to slash his taut stomach.

While avoiding the flailing limb, his wing struck the stone ceiling of the subway tunnel, causing him to fly off balance and drop to the train tracks.

He landed in a tumble then and sprang up, ready for Uttu to attack, but only a few of the babies skittered across the gravel. Cameron quickly dispatched them.

But the queen spider was nowhere to be found.

"Crap," Cameron spat, leaping into the air and onto the subway car. In the distance he saw the giant spider attempting to escape, its head still burning with divine fire as the monster ran along the wall, and then upside down on the arched tunnel ceiling.

Cameron began to run, burning blade in hand, eager to vanquish this latest demonic threat. Taking to the air, he continued his pursuit, eyes fixed on Uttu's monstrous shape, until he noticed that the lighting seemed a bit brighter as the tunnel angled to the right.

His heart began to hammer painfully inside his chest as he flapped his wings in an attempt to catch up to the monster and verify his suspicion.

The monster was heading for the crowded subway station platform.

Mallus could sense the coming of the spider before it entered the station.

Along with something else of a more heavenly nature.

Not a day had gone by when Mallus hadn't thought of the Golden City, the offenses that he'd effected against it, and the Almighty.

All in the name of envy.

He had been first lieutenant to Lucifer Morningstar, and had believed in his commander's mission with every fiber of his being, for the angels of Heaven had been cast aside in favor of the Almighty's newest creations.

How humanity had repulsed Mallus then.

But that was before the fall, before the Lord of Lords cast

Lucifer and all who had fought with him in the Great War down to the earth to live amongst the very creatures who had stolen God's affections from them.

It was the most heinous of punishments, but one that had taught Mallus the most unexpected of lessons.

Mallus shook himself from his musings as shrieks of mortal terror filled the station.

The subway patrons were in total panic as they tried to escape the loathsome beast dropping down onto the platform. Smaller versions of the spider swarmed from its back, attacking the people, whose only crime was wanting to go home after work.

Mallus knew not to become involved. A very long time ago he'd sworn to himself that his interactions with humanity would be limited, that he would not allow himself to become involved in their day-to-day existences.

Their inevitable fate would be sad enough without his forming any unnecessary emotional attachments.

He moved with the screaming patrons, heading toward the staircase that led up to the street. He was halfway across the platform when he paused, watching the spider as it flailed amongst the humans, its head burning with holy fire.

Mallus remembered how he'd once wielded the fire of God, and how brightly it had burned as it had consumed evil.

He wanted to leave, but his curiosity kept him.

The spider's senses were too keen, and it spun its burning

face toward him, fixing him in its stare with two empty sockets that boiled with gelatinous fluids that had once been eyes.

It was impossible for the beast to see him. And Mallus was certain that it couldn't *sense* his angelic nature, for he had taken great pains throughout the centuries to shield himself against both the demonic and the divine who sought his whereabouts.

Even still, the beast seemed to know he was there, and before Mallus could escape its angry attentions, the spider lashed out with one of its front legs, the hooked claw at the end slashing across the front of his overcoat and driving him to the ground of the filthy platform.

Mallus could feel the sudden warmth begin to flow. He had been sloppy. As he looked down at himself, he realized that the situation was even worse than he'd thought. His coat and shirt were torn and stained with a substantial amount of blood.

There wasn't time to check, but since his flesh was cut, there was a chance that the magickal wards hiding him from those who sought to kill him had been compromised.

And they could find him.

The Architects would know where he was.

Mallus surged to his feet, his head swimming from blood loss, and staggered back toward the wall. He needed to get out of there, needed to inspect his wound and the damage done to the wards, and repair them as necessary.

But the spider did not wish to let him go; the smell of his fallen angel's blood drew the abomination and its children to him.

Mallus leaned back against the wall; the scars upon his shoulders weren't itching anymore. He braced for battle with the demonic thing, but it did not come to be. A howl pierced the air, and with that Mallus heard the familiar sound of flapping wings.

Clutching his bleeding chest, he slid down the tiled wall, vision blurring, but before unconsciousness snatched him away, he saw the most magnificent sight.

An angel, wielding a burning sword of fire, landed atop the hellish beast, ending its blighted existence.

Cameron screamed as he descended upon his target.

Spinning his sword around as he dropped, he drove the fiery blade into the abdomen of the spider, setting ablaze some of the straggler children that still clung to their mother. The sword passed through the monster's body and into the concrete, pinning Uttu to the floor.

The creature bucked and wailed, its limbs flailing as it struggled to escape.

Cameron left his weapon pinning Uttu to the subway station floor, and flew to face the beast. He was amazed that the thing's head still burned, that it still fought to live.

Before Uttu could attack again, Cameron created another flaming blade and severed the burning head from the spider's body with one swift and decisive blow.

The spider's death throes were violent, but they eventually

calmed, and then stilled. Cameron then touched the tip of his sword to the monster's body, setting its remains ablaze.

The sprinkler system went off, showering Cameron in artificial rain. It felt good against his skin as it washed the stink of evil from his clothes and exposed flesh.

He scanned the platform for any of the wretched babies, and saw that there were none to be found. But littering the ground were the bodies of people who hadn't managed to escape and had been caught up in the spider's struggles or attacked by Uttu's children. Cameron felt a wave of guilt pass over him. He knew he had done his best, but he hadn't been able to keep the beast from the subway station.

A moan came from someplace behind him, and Cameron turned to see an older man slumped against the wall, sitting in an expanding puddle of blood. His eyes were merely slits, but Cameron could see that the man was actually alive and not a corpse filled with feasting spiders.

Cameron went to the man and knelt down beside him.

The man clutched at his chest.

"Here, let me see," Cameron said, reaching out to pull the man's hands away so that he could see the extent of the wounds. He examined the bleeding gash but also saw something else.

The man's flesh, almost every inch of it, was covered in strange tattoo-like markings.

Cameron gasped as the man grabbed his wrist in a powerful grip.

"Have to get out of here," the injured man said deliriously. "Have to go before . . . before they find . . ."

He then slipped into unconsciousness, and from the amount of pooling blood on the platform, Cameron knew that the man didn't have much time before he was gone.

But the markings—the Nephilim couldn't take his eyes from them.

Cameron knew what he had to do. He got to his feet and lifted the man into his arms. He was going to take him back to the school. Kraus should be able to heal him.

And maybe they would learn the meaning of the strange markings that covered the man's body.

Cameron called upon his wings, bringing them around to cover him and the dying man in his arms, and thought about the school that had become his home.

And the chewing out he was likely to receive upon his return.

CHAPTER FIVE

Though he'd been to the library with Lorelei many times, Dusty still had trouble wrapping his brain around what he saw.

A door that looked like it should have led to a broom closet instead opened to one of the biggest libraries that he had ever seen.

It seemed to go on forever.

Lorelei had tried to explain it. There was something about pocket dimensions and one reality being attached to another, but she would grow impatient with his confusion and just say that it was magick and leave it at that. Magick was the answer to a lot of complicated questions, he'd noticed since coming to be with the Nephilim.

"Be careful here," Lorelei said, touching his hand that rested on her shoulder, allowing her to guide him.

Since his eyesight had started to fail, Dusty had required some assistance in getting around the old orphanage, especially in the library. And most especially in this section, since they'd had a little incident with an angel falling from the heavens and through the floor. Aaron had talked about getting some wood to cover up the hole, but they'd been a tad busy lately.

They gave the opening a wide berth as they made their way to the section of the library where the most powerful books and scrolls pertaining to angel magick—*Archon magick*—were kept.

Lorelei had been bringing him here a lot lately. She was attempting to familiarize him with the various ancient writings and spells for any number of bizarre needs. From keeping the generators that supplied the school's power going to summoning doves for spells that required a life sacrifice, it seemed these texts held all of the answers.

From what Dusty could guess, the Archons were pretty powerful, scary angels.

Though, to be truthful, since getting involved in all this insanity, Dusty had yet to meet an angel that wasn't scary in one way or another.

"So what's on the agenda for today?" he asked, leaning against the table in the center of the library nook.

"The usual," Lorelei said, selecting the books she would need for whatever spells she planned to cast. As she moved swiftly from shelf to shelf, he heard the squeak of the tiny mouse that always seemed to be clinging to her shoulder.

"Let me guess," Dusty said. "We need to find the biggest, nastiest, most dangerous threats so Aaron and the others can go and kill them. Then we'll make sure that the security spells around the property are in order, and finally we'll look for Lucifer."

He watched as Lorelei's shadowy figure turned from the wall of books to face him.

"Let's not say that last one too loudly," she warned.

Lorelei had been pushing herself pretty hard to find the wayward Lucifer, and Aaron had given her explicit orders not to do it anymore. Unbeknownst to him, she wasn't listening, which partially explained the rough condition she was in. That and the spells she had been casting to calm Dusty's mind.

The images and sounds rushing through his head had quieted enough that Dusty could function, but it wouldn't be long before the static was back and Lorelei would have to help him again.

"But today we're going to do things a little bit differently," she said.

"Okay." His curiosity was piqued.

"Today I'm going to let you do the heavy lifting."

Dusty smiled, not quite sure what she meant. "What, we're moving furniture too? Or—"

"You're going to do some magick," she interrupted.

Milton squeaked, as if as shocked as Dusty was by this news.

"You're kidding," Dusty said. "What do I know about magick?"

"You were chosen to carry the Instrument, a creation of God Himself."

"Yeah. And if you remember, I was responsible for just about destroying the world," he added wryly.

"That doesn't change the fact that you were given this responsibility, and that you were able to control the Instrument's power," Lorelei said. "At least to a point."

He thought for a moment about what she said. "I don't know," he said warily.

"Why do you think I've been having you hang around me all this time?" Lorelei asked him. "The magick needed to become familiar with you. I needed to know if it would like you."

"Like me?" he repeated. "You make it sound as if the magick's alive or something."

"Archon magick *is* alive, in its own way," she told him. "It's the power of the living, and everything that ever lived, given shape and purpose."

He hated to bring it up, but if she wanted him to cast spells, then she had to know his concerns.

"I've seen what this magick can do," he said. "And I've seen what it does . . . to you."

"It takes something out of you, I won't deny it," Lorelei admitted.

"But, and I mean this with no disrespect, you're not human. If it has depleted your health this much, what will it do to me? I'm only human."

"You are?" she asked.

He was shocked by her retort. "Yeah, I am," he told her.

She turned back to her selection of books.

"You stopped being human the minute you took the Instrument into your possession," Lorelei told him. "Now get over here and lend me your arms," she ordered. "We're going to need quite a few of these if I'm going to properly teach you magick."

Gabriel noticed that it was darker than it had been yesterday at this time. That concerned him. Most of the creatures his friends fought shunned the daylight hours.

The beasts emerged into the world to hunt with the coming of night.

The Labrador sniffed around the perimeter of the property, searching for the scent of animals that lived in the surrounding woods. He remembered a time when this was his favorite thing to do, besides eating.

But he'd been simpler then. Aaron had not yet used the power of the Nephilim to bring him back from the brink of death; Aaron had not yet changed him into something more than just a dog.

These days, when Gabriel pondered such things, he wondered if he really was better off now. Before his change, complex thoughts would never have entered his mind. He'd been perfectly content to just sniff the scents of local wildlife.

Gabriel especially enjoyed the rabbits, though his joy of

chasing them had waned dramatically since his transformation. He'd come to understand how scared they were when he did that. He didn't get much enjoyment from scaring anything. The world had become far too scary on its own.

Nose pressed to the ground, Gabriel felt the presence of Lorelei's spells as he got too close to the edge of the grounds. The magickal boundaries made the fur on his neck and back stand at attention. Then he saw movement from the corner of his eye.

Gabriel thought it might have been one of the Nephilim, or maybe even a deer, but he smelled it ever so slightly in the air and recognized it for what it was.

He smelled one of his own kind.

Ignoring the electrical tingle of the magickal barrier, Gabriel surged toward the scent, only to see a small, brown shape running away.

"Wait!" he barked excitedly. Gabriel hadn't encountered another dog in these parts before, and was already thinking that he or she might have been lost, or maybe even abandoned. The thought of having canine company filled him with excitement, and he wondered if Aaron would even allow it. But that was something to consider at another time. First he wanted to be certain that the stray was okay.

Gabriel barked again, catching sight of the small dog as it ran farther from the school property.

"I mean you no harm!" Gabriel barked, in close pursuit. *"I just want to talk with you!"*

He caught a glimpse of the dog's back end as it ducked beneath the thick hanging leaves of a bush. Gabriel followed without hesitation. The branches were low to the ground, and he had to crawl on his belly for a bit before emerging into a clearing.

The other dog had stopped in the middle of the open area and seemed to be waiting for him.

"Hello," Gabriel said, attempting to keep his excitement level down so as not to scare the little dog away.

The dog did not move. He stared at Gabriel with dull, black eyes.

Cautiously the Lab moved closer, his tail wagging furiously. He'd met many other breeds over the years, and was certain that he'd never encountered another dog like this. His fur was so short that it was practically nonexistent. As Gabriel crept closer, he wondered if the dog had any fur at all. That was when he noticed that the animal's eyes didn't move as he approached.

Gabriel's hackles suddenly rose. Something wasn't right.

Then he caught sight of something long and thick attached to the dog's back end, thicker than a tail, and trailing down into the dirt behind him.

Gabriel growled and slowly backed away from the strange dog. The dark flesh around Gabriel's muzzle peeled back to reveal ferocious teeth, ready to rip and tear if necessary.

But still the other dog did not react, and Gabriel began to wonder if this was a dog at all.

Just as that doubt entered his mind, the ground beneath his paws began to tremble. Something huge and stinking of rot and death erupted from beneath the dirt and leaves.

Something that tried to eat Gabriel in one big bite.

Gabriel barked wildly, just barely avoiding the snap of massive jaws.

It wasn't a dog at all that he had tried to befriend, but some strange type of dog-shaped lure that grew out of the top of a monster's head. Gabriel found it amazing that the false dog, the lure, was somehow able to mimic the smell of another dog. The monster itself sort of resembled the toads that Gabriel used to find on his walks with Aaron through the woods back in Lynn. Only, this one was much bigger and uglier, and was now crawling from its hole to attack again.

Gabriel turned to dart beneath the bushes and return to the school and the protection of Lorelei's magickal barriers.

But the toad-thing had other ideas.

Even though Gabriel was fast, the monster was quicker. Something hard dropped from the air, striking the Lab's back, pushing him to the ground. Flailing in the dirt, Gabriel caught a glimpse of the doglike protrusion, now nothing more than a fleshy mass, being drawn back on its thick, muscular stalk.

Gabriel climbed to his feet again, but the toad would have none of it, whipping him again with the fleshy appendage. Gabriel lay there, cowering as the toad-thing dragged its body closer.

Then anger replaced fear as Gabriel realized he had no one

to blame but himself. Aaron had warned him about going outside Lorelei's magickal barrier, but the Lab had let his excitement get the better of him.

And now he was going to pay the price for his stupidity.

He would end up in the belly of this beast, and Aaron would never know what had happened to him.

Gabriel could smell the horrible stink of the monster's flesh and hear the hiss of its labored breath, the rapid-fire beating of its heart as it propelled its lumpy body at him, mouth agape to engulf him. Gabriel jumped to his feet, but he couldn't evade the attack.

The toad bit down on Gabriel, drawing the dog into its enormous mouth. It tossed back its misshapen head in an attempt to swallow him down, but Gabriel was not in the mood to be eaten this day.

Heavenly fire suddenly coursed through his body. Gabriel was burning. Inside the monster's mouth he was burning away the darkness of the beast.

Unable to contain the holy fire, the toad expelled the dog in a stream of sizzling digestive juices, roaring its displeasure. It brought its whiplike appendage down upon its enemy once more in an attempt to extinguish the divine flames.

But Gabriel would have none of it. The fire now gave him the strength to fight back. He attacked the thick, muscular tendril and tore away the fleshy hunting lure.

The toad cried out in sudden pain, rearing its grotesque mass away in an attempt to flee. But Gabriel could not let this horrible thing continue to live and feed upon some other unsuspecting dog or person.

Gabriel sprang at the monster, his body leaving a burning trail of brush behind him. He sank his teeth into the beast's accursed flesh. The taste was horrible, which made his fury all the more intense, and he bit and tore and ripped away huge pieces of the toad, filling his mouth with ash.

The monster dropped back into its hole, and that was where it died, its body quivering ever so slightly as Gabriel's heavenly fire consumed it.

Gabriel emerged from the hole as the divine fire within him began to dwindle, until there was no trace of it at all.

But he knew that it was still there inside him, waiting to be called upon again.

And as Gabriel left the burning corpse and headed back to the school and his family, he realized that it was not only the world around him that had changed—he had changed as well.

Aaron slipped the clean T-shirt over his head, catching a quick glimpse of himself in the mirror atop the old, broken bureau.

He stopped for a moment and stared at the person looking back at him.

He didn't recognize himself.

Where was the nineteen-year-old kid with the dark eyes and serious expression? He'd been replaced by someone who looked much older, and who actually had reason to wear such a serious expression. His hair was longer than usual, but who had time for a haircut when he was always out trying to save the world? Running his fingers through his dark hair, he thought that if there was ever another calm moment, he would ask Vilma to trim it for him.

He heard the sound of nails on the hardwood floor, and looked to see Gabriel standing in the doorway.

"Hey," Aaron said. "I was wondering where you'd gotten to. Why'd you let me sleep so long?"

"I was out sniffing around," he answered, somewhat agitated. *"I must have lost track of time."*

"Are you all right?" He approached Gabriel, suddenly concerned for his friend.

"Yeah," the dog answered. *"I was just out sniffing. . . . Nothing happened."* He abruptly turned and started down the corridor.

"Are you sure nothing happened?" Aaron asked, following.

Before the dog could answer, there came a strange humming sound in the air.

Aaron stopped, his hands covering his ears reflexively as his face twisted in discomfort. "What the hell is that?"

The sound seemed to permeate his skull, causing his brain to itch. In fact, he could feel his entire body tingling from the strange vibration that now filled the atmosphere. He could see that he wasn't the only one, that Gabriel was experiencing the painful sound—*sensation*—as well.

"I didn't do it," Gabriel said, ears flattening against his head.

"No, I wouldn't think you did," Aaron said, continuing down the hall to the stairs that would take him outside. "About that other stuff we were talking about . . . are you sure you're all right?" Aaron probed.

"Fine," Gabriel answered, descending the steps beside him. *"Things have just been crazy lately, and I guess it's starting to affect me."*

Aaron reached out to pat his dog's side affectionately.

"Don't make me start worrying about you, too," Aaron told his friend as they reached the exit.

Outside, the strange humming was even more prominent, and Aaron suddenly knew the cause.

"Over here," he said, already at a trot. Gabriel tagged along behind.

At the front of the property Aaron found the source of the odd sound. The giant sword of the Abomination of Desolation, which had once been the Instrument, vibrated wildly as it protruded from the ground.

"It's never done that before," Gabriel said.

"No, it hasn't," Aaron agreed, finding himself drawn to the enormous weapon.

He was not more than two feet away and reaching out to touch the trembling blade, when Lorelei cut into his mind.

"This isn't a test of the Emergency Broadcast System," Lorelei joked inside his brain. From the look on Gabriel's face, he'd heard Lorelei's voice too.

"*Could you all please come to the science lab?*" she asked. "*I've got something I think you should see.*"

The message broke off, and Aaron heard only the vibrating hum of the giant sword, and felt a slight tickling sensation in his nostril. He reached up to touch beneath his nose, and wiped away a trickle of blood. This was often a side effect of Lorelei's psychic messages.

"Shall we go see what she's got?" he asked his dog.

"*Yeah, before she calls back.*"

Aaron and Gabriel met up with Vilma at the science building. She held the door for them as they approached.

"You're awake," she said to Aaron with a sexy smile. He always found her smiles sexy, even when they weren't supposed to be.

"No thanks to you," he answered.

"Don't tell me that you didn't need it."

"Fine, I won't."

She followed them inside, and he purposely slowed so that they could walk side by side.

"Any idea what Lorelei wants?" Aaron asked.

Vilma shook her head. "Don't have a clue. I haven't seen her all day, but I bet it has something to do with the sword out there vibrating like mad."

The door creaked open behind them, and they all turned to see Melissa.

"Good! I thought I'd be late," she said, hurrying to catch

up. "What's up with the Instrument?" she then asked, following them in.

Aaron wondered where Cameron was, but was distracted by what was happening as they entered the science lab.

Since accepting that he was Nephilim, and learning about the creatures hidden in the shadows, Aaron had seen some pretty amazing things. So it was always impressive when he actually witnessed something that gave him pause.

"What is going on?" he asked.

Dusty sat cross-legged atop one of the black-topped lab tables, seemingly deep in the grip of some magickal trance. Floating in the air in front of him, slowly turning in orbit, was a globe, probably used at some point to teach about the solar system.

Verchiel was already present and stood off to the side, watching with cold, unimpressed eyes.

"What's he doing?" Aaron whispered as Lorelei came over, leaning heavily upon her cane. It broke his heart to see her this way. The Archon magick that she insisted on using to help them was slowly eating away at her. Milton the mouse sat upon her shoulder, his tiny black nose twitching excitedly.

"Was in the process of teaching him some of the basic magickal principles," she explained, eyes still locked on Dusty and the globe spinning before him.

"This looks a little bit more than basic," Vilma said.

"Exactly," Lorelei agreed. "It was almost as if I weren't

teaching him anymore but the magick was. It was like he was picking up some sort of signal from somewhere and . . ."

"The sword," Aaron said.

Lorelei looked at him.

"The sword is vibrating like crazy out there."

"I knew he had a connection to the sword, but I never expected anything like this," she said.

"How long has he been like this?" Gabriel asked, slowly padding closer to the lab table and turning his stare to the floating globe.

"Not very long," Lorelei said. "I called out just as soon as I saw the globe rise into the air."

"What do you think he's doing?" Melissa chimed in.

"I think the magick I've shown Dusty has helped him process information being broadcasted by the sword. Remember, he was the Instrument's bearer before . . ."

Small pinpricks of light began to illuminate specific sections on the globe's surface.

"Evil is spreading," Dusty said, his voice oddly magnified. Aaron had to wonder if he was totally in control, or if the sword was somehow speaking through him.

"As the daylight dims, the darkness spreads."

The dots of light now merged with other dots, covering entire landmasses.

"And spreads, and spreads, and . . . ," Dusty continued.

What had once been areas of light then turned to dark,

and Aaron watched with growing unease as the representation of the world was gradually swallowed up by blackness.

"Until the dying of the light . . . all light . . . and there is only shadow. But even that will not sustain its hunger."

Tendrils of darkness snaked out from the shiny black surface.

"And when the light of the world is extinguished, the shadow will move on, climbing higher and higher toward the ultimate source of light. . . ."

Aaron was suddenly gripped with an overwhelming feeling of dread, as he understood what Dusty was saying.

"To satisfy its voraciousness, the shadow will reach to the sky, and one by one the stars will go out, until its hunger is so great that it will feed upon Heaven itself. Then the black of nothing will hold indomitable sway over all."

As Dusty said this, the darkness began to spread from the globe, to the air around it, to the lab tables.

To lay claim to everything.

Aaron was just about to act—to do what, he really wasn't sure—when Dusty moaned. His face twisted as if in pain, and the snaking veins of shadow were pulled back into the globe, until it looked as it should.

The globe dropped to the ground with a heavy metal thud, and bounced, just missing Gabriel, who dashed away. Dented, but still intact, the sphere rolled about on the floor. Everyone stood, speechless.

Dusty unfolded himself from the position he'd taken to

work his spell, and Lorelei attended to him, making sure that he was all right.

"I'm good," he told her. "A little shaky, but good."

He climbed down off the table with her help.

"I know I'm mostly blind, but even I can see that something's up," Dusty said nervously. "What exactly did I do?"

Verchiel broke his silence.

"You were kind enough to show us that earth will be swallowed by evil, that evil then spreading to Heaven itself. I cannot express how happy I am to know not to waste any futile attempts to postpone an irreversible outcome," the angel said with a snarl.

"That's not true," Dusty said. "It's not an irreversible outcome. . . . It's only a possibility," he explained.

Aaron was curious. "What do you mean, only a possibility?"

Dusty took a moment to get his thoughts together.

"The Instrument, the sword, shows me multiple outcomes, the strongest being the most likely. But there are hundreds, maybe even thousands, of possibilities."

"So there's still a chance that we can stop this evil from spreading," Aaron said.

Dusty considered that. "Yeah, I think so."

"You're all mad," Verchiel chimed in again. The little angel of sunshine. "You saw the outcome."

"I saw a *possible* outcome," Aaron retorted.

"Darkness *will* overtake the world, and beyond. You've been out there, boy," Verchiel said. "You've seen what we're up against."

"No evil that we haven't beaten," Aaron said defiantly.

Verchiel smiled then, a cold and humorless smile. "You actually believe that you can keep this from happening?" he asked. "Have you looked around you, Aaron Corbet? Have you noticed how many there are of us and how many there are of them?"

"What was it you said to me?" Vilma suddenly asked the angel. "You either fight or die? Well, we're choosing to fight."

Verchiel's wings emerged and began to flap languidly.

"You're absolutely insane," he said. "Admirable . . . but insane. Now I understand how you beat me and my Powers. You're too damn stubborn to recognize your defeat."

"Nobody's defeated yet," Aaron said, not letting Verchiel's words dissuade him. "And I think that might be part of our problem."

Aaron squatted next to the globe on the floor. "Lorelei, or in this case Dusty, showed us where the evil will appear. Normally we would wait until it surfaced and then deal with it."

He laid his hand upon the globe and slowly rolled it around.

"I think it might be time to do things differently," Aaron declared. "A more proactive approach might serve our purpose better."

Aaron looked up from the globe.

"We're going to find this evil and destroy it before it can make its move," he said.

"Before?" Verchiel questioned.

"That's right," Aaron replied. He looked over to Dusty and Lorelei. "We can do that, right?" he asked. "There's a spell that can show us where these pockets of evil are, right?"

Dusty looked to Lorelei. "You're better at this than I am."

"Yeah," she said, stroking Milton's head on her shoulder as she considered Aaron's question. "They kinda stick out like a sore thumb. I'm sure we can rig some sort of spell to find the bigger pockets first, and then go from there."

"So we're going after this evil before it can get to us?" Melissa questioned.

"Exactly," Aaron said.

"Okay. We find it . . . but then what?" she asked.

"We give it a reason to be afraid of us," Aaron said, not really liking the cruelty he heard in his voice but knowing that it was completely necessary.

"When we find it, we kill it."

CHAPTER SIX

Aaron's words sent a chill of dread down Vilma's spine. She knew this was the way it had to be, but hearing the guy she loved speaking so violently drove home how dramatically things had changed for them.

For her.

There was a piece of her that understood these destructive times, taking to it almost like second nature. That was the Nephilim, the part of her that existed to fight evil and keep the darkness at bay.

But then there was the other part, the often scared human part that looked at all of this—what the world was becoming—and wanted to hide until it was safe again.

But her Nephilim instinct wouldn't let it. Her Nephilim told her scared human that it had to be strong, that if they couldn't work as one, the world would fall all the faster, and everyone and everything that meant anything to them would be lost.

Hearing Aaron speak about hunting down their enemies and killing them was a wake-up call. This was now her reality. And those chills of dread she felt—well, they were all just part of the package.

"He's right," Vilma said, adding her voice to Aaron's. "We hit this evil before it can hit us. Make it afraid. Maybe it'll get sloppy."

"Spoken with experience," Verchiel said sarcastically.

"Dude, was that really necessary?" Dusty asked. "Your mother not give you enough hugs or something?"

"Mother?" Verchiel questioned. "Do you have any idea who or what you're addressing?"

"I know you've got the wrong attitude," Dusty said.

"Enough," Aaron ordered. "Let's save the attitude for the enemy."

Vilma was surprised when both Verchiel and Dusty remained quiet.

Aaron looked as though he were going to continue, but he was interrupted by a cry from outside.

Vilma recognized the voice immediately. It was Cameron. He hadn't answered Lorelei's call. Vilma shot an inquisitive glance at Melissa, who quickly looked away.

Vilma dashed out toward the noise, and the others followed. She gasped as she caught sight of Cameron sitting in the grass, holding the body of another man in his arms. Their clothes were covered in blood.

"He's hurt," Cameron blurted out as Vilma knelt down beside them.

"Does any of this blood belong to you?" Vilma asked, pulling at Cameron's shirt, looking for wounds.

"Blood?" Cameron questioned.

"Are you hurt?" she asked firmly.

"No. No, I'm fine."

She turned her attention to the stranger in the Nephilim's arms. "I thought you were resting," she said to Cameron as she began to open the man's shirt.

"I went out . . . I couldn't . . . ," Cameron said quickly, and began to recount how the stranger had been hurt.

But his voice was nothing but a drone to Vilma. She stared at the bleeding gash across the man's chest, then at the strange, alien symbols that covered nearly every inch of his exposed flesh.

"What is this?" she asked almost to herself.

But she received no answer. Instead the familiar sound of a heavenly sword surging to life distracted her. She turned to see Verchiel raise the blade of fire above his head.

And prepare to bring it down upon the injured man.

Verchiel's scream of fury as he readied to kill the helpless, injured man conjured painful memories, reminding Aaron of a time not long ago when he had been the target of Verchiel's attacks.

The attacks had been vicious, but at least he had been conscious to defend himself.

Verchiel's blade had begun to descend in a sizzling arc, dangerously close to Vilma, when Aaron finally acted. His own blade of divine fire surged to life, and he thrust it forward to block Verchiel's sword. The two weapons exploded with sparks as they met, and he felt the angel's icy gaze upon him.

"You have no idea what you're doing, boy," Verchiel warned. "Leave it be and let me finish what I have started."

"I'm not going to let you kill this man," Aaron said defiantly.

He saw that Vilma had created her own blade, also ready to protect the fallen stranger.

"You talk about killing monsters, yet here you are protecting one of the greatest that ever existed," Verchiel proclaimed, fury burning in his eyes.

It was then that Aaron really looked at the blood-covered man lying upon the ground. He wasn't human. The man bore the scent of an angel.

"Who is he?" Aaron asked, pushing Verchiel back.

"His name is Mallus," Verchiel said, his every word dripping with contempt. "And next to your Morningstar, he is the greatest murderer Heaven has ever born witness to."

As the angel Mallus drifted between conscious and unconscious, he heard the voice of one he had once called brother.

And he remembered.

The war had yet to begin, but they knew that it was inevitable. The Morningstar's legions were amassing in the golden fields, waiting only for Lucifer's final order to attack.

Mallus was torn, wondering if there was any way—any chance—that war could be averted.

Lucifer had said he'd tried to explain their position to the Almighty, how the angels felt as though they were being cast aside, but even as the Lord God's most loved, Lucifer Morningstar's pleas had been rebuffed.

The Creator had told all the angels of Heaven that He had a plan and that was all that they needed to know.

But Lucifer and his minions were not satisfied with that answer. They feared what was to come . . . feared that God would no longer love them best. They felt as though they'd been left with no choice but to show their displeasure.

And so, Lucifer and his legions planned for war.

Mallus wanted to believe his Creator, but he'd seen the fires of hurt and rage burning in his brother Lucifer's eyes. And it was all because of these new creatures that God had introduced to the Garden.

These humans.

Mallus wanted to understand. He now went to Eden, to look upon these animals for himself, to see what the Morningstar and so many others of their ilk feared. Clad in armor of impending war, perched within the branches of the Tree of Life, Mallus secretly watched the humans.

The humans slept, wrapped in each other's arms, by the side of a rushing stream. Their design was fascinating but fragile. Yet as he looked closer, Mallus began to understand how special God had made these creatures.

"Hopefully you are questioning the Morningstar's madness," a voice stated very close by.

Mallus turned with a start to see that he was no longer alone. The angel Verchiel was perched upon a nearby branch.

"I wanted to see for myself," Mallus said, turning back to watch the sleeping humans. "I wanted to see if Lucifer's fears were valid."

Verchiel looked upon the humans as well. "The Lord loves them," he said. "That should be enough for us to love them too."

"But does He love them more than us?" Mallus asked.

"Does it matter?"

"To Lucifer and the others it does."

"And to you?"

Mallus continued to stare at the sleeping couple. "He gave them something special," he said after a while.

"He is the Creator. It is His right."

"He gave them a piece of *Himself*."

"The Creator calls it the soul," Verchiel explained.

"This soul . . . it makes them more like Him, closer to Him."

Verchiel agreed.

"And they can create others of their kind?" Mallus asked him. "Can this be true?"

"It is."

Mallus understood what it was that had filled so many of his brothers with such fear. "They will replace us," he said simply.

"If that is His will, so be it," Verchiel said.

Mallus suddenly felt the hatred growing in his heart. "Nothing good will come of them," he said, having made up his mind.

"That is not for us to decide," Verchiel admonished him.

"But we can show Him, tell Him how we feel."

"I see you have made your decision," Verchiel said sadly.

"I have," Mallus answered.

"Even though it will mean the death of many of your brothers," Verchiel warned.

"War is not something I take lightly," Mallus said to Verchiel. "But I would slay all of Heaven itself so as not to lose His love."

Then Mallus flew from his perch in the Tree of Life and returned to his commander and those who had sworn allegiance to Lucifer's cause.

That was the last time Mallus saw Verchiel as brother and friend.

And the first time he saw him as an enemy.

Verchiel reared back, withdrawing his sword, but he did not wish it away.

"I will not let you kill him," Aaron said with all the authority he could muster.

He watched as Verchiel stood, tensed like a cobra ready to strike. But Aaron was ready as well.

"And that is why you will fail against your enemies," Verchiel said, finally allowing his sword of fire to dissipate with a hiss and a whoosh of air. "You are not capable of making the kinds of decisions required to win this war."

"No, I'm just not going to make those kinds of decisions based entirely on your say so," Aaron retorted, lowering his own blade. "I guess it's a trust thing."

Verchiel snarled, turning, and walked away.

"I guess there's a history," Vilma said to Aaron as they watched Verchiel stalk off.

"I'd say so," Aaron replied.

Kraus was already tending to the injured angel, applying his medicines to the wound. "I've managed to stop the bleeding, but I need to get him back to the clinic," he said, standing up.

Aaron gazed at Cameron. The young Nephilim suddenly looked as though he wanted to be anywhere but there, on the receiving end of his leader's glare.

"You do realize that there isn't any room for disobedience?" Aaron asked him.

"Yeah," he said. "I understand."

"Do you really?"

Cameron nodded, then averted his eyes from Aaron's intense stare.

"Help Kraus get his patient to the clinic," Aaron ordered.

The young man helped the healer lift the unconscious angel, and the two dragged him off toward the infirmary.

"That was a little soft, don't you think?" Vilma commented.

"What did you want me to do, ground him?"

"He disobeyed an order . . . my order," she said.

"And that's unacceptable," Aaron agreed. "But we're entering dangerous times, and Cameron will be playing a very important role."

"I'm just not sure he understands how dangerous it was for him to go off by himself like that."

"If he didn't before, now he will," Aaron assured her. "Maybe we'll team him with Verchiel. That'll teach him the error of his ways."

Vilma chuckled, and Aaron was relieved to hear the sound.

From the corner of his eye, he saw Melissa approach, then hesitate.

"Everything all right?" he called out to her.

"Yeah," she said as she took a deep breath and stepped closer. "I just wanted to say that if Cameron's in trouble, then I should be in trouble too."

"And why is that?" Vilma asked. "Did you fly off on a solo mission too?"

"No," Melissa said. "But I knew he was gone . . . and I chose not to tell you."

"And you know that was wrong?" Vilma asked her.

"Yes," Melissa answered quietly, her body tensing as if preparing for the worst.

Vilma looked to Aaron, awaiting his verdict.

"Then I think we're done here," he said.

"We're done?" Melissa repeated. "That's it?"

Aaron nodded. "Go give Kraus and Cameron a hand back to the infirmary."

Melissa started to leave, then stopped. "I really am sorry," she said quickly to Aaron and Vilma, then turned and ran to catch up with the others.

Vilma watched her go. "She seems so much like a kid," she said to Aaron.

"Kid?" Aaron repeated, then laughed. "You probably only have a year or two on her."

"It feels like a long time since we were kids, doesn't it?" she asked. She moved to stand very close to Aaron. "I almost can't remember," she said quietly, and leaned her head upon his shoulder.

Aaron put his arm around her and squeezed her closer. "Do you think I'm crazy?" he asked.

"Generally?"

He squeezed her tighter, just to hear her laugh.

"Seriously, do you think this idea I'm pitching is the right one, about being proactive?"

"It's risky, I'll give you that, but at this stage what choice do we have?"

"I know," Aaron said. "The world doesn't seem to be getting any better, and unless we can step up our game, it never will. And even if we are proactive . . ."

"Now, don't you start sounding like Verchiel," she warned, hugging him tightly.

"He's not totally wrong," Aaron admitted.

"Oh, c'mon," Vilma said, giving him a shove. "If we followed his lead, we would just lie down and die now, and save ourselves the hassle. I don't buy it."

"But there are only so many of us, and way more evil creatures."

"Then we'll just have to work all the harder," Vilma declared.

"Yeah, but I'm starting to wonder . . ." Aaron gazed off in the direction that Kraus had taken their injured guest.

"Share," she ordered, looking up at him and thumping his chest with her hand.

"Our mysterious stranger. How many more of them are out there in the world? How many fallen angels weren't forgiven and never returned to Heaven? How many of them are there—and would they be willing to help us?"

Vilma looked toward the infirmary.

"Huh," she said, finally understanding his point. "Then I guess we'd better hope he doesn't die."

"Or that Verchiel doesn't kill him," Aaron added.

* * *

Bending the shadows to his will, Satan left his dwelling beneath the cold of the earth to pay a visit to his allies in his quest to order the world.

The Sisters did not seem at all surprised to see him.

"Hark, is that the king of all that flies, slithers, bounds, and crawls?" asked the first of the hunched, hooded figures.

"But why would one such as he visit three lowly ones like us?" asked the second.

"Perhaps he is eager to know of our progress?" suggested the third.

The three robed shapes huddled around an enormous stone cauldron, wafting clouds of foul-smelling smoke obscuring what bubbled within.

The Three Sisters of Umbra reached within the pot, their long-fingered hands adorned with razor-sharp claws that wove the thick, billowing smoke into shapes representative of the world of man.

A world that Satan hoped to subjugate soon.

"The darkness comes all the faster, limiting the time of light, but it is still not constant," he said.

One of the three turned her hooded gaze to him, only two burning pinpricks of light visible within the darkness of the cowl. "A tremendous responsibility to bestow upon such lowly ones as us," she said.

"But a task we assault with much vigor," said another, waving her hands through the exhaust roiling from the seething pot.

Though they were content to wear the guise of lowly subjects, Satan knew them to be far more than that. He had heard rumors that they were some of the first beings upon God's world, always lurking somewhere in the shadows, always eager to corrupt and bring about the downfall of man.

Satan wondered if they too had been wronged by the Almighty, when He'd brought the accursed light into the universe. He'd broached the subject with the Sisters in the past, but their answers had been cryptic.

All Satan knew was that their dark magicks were unsurpassed and that they were allies in his war against the light. He had a certain fondness for the three Sisters, especially since his own brothers and sisters of darkness had met with unfortunate fates during the battle when Satan had taken control of the Morningstar's form. Although he would have reduced his sisters and brothers to ash anyway if they had shown any signs of betrayal.

"Fear is high, and despair grows thick, but we still do not have enough strength to bring about the total fall of dark," said the last of the three.

All three Sisters turned their hooded faces to Satan, and spoke in turn.

"We require more energy, oh blackest of stars."

"Terror and sadness must permeate the atmosphere."

"The Fear Engines must be fed if the night eternal is to fall."

"You will have your horror and misery," the Darkstar said. "Your dearth of hope."

From a patch of shadow came an impish voice. "Master." Satan recognized his servant Scox. "Master, the Community leaders await your address."

It was time. Satan would unify the Community under his command, to speed up the fall of humanity, but first they had to learn to recognize his omnipotence.

Once more the Sisters spoke.

"You are summoned, oh darkest of stars."

"Do not dally, for there is much to be done to make the world yours."

"Show them who you are. . . . Show them who they must serve."

The Darkstar spread his wings in a whoosh of stagnant air, eyeing the three as he prepared to leave.

"I will do my part, and you will do yours," he commanded, using his wings to lift himself from the ground toward the patch of shadows that would transport him to the gathering of fiends.

A gathering of those who would soon call him king.

Scox turned his long neck toward the sounds coming from the next chamber.

Those representing the various races of the Community had been congregating there for some time, and they were not happy to have been kept waiting.

"Master!" he called again into the patch of shadow.

There were terrible screams from the chamber beyond, and

Scox knew that one of the Community members had probably become hungry and made a meal of another.

Such a volatile gathering, the imp thought, knowing full well that the Community races had issues sharing a world, never mind gathering in the same room. Scox was about to call for his master once more, when the patch of shadow started to undulate like a storm-swept ocean.

Satan, the Darkstar, emerged in all his glory, his wings unfurled.

"They're waiting," Scox said, wringing his hands.

Satan glared. "They've yet to realize that it is their duty to await me and my commands." He swiped at imaginary pieces of dust upon his armor.

"Yes, I suppose," Scox agreed as the sounds of disquiet wafted from the vast room beyond.

"And do I look the part of ruler?" Satan asked the imp.

Scox averted his eyes as he bowed his horned head. He knew only flattery would be welcome.

"When the Community sees you, they will think of nothing more," the imp spoke.

Satan glanced toward the doorway that would take him out into the chamber.

"This will be a historic moment," Satan spoke. "When all beasts spawned in shadow at last recognize me as their lord and master."

Scox again bowed his head, his clawed hands clasped reverently to his chest. "I'm certain it will be glorious," he added.

Satan flapped his wings once more, ruffling the slick, black feathers, and strode out onto a platform of ice and rock.

Scox followed, but only went out so far, watching from the sidelines.

The gathering of monsters went eerily quiet as Satan reached the center of the stage. Scox extended his neck to look out across the vast amphitheater at those in attendance. All eyes—if they had them—were fixed upon the Darkstar.

"Citizens of the nether," Satan began, his powerful voice reverberating through the vast underground auditorium. "For countless millennia our kind has been forced to hide from the light of the world and our divine enemies," Satan extolled, slowly pacing back and forth upon the stage. "But a plan has been formulated, and carefully executed."

Scox couldn't believe his eyes. The Darkstar had the Community's rapt attention. Perhaps they would recognize him as their leader after all.

"And at last it has come to fruition."

Satan spread his wings and raised his arms.

"I have orchestrated that plan, and I am here to bestow upon you that which has been denied to each and every one of your myriad species. I am here to give you what you have never been able to win for yourselves, no matter how hard you have tried."

Satan slowly scanned his audience, and Scox believed that his master was attempting to make a personal connection with each and every one of them.

"I give you," his voice boomed like thunder, "the world."

Satan's words were followed by gasps from the beasts and fiends, and Scox watched the various monsters muttering amongst themselves.

His master smiled from the stage.

Suddenly a lone voice spoke from the crowd.

"And what is expected of us? What do you require for such a prize?"

The mutterings, squeaks, and growls grew in intensity, supporting the question.

"What do I . . . ," Satan asked, bringing a metal-gauntleted hand to his armored chest, "expect of you?"

The Darkstar paused for effect. Scox could practically feel the anticipation growing from the bestial crowd.

"Your adoration," Satan announced, again starting to pace. "Your absolute obedience."

He paused again. The Community hung on his every word.

"And for you to call me king."

The vast chamber became very still as Satan's words began to permeate.

Scox was unsure what he had expected. Jubilant cheers? Cries and howls of excitement? He'd certainly never expected what followed.

As Satan waited for a response, an armored demon sprang up onto the stage. At first it seemed that the demon would kneel and swear its allegiance, but then it drew its sword.

"I'd just as soon die before swearing my loyalty to the likes of you!" the demon raged, charging Satan with a sword caked with the blood from previous kills.

Scox gasped.

The blade descended toward his master's skull, but Satan was faster.

"Don't let me keep you," Satan said, reaching out with blinding speed to grab the demon's wrist. He snapped its arm like a twig, causing its weapon to clatter to the ground.

Scox winced as Satan tore the demon apart, limb from limb, until only a pile of bloody pieces remained.

Finished with his gruesome chore, the Darkstar looked out to the crowd.

"Anybody else?" Satan asked, wiping his gore-covered hands together. "Would anyone else rather die than serve me?"

The chamber erupted into total chaos. Monsters of every conceivable size and shape charged en masse toward the stage.

Scox knew that it was best to flee the scene, but he found himself frozen in place, watching the symphony of violence that unfolded before him.

The beasts rushed Satan in a tidal wave of snarling, hissing, wailing fury that surged onto the ice stage with only one intention. Scox watched his master, marveling at the fact that Satan did not move from where he stood as the tsunami of violence bore down upon him.

Satan threw open his arms and wings in a welcoming gesture as the creatures of darkness who refused to recognize his authority attacked with the utmost ferocity.

They piled on him, weapons—as well as fangs and claws—ready to dispatch death upon the one who wished to rule them all.

Scox stood transfixed as his master was engulfed. He was tempted to cry out but feared the beasts would turn their rage on him.

So he remained quiet as the scene unfolded before his eyes. Scox never would have imagined so many different species of beast working together toward one goal: the murder of one who dared to proclaim himself king.

After so many centuries of ruling themselves, these creatures of the darkness did not respond well to the Darkstar's authority. It had been an interesting concept, but one that was doomed to fail—not that Scox had ever mentioned that to his master. To do so would have most assuredly courted his demise, and he quite enjoyed being the last of his species.

Scox was considering retreating, when there was a sudden flash of darkness.

Instead of an explosion of light, there came an outburst of shadow. Bodies flew in every direction, discarded and torn asunder by the mysterious detonation.

Covered in the blood of his master's attackers, Scox

craned to see what had happened. If he hadn't already been cold-blooded, the servant imp's blood would have frozen to ice from the sight. The crowds of murderous fiends had been driven back, corpses forming a ring of death around the Darkstar.

His glistening wings of ebony black unfurled, and he held a sword whose blade was as black as night.

The creatures of the darkness were as stunned as Scox, falling back at the sight, gasping as Satan then stood, surrounded by carnage.

"It doesn't need to be this way," Satan spoke in the calmest of voices. His voice was so soft and bereft of emotion that he could have been asking for a goblet of virgin's blood or the time of the next full moon.

Scox understood what he was doing. Satan was giving them another chance to accept him as their ruler.

Another chance to live.

And for a moment Scox believed that they were considering his master's offer.

Accepting Satan's mercy.

But beasts such as this seldom used their brains, being so caught up in their lust for blood.

It was a Duergar troll, the largest of the troll species, and the most vicious, who raised its ax above its head, and with a roar inspired those still alive to attack once more.

Scox saw the look upon his master's face as they charged

again. He was disheartened with what was about to occur, but he would protect himself—his mission—at all costs.

He would prove a point to the survivors.

Since the Duergar reignited the frenzy, it was only right that it was the first in this new wave to die. Scox didn't know if trolls believed in anything beyond the life they lived, but whatever they believed, the Duergar was now confronted with it.

Satan showed no mercy. His blade of darkness sliced through the tough leathery skin and internal workings of the Duergar, cutting it in half.

It was as if the troll's blood fueled the others' stupidity, and they began to throw themselves at their enemy. Satan met their attacks, his blade of shadow cutting them down, one after the other.

And still they came at Satan. It was as if they had committed to this act, and would see it through no matter how futile.

Scox wondered if his master would have shown mercy if one of the monstrous Community had laid down its weapons, sheathed its claws, and bowed its head, swearing allegiance.

Would the Darkstar forgive their indiscretions against him?

This was a question perhaps for another time, for none appeared ready to give up without a fight. Demons, trolls, goblins, and giants fell before the Darkstar. Satan never seemed to tire, never seemed to falter.

The chamber became choked with the smell of blood, and offal, and fluids of every conceivable consistency, and Scox could only watch as the Community was cut down.

Then Satan left the stage, swooping down to slay those that sought to escape his justice. They died as all the others had, quickly, painfully, choking on their life fluids.

Armor stained with the lives of those he had wished to lead, Satan walked amongst the fallen, seeking out those who still clung to life, and making certain that they clung no more.

As he drove the end of his glorious black blade through the throat of a struggling frost giant, Satan turned his gaze toward the stage.

To where Scox knelt in a pool of blood.

The imp's eyes locked with his masters, but he remained silent, waiting for his lord to be the first to speak.

"Well," Satan said as he looked back at the carnage that he had caused. "That certainly could have gone better."

CHAPTER SEVEN

Jeremy dreamed of Vilma.

Her lovely dark hair, her bronze-colored skin, her wings of fawn dappled with flecks of white and black.

They flew together, high in the air above a fantastic city of golden spires. She teased him, attempting to evade him with some pretty brilliant aerial acrobatics, but he was a determined soul and matched her maneuverability.

But he didn't want it this way. Jeremy didn't want to catch Vilma. He wanted Vilma to willingly come to him. He wanted her to know how right they were together. He wanted both of them to want the same thing.

She dove down to the city skyline, weaving in and out between the towers that seemed to be made from gold infused with the power of the sun. Jeremy considered letting her go about her business. Then he saw her chance a look, to see if he was still there. Vilma smiled that smile that drove him mad, and Jeremy flapped his wings all the harder to catch up with her.

With a smile like that cast in his direction, he would never give up the chase.

The wind rushed in his ears as his wings flapped harder and faster. Vilma was almost in reach. He soared above her, looking down at her delicate yet powerful wings, the glorious musculature of her back that allowed the appendages of flight to move with such flawless efficiency. His eyes continued their journey over the beauty of her details, the long, muscular legs that—

The tower needle seemed to appear from out of nowhere, but he knew he just hadn't been paying attention.

Almost striking the antennae, Jeremy narrowly averted the potentially deadly situation, but found himself spiraling toward the ground. Though barely able to control his descent, he managed to get some air beneath his wings just before he would have crashed through a rooftop. It wasn't graceful, but it beat breaking a leg or wing.

For a moment he lay there on the roof, stunned, reviewing what had just happened, and how Aaron would have berated him for not keeping his head in the game. Jeremy remembered Vilma's muscles flexing and releasing beneath her skin of golden brown, the delicate line of her back, and the way her bottom . . .

He closed his eyes and smiled, holding on to the memory with both hands. His head was in the game all right.

Sitting upright, he checked himself to be sure he'd survived the awkward landing unscathed. He had. Getting to his feet with a moan, Jeremy glanced up to see an image of absolute beauty flying toward him at a decent clip.

He considered diving out of the way but decided to hold his ground. What did the Americans call it? Playing chicken.

Yeah, that was it. Playing chicken.

He'd play the game to see who would blink first.

She hit him like a runaway train, driving them both back along the roof in a tumble of arms and legs. Vilma lay atop him, looking down into his eyes, and Jeremy was startled by her intensity.

He struggled to say something, but could only concentrate on the feeling of her weight pressing against him. Vilma's wings fanned ever so slowly on either side of them.

Vilma looked as though she were about to make a smart-ass comment that he should look where he was going.

But instead her face darted down to his, her lips hungrily seeking out his own. He'd thought the kiss he had stolen from her on the school grounds had felt amazing, but now he knew how wrong he'd been. This kiss was electrifying.

Jeremy kissed her back, his arms circling her delicate yet muscular body as his hands ran along her back, and onto her wings.

It was as he'd always imagined it would be. He had an overwhelming feeling that this was right, and from her reaction to him, he knew she felt the same way.

They were supposed to be together.

* * *

Jeremy wasn't sure at first what woke him. The feeling of Vilma's lips pressed to his slowly began to diminish, and he tried desperately to hold on to the memory of them for just a little bit longer.

He was disappointed that it was only a dream. But what a dream! His body was slick with sweat, and he could still feel his heart beating triple time behind his ribs. He'd dreamed of Vilma often but never with this intensity.

But the telly in the other room blared as if it were in the room with him.

"The bloody hell," Jeremy grumbled, throwing his feet over the side of the mattress and heading toward the door. They'd had a right difficult time getting the exceptionally crabby Baby Roger to go down for the night, and if he should be awakened, there would most certainly be hell to pay.

Throwing open the door, Jeremy was assaulted by how loud the television was actually playing. Cursing his mother for her lack of common sense, never mind for awakening him from the most spectacular dream he'd ever experienced, he prepared some choice words for old Irene. As he reached the end of the short hallway and entered the small but cozy living room, he stopped. The telly channels were switching, but there was nobody in the room.

"Mum?" Jeremy called out, his eyes going to the overstuffed chair where she usually sat, but the seat was empty.

Like some sort of zombie he lumbered forward into the

living space, coming up against the back of the equally over-stuffed sofa and looking over the side.

Nestled in the corner of the couch, back propped up against two pillows, sat Baby Roger. He was holding the television remote in two chubby hands and pressing the buttons, watching as the programs ticked past.

"Oh, my," was all Jeremy could say as he watched the infant, almost convinced that this was yet another dream.

Until Roger noticed him standing there.

The baby looked at Jeremy with large and strangely intelligent eyes.

"Would you be so kind as to get me a bottle, Jeremy?" Baby Roger asked before turning back to the television. "I'm absolutely famished . . . and I think I may have soiled myself."

Jeremy was numb with shock, capable of only staring in disbelief.

Baby Roger glanced at him briefly, smiling a toothless grin and waving a chubby hand. "Jeremy, I have my needs."

The Nephilim broke the paralysis that had held him in place, stiffly turning away from the baby and lurching toward his mother's bedroom, screaming for her as he had as a wee child when the bogeyman had come for him in the night.

Aaron stood silently in the doorway, watching Lorelei struggle.

She leaned against one of the lab tables, rubbing her left palm, which was now twisted like a claw. Her expression told him that she was in great pain, and he felt that sorry, helpless feeling in the pit of his stomach. He knew that he was at least partially responsible for her declining health and that there was no way he could make her better.

The spells she cast, the spells that ravaged her body, were essential for their survival, and the survival of the world.

He stepped a little bit farther into the room and cleared his throat.

Lorelei immediately turned to him, a smile on her face as if everything were perfectly fine. But Aaron knew otherwise.

"I didn't see you at supper, so I brought you a sandwich," he said, placing the paper plate he'd been carrying on the table in front of her.

"Thanks." She pulled the plate toward her with her injured hand. "Did you make it?"

"Yeah," he said. "Ham and cheese with a little mustard. . . . That's right, isn't it?"

"Perfect." She picked up one half of the sandwich and took a bite. "I used to be a mayo girl, but since I started playing with Archon magick, my taste buds have gone the spicier route." She chewed for a bit, wiping the excess mustard from the corners of her mouth. "I wonder why that is."

"I don't know," Aaron said with a shrug. "Maybe the Archons like mustard."

Lorelei laughed. "Yeah, maybe it is something as simple as that."

Aaron looked around the lab. "No Dusty?" he asked.

Lorelei broke off a piece of crust and fed Milton, who was sniffing around her plate.

"The boy's exhausted," she replied, taking another bite. "That was his first real try at magick, and it certainly took a lot out of him. I told him he should get some rest, that he would probably be needed again soon."

Aaron pulled one of the metal stools from beneath the table and sat down beside Lorelei. "So this is good for you, right?" he asked.

"What—the sandwich? It's great."

Aaron laughed, but the seriousness of his question quickly drove the laughter away. "No, this business with Dusty being able to work the magick. This allows you to take it a little slower, right?"

Lorelei started on the second half of her sandwich. "That all depends," she said, peeling away some crust and popping it into her mouth. "We've got a lot going on here, and now with two of us being able to do the spells—"

"You've already done some serious damage to yourself, and it's only going to get worse," Aaron interrupted her. They had talked about this many times before, and every time Lorelei would agree with him, tell him that she planned to slow down, but she never did.

And she continued to die by inches.

"I know you're concerned, but you don't have to be," she

told him around a mouthful of ham and bread. "This is what I signed up for, what I'm here to do, with you guys."

"But I don't want you to—"

"Every day you and the others are out risking your lives to make the world better, like it used to be," she continued, ignoring him. "Any one of you could have an off day or night and not make it back here. Those are the risks *you* take to be what you are."

She popped the last bite of sandwich into her mouth and chewed well before speaking again. "And these are the risks that *I* take."

Aaron was going to argue, but he knew it would do little good. If there was one thing he had learned about Lorelei, it was that the word "stubborn" was far too soft to describe her.

He nodded, begrudgingly accepting what she had to say.

"So," he said, changing the subject. "What do you think of my plan to be proactive instead of reactive?"

"I think it's as good a plan as any," she told him. "We need to make some headway somehow, and that sounds like it might be the way."

As she spoke, he noticed a tray of bloody doves on the counter behind her.

She followed his gaze. "I took a little psychic walk not too long after our meeting," she began to explain. "I wanted to see if I could find some of the larger nests of beasties in the world, and I realized that many of these threats showed no signs of even being on the planet."

She held up a finger before he could start to question.

"Until they were," she added.

"They weren't here, until they were," Aaron repeated, confused.

Lorelei nodded. "Exactly."

"I don't understand. Are you saying that they're coming from someplace else?"

"Not all of them. There are always those random creatures hiding at the bottom of a mine shaft, or swimming in the deepest parts of the ocean, but the majority of these creatures are opening passages from another place to come here and raise some hell."

"And then they go back to wherever?" Aaron asked.

"Most likely."

"So what do you suggest? Can we find and close these passages?"

Lorelei leaned forward on her cane as she thought for a moment. Milton jumped from the lab table onto her arm and climbed back up to his place upon her shoulder.

"They'd probably just figure out how to open them again," Lorelei said.

"Then we'll have to stop them when they try to cross over," Aaron stated.

"Yeah, I think that's the best," she said.

"When they open these passages, we'll be waiting," he said. "And we'll see how much they like somebody going into their space."

"Raising some hell on the other side," Lorelei said with a smile.

"We'll give those beasties a real reason to be afraid of us," Aaron added.

He started to get down off the stool, remembering that there was someplace he needed to be.

"We'll start tomorrow," he told her. "We'll split into teams so we can cover more area."

"Sounds like a plan," Lorelei replied with a smile.

Aaron started for the door, but then paused. "Anything on Jeremy or my father?" he asked.

"No," she said. "But now that I have Dusty to help, there are a few locating spells that I want to try."

Aaron was good with that answer. He felt in his gut that they hadn't been deserted by either of the two, and he wanted to do everything in his power to see that the two men were found.

"And, Lorelei?"

She looked at him.

"Try to get some rest."

The Archon magick user smiled her sly smile as she answered, "Aaron, you of all people know there's no real rest for the wicked."

Vilma had taken a shower, hoping that the hot water and soap would somehow wash her dream from her mind. But she met with little success.

She couldn't get the kiss she'd shared with Jeremy in her

dream out of her head. That would teach her to slow down for a minute. She hadn't even known she was falling asleep.

The dream had been strange. Jeremy had pursued her as they flew over some strange, almost futuristic city. She remembered feeling excitement as she flew—and as he got closer to catching her.

She wanted him to catch her.

Vilma swore beneath her breath, hanging her towel on the rack and then getting herself dressed. It was crazy; she didn't have any feelings for Jeremy. It was Aaron whom she loved.

Then why dream? a nasty voice asked from the back of her mind.

She remembered flying down to tackle him on a rooftop, and that moment's hesitation before . . .

Vilma's lips tingled with the memory, and she reached up to touch them.

"This is so crazy," she said to herself.

She would have been lying if she'd said that she wasn't concerned about Jeremy. It had been weeks since he'd disappeared without a trace. But her heart raced with the thought of the dream—the thought of him. Her skin prickled as if caressed by a cool breeze.

"Enough is enough," Vilma said aloud, pulling on her jeans.

"What's enough?" asked a familiar guttural voice from the doorway, and Vilma looked up to see Gabriel standing there, his tail wagging.

She grabbed a clean blouse from a pile of folded clothes and started to put it on.

"This day . . . this life . . . ," she grumbled, buttoning her shirt.

"That doesn't sound so good," the Labrador said, padding into the room.

"I'm sorry, Gabe," she said, bending down to pet him. "I'm just a little stressed right now."

"Want to talk about it?" he asked, turning his brown soulful eyes to hers. She was tempted to talk to him about the dream, and about Jeremy, but she didn't think that she could.

"Thanks, but I'm okay," she said instead. She hugged his thick neck, and bent forward to kiss his blocky head. "I've got to go."

"Where are you going?" the dog asked with a curious tilt of his head.

"Aaron and I are going out."

The dream was there, at the periphery of her thoughts. She could feel Jeremy's hands upon her back, stroking the sensitive feathers of her wings.

"You're going on a date?" Gabriel asked.

She pushed the dream as far away as she could, but could still see it—*feel it*—off in the distance.

"Yeah, you could call it a date," she said, and smiled at the dog.

"That's nice," Gabriel said, sitting at her feet and wagging his tail. *"You two need some time alone."*

"Yeah," she said. "I think we do."

*   *   *

Lucifer remembered the love of his God, the love He had for all of His angels.

Although He had loved Lucifer most of all.

Adrift in this mindscape of the past, Lucifer Morningstar tried to look away. He would have preferred not to remember this time in his distant past, but it appeared the choice was not his.

He saw himself as he had been, the Son of the Morning, sitting by his Creator's side as He established order from the chaos of nothing, the cold darkness driven away by His divine light.

How proud Lucifer was.

He heard the choirs of angels singing in praise of Him, their celestial voices raised to the Lord God as He created the universe and the planets that would populate it. Oh, what a time it was, and Lucifer wished that the moment could be frozen in a perpetual loop to be played—lived—over and over again.

That was when he was the happiest, when all who had been created to serve Him were the happiest.

Lucifer tried to move on to some other time in his existence, for he did not want to see what was to follow. But this memory continued.

The Almighty had crafted a place like no other. Such attention He paid to this world, as if it were to be a jewel in His crown of glory.

"What is this place?" the Morningstar asked his Master.

"It is to be the home of my latest creations," God replied proudly.

"And what shall they be?"

"They shall be my greatest achievement," the Almighty lauded. "Through them, all that I am and all that I shall ever be will be exemplified."

"But what of us, your angels?"

"You shall always have a place," God said, and continued about His task, making sure that this new world—this Garden—was perfect for His newest creations.

Lucifer watched this vision, transfixed, as God took up mud and dust and dirt and fashioned this new creation.

And then He breathed life into what had none, life and a piece of Himself.

"I present to you the first of humanity," the Lord of Lords said proudly to His angel, who had once been His most loved.

Who had once been, but was no more.

That was the moment when Lucifer Morningstar first knew the feeling of hate.

A hate that would gestate over time, giving birth to his fall and destruction. But from this fall there would also come a gift.

A gift of salvation.

Verchiel waited for the healer and the two Nephilim to depart and leave their patient unattended, before he stepped from the darkness.

Mallus lay upon the cot, his dire wound tended to by Kraus's expert hands. If there was ever a human amongst them who understood the biology of the angelic, and could save Mallus, it would certainly be Kraus.

Verchiel loomed over the unconscious fallen angel, resisting the urge to strike him dead. How long had he and the Powers searched for this criminal of war, often coming close but never able to lay hands upon him?

Gazing down at the powerful magickal sigils tattooed on Mallus's flesh, Verchiel now understood why. He extended his hand, holding it over the markings, feeling the magick emanating from them in waves. If it hadn't been for the wound in his chest that had broken the patterns scrawled upon his flesh, Mallus would have remained completely invisible to him.

But now . . .

"I think I wanted you most of all," Verchiel said in a soft, menacing whisper. "Even more so than the Son of the Morning."

Verchiel had a brief, painful flash of memory. The battlefields of Heaven, awash with the blood of brothers; Mallus's leering face, speckled in gore, looming above him, a spear of fire ready to be brought down.

Verchiel experienced that wave of helplessness again, which fueled his present anger. A fiery sword came to life in his grasp as he looked upon the injured criminal.

It was then that he saw that Mallus's eyes were open. They

were little more than slits, and Verchiel was unsure if the angel was fully conscious.

Until his mouth began to move.

Mallus's lips quivered ever so slightly. He was trying to speak. Leaning closer, Verchiel attempted to hear the angel's words.

They were soft, barely a whisper, but Verchiel understood.

"Do it," Mallus urged. "For what I have done . . ."

Verchiel clutched the burning sword hilt all the tighter as the blade hissed and burned brighter, fueled by his emotions.

"Kill me."

And even though there was nothing he would rather have done at that very moment, Verchiel refrained. Was it that he wished the angel to continue to suffer for his sins, or was it something more . . . something that went back to another time when they were brothers beneath the loving gaze of the Creator? Verchiel could not bear to think of it any longer. He wished his weapon away and stepped back into the darkness from which he had come.

Before he could change his mind.

Aaron opened his wings, releasing Vilma from his arms.

"Can I open my eyes now?" she asked with a smile, eyes still tightly closed.

"Go ahead," he said.

She opened them and looked around, nose wrinkling at the funky smells.

"Where are we?" she asked.

Aaron took her hand, leading her out from behind the Dumpster at the far side of the parking lot, and toward the building across from them.

They passed an open screen door and could hear the sounds of people talking, and smell the delicious aromas wafting out from vents in the building's roof.

"Is this a restaurant?" she wanted to know as they rounded the building to the front entrance.

"It's nothing fancy," he told her.

"We *are* at a restaurant," she said, and he could hear excitement in the tone of her voice.

Aaron let go of Vilma's hand to open the door for her, gesturing with a sweeping motion for her to go inside.

"I can't believe you," she said. "Why are we doing this?"

The hostess at the wooden lectern at McKinney's Grill greeted them and gathered two menus, directing them to follow her to a cozy booth at the back of the restaurant.

"Here ya go," she said as they seated themselves, and she handed them each a menu. "Kathy, your waitress, will be right over. Enjoy your meal."

They thanked her, and Aaron opened his menu.

"What are you doing?" Vilma asked him.

He lowered his menu to find her looking at him, surprised. "What do you mean?"

"Why are we doing this? Why are we here?"

"Answer me honestly," Aaron said. "Have we ever been on a date? A real date, where we weren't killing something that crawled from a sewer or attacked a school bus or something?"

She thought for a moment. "No, not really, but—"

"Well, here we are, then," he told her. "Our first real date."

"I can't believe you," Vilma said, shaking her head but smiling at him.

"Get whatever you want," he told her. "The sky's the limit."

She laughed, and Aaron just about melted. Now, that was a sound that he wished he could hear more often.

Aaron looked around the dining room. Many of the tables and booths were empty, but there were some brave souls who had ventured out to grab a bite. He could only imagine how the insanity in the world was affecting businesses like this one. Who wants to leave the house, when you risk being eaten by something?

As he craned his neck, he could see inside the next room. Nearly all the bar stools were taken. Those patrons were glued to the news broadcasts of the latest horrors to befall the darkening world.

"Hey," he heard Vilma say.

He smiled as he turned his attention back to her.

"So, was this spur of the moment, or what?" she asked him.

"Yeah, kinda," he said. He focused on his menu, trying to figure out what he felt like eating. "It just felt more important over the last few days and all."

"Does it have anything to do with your new proactive plans?" Vilma's demeanor became very serious. "Are you afraid that one of us might die?" She paused for a heartbeat. "That we have to have at least one real date before it's too late?"

"No," he said, reaching across the table to take her hand. "Not at all." Aaron was lying but felt it was the acceptable kind of lie. He didn't want to scare her, or make a potentially bad situation even worse.

What he was planning, what he was planning for all of them—it was risky. Who knew what the repercussions might be? He was desperate for a few special moments alone with Vilma, before everything that they knew slipped away into the darkness.

"I wish we'd done something like this sooner," he told her. "But now seems just as good a time as any."

They were still holding hands when their waitress arrived.

Kathy was an older woman with bleached blond hair. Just by looking at her, Aaron could tell that she'd worked at McKinney's for a very long time.

"Sorry to keep you waiting, kids. Do you know what you'd like?" she asked.

Vilma ordered a house salad and the chicken piccata with a ginger ale.

He ordered the rib eye, medium rare, a house salad, and a soda water with lime.

Kathy wrote it all down, then excused herself to put in their order and get them some rolls and butter. They thanked her as she went off, and Aaron realized that they were still holding hands.

No wonder Kathy had looked so amused.

"You have to promise me something," Vilma said suddenly to Aaron.

"And what's that?"

"You have to promise that this isn't the last time we do something like this."

"Oh, so you like the good life, eh?" he joked.

"We could be sitting waiting for a bus, just as long as we're together," she said seriously. "And just as long as the promise keeps you from getting killed."

He ran his thumb gently over her knuckles.

"Waiting for buses," he repeated with a nod. "Why didn't I think of that? It would have been a lot cheaper than McKinney's."

That made her laugh, but Aaron could tell that Vilma was still waiting for him to say it. "I promise," he finally said, feeling something twist in the pit of his stomach. "But you have to promise me the same thing."

"I promise," she said.

But Aaron recognized the look in her eyes, and understood that they both knew these were promises they weren't sure they could keep.

CHAPTER EIGHT

The Architects had been searching for Mallus ever since he had abandoned their cause. Somehow he had managed to keep himself hidden, but the Architects were patient, knowing that there would come a time when he could hide from them no more.

Once, the Architects had seen something special in the one called Mallus. His beliefs had mirrored their own. They had welcomed him into their fold and had given him purpose. But something had happened.

Something had turned him from the path they had paved for him.

The path to the future.

No longer serving the Architects' purpose, Mallus had become a threat. As resourceful as they knew him to be, he had managed to elude the many Agents sent to find and eliminate him.

Until now.

Mallus had suddenly reappeared, the familiar thrum of his life force resonating along the strands of invisible webbing that enwrapped the world.

And the Architects had immediately dispatched an Agent to kill him.

Agents were relentless in their pursuit, never resting until they found their quarry. But once they did, once their purpose was fulfilled, their lives ended.

This particular Agent had waited patiently for its prey to surface. Now it stood on the periphery of a wooded property, its skin-tight suit blending with the environment, making it invisible to the eye. It tilted its masked face ever so slightly to the cool evening air, tracking the scent of its quarry.

The Agent could tell that Mallus was close, and that he was gravely injured. But it also caught the scent of angelic magick surrounding the land. The Agent squatted down next to the magickal boundary and leaned in close, its mind processing the aroma and determining that it was an Archon spell that protected this property.

Searching its memory with great speed, the Agent found a counterspell that would deaden an area large enough for it to enter without setting off any defensive alarms. Swiftly, silently, it followed Mallus's scent. The Agent clung to the shadows, careful not to be seen. The Architects desired the fallen angel to look as if he'd died of natural causes. His current injuries would be the perfect cover for the real cause of Mallus's demise.

The smell of the traitor grew stronger as the Agent neared a stone building. Pressed against the sides of the structure, it found a window, open just enough for it to slip over the sill and inside.

The Agent was close now. Mallus was in a nearby room, but the Agent's preternatural senses picked up the scent of another. It was a human, who would pose no threat to the Agent.

Noiselessly the Agent found its way into the room. The human sat at a desk, writing, occasionally looking into the adjoining room at Mallus's still form. The angel was lying upon a cot in a deep, healing sleep. The Agent extended a needle from the tip of one of its gloved fingers and crept silently behind the man. It pricked the back of the man's neck and injected him with a mild sedative that would render him unconscious almost immediately.

With the human now fast asleep, his head resting on his notes, the Agent turned its attention toward Mallus. Considering that its prey had avoided elimination for so long, the Agent was surprised how easy its mission was going to be.

From a sheath on the side of its leg, the Agent withdrew a Blade of Gleaning and prepared to drive the supernaturally sharp knife into the skull of its prey. The blade would extract information that the renegade might have collected and retained during the years when he'd hidden from the Architects.

The Architects needed to know everything that Mallus had

done—where he'd gone, why he'd turned on them, and who else might now know of their existence and plans.

The Agent leaned in close to find the best place to insert the blade, and noticed the sigils tattooed upon the fallen angel's body. The markings were powerful magicks, that had successfully rendered Mallus invisible to prying eyes.

These sigils had been an ingenious plan, as long as the marks had remained intact.

The Agent surmised that the bloody bandage covering Mallus's chest concealed not only a grievous wound but broken sigils, which allowed the angel's presence to again be felt.

The Agent breathed in the scent of the angel who had defined its purpose for so long, then brought the knife up behind the angel's ear. As the tip of the Blade of Gleaning touched the angel's pale flesh, the Agent considered what it would be like to have fulfilled its purpose and no longer exist.

It found the unknown strangely exciting.

"You might want to step away from him," said a voice from behind it.

The Agent turned toward the sound. A lone figure stood in the doorway. He had a strange stink about him, both earthly and divine.

A Nephilim.

All in all Aaron had a great night.

He and Vilma managed to enjoy their meals, both cleaning

their plates. They split a huge slice of mud pie, and were so full by the last bite, Vilma thought that she might pop the top button of her jeans, while Aaron just thought that he might slip into a food-induced coma.

They lingered for a little while after Aaron paid the bill, before they both admitted that it was time to head back.

Outside in the parking lot, they kissed, a long, loving kiss that reminded Aaron how much he wanted to live. Vilma grounded him. She made his life make sense. It was that simple, and complex at the very same time.

"I love you, Aaron Corbet," she said as their lips parted and she looked deeply into his eyes.

"And I love you, Vilma Santiago."

Then they walked arm in arm to the back of the parking lot, searching out a patch of darkness to conceal their departure.

It wasn't late, but it was deathly quiet back at the school. Vilma started to lead Aaron back to the dormitory, but something made him stop.

"Aren't you coming?" she asked him.

He looked over to the infirmary building. "I think I'm going to check in with Kraus," he told her. "See how our mysterious patient is doing."

Vilma nodded slowly as she released his hand. "Don't be too long," she ordered.

"I won't," he said.

"I'll wait up for you," she added, a hint of a lascivious smile playing at the corners of her lips.

"You'd better," he warned jokingly, watching as she turned from him, continuing on her way.

So there he was, standing in the doorway of their patient's room, Kraus asleep at the desk nearby. Aaron stared at the bedridden casualty across the room, but saw so much more.

A figure made of shadow leaned over the unresponsive angel, holding something that glinted in the faint light of the infirmary room.

"You might want to step away from him," Aaron then said.

And the masked figure turned toward him, knife in hand.

The figure was there one second, and gone the next.

Aaron was thinking it had somehow teleported away, when he suddenly caught a flash of light heading straight for his left eye. He dove from the path of the blade, crashed into the front of a supply case, and shattered one of its glass panels. He looked to where he thought his attacker would be, but still did not see it. Then came the crunch of glass, and Aaron again found himself under attack.

Somehow his attacker was able to blend with the environment. It took everything that Aaron had to distinguish the shape that slashed and thrust its knife at him.

From his training Aaron knew that the best way to deal

with this situation was to grab hold of the attacker. If he could touch it, then Aaron could fight it.

But the figure's costume was strangely slippery, as if covered with some sort of grease, and Aaron was thrown off balance. The two grappled briefly as Aaron tried to regain his footing. The blade came dangerously close to him again.

Suddenly, like a switch being thrown, the angelic aspect of Aaron's nature kicked in. He felt the warm flush as divine fire engulfed his hand, which held the attacker's blade at bay. There was a flash of orange flame, and the stink of cooking meat filled the air.

But his attacker did not even cry out.

The two continued to struggle, until the attacker's hand burned away and the blade clattered to the infirmary floor. The attacker disappeared into the shadows, leaving Aaron with a handful of ash.

Disgusted, and a little unnerved, he tossed the remains to the floor.

A rattle and clank sounded nearby. The drawer on a wheeled cart opened to expose surgical tools on the inside. Aaron reacted, ebony wings exploding from his back as he leaped across the room, but the scalpels were already in flight and sank into the soft flesh of his shoulder.

Aaron crashed to the floor and ripped the three surgical knives from his right shoulder. It took far more effort to remove them than he would have expected, the blades having been thrown with such strength that they had buried themselves deep into the muscle.

He dropped the bloody tools to the floor, and he carefully scanned the room for his foe. There was a sudden weight upon his back, and Aaron felt a rock-hard forearm slip about his throat, viciously hauling him backward. His oxygen was immediately depleted, and tiny explosions of color danced before his eyes. With great effort Aaron tensed the powerful muscles in his back, flexed his expansive wings to their fullest, and tossed the invisible threat away.

Rubbing at his bruising throat, Aaron listened for where his attacker had fallen. A file cabinet in the corner of the room tipped over, spilling old records from the facility's previous occupants. The papers spread across the floor and crinkled under the invisible attacker's step.

Aaron sprang from the floor just as something rough and jagged slashed across his face. The Nephilim recoiled and fell backward. His foe was using the jagged stump of his own arm as a weapon.

What is this thing? Aaron wondered as a surgical saw flashed through the air at him. He was driven back toward the wall as the silver blur slashed at him, barely missing. Aaron worked his way to the door as he concentrated on bringing forth a sword of flame to block the relentless attack. Then the saw blade bit savagely into his already injured shoulder. Aaron let out a piercing scream and his fire sword sizzled to nothing as his concentration was temporarily broken. He tried to pull himself together, to rouse another weapon, but the saw was already coming at him again.

Anger and fear coursed through Aaron, and a sword materialized in a rush of fire. He was ready to continue the fight. But there was no longer the need, for the saw was suddenly yanked back and away.

The mysterious patient had risen from his bed and stood behind Aaron's attacker, arm wrapped around the nearly invisible foe, restraining him.

Aaron was about to go to the patient's aid, when he saw a flash of something silver and the patient wielding the attacker's knife. The injured man plunged the weapon deep into the back of their foe's neck with the sickening sound of metal rubbing against bone.

"No!" Aaron cried as he realized what had just happened.

The patient let the body slip from his arms to the floor. With the attacker dead, Aaron could now see its form. Whatever magickal qualities had kept it hidden were fading.

"Did you have to kill him?" Aaron asked, kneeling beside their fallen foe.

The patient stared at the blade that he'd used against the attacker. It crackled with energy.

"If I hadn't, the Agent wouldn't have stopped until we were both dead," he said. He then stumbled backward, catching himself before carefully sitting at the end of his cot.

Aaron stared at the corpse and realized that it was wearing a skin-tight suit. He fumbled at its throat, found the edge of its mask, and pulled it off to reveal the face beneath it. He gasped at what he saw. Aaron had seen illustrations in books, interpretations in movies, and statues at museums, but this was the last place he'd ever expected to see a Neanderthal.

"Much easier to augment than the more evolved members of your species," the patient said. He rubbed at his bandaged chest.

Aaron stared at the apelike features of the primitive man, and again wondered if his own existence could get any more bizarre. He looked away from the dead Neanderthal to the patient, who stared at him strangely.

"What?" Aaron asked.

"Nothing," the patient said, barely able to tear his gaze from the Nephilim. "It's nothing."

But Aaron new that it wasn't.

"So you have some explaining to do," Aaron said as he rose to his feet.

"Yes," the patient said. "I believe I do." He peeled the bandage away from his chest and examined the pink, puckered skin where his nearly fatal injury had healed. Cautiously he touched the scar that slashed through the elaborately tattooed sigils.

"But first I need a needle and some ink before we have any more unwelcome visitors."

Baby Roger spastically attempted to bring the spoon up to his hungry maw, but more of the creamed peas and corn landed on his chin than in his mouth.

"Damn it!" the baby shrieked, tossing the spoon away from the high chair in frustration. "Somebody feed me this instant!"

"You said you could do it yourself," Jeremy said, sitting at the small kitchen table, his mother across from him.

"Well, obviously I'm having some difficulty," Roger retorted, his chubby hands wiping at the food that adorned his face, before he eagerly shoved his fingers into his mouth to noisily suck on them.

Jeremy got up from the table to retrieve the spoon. "Could you explain again how you're talking?" he asked.

"I already told you, I don't know . . . yet," Baby Roger said. The child watched Jeremy as he approached. "You're not going to use that spoon to feed me, are you? It's filthy. Get a clean one."

"I wasn't going to use it," Jeremy said, annoyed.

"Well, see that you don't," the baby scolded. "And hurry up. I'm starving."

"How could you be starving? You haven't stopped eating all morning," Jeremy's mom said as she sipped her tea.

"I'm a growing boy, and all that nonsense," Roger declared. He started to blink his eyes rapidly, looking around the cottage.

"What's wrong?" Jeremy's mother asked, standing up, a look of concern on her face.

"Color," the baby said, still blinking rapidly. "I can see colors now. Fascinating."

Jeremy pulled his chair closer to the high chair. He'd taken a new spoon from the silverware drawer and was ready to make another attempt at feeding the hungry child.

"Are you ready?" Jeremy asked, plunging the spoon inside the jar of baby food.

"I couldn't be more ready." Roger tilted his round head back as he opened his mouth. "Solids are far more satisfying than formula."

Jeremy took a spoonful of the disgusting-looking mixture and stuffed it into the child's mouth. Roger immediately started to cough and gag.

"What's wrong" Jeremy asked, startled by all the fuss. He looked to his mother for help.

"You nearly choked me!" Baby Roger wailed. "You practically shoved that spoon down my throat. Gently, Jeremy. Remember, I'm just a baby."

Jeremy stuck the spoon back into the jar for another go.

"Yeah, you're just a baby, all right," he muttered.

"And what is that supposed to mean?" the baby asked as Jeremy gently brought the spoonful to Roger's mouth and tipped it.

"I mean that you're just a few weeks old," Jeremy said, again delving into the jar. "You're not supposed to be talking, never mind speaking in full sentences."

Roger had some more of his food. "I must admit, the situation here is rather unique," the baby said.

"I'll say," Jeremy's mother agreed. She got up and poured

herself another cup of tea from the electric pot on the counter.

"The only thing I can assure you is that there is a reason for all this," Baby Roger said, opening his mouth again in anticipation.

Jeremy did as was expected, shoveling in more peas and corn.

"We just need to know what that reason is," Jeremy said.

"And you'll know as soon as I do," Roger said, turning in his high chair to watch the telly. "I do so hate to miss anything," he said, craning his neck to see.

"Considering that you couldn't speak a word before bedtime last night, I'd gather you haven't missed much," Jeremy's mother said as she sipped her fresh cuppa.

"But that's the wonder of television," Roger said, taking another bite of his food before turning again in his chair to see into the small living room. "There's so much it can teach you. Twenty-four glorious hours of information. I wouldn't be half the baby I am now without it."

"And you knew to put the telly on to get this information, how?" Jeremy asked. He dug at the last of the jar's contents and got another spoonful.

Roger turned back to him, considering the question. "I really don't know," he said. "It was something akin to instinct."

Roger thought seriously as he gummed his last bite of peas and corn. "Something told me that I needed to proceed," the baby said. "And I did what was required of me, escaping that silly crib, and locating the remote control."

The baby turned in his high chair to see the television again.

"It was like being immersed in a fountain of knowledge," Roger said wistfully.

"A fountain of something," Jeremy commented sarcastically as he got up to throw away the empty jar of baby food.

"So now what do we do?" Jeremy's mother asked. "This is obviously happening for a reason."

"Exactly," Baby Roger said. The child stroked his chubby chins of baby fat with an equally chubby hand. "We'll just have to wait until—"

Roger's face suddenly twisted in a grimace of pain, and he began to wail like the damned.

"What's the matter now?" Jeremy asked. He was reaching the end of his rope with all this bizarreness.

Baby Roger stuck one of his tiny fingers inside his drooling mouth and started to probe around.

"Damnation," he exclaimed. "I'm cutting a tooth!"

CHAPTER NINE

Verchiel would rather not have remembered this scene, but recent conditions made it difficult not to. The battlefields were covered with the bodies of those who had fallen in combat, some hacked and bloody, others burned, their simmering flesh sending clouds of oily black smoke to hover like storm clouds above the yellow fields.

Verchiel stared down at a brother, turned enemy. The blade of his burning sword was buried deep within the angel's twitching breast. His foe still lived, but it was only a matter of time before the fire that coursed through his dying form turned his beating heart to ash. Verchiel placed a golden boot upon his enemy's chest plate and leaned back to pull the blade from his heart. He watched the life go out of his brethren's eyes.

"Was it worth it?" Verchiel asked as the dead angel's flesh began to bubble and blacken, burning from within. He did not know how many he had slain since the war had begun, but he'd asked the same question of every one who'd fallen beneath his ferocious onslaught.

Another angel in service to the Morningstar's cause dropped down from the smoke-filled air, a blazing mace cutting a fiery swath through the sky. A shield of concentrated flame came to life upon Verchiel's arm, absorbing the impact of his adversary's strike.

The two leaped into the air to continue their battle. Verchiel lashed out with his own weapon of flame, slicing into one of his opponent's feathery wings and sending him spiraling to the ground below.

He watched as his foe landed, then he dropped down like a hungry hawk to finish his prey.

The war had made Verchiel cruel. As the enemy angel attempted to rise, Verchiel lashed out with his blade, cutting away part of the angel's wing. The angel cried out pitifully, falling back to the ground that was already saturated with blood. Seeing the ground damp and smelling that nauseating coppery odor just inflamed Verchiel's anger. He continued to hack at his foe, until the angel struggled no more, lying still—dead— upon the ground.

"Was it worth it?" asked a voice from someplace very close.

Verchiel spun around, his wings spread wide, eager to fight once more.

A spear of fire, thrown from the cover of oily black smoke,

plunged into his chest, carried him backward, and pinned him to one of Heaven's delicate trees. The bark was now spotted and black. The blood that had been spilled was poisoning its once beautiful growth.

The spear burned him. Verchiel could feel his flesh starting to wither as an inferno began to rage on the inside. With a scream of agony he grabbed the shaft with both hands and fought to remove it.

A familiar figure emerged from the smoke of the battlefield.

Mallus stood before him, the flesh of his smooth, pale face speckled with the blood of the righteous who'd been struck down by Lucifer's madness.

"You didn't answer my question," Mallus observed as Verchiel continued to struggle.

"You mock me," Verchiel growled, already feeling himself burning from the inside out.

"Mockery, Verchiel?" Mallus asked. "I've but asked you a question. Was it worth it?"

"You use my words against me," Verchiel said, the smell of his own burning flesh filling his nostrils.

Mallus watched him burn for a moment, then reached out and pulled the spear free.

Verchiel gasped and dropped to his knees. Every ounce of strength he had left was struggling to quell the divine fire burning within him.

"I simply asked you a question, brother," Mallus said. "It

came to me as I watched you on the battlefield, murdering the heavenly family with such cold ruthlessness." Mallus paused, a snarl appearing upon his handsome features. "Was it worth it, Verchiel?" he asked again. "To become a monster?"

A sword of fire came alive in Mallus's grasp, and Verchiel knew that he did not have the strength to fight back. It was taking everything that he had to hold the fire inside him in check.

Verchiel struggled to his feet and the two angels stood opposing each other, eyes locked. Mallus's sword continued to burn, the fire crackling and snapping in anticipation of its next murderous act.

Finally Verchiel could stand it no more.

"Kill me," he demanded. "Kill me now."

But Mallus did not. Instead he turned his back upon Verchiel and walked away. "That would be too easy," he called back as he became lost in the smoke of the battlefield. "For me, and for you. We both need to see the future we have wrought."

Verchiel stirred angrily from the assault of memory, sensing that he was no longer alone.

"What is it?" he asked.

"Aaron wants us to come," Gabriel said.

Verchiel rose from where he crouched upon the altar, to look upon the animal with disdain. "Where?" he asked with a sneer.

"The infirmary," Gabriel answered, averting his gaze from the angel's stare. *"He wants us all there."*

"And he sends a dog as his messenger?" Verchiel asked. "If I were the sensitive type, I would be offended."

Verchiel bore down upon the dog. He would have been lying if he'd said that he didn't get a certain perverse pleasure from this dog whose entire makeup had been rewritten by the emerging power of the Nephilim, Aaron Corbet.

What a waste.

"Aaron didn't mean to offend you," Gabriel spoke, eyes still on the ground. *"He just told me to come get you."*

"And you have," Verchiel said.

"Yes," Gabriel agreed.

"So why are you still here? You have done what your master asked of you."

Gabriel turned to leave, his ears flat and his tail curled between his legs. *"Sorry,"* he said in passing.

"You are at that," Verchiel sniped. "You and the boy who pretends to lead this loathsome band of miscreants, who think they are going to save the world." Verchiel chuckled. "If it weren't so pathetic, it would be amusing."

He recoiled as the dog crouched, low and menacing, before him. Sparks of divine fire popped and snapped from the dog's raised hackles.

"Aaron is a leader, and those he leads are great warriors, whether or not you have the eyes to see it. You've been asked by our leader to attend a gathering. Come or not. It's entirely up to you."

And with those final words Gabriel trotted toward the door at the end of the aisle.

Leaving Verchiel to wonder if perhaps the animal had been changed far more than anyone realized.

THE MARIANA TRENCH
36,201 FEET BENEATH THE PACIFIC OCEAN

This had always been his favorite of the churches erected to worship him.

Built in the earliest days of the earth's existence, it had been a towering structure, rising up into the sunlight, reaching for Heaven. But that had been before the great oceanic upheaval that had swallowed the island and the church that had been built upon it.

He who now called himself Satan had always mourned the loss of the impressive structure, for none of his other worshippers had ever been able to capture the glory of this temple.

The high priests and their followers who had prayed here could barely be considered human, but they had understood the power that he wielded, and had prayed that he would grant them supremacy over the newly emerging race that would soon be known as humanity.

Satan had so regretted disappointing his faithful, but it had not been the time to challenge the God that was still eager to define the world. And so he had allowed his followers and his church to be pulled down deep below the depths. For he was patient, and he knew that his time would eventually come.

Or at least, that was what he used to believe.

Satan was unfamiliar with the emotions that now caused his life fluids to roil, by-products of this newly acquired corporeal form, but he understood that it was rage.

Rage caused by the Community's rejection of his leadership.

He had hoped that remembering another time, another faithful group, would calm his fury, but the memory only served to inflame his fury all the more.

The Darkstar lashed out at his surroundings. Divine fire tainted by his own corrosive darkness leaped from his hands to decimate the ancient stone, causing pillars to tumble and shatter upon the church floor.

Do they not realize who they are rejecting?

A great stone idol carved in his countenance was the next object to experience the Devil's wrath. Satan rose upon wings of black and flew at full speed toward the idol. His armored form crashed into the statue with such force that it reduced the statue to dust.

Satan crouched upon the altar, which had grown thick with green algae over the years. He eyed his surroundings, deciding what would next feel the touch of his anger.

"Such a beautiful place of worship," said a voice as dry as dust.

"A shame to see it treated in such a manner," said another.

"Whatever did it do to deserve this?" another wondered aloud.

Satan knew those voices. "Show yourselves, hags," he demanded. He scanned the shadows of the vast temple.

The Three Sisters of Umbra slowly hobbled from their place of concealment.

"Such anger," said one, shaking a long clawed finger at him.

"Is this the way to vent such fury?" asked the second.

"What real purpose does this destruction serve?" questioned the third Sister.

Satan launched himself into the air, almost hitting the curved ceiling of the domed roof before landing before them.

"How dare you question me?" he growled, fist clenched before him.

"We mean no disrespect, oh king," one of the Sisters said as she bowed her hooded head, clawed hands folded before her.

"We sensed your anger from afar and came to see if we could assist you," said another, equally repentant in tone.

"Perhaps if we were made privy to what causes you such ire," suggested the last of the three.

The Darkstar turned his back upon them and strode away.

"Things do not go as I designed them," he began, not really sure why he was confiding in them, but finding it strangely comforting. "Those who should worship my prodigious countenance have instead decided to try to destroy me."

He stopped, clasping his hands behind his back, taking in the grandeur of the ancient temple built to his former glory.

"They do not realize what I am, who I am, and what I

can do," Satan continued. "They have forgotten the power that spawned their like. They believe that they have always been here, waiting in the shadows for the world to be ready for them." He turned to face the Sisters. "They do not recognize who has prepared the world for them."

The Sisters leaned together, their hooded heads close as if silently communicating.

"What words of advice do you have for me?" he asked.

"Those of the Community are stubborn," said the first Sister.

"They do not take kindly to the new, even though it is very old," said the second.

"They must be shown your power, your supremacy," the third said.

"Well, I killed many of them quite recently," he said.

The Sisters considered this.

"A strong start to making your point," the first praised.

"You showed them your strength," the second added.

Satan stretched his wings of shadow.

"I want to kill them all," he said with a snarl. "Each and every one of them."

One of the Sisters shambled toward him, clawed hand emerging from within the folds of her robes as she held up her finger. "But now you must show them your restraint."

Another lumbered forward to join her Sister. "You must show them that you are stronger than their petty insecurities."

The third joined the others. "Show them who you truly are."

Satan did not care for their advice, finding it all too obvious.

"They know who and what I am. How could they not?"

The Sisters of Umbra huddled together once more. He felt his annoyance grow.

Finally a Sister said, "You will have a chance to prove your supremacy."

"It will come in time," said a second, with a slow, assured nod.

"But until then you must look the part," said the third.

This made Satan laugh. He spread his armored arms and presented himself to the three hags.

"Do I not look like a king? Do I not look as lovely as any god?"

"You blind our poor old eyes with your majesty, Star of the Dark," one said, raising her hands to cover the front of her hood, as if his form were too much to look upon.

"But the Community, they are a materialistic lot," said another.

"Measuring worth in material gain, gold, land, bone, blood, and meat," added the third. "How do you show them you are king?"

"By not killing each and every one of them," Satan snarled.

"Yes, yes, that shows mercy. But how do you impress them?" a Sister asked.

"How do you show them your godly stature?" asked another.

He pondered about that for a moment but had no answer. "Enlighten me," he ordered.

The Sisters turned the darkness of their hoods to one another before setting their glowing stares on him.

"A dwelling," suggested one of the three. "A dwelling to demonstrate your magnificence."

"A dwelling crafted to honor you as a god," said another.

"Now, where could such a structure be found?" asked the third, extending a clawed finger inquisitively.

Satan looked about the great church. In spite of the damage his earlier rage had caused, it was still quite a sight to behold.

"This church," he stated. "You believe that this church will impress the Community enough that they'll follow me . . . worship me?"

"In time, yes," they all agreed as one.

"But it cannot remain deep beneath the ocean waves," said a Sister.

"It must be visible for all to see, human and inhuman alike," said another of the Sisters.

"It must be raised." The third Sister held her spindly arms toward the ceiling.

"Raise it up!" exclaimed the three together, their arms up. "Raise it up!"

And Satan, the Darkstar, agreed that that was what he would do.

Yes, he would raise it up.

* * *

Lucifer Morningstar felt the weighty penance of God's anger writhe within his chest.

All the rage, pain, and sorrow of Lucifer's actions, and of those who had stood with him against Heaven, had been collected by the Lord God into a seething, crying, screaming miasma of emotion.

And He had placed it inside the Morningstar so that he might remember what he had done, and suffer for it.

Lucifer Morningstar had then been cast down, his body thrown from the heavens to earth so that he might learn from his grievous mistake.

The Morningstar experienced it all again, deep within the prison of his subconscious mind. Even after the crushing defeat at the hands of God's legions, even after having what could best be described as *Hell* placed inside him, Lucifer had still been too stubborn—too vain—to admit that he had been wrong.

In those early days of exile, Lucifer had viewed himself only as the loser of a war, and would have taken up arms again in an instant if he and his armies had not been so thoroughly routed.

He loathed humanity and all that they stood for. How could such foul creatures have so captured the love of the Almighty?

That question had seethed within his mind as he had wandered the world of man for countless ages.

And he still had not been able to understand it.

Until *she* had come into his life.

Lucifer watched as the landscape of his subconscious memories shifted and changed. All the places he had been in his seemingly eternal exile morphed before his eyes.

He knew where his visions would stop, and found himself both dreading and anticipating what he was about to relive. The air was lush with the aroma of freshly cut grass. And it was all there, just as he remembered. The park crowded with people on their lunch hours, some sunning themselves during the first real warm day of the season, others walking their dogs.

Lucifer saw himself as he had been that day, a wanderer. He had been sitting beneath a tree, and he distinctly remembered feeling a sensation akin to serenity.

And as if in reward for opening himself to a peaceful calm, a golden-haired dog approached him and dropped a stick at his feet.

"Brandy," Lucifer said aloud, watching the scene from his memory play out. "The dog's name was Brandy."

He'd attempted to ignore the animal, but she had insisted, barking for him to pick up the stick and throw it for her. Lucifer had almost spoken harshly to the dog, but he didn't want to spoil his moment of placidity. Besides, what would it hurt?

So he picked up the stick, wet with the dog's saliva, and tossed it as far as he could. He watched as Brandy bounded off in pursuit. He marveled at the beauty of her design, at her interaction with the world around her.

The retriever quickly snatched up the stick from the grass

and was heading back toward Lucifer, when she stopped to interact with a human.

A woman.

And Lucifer found himself enjoying the beauty of her design as well.

The dog bounded away from the woman and raced back to him, the stick clamped tightly in her jaws.

The woman followed, and Lucifer recalled the strange feeling of his heart fluttering.

"I'm sorry. Is she bothering you?" the woman asked him.

Lucifer saw that she was even more beautiful in this memory than he had remembered. He watched the expression on his own face as she spoke to him, petting the dog that had again dropped the stick at his feet.

"Her name is Brandy," she told him, and they started to talk.

He wasn't sure exactly when the Lucifer Morningstar of old—the angel of Heaven who had led a revolt against his Creator and been cast down to live amongst the very creatures that he despised—started to die.

But he guessed that it was right around the time when the beautiful woman told him her name.

"I'm Taylor," she said, extending her delicate hand to Lucifer.

"Taylor Corbet."

CHAPTER TEN

Mallus looked down at the lines of the sigils tattooed upon his chest, and at the new pink scar that broke them.

"It appears that you've healed quite nicely," Kraus said, leaning in to examine the wound.

"With your help, of course," Mallus said. "And for that I thank you."

Kraus bowed, stepping away to stand in waiting against the wall.

Mallus dipped the point of a needle into a puddle of black ink that he had made by breaking open a ballpoint pen. Then he went about repairing the sigils, hoping to restore the magick that had once flowed from them. Mallus dug the needle into the fresh scar tissue, pushing the ink below the new skin.

"Does that hurt?"

Mallus looked up to see the Nephilim Aaron observing him.

He dipped the needle into the black ink once more. "Not really," he said, poking the scar tissue again. "But when it does hurt, I just think of the pain if the Agents find me, as it will be much more permanent."

Mallus paused, staring at the boy. He'd heard about this Aaron Corbet. He could see the resemblance to his father almost immediately in the way that he carried himself, the way he fought in battle. He had no doubt that this was the Morningstar's son, but Mallus saw that the Nephilim had acquired his mother's traits as well.

Taylor.

It had been a very long time since he'd last thought of her, the human who had somehow managed to quell the Morningstar's fury.

The human who had transformed Mallus as well.

How is it possible? he thought, continuing to poke at his flesh with the needle, injecting the ink beneath his thick rope of scar tissue. She had been human, something that he had despised with every iota of his divine form, but still, somehow, she'd manage to touch them both.

Bringing the needle back to the ink, he glanced at Aaron, unable to stop the flood of memories that poured over him.

Mallus had still been working for the Architects. He'd actually been searching for his former leader, the Morningstar, and had found him in a human city, in a park. He'd been just about to make contact, when he'd seen the Morningstar and the human woman together.

At first Mallus had believed she was some sort of wicked enchantress. How else could she have controlled and manipulated one of God's mightiest angels? And then he'd realized there was no magick present.

She was just a woman.

How was it possible? Mallus wondered again, continuing to repair the sigil that would hide him from those he'd once served with relish.

"That's Archon magick," said a woman's voice, interrupting his reverie.

Mallus looked up from his work to see a female Nephilim enter the room, walking with the help of a cane. She was accompanied by a young man. At first glance Mallus thought the woman rather old, but then he caught a whiff of magick upon her. It was slowly eating her alive.

"Malakim, actually," Mallus corrected her, making reference to the powerful angelic beings that had taught the Archons to use the forces that would define their magick.

The woman moved closer, her eyes following the lines etched upon his flesh.

"These are amazing," she said, reaching to touch the marks with slightly trembling fingers.

"This is Lorelei," Aaron introduced her. "She's our resident magick user."

"But for how much longer?" Mallus asked softly so that only she would hear. He watched her eyes. A tiny rodent watched him from beneath lengths of the woman's snow-white hair.

"Long enough to do what I have to," she said, meeting his stare.

This one was strong, but fading fast.

"And him?" Mallus asked Aaron as he looked away from Lorelei at the man who had entered the room with her.

"That's Dusty," Aaron replied. "He's new here."

Mallus studied the young man, not sure what to make of him. That one would bear watching.

Mallus turned his attention back to the task at hand, restoring his sigils. It felt as though they could be working again, but he wasn't completely sure.

A yellow dog trotted into the room, followed by three more Nephilim, one being the boy who had brought him here. Mallus caught a whiff of something coming from the animal, something that aroused his senses. Something had happened—*was happening*—to this animal.

"This is Vilma, Melissa, and you already know Cameron." Aaron introduced the Nephilim, then motioned toward the dog. "And that's Gabriel."

Mallus set the needle down and dabbed at his chest with a damp cloth. What an interesting lot. "Are we all here?" the angel asked, knowing full well that there was still at least one more to arrive.

"Where's Verchiel, Gabriel?" Aaron asked the yellow dog.

"I told him you wanted to see him," the dog growled in his canine tongue.

Mallus could feel Verchiel's approach before he'd even appeared. It came as a sudden electricity that made Mallus's every instinct cry out to flee.

And then the angel emerged from behind his wings to stand in the corner of the room, glowering at them all.

"Glad you could make it," Aaron said with sarcasm.

"What do you want?" Verchiel asked with a sneer.

"We need to talk," Aaron said, looking at them all.

"I don't think that's wise," Verchiel said, directing his attention to Mallus. "Especially with that one present."

Mallus chose not to respond. The former Powers leader was seemingly still upset with Mallus for not ending his life when he'd had the chance. But if Mallus had done that, then this gathering would never have taken place, and the Architects' machine would have rolled on.

"That one has a name," Aaron announced. "His name is Mallus, and just a short while ago he was attacked in the infirmary."

Lorelei immediately reacted. "But the defenses weren't—"

"Somehow it found its way through the defenses," Aaron cut in.

"Your defenses are nothing to an Agent," Mallus announced.

Aaron walked over to the corner of the room, where something had been concealed beneath a blanket. He reached down, dragged the object into the center of the room, and then pulled away the cover for all to see.

Mallus watched as they saw the face of their enemy—their true enemy—for the first time. Gabriel growled.

"Who is he?" Melissa asked.

"Dude looks like a caveman," Cameron said, laughing nervously at the sight of the corpse.

"That's because he is," Mallus responded. "Or at least he was, until his masters had their way with him."

That got their attention.

"Masters?" Lorelei questioned. "And who might they be?"

"Ah," Mallus said, pausing for a moment to consider what he was about to do. He studied them all, their expressions tense with anticipation. They hadn't a clue as to what was happening around them, what was *really* happening to the world, and who—what—were responsible.

So why now? Mallus thought. Why not just keep going as he had been, hiding from his former employers, hating what was happening, but powerless to act.

Why should he risk so much now? Was there even a point?

His thoughts again drifted back to that day in the park, to Lucifer and the woman—Taylor. He guessed that that's where it had started, and now it would come to an end, with Aaron.

Mallus stared at the Nephilim, marveling at what he sensed in that one. Was Aaron Corbet to be humanity's chance to survive?

They were all waiting for Mallus's response.

"What do you know about the Architects?" Mallus finally asked.

There was no turning back now.

AUGUST, A.D. 79
POMPEII

Mount Vesuvius had erupted for two days. The air over where the great Roman city of Pompeii had stood was now filled with choking clouds of poisonous gas and ash.

Mallus found himself drawn to the scene of this great disaster.

To the site of more than two thousand human deaths.

He had flown through the shroud of ash spewed out by the volcano, listening to the sounds as the inhabitants had cried out to their gods for salvation. But there had been no one to help them as the air had become superheated and their bodies had been buried under ash and pumice.

The ash clung to him too, so he soared above the disaster and simply shook off the white-hot volcanic spew like a dog shaking off a summer's rain.

He liked to think of these kinds of disasters as being God's way of expressing His displeasure with humanity. But deep down Mallus knew that it wasn't true. This was just a natural disaster.

And he should learn to enjoy it for what it was, and the damage that it caused.

As Mallus walked atop the cooling layers of lava, he tried to visualize the city as it once had been, where the bathhouses had once stood, where the markets had teemed. Now there was nothing. Everything had been buried beneath a blizzard of black snow, twenty feet deep.

Through the thick haze Mallus caught sight of movement. He knew that nothing human could have survived the still blazing temperatures and air inhospitable to fragile lungs. He summoned a sword of fire.

Using his wings to fan away the gas and smoke, Mallus charged at his unseen foe, eager to be the first to strike. He swung out with his sword of fire, aiming for where he imagined his enemy might be, and found his blade of divine flame captured in a powerful grip.

Mallus attempted to pull back his weapon, but it was held fast. His wings continued to beat the air, and finally the thick, poisonous clouds parted to reveal the strangest of sights.

It was human in shape, but it appeared to be made entirely of ash—the same ash that now hid Pompeii. Thinking quickly, Mallus brought forth another weapon, a battle mace, and smashed his opponent's featureless face with all of his heavenly might.

The ash broke away, to reveal a blazing red eye peering out from the blackened eye socket of a human skull.

What madness is this? the fallen angel thought, just as the ashen figure latched on to his throat with its other hand and drew him close.

"Will you serve the makers of the future?" rattled a voice from somewhere deep within the attacker's charred throat.

Mallus spread his wings, struggling to free himself from the painful grip upon his neck, but the figure held fast and slammed him against the still cooling ground.

"Will you serve the makers of the future?" it asked again.

"You speak in riddles, monster," Mallus rasped, still fighting to be free. "I serve only my own interests now that I have been abandoned by God."

The single eye burned brightly. "Will you serve the makers of the future?"

Understanding that this thing that held him wielded enough power to end his existence, Mallus had no choice but to answer, giving his enigmatic attacker what it sought, in hopes of gaining an opportunity to escape.

"Yes," Mallus hissed. "I will serve the makers . . . the makers of the future."

In an instant his attacker was gone, and the still seething layers of ash beneath his back began to crumble, giving way to his weight. Mallus fell.

He tried to slow his descent, but his wings were useless as he continued to plummet. It felt as though he were falling for days; the passage of time suddenly had no meaning.

Then as quickly as his descent had begun, it stopped.

Mallus found himself standing in a world of total darkness. Even the divine fire that coursed through his veins could shed no light upon his surroundings. The flames that he summoned were quickly suffocated by an all-encompassing dark.

After a time the infinity of blackness was all that he knew, all that he could remember. He felt himself being taken apart, atom by atom.

And just as he felt his life about to cease, a voice called out.

"Will you serve the makers of the future?"

"Yes," he answered, his voice strained and dry after days . . . months . . . years . . . of disuse. He thought he had answered the question immediately, although time had become meaningless in the black of nothing, and he realized that it might have taken a century or more for him to respond.

A golden light then shone upon him, bathing him in a warmth akin to the praise of the Lord God Almighty, and Mallus felt the atoms of his form taken from the shadows and reassembled, not as he had been before . . .

But better.

An envoy of a new beginning . . . an agent of the future.

From the darkness they emerged, like multiple suns rising to chase away the eternal dark. These globes of golden fire were covered in multiple sets of staring all-seeing eyes, and these eyes were all turned to Mallus.

"We are the Architects, and the future is ours to build." The spheres spoke in unison. Their voices sounded like the most beautiful of heavenly choirs raised in exaltation.

Mallus could not take his eyes from the magnificent beings. He had heard of the Architects but had always questioned their existence, as did all the angels of Heaven.

The Architects were supposedly the very first of God's creations, produced to aid Him in the task of plotting out the universe. Once they had served their purpose, the Almighty had reabsorbed the Architects into His being. Then He was said to have used them in the creation of the angels themselves.

But somehow the Architects had emerged again, and Mallus reveled in the presence of their power.

"The Architects have watched you, angel, and have seen the depths to which you have fallen." Their voices rose in a cacophony of sound. "But we have also seen your potential."

Mallus was speechless, and all he could do was stare.

"We see in you an ability to serve us."

"Yes," Mallus said, his voice barely a whisper.

"The ability to perform as one of our Agents out in the world . . . to serve a greater goal . . ."

"Yes," Mallus said again.

The orbs of fire continued to spin in place, but the thousands of eyes were still fixed upon him.

"But first you must prove yourself worthy to serve our lofty goals."

"Anything!" Mallus screamed, for whatever they asked of

him would be better than the eternal blackness in which he'd been lost for so long.

"Your task is of the utmost importance to our cause," the Architects said.

"Tell me," Mallus begged.

"There is an angel second only to the Lord God," they said. "He is the Metatron, and he is God's voice, God's will in the world."

Mallus waited to hear what they required of him.

"You must kill him for us."

Closing his eyes, Satan reached out to the shadows around the temple and beyond, entwining himself in their fabric, making himself a part of the darkness.

He knelt within the place of worship. The Sisters stood in a circle around him, their hands clasped together, lending him their unnatural strength.

The Darkstar allowed his essence to permeate the ancient rock and soil deep beneath the churning sea that had held the church in its grasp. Then he spread his arms and wings and tossed back his head as he forced his will upon the ocean landscape.

He was the rock and mud of the seemingly bottomless trench, and the rock, mud, and trench was he. With a grunt of exertion Satan flexed his muscles, feeling the underwater landscape respond in kind. Careful to not damage his place of worship, he used his connection to the ocean floor and raised the temple on a volcanic plume of molten rock.

Though the crushing waters sought to enter the long-buried place of worship, he kept himself and the Sisters dry by weaving a barrier of darkness around the structure as it slowly pushed through the murky depths on a growing platform of cooling igneous rock.

The ocean around the rising church did not care for Satan's dark influence and attempted to show its displeasure, unleashing angry seismic activity to thwart his actions. It was as if the ocean floor had gone to war. Mountains of rock jutted up through the strata as the sea grew black with swirling sediments.

The rushing waters around the church were like the chaos Satan imagined for the world when its occupants truly learned of his existence. Life upon the planet would either accept his omnipotence or pay a horrible price.

An island of smoldering black rock emerged from the roiling waters to present itself to an unsuspecting world. The bubble of darkness that had covered the expansive church disintegrated in the fading sunlight as the temple was again exposed to the air.

"It is risen," Satan said within the halls of his church.

The Sisters of Umbra laughed with joy, raising their hands and bowing their hooded heads in praise.

"Praise be, it is risen," they said as one.

Satan was weary from his exertion, but euphoric. Now everyone would know of him. He no longer had to hide in the shadows of the frozen earth.

The new lord and master had arrived.

And long would he reign.

CHAPTER ELEVEN

S o these Architects," Aaron asked into the silence of the room, after Mallus had paused in his tale. "Are they angels, or something else?"

Mallus opened his mouth to answer, but Verchiel interrupted him. "They're neither," the former Powers leader said. "They don't exist. They're fairy tales fabricated by overly creative minds to explain things that are unexplainable."

Mallus turned his gaze to the angel. "And yet I served them for centuries."

Aaron could feel the tension between the two and attempted to defuse it.

"Then why wouldn't Verchiel know about them?" he asked. "He's been on the earth a good many years. Why wouldn't he have encountered the Architects?"

Mallus smiled briefly. "Probably because they didn't want him. To allow him to be aware of them would have interfered with their grand schemes."

"Which are?" Lorelei asked, leaning heavily upon her cane.

Mallus looked down at the floor, shaking his head ever so slightly. "They didn't share that with me. They simply expected me to carry out my assigned tasks.

"At first they seemed to be random acts, but when I began to figure into other Agents' assignments, patterns began to emerge." Mallus paused, making certain that they all were listening. "The Architects have led the world to this," he said, gesturing toward the world beyond the infirmary windows. "This is all part of their plan."

Verchiel scoffed. "Madness," he said, folding his arms defiantly. "Why would any being of a divine nature plan for a fate such as this?"

"Perhaps a greater plan is in motion here," Mallus answered. "I had yet to figure it out before I left their service."

"And why the change of heart?" Aaron asked.

"Yeah, for somebody who liked to see towns covered by volcanic ash, why would you care about destruction now?" Cameron followed through.

"Perhaps I saw something of this world and its inhabitants that made me realize I had made a mistake," Mallus said, focusing his gaze on Aaron.

Aaron was suddenly uncomfortable. It felt as though the fallen angel were looking right into him. It was weird, and it was the second time Mallus had done it.

"How do we know that this isn't all some sort of clever deception?" Verchiel asked, distracting Aaron. "How do we know that Mallus doesn't still serve these mysterious Architects and isn't just using us to further their agenda?" He smiled slyly, and Aaron was reminded again why the angel was such an asshat.

"I don't think being seriously injured in a subway station was part of a master plan," Cameron responded.

Mallus stood up from his chair, and faced Verchiel.

Aaron and Gabriel were already on the move, positioning themselves between the two.

"All right, guys. Why don't we—" Aaron began.

"If I were still in service to them," Mallus said, ignoring them, "would I have done this?" He turned his bare back to them, revealing the angry scars upon his shoulder blades.

Where his wings had once been.

"You cut off your own wings," Melissa gasped in a horrified whisper.

"If I were to leave the Architects, I had no choice," Mallus said, the pain of his loss obvious in the timbre of his voice and the sorrow in his eyes.

"Every angel's wings are distinct, like a person's finger-prints," Lorelei explained to the group. "Each gives off its own unique magick."

"Aye," Mallus agreed. "They would have been able to find my trail whenever I used them. I had to be sure that I would not be followed." He then looked down at the elaborate tattoos on his chest. "The loss of my wings and these sigils have rendered me nearly invisible to my former masters."

"Until you were injured," Aaron added.

Mallus nodded. "Until I was injured. One of the sigils was interrupted, sending out an invisible alarm to those whose only purpose was to watch for me."

He gestured toward the corpse on the floor.

"His sole task was to find and eliminate me. And now that he is gone, I'm sure another has been given the same task. But we are in luck."

Mallus produced the Agent's knife. "We have its Gleaning Blade."

Lorelei hobbled forward for a closer look. "May I?" she asked.

"Careful of its point," Mallus said. "Just a prick is enough to devour everything stored in your brain."

She admired the weapon, turning it in her hands. Dusty came to stand beside her.

"The Agent was going to use it on me," Mallus said. "To find out everything I've learned, seen, and heard since leaving the service of the Architects. But the Agent never got the chance, ending up a victim of its own weapon."

"You killed him with this?" Dusty asked the angel.

"I did."

"Then everything he knew . . . ," Dusty began, staring at the dead Agent.

"Is now stored within this blade," Lorelei finished.

"It is," Mallus agreed. "And that is a very good thing for us."

Verchiel stalked toward Mallus and then stopped, his face inches from the fallen angel's.

"Verchiel, stand down," Aaron ordered, although he expected his words would have little effect on the stubborn angel.

"It's all right, Aaron," Mallus said, staring straight into Verchiel's eyes. "What is it now, Verchiel?"

"Why do you tell us this? You've been on the run for centuries. You've known of the Architects' plans for far longer than that. Why share all of this with us now?"

"Until now I didn't think that the world had any chance of surviving what the Architects had in store," Mallus said.

"But something changed your mind." Verchiel had a curious gleam in his eye.

"Yes," Mallus answered with a nod. "He changed my mind." He pointed at Cameron. "I'd heard that some Nephilim had survived the Powers' crusade to exterminate them, but I never gave it any more thought than that . . . until that one saved my life and I saw the Nephilim's potential."

Mallus turned to Aaron again.

"And then I discovered who was leading them, the son of my former commander, the angel for whom I fell from the grace of Heaven—Lucifer Morningstar."

Aaron immediately felt uncomfortable.

"You have given me the courage to act as I should have acted long ago," Mallus said. "There have been others fighting this fight, but their victories were few and far between. It all seemed so very pointless." His shoulders slumped in regret. "It was easier to do nothing and remain invisible than to protect what time humanity had left."

"But now that you've met us, you think there might be a chance to fight back?" Aaron asked, not really sure he believed Mallus. "Have you seen how many of us there actually are? This is it." He gestured around the room.

Mallus nodded. "Although I believed there was no hope before, now I see a glimmer of possibility. Just a glimmer, mind you, but a glimmer nonetheless."

"So you're saying that we haven't even met the real enemy yet," Cameron said.

"Exactly," Mallus replied. "And that's how they prefer it. The Architects are guiding actions from the shadows to eventually realize their goal."

"Which is?" Melissa asked, arms folded nervously across her chest.

"That I cannot answer," the fallen angel said. "But from what I could gather while in their service, it does not bode well for humankind."

Aaron felt his anger begin to rise. This was all getting to be too much for him. Wasn't it bad enough that they'd failed to prevent the earth from being cut off from Heaven, that they were paying the price as daylight steadily diminished and humanity was at the mercy of the monstrous things that had emerged from the shadows to lay claim to the planet? Now there was more?

Aaron just couldn't take it anymore.

"This is bullshit," he said, shocking the others with his outburst.

Vilma looked at him, fear in her eyes. "Aaron?"

"I said this is bullshit," he repeated. "How much more can we do? We Nephilim were supposed to be God's greatest achievement, but we've been hunted down to near extinction, and now we can barely perform the function we were created for."

Vilma grabbed hold of his arm. Her touch brought him a certain amount of solace, but not enough to silence his rant.

"Now we're being asked to stop godlike angels that have been crafting their will behind the scenes since before creation?" Aaron continued. "It's just too damn much, and I'm beginning to believe that your not killing me"—he pointed to Verchiel, who seemed startled by the attention—"was the worst thing that could have happened to me."

Aaron suddenly stopped, stunned by what had just poured from his mouth, but feeling no regret.

"I need some fresh air," he said then, leaving the room, and leaving the fate of humanity—the fate of the world—hanging in the balance.

But at that moment he just didn't have the energy to care.

* * *

The Morningstar had never imagined that he would care so much.

As he watched the vision, he was again reminded of the depth of emotion that he'd experienced in the presence of Taylor Corbet.

How was this even possible? he wondered, observing snippets of the life they had started together. He had once been a self-centered monster who had allowed his feelings of jealously to spread like a cancer through the hierarchy of Heaven. How could he have fallen so deeply in love with a human woman? How could he possibly have been in love with one of the creatures that had stolen away God's love for his kind?

But perhaps in growing to love her he had learned something that the Almighty had tried to convey. Humanity *was* something special, and to love them was to truly love Him. For the spark of God was in each and every person, although it seemed that Taylor Corbet had more of Him in her than many of the others.

Lucifer could never really say for sure what it was that set her apart from everyone else, but whatever it was, the Morningstar embraced it. And in doing so, he embraced the world. With Taylor Corbet's love he was able to set aside his anger and see the grave mistake of his actions.

And begin his journey on the long road to redemption.

Other than when he was with the Almighty Himself, Lucifer had never been more happy in the presence of another being. The life he had with Taylor was simple but whole. He lived not as the Morningstar but as a human, and his admiration of God's greatest achievement grew.

But the way to atonement was not an easy path. It was filled with great pain, and sacrifice. Lucifer still had a great price to pay.

He had been with Taylor for little more than three years when he had begun to sense that those he had wronged, those who hunted him, were close. And for the safety of the woman he'd grown to love, he'd had to leave. He knew that these Powers would show her no mercy. They would derive great pleasure in taking her from him.

So Lucifer left in the early hours of the morning, without saying good-bye, without telling Taylor how much he loved her.

She had become his universe. She had saved him from himself, and for that he would be forever in her debt. But he never had a chance to tell her that, for his sins were catching up with him, and he'd had to flee.

Lucifer watched, and remembered the sinking feeling of despair he had experienced as he'd left the life he'd made for himself with Taylor. But that despair was even worse now, for he knew that it was not only Taylor Corbet whom he had left that fateful morning.

But his unborn son as well.

Mallus started to follow Aaron out, but the other female stopped him with a firm hand on his arm.

"Maybe you should give him a minute," Vilma said.

The fallen angel considered this, then withdrew his arm from her grasp.

"I need to speak with him further," he said, again starting to follow.

A sword of fiery red suddenly blocked his way.

"And I asked you to give him a minute," she said in a semi-threatening tone.

He liked the spirit of these Nephilim, and the more time he spent with them, the more hope he had. He knew the Architects would have prepared for every contingency, but there was something he admired about these young half-breeds that he couldn't quite put his finger on.

Something that made him believe in the impossible.

"Please," he said to Vilma. "I think I might be able to help him."

"You've done an awesome job so far," she said angrily.

So he waited for her approval, as the others watched. Mallus knew that if he went against her wishes, he would not only have to deal with the female's wrath but the wrath of all the others—including Verchiel.

Again he briefly wondered how the former leader of the Powers had come to be here amongst those he had once called abominations. But who was Mallus to question, for here he was attempting to save humanity.

"Take it easy on him," Vilma finally said, and her sword

disappeared in a searing flash. "We've been burning the candle at both ends these days, and we're all a little fragile."

"Fragile," Mallus said, sensing their potential for ferocity. "That couldn't be farther from the truth."

Then he strode from the room in search of their leader.

Mallus found Aaron perched atop a swing set in an old, decrepit playground. He watched the young man sitting perfectly balanced across the metal bar, staring off into space.

The angel wanted to tell him that the answers were to be found within oneself, in the choices that one made.

He was transported back to the time when it had all changed for him, when Mallus had observed the Morningstar and Taylor Corbet together in the park. How long he had watched them, Mallus could not remember, but it was long enough to have instilled a change in him, although he'd been unable to admit it at the time.

The Architects had wanted Lucifer Morningstar in their ranks, and it had been up to Mallus to approach him with the request.

Aaron interrupted Mallus's thoughts. "I know you're there," he called out.

Mallus pushed the memory aside and approached the Nephilim.

"If you've come out here to tell me more stuff that I should be fighting you can forget it," Aaron said, refusing to look at him. "I've got way too much on my plate right now."

Mallus decided to dive in headfirst. "It was seeing you, and realizing who you were, that gave me the notion that there was still a chance for the world."

"Yeah, yeah," Aaron said, jumping down to the ground. He picked up a handful of pebbles at his feet and threw them at the rusted merry-go-round in the center of the play area. "I'm the savior . . . the Chosen One . . . yadda, yadda, yadda."

A pebble hit the old ride with a metallic clatter.

"I wasn't even sure that you had survived," Mallus said.

Aaron looked at him, confusion in his gaze. "Survived?" he asked. "What, the Powers' attacks?"

Mallus stepped closer, shaking his head. "After you were born, I made sure that you were safe by putting you into the system."

Aaron turned toward him, the weight of Mallus's words starting to permeate. "You put me into the system?" he asked. "What the hell are you talking about?"

"At that time, your mother was in true danger," Mallus explained. "She was the one who needed my help to survive."

"My mother?" Aaron stepped toward him. "My mother died giving birth to me."

Mallus smiled. "That's what I wanted everyone to believe."

"What are you saying?" Aaron demanded. His wings of ebony stretched from his back, and angelic script appeared upon his taut, muscular flesh. Mallus stood in awe, reading the names and remembering those whom he'd fought alongside, those who had fought for the beliefs of the Morningstar.

Aaron was even more of a spectacle than Mallus had originally believed.

"What do you know about my mother?" Aaron demanded, his voice raging with suppressed angelic might.

"I knew that it was only a matter of time before they came for her, the human woman who had tamed the Morningstar," Mallus explained. "And then when I found out she was with child—*his child*—I knew what had to be done."

"You knew my mother?" Aaron asked incredulously.

Mallus laughed softly. "Let's just say I admired her from afar. I saw a power in her . . . and the more I saw, the more I was changed as well."

He had the young man's rapt attention.

"It was she, your mother, who swayed me from serving the Architects," he continued. "If the Morningstar could live amongst them, love one of them, then who was I to want them dead?"

"You . . . you're saying that she didn't die?" Aaron asked.

Mallus shook his head. "Not then," he explained. "Fearing for her safety, Lucifer departed before learning that she was with child. I felt a certain responsibility to my former commander, as well as the woman he had come to love—and besides, I knew how valuable she and her unborn child could be to the Architects."

Mallus went to sit upon the merry-go-round, and Aaron followed eagerly.

"I watched her through her pregnancy, shielding her from danger, and when it was time, I was with her."

"What did you do?" Aaron asked, desperation in his tone.

"She did die giving birth to you," Mallus said.

"But you—"

"My concern at first was for you," he said. "I knew that at birth you would be just a normal child, and I made sure you were put into the foster system, where you would be cared for." Mallus looked at him then. "I knew that once you reached maturity, problems would arise. But that was a worry for another time."

"My mother . . . she was dead?"

"She was," Mallus acknowledged. "But not for long. Her body was taken to the hospital morgue, but there was still enough of a spark within her for me to work with. I fanned the flame of her life. I restored her."

"But if you were afraid that the Architects might—"

"I was afraid, but I also saw the benefit of keeping her alive," he said. "After all, she was the human woman who'd tamed the Morningstar."

"Where did she go?" Aaron demanded. "What did you do to her?"

"The Architects had enemies. They still do. I contacted those enemies and told them who she was. They took her away."

"Somebody took her? Is she still alive?" The boy was growing frantic.

Mallus shrugged. "Truthfully, I do not know. That night was the last I saw of her."

"Who did you give her to?" Aaron asked, tension in his voice.

"There wasn't a choice, Aaron," Mallus said. "The Architects would have used her as a bargaining chip with Lucifer. I did what I thought was best for her . . . and for you."

"Yeah," Aaron said, the names on his exposed flesh starting to fade as his wings receded. "I've been doing just awesome, thanks."

"But you are," Mallus said. "This world would have spiraled downward far more quickly if it weren't for you and the others."

"But we're still spiraling," Aaron said. "There doesn't seem to be any way to stop it."

"If this were any other night, I might have agreed with you," Mallus told him.

"What do you mean by that?" the boy asked suspiciously. "What else are you going to spring on me?"

Mallus could feel his hope for humanity actually rise. "I know . . . things," he said.

"Yeah?" Aaron questioned. "What kinds of things?"

"The kinds of things that could be dangerous to our enemies."

"Do you really think we have a chance against the Architects?" Aaron asked.

"The Architects are the endgame," Mallus said. "First we have to beat back the threat of darkness and the creatures that thrive in it."

"And what are our chances with that?" Aaron wanted to know.

Mallus looked at the son of the Morningstar and Taylor Corbet and felt something stirring inside him. He knew it was hope, but he didn't want to give it a name, for when something was named, it was easier to take away its power.

"Let's return to the others," Mallus said, turning back toward their meeting place without answering Aaron's question. "There's quite a bit that we still need to discuss if any of this is going to matter."

CHAPTER TWELVE

Satan flew above his risen church, reaching out with his mind to all who called the darkness friend.

He was summoning them so they could see his power. This was their chance to accept his divinity and sovereignty over all who lived in the shadows. For those who did not answer the call, who would not bow down to him in fealty, there would be a terrible price to pay.

He soared over the spires of his citadel and over the still churning seas. After only a few short hours in the sky, the sun was already waning, the darkness ready to claim the day and turn it to night.

After touching down upon the newly formed island that held his place of worship, the armored monarch strode through the front entrance to find the three Sisters awaiting his return.

"It is done," he proclaimed, moving toward the empty throne at the front of his temple.

"Now we wait for the replies to come," said one of the Sisters.

"Many will see that you are the one," said another.

"While some will need persuasion," the third added.

Satan sneered. "Those who doubt my credentials will be persuaded by death," he proclaimed.

The Three Sisters of Umbra stood before him, their faces hidden by the hoods they wore, but he knew that they were staring at him.

"What?" he demanded. "What do you disapprove of now?"

One of the Sisters shambled forward. "It is not that we disapprove, oh Star of Darkness," she cooed. "It is simply that we believe there might be a better way to draw allies to your side."

The other two bowed in agreement.

Satan did not want to hear it. He'd already experienced the scorn of the Community, which no one of his power should have to endure. Destroying them would be far more satisfying.

But perhaps swaying opponents to his side instead of relying on genocide was an option to consider. Certainly it might increase the number of soldiers able to fight for his cause.

"Tell me," the Darkstar said, reclining on his throne of marble. "Tell me of a better way."

Aaron and Mallus found the others in the TV room, engrossed in the news.

"Outbreaks are escalating," Vilma said nervously. "The news anchors can barely keep up with the information that's flooding in."

"And none of it is good," Gabriel grumbled.

"The increase in the hours of darkness is providing the perfect environment for evil to fester," Verchiel said, arms folded across his chest as he stared at the horrific images from all across the globe.

Mallus's eyes were riveted to the television screen as well. "If things continue the way they are, there will be no reprieve in the form of daylight," he said. "Soon there will be only darkness."

"We've tried to use Archon magick to stop the progression of night," Lorelei said. "But encroaching darkness seems to be a result of the severed connection with Heaven."

Gabriel walked toward Mallus.

"So what's causing the darkness to grow, and where can we find it so that we can stop it?" the dog wanted to know.

"If only it were that easy," Mallus said. "Long ago, when I was still in service to the Architects, they employed powerful magickal machines called Fear Engines."

"Let me guess," Cameron spoke up. "They make people afraid."

"No, they do not make fear. They collect it," Mallus corrected. "These engines use fear as a power source to perform complex acts of magick."

Verchiel slowly looked away from the television and fixed the angel in his icy stare. "So as fear around the globe intensifies, so does the level of power available to our adversaries."

"Yes," Mallus said. He pointed to the television screen. "This is making them very powerful indeed, powerful enough to eventually stop the sun from shining."

"Then our response should be simple and direct," Verchiel said. "Find these Fear Engines and destroy them, depriving our enemies of power."

"Unfortunately, it's easier said than done," Mallus said. "The Fear Engines are hidden all over the world, and the Architects have employed their most powerful magicks to keep the machines from being detected."

He then looked to Lorelei. "No offense to your talents, but even if you could locate the engines, it would take far too much time."

Aaron's frustration soared. He was about to beg Mallus for some idea, when a proposition came from the most unexpected source.

"She probably couldn't do it, but what about me?" Dusty asked.

Mallus looked at the young man in surprise. "You?"

"I'm still pretty new to all of this stuff, but I think I could—"

"But you're human," Mallus interrupted. "We deal here with matters of the divine. How could you possibly—"

An earsplitting noise suddenly filled the air, its vibrations resonating to the very cores of their beings.

"I may look the part, but I think I stopped being completely human the first time my hands touched the Instrument," Dusty said, gesturing to the window and the giant sword sticking up from the ground outside. The sword vibrated, and the sound grew louder as it did.

"The Instrument?" Mallus asked. "You . . . ?"

"It was given to me," the nearly blind young man said. "And I still have quite the connection to it."

Mallus seemed to be reconsidering. "If the Instrument's connection to the world could be tapped—"

"It can," Dusty cut in. "I've already done it."

Lorelei now stood beside Dusty, a look of concern upon her face.

"Are you sure?" she asked. "We don't really know what this means, or what it might do to you."

"It's all right," Dusty reassured her. "I'm tired of fighting it. If the Instrument wants to show me things, let it show me where those engines are."

"If we can locate the engines, we may be able to destroy them," Mallus said excitedly.

"'May be able'?" Melissa asked.

"The Fear Engines will be heavily guarded," Mallus explained.

"Then we'll just have to deal with that first," Cameron said, and Melissa nodded her agreement.

"Something tells me it won't be easy," Vilma said.

Gabriel had started to whine, coming to stand very close to his mistress, leaning against her.

"The Architects will make nothing easy," Mallus said.

Aaron couldn't say that he was happy with what they had to work with, but he wasn't complaining; at least they had a lead. He had already started formulating his battle plans.

"As soon as we determine the engines' locations, we'll break into teams," Aaron informed the group. "Melissa and I, Vilma and Cameron, Verchiel and—"

"I'll go alone," Verchiel said. "Unless you want to team me up with the dog."

The former Powers leader looked to the animal, and a look seemed to pass between them. Aaron would have to ask Gabriel what that was all about, as soon as they had a moment together.

"Dusty, what are you going to need in order to—" Aaron began, but was interrupted.

"You will not be going with them," Mallus informed Aaron.

"What are you saying? I'm the leader of this group."

"You'll go with me," the fallen angel said. "A very long time ago I committed a great error, which must be addressed if what we're about to attempt here is going to matter.

"You, Aaron, are going to help me correct that error for the benefit of the world."

* * *

"Damn it!" Baby Roger screeched, swatting aside the pile of blocks that he'd precariously erected in the sitting room.

"Now, then," Jeremy's mother said, going to the angry child. "Where did you hear such language?"

She leaned over, picked up the mewling babe, and carried him to the sofa, where she bounced him on her knee.

Jeremy watched from the kitchen, a tension growing in the air. Baby Roger's outbursts had become quite common of late, and needless to say, that meant sleep was at a premium. He drank his cup of tea as his mother attempted to calm the child.

Good luck with that.

"Stop bouncing me!" Roger demanded, his intense stare fixed upon the older woman. "Do you know how hard it is to think with your insides all jostled like that!"

"Sorry, luv," she apologized.

Jeremy was about to step in to reprimand the little monster, but what would it matter? He and his mother had both been trying to get Roger to behave for days, but there was no talking to him.

"Maybe you need your nappy changed?" his mother suggested, about to stick her finger down the back of the child's undergarment.

"I do not need my nappy changed!" he bellowed. "And if I did, I'd tell you to do it and do it quickly!"

Jeremy's mother looked in his direction and rolled her eyes. "I'm sure you would," she said.

Jeremy stepped into the room. "What is it this time, Rog?" he asked. "Blocks not lining up the way you like? Have a little patience, mate, Your hands are still developing and all."

"It's not the damned blocks," Roger said, though he was looking at the wreckage. "It's much deeper than that."

Jeremy knew where this was going. This same conversation had been happening more frequently over the last day or so.

"I wish I could remember," the baby said. "I know the information is in here." He smacked his head with a chubby hand. "But I can't access it. It's almost as if something is trying to keep it from me."

"No sense beating yourself up about it," Jeremy told him. "It'll come to you when it's time." He wasn't sure that's what Baby Roger wanted to hear, but it was the only advice he had to offer right now.

This child was somehow very important to the world, and Jeremy and his mom had been chosen to safeguard him. Seeing how crazy things had become out there in the world, he knew that a revelation was inevitable. The three of them would just have to be patient until it chose to manifest itself.

Jeremy's mother sat Roger on the couch and stood up.

"Where are you going?" the cranky Roger demanded. "If I wanted to be set down I would have told you that!"

"Hold on now," she said, heading for a bag that had been stashed in the corner by the telly. "You're getting smarter every day. Maybe you just need more of a challenge."

Roger folded his arms across his chest and glowered.

"Oh, yes, a challenge is all that I need, thank you very much," the baby muttered, watching as the woman retrieved the bag and brought it to a blanket that had been spread out on the floor.

"Bring him over here, would you, luv?" she asked Jeremy.

Jeremy set his nearly empty cup of tea down and went to the baby.

"I do not wish to return to the blanket," he declared as Jeremy picked him up. "Put me down this instant!"

"Yeah, yeah, yeah," Jeremy said, having heard the baby's complaints before.

Jeremy set the child down next to Irene.

"Now, let's see what we have in here," she said, looking inside the satchel.

"Perhaps there's a club in there, and I could beat you both with it," Roger said, his sarcasm getting nasty.

Jeremy couldn't help but be amused, and stifled a laugh. "Careful there, Rog, or we'll put you up for adoption," he warned the baby.

"Adoption," Roger repeated. "Sweeter words were never spoken. At least it would get me away from the likes of you two simpletons."

Jeremy's mother removed a colorful puzzle from within the bag and dumped all the animal-shaped pieces onto the floor.

"What the devil are you making a mess for?" the baby asked,

reaching down to pick up a piece that was shaped like a monkey.

"You're supposed to put the monkey where it belongs," Jeremy's mother told the child, gesturing toward the board before him.

"I'll put it where it belongs," Roger grumbled, tossing aside the monkey and then sliding the board away as well. "I have no interest in such nonsense," he stated. "Pick me up this instant, or I will—"

Jeremy's mother removed something else from the bag.

"I had one of these when I was just a little girl," she said happily.

"They actually had items such as that during the Cretaceous period?" Roger asked with a nasty smirk.

Jeremy leaned forward and flicked the baby's substantial earlobe. "Be nice."

The child shrieked in rage. "Do not lay your hands upon me!" he warned, and then watched what the woman was doing.

She held a brightly colored wooden object, with what appeared to be a peasant girl painted upon it. Jeremy's mother opened up the object and removed another, smaller object from inside. It was painted with the same image of a little girl. She opened the second object, revealing yet another, even smaller painted wooden figure.

"What is that?" Baby Roger asked, his eyes fixated upon it.

"It's a Russian nesting doll," she said. "I used to love to play with mine."

It had been quite some time since Jeremy had seen his mother smile like that; the wooden dolls must have brought back some pleasant memories.

Roger leaned forward as the last of the dolls, a tiny baby, was removed from inside the body of the previous doll.

"They all fit into each other," Roger stated. "One inside the other."

The baby really seemed taken by this.

Jeremy's mother was now in the process of putting them all back inside each other, and Roger watched, absolutely fascinated.

Finished, she placed the single beautifully painted doll into his lap. "You try it," she said.

There were no complaints this time. Roger reacted without a single word. After some difficulty he managed to open the first and largest of the dolls, and then removed and opened the one inside that. After a few minutes he held the single piece of wood that was painted to look like a baby. He studied it for a moment.

"Yes," he said finally, as if talking to the wooden child. "It's all starting to become clearer."

He picked up the largest doll and held that in his other hand. Roger's head turned as he looked from the largest doll to the smallest doll.

"Yes," he said again, placing the baby inside the empty body of the larger doll with a hollow *clunk*.

"Much . . . clearer."

CHAPTER THIRTEEN

Dusty stood before the giant sword. He could see little more than a darkened outline through the milky haze that obscured his vision.

"Are you sure about this, Dusty?" Aaron asked from beside him.

Dusty could hardly hear the question. The emanations from the Instrument crowded his head. "I'm good," he managed, momentarily turning his failing eyes from the vibrating blade toward Aaron's voice.

The Instrument had been plunged deep into the flesh of the earth by the monstrous Abomination of Desolation, and was now tuned with the new horrors of the world. It saw everything that happened across the globe, and wanted to share all of that news with Dusty. The sword could also see the future, and wanted to show him the multitude of those possibilities too.

That was more than enough to drive a normal person insane, but Dusty wasn't normal. He hadn't been normal since he'd come to possess the Instrument. If he'd had the choice, he would have broken the psychic connection with the great weapon, but Dusty knew that wouldn't happen until he was dead.

He felt Lorelei's hand upon his shoulder. "Just let me know when you're ready," she said into his ear.

Dusty didn't want to do this, but he owed it to his new friends, and the world. *Who knows*, he thought hopefully. *Maybe whatever I do today will free me from the damn Instrument tomorrow.*

It was worth a shot.

"I'm as ready as I'll ever be," he said over the nauseating hum inside his own head.

Lorelei was going to use her magick to help him focus, to keep his mind from spinning into oblivion with the Instrument's millions of visions and alternate realities. Dusty could faintly make out the scroll containing the spell and Lorelei's copper bowl as she set them on the ground next to him. She'd also brought a dove for sacrifice (*How many of those poor things bite it in a week here?* he had to wonder) and the globe from the science room to use as their map.

"Remember," Aaron said. "We get the locations of the Fear Engines, and then that's it. Break the connection as quickly as you're able. No need to put yourself at any more risk than absolutely necessary."

Dusty nodded. Part of him wanted to scream that simply being near the sword was a huge risk, but there wasn't any point in making Aaron feel worse than he probably already did.

Dusty turned his focus to the blade before him. "Ready when you are," he said to Lorelei, who dropped the last of her special ingredients into the bowl.

The contents of the bowl began to smoke, and Lorelei picked up the small rolled scroll and started to quietly read from it.

Dusty opened his mind to the Instrument—and almost immediately wished that he hadn't. He felt as though he were drowning, drowning in sheer terror. Images bombarded him, barely giving him the opportunity to process one before another replaced it. It took everything he had not to scream, everything he had not to search out the nearest jagged rock and cut his own throat.

Anything to make the visions stop.

Dusty could hear Lorelei, far off in the nightmarish distance, telling him to focus on her voice. She was persistent, demanding that he hear her and follow her commands. Amidst scenes of a world of horror, bloodshed, and unnatural death, Dusty zeroed in on her voice. He concentrated, finally feeling the onslaught begin to subside.

He felt like he was in a whirlpool now. A numbing coolness was all around him. The images were still with him, still clamoring for his attention, but suddenly he had the strength to sort them.

To assess them one at a time.

Lorelei instructed him to observe the nightmarish scenes unfolding before him and to visualize the fear they caused, then follow that fear. The imagery was devastating, and painted a picture of a world Dusty wanted nothing to do with.

Humanity was in danger. The darkness stretched to claim more and more of the earth. Dusty watched as tendrils of fear began to snake up into the ether. That was what he needed to track. Those threads of emotion would lead him to the engines.

Dusty followed those paths, and the trails ended in the strangest of places. But there they were, the engines throbbing with collected fears.

"I've found them," he exclaimed, nearly losing his concentration. *Focus,* he told himself.

Before he could gain his composure, the Archon magick was inside him. It flowed through Lorelei and into him. The magick was like liquid lightning, singing in his veins and boiling his blood. Dusty screamed as the magick punched through his fingertips, engulfing the old globe. The tin globe exploded, sending jagged pieces of metal whizzing through the air.

The magick was wild. Tendrils of energy pulsed from his hands, striking the earth, worming down into the soil. The ground churned as a huge section of dirt, rock and grass rose up into the air. The soil took on a spherical shape, a representation of the planet, spinning slowly as it hung in the crisp New England air.

"There!" Dusty yelled as a column of light erupted from the magickal globe, followed by another, and another after that.

Three beacons of light, marking the locations of the Fear Engines.

Lorelei was impressed.

Dusty was handling the Archon magick like a pro. It had left her body when it had been summoned, and had flowed into the waiting receptacle that was Dusty.

She still held the leash, but was shocked and delighted to see how the ancient magick was taking to the young man. She could not help but think about the day when the magick would no longer listen to her commands, but would turn on her like an angry dog, beaten one too many times by its master. Then the magick would utterly consume her.

And then it would be up to Dusty to help the Nephilim with their mission. Watching as he located the Fear Engines with pillars of light, she saw someone who was certainly up for the task. With a little more training, he would be just as good as she was.

Maybe even better.

Lorelei could sense Dusty's enormous potential. He had the ability to hold and control vast amounts of powerful magick. It made her inevitable death that much easier to accept.

It also made her more willing to take a chance. As she

watched him wield the power of her spell, Lorelei was tempted. If Dusty was able to locate the Fear Engines that had been hidden by powerful magicks, could he also help her find the wayward Lucifer?

It was certainly something to consider. His disappearance gnawed at her, making her all the more determined to find the missing Morningstar.

With Dusty's help, she hoped to solve the mystery, to the benefit of them all.

Aaron approached the spinning ball of earth, his eyes focused upon what could best be described as the hot spots. There didn't appear to be any particular rhyme or reason to their placement, but then again, he had never been part of a secret gathering of angelic beings that wanted to see humanity go extinct.

"Does this look right to you?" Aaron asked as Mallus came to stand beside him.

The others had stepped up for a closer look as well.

"As right as anything the Architects might have their wings in," the fallen angel said.

"Why these places?" Aaron asked as the globe slowly spun, revealing the three locations. "Why in these particular spots?"

"You're asking me to think like them," Mallus said. "I haven't a clue. Perhaps they have some special meaning to the Architects, or maybe they mean absolutely nothing at all."

"In the long run it doesn't really matter," Vilma said, watching the beams of light. "We just need to get to these places and take care of the engines."

"Right," Aaron said, trying to make up his mind as to how they should proceed. "Since we really haven't a clue as to what we'll be up against, I want us to go in teams." He stopped to study the earthen globe for a moment. "Vilma and Cameron, you'll go west. Verchiel and Melissa, I want you to go east." He paused again, collecting his thoughts. "Since I have to go with Mallus, one team will have to do double duty—"

"I'll do it," Gabriel barked, interrupting him. *"I'll go."*

Aaron smiled at the good-hearted nature of his dog's offer. "That's all right, buddy," he told the animal. "We can—"

"I can do it," Gabriel insisted, his stance stiff, his gaze intently upon Aaron.

"Gabriel, I know you want to help, but—"

"I've changed, Aaron," Gabriel spoke. *"More than you realize."*

And before Aaron could question him further, Gabriel decided to show them all.

At once the Labrador's body began to glow, sparks of divine fire leaping from his golden fur, which looked as if it shifted and moved. Strangely enough, it reminded Aaron of a wheat field caressed by the wind.

The dog seemed larger and fiercer, and suddenly Aaron was afraid. Where was the sweet animal that he loved with all his heart and soul? Where was the dog that meant so much to him that he'd brought him back from the dead?

And then it hit him. "I did this."

The dog looked up at Aaron with eyes flecked with golden fire.

"Yes," he said. *"I knew that you had changed me, that I had become smarter than other dogs, but this was totally unexpected."*

Aaron didn't know what to say. He knelt in front of Gabriel.

"I had no idea that—"

"Neither did I," Gabriel said. *"It just kind of happened when I was attacked outside the school's barriers."*

Aaron reached out to pet the animal, but hesitated.

"Please don't be afraid of me, Aaron," the dog said sadly.

Aaron threw his arms around the animal's large neck in a hug. He had a sudden, painful sensation, but it quickly dissipated as Aaron felt his body assuming his more angelic guise, somehow triggered by his contact with Gabriel.

"I could never be afraid of you," he said.

"I do so hate to break up this charming emotional display," Verchiel chided, "but the earth, if I'm not mistaken, is still in danger."

Aaron released his dog and stood. Gabriel's gaze followed him, waiting for Aaron's decision.

"Gabriel will take the last of the engines," Aaron said.

The dog nodded, divine fire sparking around his head. *"I won't let you down."*

Aaron retained his fearsome angelic form and stared at his

friends, his fellow Nephilim, his soldiers. His gaze lingered upon Vilma longer than the others, a message passing between them as their eyes momentarily locked.

He loved her, plain and simple, and she loved him back. But in order for that love to survive, and to become even greater than it already was, a world needed to be ordered.

That was their mission.

Their purpose.

"Be careful," he told them all. Suddenly he realized that this could be the last time he saw some of them alive. He wanted to say more, but there wasn't time.

One by one the Nephilim took on their angelic guises, spreading powerful wings, wrapping themselves within their feathered embrace, and then they were gone.

Gabriel was the last to go.

"I love you, Aaron," the dog told him in his kind doggy grumble. *"Thought I'd like to tell you that, just in case."*

It took everything that Aaron had not to beg him to stay. "I love you too, Gabe," he managed before his voice cracked with emotion.

Gabriel's stance then stiffened, and he shook his canine body as if shucking off water. Golden fire swarmed around the dog's form like eager fireflies, until he disappeared, until there was only the light of the divine.

Then that too winked out; the dog, and the fire, were gone.

"Are you ready?" Mallus asked Aaron.

Aaron managed to tear his eyes away from where Gabriel had been.

"Yeah," he told the fallen angel. "As ready as I'm going to be. Where are we going?"

Mallus stepped closer to him and grabbed his wrist in a powerful grip.

"Do you see?" the angel asked.

For a brief moment Aaron didn't understand. Then an image, as clear as day, appeared in his mind.

"Yes, I see," Aaron replied.

"Then let us be gone."

Mallus stepped closer as Aaron stretched out his wings of black, and enclosed them both.

The globe spun as Dusty stood, shivering, in its shadow.

"Are you all right?" Lorelei asked, still managing the Archon spell that held the young man in check.

"Yeah," he said, though there was strain in his voice, "but I think I'm ready to be rid of this connection."

"Wait," she said, limping forward, leaning upon her cane.

Surprised, Dusty turned his milky eyes in her direction.

"Can you hold on for just a little bit longer?" she asked as she approached him.

"I'm not sure that I can—"

"I need to ask you a favor," Lorelei interrupted.

His eyes blinked. "Okay," he said cautiously.

"I need you to let me in," she said. "I need you to let me see what the Instrument is showing you."

Dusty slowly nodded.

"I have to find him," Lorelei said.

"Lucifer," Dusty stated.

"If things continue as they are . . ." She paused, considering the future. "We need him," she finished with finality.

"Are you sure you're strong enough to handle this?" Dusty asked her.

She stood on the periphery of his connection to the sword, wielding the Archon magick and feeling the intensity of the power that radiated from the sword. In all actuality she wasn't sure if she *was* strong enough, but she knew for certain that soon she wouldn't be.

But now . . .

"As sure as I'll ever be," she told him.

Dusty accepted that, and she watched him change his stance, readying himself for what was to come.

"What do you need me to do?" he asked.

"Just hold on for a little longer," Lorelei said. "And I need you to let me into your mind."

It felt as though Lorelei were sticking her head into a rushing stream, only there were multiple currents, each traveling at about a hundred miles an hour along different routes. For a moment she hesitated, tempted to draw back, fearing for her safety. But then she considered the safety of her friends and of the world, and then she immersed herself.

At first she thought she was going to be torn apart. Then she felt herself begin to slide into Dusty's mind.

Oh, the sights she saw. Lorelei wanted to so look away, but there was no stopping now. The more she saw, the better she was able to let herself drift.

"Lorelei," she heard her name called forcefully.

She chose to ignore it, knowing that whoever was calling her could do little to change the path of the world.

"Lorelei, it's me," the voice said again, and she remembered Dusty. "I'm not sure how much longer I've got. I'm getting tired and . . ."

Dusty, she thought, remembering the young man and how his gift—*or was it a curse?*—was allowing her to see everything that the sword saw, every darkened pocket of the world.

Images that had been hidden from her magick.

And then she remembered why she was there in Dusty's mind.

"Dusty!" she called out, hoping that she had strength enough to lend him. "Just a bit longer, Dusty."

She pulled herself together. Her time was limited, so she tried to see as much as she could, scanning and discarding one nightmarish vision after another.

"Where are you, Lucifer?" she called out in frustration. "Where have you gone?"

Lorelei felt a powerful tug upon her psyche. Dusty was

weakening. Her time was up, but still she searched, exposing herself to sights that would have driven a lesser being to madness.

Dusty was screaming now, no longer able to contain her presence within his own. She was about to withdraw, when she saw a flash of darkness. A star of black twinkled amid a sea of nightmares.

"I'm sorry," she told her agonized host, forcing herself toward the mystery.

Lorelei extended her already damaged and fragmented psyche, but she was running out of time. She could feel Dusty failing, the Instrument's relentless pummeling driving him to destruction. All she needed was a moment more to see what was lurking inside this vision.

Lorelei pushed, and felt the fragile exterior of the darkened star shatter like an eggshell. She was disappointed to see that there was only more darkness within, and was turning to depart, when she saw it.

When she saw him.

Lucifer Morningstar, curled in the fetal position, floated in a sea of total black. She saw his face twitch, and his mouth grimace as if he were locked in a nightmare. Knowing that her time was precarious, Lorelei reached out to take hold of her friend and mentor, desperate to wake him from his slumber.

"Lucifer!" she cried. "Lucifer, we need you!"

And then the magickal tether that had held her to the visions of the Instrument yanked her back.

But not before she saw that Lucifer's eyes had opened.

Lucifer's life had returned to darkness once he'd left the woman he loved, but he did not let it control him as it had before. This love had changed him, and even though despair flowed through him, he did not let it affect him.

Lucifer remembered how it had felt, the torture of no longer having Taylor in his life, but he knew that it was for the best. His enemies were many, and they wanted nothing more than to wound him using that which he loved most.

As he had struck out against God and Heaven.

Lucifer had initially sought peace in the monastery of Crna Reka, in the Serbian mountains. He had hoped that removing himself from the world would be enough to please his enemies, but of course it wasn't.

The fallout from betraying God had followed him like a rabid beast, dragging him from his hiding place, his place of solace.

What if Verchiel and his Powers hadn't come for me? Lucifer pondered, immersed in the memory. *What if I was allowed to hide, wrapping myself in the darkness like a cloak?*

Like a protective cocoon.

Lucifer did not want to remember anymore, and forced himself to fall into a deeper subconscious world. This was where he belonged, where he could do the least damage to those he had grown to care for, those he had dared to love. This was where he would stay, letting the chrysalis of shadow grow thicker and stronger, protecting him from the world.

And protecting the world from him.

He wasn't sure how long he'd been asleep in that darkened embrace, but there came an insistent rapping as if somebody knew he was inside. Lucifer tried to ignore it, to return to the solace of sleep, but the knocking persisted.

And then, the unthinkable occurred.

Whatever—whoever—was outside his place of solitude cracked the exterior shell, exposing him, and he heard a voice that was strangely familiar.

"Lucifer!" it cried, temporarily rousing him from his numbed state, tempting him to open his eyes.

"Lucifer, we need you!"

An image of Lorelei filled his head, beautiful, powerful Lorelei. He'd almost forgotten her, forgotten all of the Nephilim. Visions of those who were trying to safeguard the world suddenly flowed through the cracks in his cocoon.

Then, as quickly as she had arrived, Lorelei was gone. But she had left a trail for him to follow back to the world from which he'd been taken.

It dawned on him then, a blow as crushing as when he'd realized the angels were no longer the Almighty's favorite.

If he could follow the trail back to the Nephilim, then so could somebody else.

Something else.

Lucifer's eyes snapped open, and Lorelei's ghostly image reappeared for an instant before she winked away. He tried to warn her, to tell her to guard her location before it—the evil power that had stolen his body—could follow her.

But it was already too late.

The darkness that had been Lucifer's solace was now filled with the laughter of his foe.

Satan's eyes snapped open.

Since the Abomination of Desolation had severed the earth's ties to Heaven, humanity had been gradually succumbing to the encroaching darkness. Their efforts to halt the onslaught of shadow that would eventually befall them were pitiful.

But there had been a wrinkle.

The Nephilim.

Satan did not fear the half-breeds, but he knew that they were striking out against his denizens of night, inspiring fear in those who should have been swearing their allegiance to him.

"You smile, oh lord," said one of the Sisters who stood before him.

"What did you see, oh Darkstar? " questioned the second.

"Was the path to the Community's fealty made clear?" the third Sister wanted to know.

Satan rose and fanned his wings.

"It was," he told them. "The Morningstar has provided me with a gift to entice those who have yet to admit that I am their lord and master."

He descended the marble steps from his throne to the court below, the Sisters fleeing from his path.

"Lucifer had attempted to hide them from me," the Darkstar growled. "These children of the fallen, these Nephilim."

"Horrible things," commented one of the Umbra Sisters.

"Thorns in the sides of so many of your blessed Community," said another.

"If only someone could exterminate them, remove this winged obstacle."

Satan smiled. "If only," he said, and began to laugh, a vision of the slaughter to come traipsing through the fetid fields of his mind.

CHAPTER FOURTEEN

The despair was so heavy in the air that Aaron could almost taste it.

He parted his wings, to find himself in the center of a deserted street. Instinctively he knew that he had arrived in the city of Detroit.

"Is this right?" he asked Mallus, who stepped from the embrace of Aaron's wings.

Mallus looked around. Cars burned in the road, with bodies strewn beside them. "Yes, this is where we're supposed to be," he confirmed.

"Something isn't right here," Aaron observed, unnerved by the boarded-up storefronts. "Where is everybody?"

"It wasn't like this section of town was bustling to begin with," Mallus said, strolling past abandoned buildings unhindered by foot traffic. "But evil has a tendency to lock on to despair, and it made this part of the city its home."

It was then that Aaron heard the first evidence of life. A scream of absolute terror carried on the night winds. He stopped, eyes scanning the area in search of the source.

Mallus's hand took hold of his arm, urging him on.

"We've no time for—"

Aaron yanked away his arm, feeling the sigils of his birthright rising to the surface of his flesh. "There's always time," he protested, his wings splaying as he prepared to take flight.

Mallus looked as though he would argue, but then resigned himself to Aaron's decision.

"That's where we're going," he said, pointing to a rundown building, its windows shuttered with random pieces of wood. A peeling sign hanging from a metal post read, BLESSED ANGEL NURSING HOME.

"Of course it is," Aaron replied, springing into the air, senses attuned to any further activity.

There were more screams, and he immediately found the source on the next street over. A tenement was burning. Flames and thick black smoke billowed out from broken windows. At first Aaron thought it would be a simple rescue mission, but then he caught sight of the street below.

People streamed from the burning building, believing they were running to safety, but there were things waiting for them—short, armored creatures with reptilian faces.

Goblins.

Some held burning torches in their clawed hands, and Aaron knew the goblins must have set the building ablaze. They leaped, snatched up their prey, and dragged them, screaming and struggling, into the shadows.

Soaring overhead for another look, Aaron could see a kind of swirling passage in the darkness behind the goblins. The building's inhabitants were being forced through the portal to a fate he would rather not consider.

Aaron brought forth an awesome sword of fire. The light from his weapon alerted the beasts below, and their bulbous eyes glistened as he swooped down amongst them.

"Angel!" one of the goblins barked in the tongue of its species as it yanked a short sword from a leather scabbard at its side.

Aaron landed on the street between the burning tenement and the goblins. The foul creatures rushed at him, murder in their monstrous gazes, but he was ready. The pulse of the divine throbbed in his veins. The goblins screeched their battle cries, attempting to scare him with their ferocity, but Aaron felt no fear.

This wasn't the time for fear; it was a time of battle.

Aaron counted nine goblins in the initial attack, all wearing filthy, blood-caked armor and wielding a variety of swords, knives, spears, and axes. Aaron propelled himself into the fray with his own battle cry, and collided with the first of the attackers, knocking them backward to the street. He swung his blade, the sword hissing eagerly as if knowing it would soon bite deep into the flesh of its enemy.

The goblins were ferocious in their attack, but they were nothing before a soldier of Heaven. Aaron did not stop moving. He pushed through the opposing force, his sword hacking through the goblin armor as if it were made of paper. The ground became slick with goblin blood as the creatures dropped, piling up around him as he fought.

And then above the moans of dying monsters, Aaron heard something that did not belong, something that momentarily distracted him. He scanned the area and caught sight of a goblin soldier carrying a car seat by its handle. The goblin crept close to the shadows of the abandoned buildings as the creature made its way toward the passage.

A goblin knife bit into Aaron's shoulder.

He cried out as his attacker laughed. Furious, Aaron pulled the knife from his shoulder and leaped into the air, fashioning his sword into a spear. While the goblins gazed up at him, Aaron threw the spear amongst them with all his might. The weapon detonated upon impact with the ground, and an explosion of divine fire cascaded outward, consuming the goblin horde and leaving only ashen bodies in its wake.

Aaron allowed himself a moment's pleasure, then saw that the goblin with the baby was still hurrying for the shadowy passage. Aaron arced his body downward, flying mere inches above the filthy street. Goblins tried to catch him, but he was moving too fast and scattered them like bowling pins.

The goblin with the baby saw Aaron's approach, the creature's bulbous eyes growing even larger as it realized that it was the angel's objective. Aaron beat the air with his wings, increasing his speed, but the goblin charged ahead.

Aaron extended his hands as he drew near, watching as the goblin wrapped its arms around the car seat while the baby wailed in fear; and then the goblin jumped into the yawning blackness.

The goblin shape disappeared within the magickal passage, but Aaron would not give up—could not give up. He landed and reached into the darkness. It was cold in the void, and the feeling went out of Aaron's arm, but he managed to grab hold of the metal collar of the goblin's chest plate. Using all of his strength and the powerful flapping of his wings, he dragged the goblin, still clutching the car seat, from the abyss.

His arm painfully numb, Aaron released the struggling goblin's collar and sent the beast and the car seat tumbling to the ground. He quickly scooped up the shrieking infant, still strapped tightly into the seat. Other than being scared, the child didn't appear to be injured.

"That's all right, little guy," Aaron said softly. "We'll see what we can do about finding your mom and—"

The goblin leaped upon his back.

"You will not deny the Darkstar his feast!" the goblin wailed, pulling a dagger from a small scabbard on its side.

Aaron reacted instinctively, flexing his wings and tossing

his attacker away. Then he gently set the car seat down and turned to the creature.

"His feast?" Aaron asked, stalking over to the goblin, which was pulling itself to its feet, still clutching a dagger. "You were going to feed that poor little kid to somebody?" He pointed toward the car seat, catching a glimpse of a woman using the distraction to snatch up her crying baby and race away.

The goblin lunged, but Aaron captured its wrist, halting the progress of the knife mere inches from his chest.

"Not just anybody," the goblin grunted with all his might. "The Darkstar."

Aaron savagely bent the goblin's wrist to one side, snapping it like a pencil. The goblin wailed in pain as its knife clattered to the street.

"The Darkstar?" he asked the goblin, squeezing the creature's snapped bones. "What's so special about this Darkstar?"

The goblin looked up with something akin to euphoria in his protruding eyes. "He is the lord of us all," it said in a reverent whisper. "He will lead us from hiding to claim this world as our own."

"Lord of who?" Aaron asked, putting more pressure on the goblin's wrist. "The goblins?"

"Do you have feathers in your ears as well, angel?" the goblin screeched. "He is the leader of us all—of us all!"

Slowly the full meaning of what the goblin was saying unfolded for Aaron.

They had a leader. Not just the goblins, but all of the creatures that the Nephilim had been fighting.

And now Aaron knew its name.

The door to the nursing home was open, and Mallus stepped into the lobby. The electricity was out. Emergency lights only faintly illuminated the gloom.

There wasn't anyone at the reception desk, and the thick layer of dust on the counter made him wonder when was the last time there had been.

Pulling up the sleeve of his coat, he looked at the squiggling horizontal sigil that had been tattooed on his wrist. It was rippling like the surface of the ocean caressed by the wind. He was in the right place.

Mallus found the stairwell in the dim glow of the emergency lights. He climbed the steps, paying close attention to the sensation in his wrist. The closer he got, the more severe the tingling became.

By the time he reached the second level, it felt as though the sigil were ready to tear itself from his flesh. He stood on the landing, peering through the small window in the door at the second-floor hallway. This floor seemed deserted as well, but the sigil told him otherwise. Mallus opened the door.

"Tarshish," he called out. "Tarshish, it's me."

He waited for a response, but there was only silence. Starting down the corridor, Mallus passed empty room after empty room, and began to wonder if the sigil on his wrist, which aided in finding the Malakim, had somehow been tampered with.

An old woman wearing a heavy pink bathrobe and slippers shuffled around a corner at the end of the hallway and came toward him. She had a wig upon her head like a hat, tilted jauntily to one side, wisps of white sneaking out from beneath the artificial brown.

"Hello," Mallus said in his most soothing voice. "I was wondering if you can help me find my friend. His name is Tarshish."

Bolts of pure magickal force crackled from the old woman's arthritic fingers, catching Mallus square in the chest and tossing him violently to the floor. His shirt was shredded, and his skin smoldered where the magick had touched him. He scrambled to his feet.

The woman continued her approach. Her robe was now burning with a supernatural fire, and her hands that had discharged the magickal blasts were burned and blackened. She came at him with arms outstretched, attempting to pull him into her fiery embrace. But Mallus drove a kick into her belly and sent her sprawling to the floor, where she exploded into ashes.

There was more scuffling and moaning. Other nursing home residents, their bodies alive with magickal energies, emerged from rooms he'd thought were empty. They came at him in a wave, launching magickal fire from their hands, mouths, and eyes. It was at times such as this that Mallus really did miss the protection of his wings.

He leaped behind the nurses' station, magick exploding all around him as he reached into his coat and withdrew the Gleaning Blade. He hadn't wanted to use the weapon, preferring to keep it safe in case it might provide them with new knowledge, but right now he could think of no better use. He closed his eyes, took a deep breath, counted to three, and then sprang up onto the counter, slashing at the closest attacker.

The old man reared back with a grunt, his throat slit from ear to ear, leaking not blood but supernatural energies. Energies that ignited not only the man but at least five others near him as the power was unleashed.

Mallus leaped from the counter, dodging bolts of destructive power that tore up chunks of the ancient linoleum. He lashed out with the blade, cutting and stabbing.

The energy built, then exploded, picking up the fallen angel and tossing him down the length of the corridor like a rag doll. He bounced off the wall and landed in a smoldering heap upon the floor.

Mallus lay there for what seemed like hours, his body seared by supernatural energies. Finally he was able to push himself up from the ground. The hallway was silent and blackened with ruin. Not a soul moved.

Someone coughed, and Mallus was immediately on alert. He faced the open door in front of him, squinting into what appeared to have been the nursing home's activity room. It was filled with tables littered with magazines and half-finished puzzles. A big-screen TV sat in the corner, with several vinyl-covered recliners in front of it. All were occupied by elders, their dull eyes fixed to the empty screen as if they were watching the most riveting program imaginable. He heard the cough again.

Mallus carefully entered the room, searching the gloom for signs of life.

"I shoulda figured it was you," said a voice from behind him. It sounded as though its owner had gargled with broken glass.

Mallus spun, mystical blade at the ready.

A wheelchair-bound figured sat in front of a card table. The man held a puzzle piece in his hand and was searching for its proper place.

The fallen angel cautiously stepped closer. "Tarshish?" he asked, not sure what form the Malakim might be wearing.

"That's right," the old man said, snapping the puzzle piece into place.

Mallus could now see the picture on the puzzle. It was a desert scene, pyramids rising up from the sand under a setting orange sun.

The old man looked up from the unfinished puzzle. Mallus could feel the ancient being's eyes upon him, scrutinizing the markings that he had put upon Mallus's flesh a very long time ago.

"Who touched up your ink?" the old man asked, looking back to his puzzle and picking up another piece. "Looks like crap."

CHAPTER FIFTEEN

Verchiel recognized where he was by the smell in the air, and the feel of the sand beneath his feet.

This was where the village had been, where he had heard a supposed prophet speak lies—*revealed as the truth*—about the Nephilim and their Chosen One, who would forgive the fallen angels, allowing them to return to Heaven.

This was the accursed village that Verchiel had wiped from the face of the earth.

"Where are we?" Melissa asked, hand upon her brow, shielding her eyes from the ferocity of the setting sun as she gazed about her desert surroundings.

"A cursed place," Verchiel replied, remembering not only what he had done here but his recent memory of the old prophet.

"You know this place?" the girl asked.

Verchiel ignored her question, scanning the desert for a

sign of where they were supposed to be. In the distance he saw what appeared to be an encampment, and started toward it.

"Is that some sort of archeological dig or something?" Melissa asked, running to keep up with Verchiel's powerful strides.

"It appears that way," he said, keeping his eyes on the encampment, searching for signs of life. He saw none.

They came up over the dune to a view of the camp—tents of varying sizes and purpose on one side, trucks and Jeeps on the other. It appeared from the buildup of sand upon the vehicles that they had not moved in quite some time.

"Hey, Verchiel. Over here," Melissa said, walking over to where a more solid structure had been erected.

He followed the girl, searching the area with a scrutinizing eye in the hopes of discovering what had happened to the camp's inhabitants. He learned nothing other than that they were not there.

Verchiel considered that maybe the site had been abandoned, but then why would they have left so much behind? Inside a food tent, tables were still set for supper.

"Take a look at this," Melissa said, holding open a heavy tarp so Verchiel might follow her inside.

Verchiel passed through the opening. An excavation site lay before him. The hole was large, with ladders leaning against the inside walls down into what seemed to be an open passage. The former leader of the Powers remembered how the village had looked before he'd called his wrath upon it.

"Should we go down?" Melissa asked.

Verchiel didn't bother to answer, grabbing onto a ladder and heading down into the passage.

"Guess that's a yes," the girl said as she followed.

The excavated corridor had been shored up with wooden planking, and flickering lights hung from the ceiling. A generator droned somewhere ahead of them.

Verchiel found the first of the camp's inhabitants sticking up out of the dirt floor.

"Is that a boot?" Melissa asked, stepping around the angel for a closer look.

Verchiel could only stare.

She tried to pick the boot up, and was surprised as it came away to reveal a dirty foot.

"Oh, that's not right," Melissa said, backing quickly away.

"No, it's not," Verchiel agreed.

Giving the filthy foot a wide berth, they headed farther into the tunnel.

Typical survival instincts would have encouraged the fight-or-flight reaction in most people, anything to avoid the possibility of impending death. But Verchiel was of the host Powers, and such instincts were not part of his makeup. All he knew was that he had to confront the danger and eliminate it. He glanced at the girl accompanying him, and could tell that she was struggling with her own survival instincts. He could practically feel the fear radiating from her.

"What?" she asked, catching his stare.

"You're afraid," Verchiel said, amused. *These are the powerful angelic warriors who are supposed to save humanity from harm? What was the Lord God thinking?*

"Yeah, so?" Melissa said. "Hasn't stopped me, though, has it?"

She did have a point.

"No, it hasn't," Verchiel agreed, momentarily considering the Nephilim's courage.

"Then you shouldn't worry about it," she added, continuing on.

The passage opened up into a much larger area, and Melissa stopped to take it all in. She turned slightly as Verchiel joined her.

"What is this?" she asked.

"Obviously what they had been rooting around to find in the dirt and sand," Verchiel said, knowing exactly what they were looking at.

He remembered the place as if he'd seen it only days prior, not thousands of years before. It was the marketplace where he and the Powers had meted out punishment for the lies of a supposed prophet.

"They've uncovered a section of the market," Verchiel said.

Melissa stepped farther into the room. "It was buried," she said, squatting down to brush at a section of floor, revealing the broken pieces of a clay pot sticking up from the ground. "Swallowed up by the desert and the passage of time."

Verchiel remembered his rage, and how he'd called the

power of Heaven's warriors upon the settlement and those who had provided that damnable prophet a safe haven.

The Powers had left no one alive, and had reduced the city to rubble. He was surprised to see even this much left intact.

"Removed from the eyes of God," Verchiel said softly.

"What? You're saying that all this destruction happened for a reason?" she asked, slowly rising.

"I'm saying that this place offended the Creator, and it was erased from His sight."

"You seem to know an awful lot about this place," Melissa observed.

"Yes, I do," Verchiel agreed, finding it strange that a Fear Engine was here, of all places.

Before the female could prod him further, he began his search in earnest, extending his senses outward, searching for a sign of the infernal machine and what fate might have befallen this excavation.

There was another passage leading away from the market-place dig, and Verchiel ducked into it, following a line of black electrical cables toward the growing sound of a roaring generator. This passage opened into a larger chamber that held the generator. Large spotlights had been erected around the circular cavern to illuminate a complex mural—a painting depicting the prophecy of the Nephilim.

Verchiel froze, remembering the strange dreamlike memory

he'd had back at the school, when he'd seen this very painting, and how it had seemed to go on and on.

"What is this?" Melissa asked over the rumble of the generator. She moved closer to examine the simple figures of angel and mortal woman joined together to form what Verchiel and the Powers had seen as abominations in the eyes of God.

It was all there, the birth of the Nephilim and the coming of a Chosen One, a savoir for them all.

Aaron Corbet.

"This is about us," Melissa said excitedly.

But there was more here, more than what Verchiel remembered seeing or hearing. Images depicting the Nephilim in the midst of combat against a demonic foe, a world surrounded by darkness.

Verchiel found himself drawn to the crude paintings, finding images that had yet to be cleaned of a millennia of dirt.

"This is about the Nephilim," Melissa said again, looking at him, waiting for a response, but he could not respond—for he could not take his eyes from the area of the mural that was still obscured.

What might lie beneath it?

A story that went on and on . . .

Willing his hand full of divine fire, Verchiel slowly brought the flame closer in an attempt to see what was hidden. He could hear the female chattering on, but he chose to ignore her, his curiosity piqued beyond measure. And as the light shone through the dust, Verchiel suddenly realized that the girl had fallen silent. He glanced from the mural to her and saw a most curious thing.

The walls and the floor of the underground chamber had come alive. The surfaces of both churned and swirled like ocean water. Melissa had been washed against a nearby wall, her body nearly immersed in the now liquid rock and sand.

As the once solid surfaces continued to ebb and flow, he saw other bodies—those of the missing archeological team—floating too. Then the floor before him surged into the guise of a king cobra, and Verchiel caught sight of something else amongst the ancient layers.

A device of both metal and flesh.

An infernal machine . . . collecting the fear of the world.

Vilma appeared in an alley between two old brick buildings, her senses immediately tuning in to her surroundings.

Cameron materialized just to her right, his brown wings parting to reveal his burning sword in hand. He was tensed, ready to fight.

"You might want to put that out," Vilma said, pulling back her wings. "We don't want to draw attention to ourselves if it isn't necessary."

Cameron hesitated for a moment, but seeing no immediate threat, he did away with his blade and wings.

The air was cool, and thick with the smell of pine. It made Vilma think of Christmas, an alien thought for her of late. She strolled casually to the mouth of the alley and looked out at the street beyond.

"Seems pretty quiet," she said as Cameron joined her.

"Smalltown, USA," he said. "I wouldn't consider this the best place for a Fear Engine."

"But this is where the map said it would be," Vilma said, checking out the street that was vacant of life. She closed her eyes briefly, breathing in the sweet smell but extending her senses outward, searching for a sign of anything out of the ordinary, for anything that did not feel right.

As it turned out, she didn't have to search at all; it came looking for them instead.

The canine-like beasts appeared at the end of the street, beneath the traffic light that pulsed red like a heartbeat. There were quite a few of them, and at first Vilma thought they might have been a pack of stray dogs. But when they stood upon their back legs, snouts lifted to the night air, she knew otherwise.

"What the hell are those?" Cameron asked, a sword of fire reappearing in his hand.

"Your guess is as good as mine," Vilma answered, watching as the pack caught their scent on the wind and, one after another, began to howl, before slowly stalking down the center of the street directly for them. "Werewolves, maybe?"

"I suppose werewolves is as good a guess as any," he said. "What do you want to do?"

She really wasn't sure if throwing down with a pack of were-beasts was going to help them find the Fear Engine, but then again, maybe the wolves had some sort of connection. Who knew?

Vilma didn't know what to do, and was about to suggest that they take to the relative safety of the air, when she heard a voice call out to them.

"Hey! Hey, you two!"

Both Cameron and Vilma turned. A girl in torn jeans and a faded red hoodie frantically waved at them, and a younger boy peered out from behind her.

"You don't want to stay out here if you know what's good for you," the girl called through cupped hands, and then gestured for them to follow.

"What do you want to do?" Cameron asked Vilma, his eyes glued to the cautiously advancing pack.

"I say we follow the kids," Vilma replied. "They probably have a better idea than a pack of werewolves where this engine is."

"I don't know," Cameron countered. "Monsters . . . Fear Engines . . . the two might go hand and hand."

"Yeah, but we don't even know if they can talk," Vilma said, gesturing toward the pack.

"That's a good point," he said. "Do you want to kill a few?"

"Are you that desperate to kill something?" she asked him. "What's it been, a few hours?"

He smiled at her, turning away from the wolves and extinguishing his sword. "You're no fun."

"I'm sure we'll have plenty of fun pretty soon," she reassured him as she ran to catch up with the two kids.

She and Cameron darted around the corner at the end of the main street, the unnatural sounds of the werewolves' cries chasing them. The two kids scurried ahead, the boy pushing a shopping cart as the girl stopped and waved them all into a passage between an old-fashioned pharmacy and the Laundromat.

"C'mon, c'mon," the girl urged.

Vilma ran to catch up, giving the boy a smile as she passed him. "Wait up," she called to the girl, who stopped and turned when she was halfway down the alley.

"What are you doing out here?" Vilma asked. "Especially with things like that roaming the streets," she said, motioning over her shoulder at the sounds of the pack in the distance.

"We needed some supplies," the girl said. "I didn't realize what time it was, and stupid Ryan wanted to look at the comic books."

"I only looked at three," Ryan said, coming up behind them with his cart.

Vilma could see some plastic bottles of water, canned goods, and candy bars in the basket of the cart.

"You can't even read," the girl retorted fiercely. "You just look at the pictures."

"I can too read, Jinny," the boy protested.

"Yeah, sure you can," the girl said sarcastically before turning her attention back to Vilma. "So, what are you and your boyfriend doing here?" she asked. "I ain't never seen you two around here before."

"He isn't my boyfriend," Vilma said, not quite sure why she felt the need to respond to that so quickly. She thought of Aaron, then Jeremy. *So frustrating.* She wished she knew what it all meant.

"Uh-huh," Jinny said with a devious smile.

Cameron laughed. "Seriously, I'm not," he said.

"*K-I-S-S-I-N-G,*" Ryan sang, and then started to giggle.

"Shut yer trap, Ryan," Jinny ordered, and the boy went quiet, though he was still smirking.

"We're looking for something," Vilma explained. "It's a kind of machine." She realized that she hadn't a clue as to what this Fear Engine even looked like, though she was certain she would know what it was when she saw it.

"A machine?" Jinny asked.

"Like a robot?" Ryan asked. "Are you looking for a robot?"

Vilma shook her head.

"It's a machine that collects fear," Cameron started to explain. "We heard that it's somewhere around here, and we came to stop it."

Jinny thought for a moment. "I don't know about any fear machine," she said. "But maybe Father Donnally at the church does."

"Father Donnally?" Vilma asked.

"He's been looking out for us since the nighttime started to get so long and those things started to show up," she said, referencing the wolves. "We've been staying at the church."

"With everybody who didn't get eaten," Ryan added.

"Shut up, Ryan," Jinny ordered. "You're not supposed to talk about the sad stuff."

The boy looked away from her scathing glance.

"Do you think we could meet Father Donnally?" Vilma asked.

"Yeah, I think it'll be all right," Jinny replied.

"Excellent," Vilma said. She looked at Cameron, who had turned back toward the mouth of the alley.

"We should really get moving," he said.

"C'mon. The church is this way," Jinny said, heading down the alley. Ryan started the shopping cart rolling again with a grunt, and they all followed.

Jinny stopped at the corner and peeked out, just in case. "Looks good," she said, motioning for them to follow.

They emerged from the alley into a quaint common area. Vilma could see metal benches, picnic tables, and even a white gazebo off in the distance.

"It's across here," Jinny told them, making her way across the overgrown grass, underneath a dark, cloud-filled sky.

Ryan was having some difficulty pushing his shopping cart over the grass, and Cameron hung back to help him drag it along.

"What are you doing?" the little boy asked suspiciously.

"I'm giving you a hand," Cameron said, careful to watch where he was going as he pulled.

"Well, quit it."

Cameron laughed, surprised at the outburst. "Seriously?" he asked.

"I ain't foolin' around," the boy growled, giving the cart a violent shake for him to let go.

"Fine," Cameron said, obviously a little hurt by the kid's rejection of his aid. "Hope you pull a groin muscle or something."

"You're a groin muscle," Ryan said, straining to push the cart past him.

Vilma caught Cameron's eye and shrugged, giving him that *Whata ya gonna do?* look.

He saddled up alongside her as they followed their escorts across the common.

"I sure hope we're not wasting our time," Cameron said.

"We have to start somewhere," Vilma answered. "I haven't been able to pick up any unusual vibrations. If Father Donnally knows anything, it'll be a help."

"It's right over there," Jinny said, pointing out the old, white church across the street.

There were no cars on the road, so they were able to cross without any difficulty.

"We'll take you in the back way," Jinny said, walking up the path that split off and snaked around to a parking lot.

Vilma looked for a sign that gave the church's name and

denomination but could find none. *Odd,* she thought briefly.

"Father Donnally won't get mad at you for bringing back strays, will he?" Vilma asked Jinny, only partially joking.

"Naw," Jinny said. "I bet he's gonna be pretty happy to see you."

"So you and the others have been safe here?" Cameron asked, giving the church a once-over.

"The monsters leave the church alone," Jinny said, opening up the back door.

Vilma guessed that made sense. Churches were holy places, and evil creatures weren't necessarily known for their purity.

Ryan gathered up the things from his cart. He was having some difficulty carrying it all, but he managed.

"I'd offer to give you a hand," Cameron said, holding the door open for the kid, "but I wouldn't want you to get your panties in a bunch."

"You're a fart head and you smell," Ryan said, struggling to keep from dropping any of his supplies.

Vilma waited for Cameron as he pulled the door shut behind them. They stood in a kitchen area.

"We'll let Jinny go in first to let them know that we're here," Vilma said.

"Hopefully Father Donnally's more pleasant than Ryan," Cameron said.

"He is a charmer," Vilma agreed. She could hear Jinny

speaking with someone just beyond the doorway, but she couldn't make out what was being said.

"You ready?" Vilma asked Cameron.

"Sure," he replied. "Let's hope your hunch is right and this Donnally guy can help us."

They stepped into a short corridor. Just beyond it Vilma could see the inside of the church, where some of its parishioners sat.

She and Cameron walked through the doorway and into the church, feeling everyone's eyes upon them. The church was dark, the altar lit only by a few flickering candles. They slowly walked down the center isle as the parishioners watched them from the wooden pews.

"That's them," Jinny said to an older man dressed in the white robes of a priest at the altar.

Vilma's eyes darted around the church. There was no religious iconography, which she found a little weird. Where were the crucifixes? The statues?

Father Donnally stepped down from the altar, all warmth and smiles. "Welcome, welcome," he said as he walked closer.

He was a pleasant-looking man, with salt-and-pepper hair and red, flushed cheeks. Vilma immediately felt at ease.

"Jinny was certainly right. You two are special." He stopped about four feet away and clasped his hands together, looking from Vilma to Cameron. "So special. So very, very special."

Vilma was about to thank him for his kind words, when

she was struck from behind. She fell to the floor, a sound like the buzzing of an alarm clock filling her head. She wanted to warn Cameron, but through a blur she saw that he was on the floor beside her.

Then Ryan came into view, holding a hammer in one hand and smacking it against the palm of the other. The boy smiled as he bent over Cameron and whacked him viciously across the side of his head, knocking him out cold.

Vilma tried to bring forth the power of the Nephilim as the boy headed to her, but she wasn't fast enough.

"*K-I-S-S-I-N-G*," she heard the little boy sing as the hammer struck her head.

And then she heard nothing.

Gabriel appeared, his legs wobbly.

Sure, he had traveled with Aaron before. Aaron had held him and wrapped his wings around them both.

But Gabriel had never done it on his own. . . . He hadn't even realized that he could.

Until he did.

The knowledge came to him, a result of his new form. As he steadied himself from his journey, Gabriel wondered off-handedly what other new talents had yet to manifest.

The Labrador studied his surroundings, turning his nose to the air and sniffing. There was a stink, but not necessarily one caused by the supernatural. He stood on the outskirts of a forest, peering out through the meager foliage at what appeared to be some sort of factory.

He padded toward the chain-link fence surrounding the property and, closing his eyes, imagined himself on the other side. There was a crackle of energy, the sound of air collapsing in upon itself, followed by something akin to the rumble of thunder, and then he was standing in the empty parking lot on the other side of the fence.

Interesting, Gabriel thought as he trotted across the cracked and uneven blacktop. The more he used this new traveling ability, the easier it seemed to become.

And the closer he got to the factory, the stronger the disturbing smell became. It was a pungent chemical smell, and it seared the inside of his nostrils and throat.

The dog paused for a moment to sneeze, and noticed for the first time the objects that littered the ground in front of the building. Cautiously Gabriel stepped closer to one. It was a dead bird. And not too far from that were a number of dead squirrels and a dead rabbit, its legs sticking out stiffly, its head twisted to one side. The expression on its face made it clear that its passing from life had not been pleasant.

Gabriel could see dead animals all around the perimeter of the building. He wondered if the toxic stink had anything to do with it.

No matter, he thought, approaching the seemingly

abandoned building. He was sure that this was where he was supposed to go to find the Fear Engine.

Climbing the broken concrete steps, noting the flattened bodies of long-dead sparrows, Gabriel approached the main entrance. Heavy pieces of plywood had been nailed over the doors. A NO TRESPASSING sign, written in a language he did not know but still could understand, was posted prominently.

Gabriel sniffed at the bottom of the barricaded door, but could only smell heavy chemicals and the aroma of decay. The dog wondered how much death he would find inside.

Trotting down the steps, and going around to the side, Gabriel searched for another entrance. At the side of the building, he found a heavy metal door, seemingly used for deliveries at one time, but it was locked with a padlock. There was a small window in the door, one that he could reach if he stood on his hind legs. It was as good as if he had a key, he thought.

Standing up to peer through the window, Gabriel saw a dust-covered security desk and chair. Gabriel then closed his eyes and wished himself on the other side of the door.

The noxious smell was even stronger inside the building, but he did not let it deter him from his search.

He passed offices, not stopping to investigate, for he doubted a device that collected fear would be stored there. He soon came upon a security door that was hanging from its hinges. A walkway extended beyond, disappearing into total darkness.

This is more like it.

Gabriel allowed some of his angelic power to flow through his body, illuminating his fur so that he could see. Cautiously he proceeded down the walkway. From the shadows beyond the reach of his light, Gabriel heard the scrabbling of animal feet and was curious as to why these creatures in the factory's shadows had not shared the same fate as the animals outside.

At the end of the walkway, he found another heavy door, only this one was closed. Gabriel stood on his hind legs and peered through the cracked window. A metal stairway led down to the ground.

After transporting himself to the other side of the door, Gabriel carefully made his way down the metal stairs to the floor of the factory. His fur still crackled with divine fire, casting eerie shadows upon the floor and walls. The place appeared to be deserted. Whatever equipment this factory used to house had been removed, and all that remained were the twisted, rusted pieces of whatever couldn't be salvaged.

Gabriel caught the sound of movement in the shadows.

"Hello?" he barked.

He knew that Aaron and the other Nephilim could speak in the language of all living things, and wondered if he might be able to do the same.

"Hello, are you there?"

There was some sort of response, but he couldn't make it out. He stepped farther out onto the floor of the factory.

"I don't mean you any harm," Gabriel said to whatever was hiding. *"I just want to talk to you, if it wouldn't be a bother."*

Nothing wrong with being polite, he thought, his intense gaze trying to penetrate the shadows.

Something skittered across the floor with a hiss.

"Hello?" he called out again. *"Will you speak with me?"*

"The light," croaked an animal voice. *"The light, it . . ."*

"Does it hurt your eyes?" Gabriel asked. *"I'm sorry."* He pulled back upon his gifts, dimming the glow from his fur. *"Is that better?"* he asked. *"Will you speak with me now?"*

"Speak," said another voice, different from the first. *"Speak now."*

There seemed to be multiple voices, all whispering and muttering at the same time.

"I'm sorry. I can't understand you," Gabriel said, eyes attempting to pierce the curtain of black around him. *"Would you show yourself to me? I mean you no harm."*

"No harm," answered a whispering voice. It was indeed closer, and Gabriel stayed where he was so as not to frighten the speaker away.

"That's it," Gabriel urged. *"Come closer so we can talk."*

He heard the sound of nails clicking on the concrete floor, and he waited patiently as the factory animals seemed to move closer. His nose was working, trying to sniff out his surroundings, but all he could smell were chemicals and rot. Then the voices grew louder, all talking at the same time, and he wondered how many beings might actually be there.

Gabriel felt the thick hackles of fur around his neck rise at the potential for danger.

"It sounds like there are a lot of you," Gabriel said. *"Do you live here in the factory?"*

There was a soft sound that could have been a chuckle.

"Live here . . . ," one voice said, followed by more sounds like laughing.

The smell of decay was getting stronger, overpowering the chemical stench. Gabriel squinted into the shadows, but the factory residents stayed just beyond his field of vision.

The room was suddenly quiet again, and Gabriel wondered if they were waiting for him to speak next.

"Are you there?" he asked. *"I'm looking for something. A strange machine. Have you seen it, perhaps?"*

"Machine," whispered a voice, closer now.

"Yes, a machine," Gabriel urged. *"Do you know what I'm talking about?"*

"Machine. Yes," said the multiple voices.

"Can you tell me about this machine?" Gabriel asked with growing optimism. *"Or perhaps you can take me to it?"*

There was a scrabbling in the darkness before him, something sounding much larger than rats, maybe squirrels or raccoons.

"Protect," said the voices.

"Protect?" Gabriel asked. *"Protect what?"*

"We protect the machine."

Suddenly Gabriel knew that he was in grave danger. He quickly tapped into his angelic ability, his body glowing brightly with the light of Heaven.

He yelped in terror at what he saw before him.

It was huge and terrible, a body of not a single thing but many things—the twisted bodies of raccoons, feral cats, squirrels, rabbits, rats, and other animals that Gabriel would have to get closer to identify. They were all somehow linked together into one massive body—one powerful, horrible life-form with one singular purpose.

To protect the Fear Engine.

CHAPTER SIXTEEN

Mallus pulled a plastic chair from a stack in the corner of the television room and dragged it over.

"Mind if I sit?" he asked Tarshish.

The Malakim didn't answer right away, slipping another puzzle piece into place.

"Go ahead," the ancient being finally said. "It's a free country. For now."

As he sat, Mallus noticed that the image on the puzzle was now of a picturesque town with the quintessential white steepled church in the foreground.

"It's been a very long time," Mallus said.

"It certainly has," Tarshish agreed without looking up from his puzzle.

"How have you been?" Mallus asked.

Tarshish raised his ancient eyes for a moment. "Livin' the

dream," he replied, his voice dripping with sarcasm. His eyes dropped back to the puzzle. "You?"

"If this were any other day, I would have said the same," Mallus said. "I would have said something about keeping out of sight and trying to enjoy what little time this world has left."

Tarshish stared at him again, his eyes dark, like polished stones. "But today?" he asked.

"Today . . . ," Mallus began. "Today I have hope."

The ancient figure laughed as he leaned back in his wheelchair. "And where would you have gotten a thing like that?" he asked. "Have you looked outside?" Tarshish gestured to a window on the far side of the TV room. "The clock is most definitely ticking."

"I know," Mallus agreed. "But I've seen some things . . . met some people . . ."

"What, did you find Jesus or something?" the old being asked, and then laughed again. He laughed so hard that he started to cough. It sounded as though his lungs were about to land in his lap.

"Do you need some water?" Mallus asked.

Tarshish continued to cough and gag and cough some more, gesturing with his long-fingered hand that he would be fine.

Mallus waited for him to regain control, then spoke. "I've seen what's going on out there, and it makes me sick to think that I was once part of it."

Tarshish breathed raggedly as he stared at Mallus. "That *we* were part of it," the old soul added.

Mallus acknowledged that with a nod. "It's been a long time since I thought I could help," he said. "A long time since I thought I might be able to stop them."

"You can't stop the Architects," Tarshish said gravely. "We made sure of that, if you recall."

"I know," Mallus said, the memory of what they had done rising up like some huge behemoth from the deepest depths of the sea. "And we were pretty damn proud of ourselves too."

Tarshish looked around the room, gazing at the old folks sitting in their chairs watching the blank television screen.

"And why wouldn't we be?" he asked, his voice tinged with sadness. "How many folks get to say that they killed a part of God?"

Tarshish remembered the war in Heaven, and the bitter taste that it had left in his mouth, and the mouths of all God's divine creations.

The Lord God desired to set the world of His man on the right path, to stem the discordance seeded by the Morningstar.

This new creation—this Metatron—was to be His solution.

The Almighty chose one of His beloved pets to wield this power of change. The human's name was Enoch, and the Lord of Lords told the devout but frightened human that he had been chosen for a very special purpose.

Tarshish recalled how Enoch averted his eyes from the sight of his Creator, begging to know why he had been selected, and what he was to do with this frightening honor.

God explained that He had seen something within Enoch, something that had rekindled the Creator's faith in humanity. Tarshish laughed inwardly at that, recalling how disappointed the Almighty had been by the actions of the first humans in the Garden.

As far as the Malakim was concerned, humanity was a failure, and no matter how much time and effort the Lord put into His precious little apes, they would always disappoint Him. But that was an opinion Tarshish chose to keep secret from his Malakim brothers, for they could not imagine their Creator as fallible.

The Almighty then bestowed upon Enoch a gift unlike any other, taking all that was good about His angels and merging it with all that He loved of humanity. Then He added a piece of His own godliness. This new being, the Metatron, was above all other creations, except, of course, God Himself.

The Metatron would be an aspect of God, residing upon the earth, guiding humanity toward the zenith of its potential.

God sent Tarshish and his fellow Malakim to the world of humanity to watch the Metatron, to record for Him the sensations and wonders of an emerging paradise. It was then that Tarshish finally shared his doubt with his brothers. They were outraged by Tarshish's lack of faith and disavowed him, using powerful angel magicks to wipe away their memories of his existence.

It was a punishment meant to make him realize the severity of his doubts, but it only strengthened Tarshish's resolve. As he lived amidst man during the earliest days, watching as things were secretly guided by the Metatron, he had to wonder when it would all come crashing down.

He never realized the role he would play in that downfall.

The power of his doubt brought Tarshish to the attention of the Architects. He stood before them, in awe of these first angels that he had never truly believed existed.

The Architects had been amongst God's first creations. They were beings so powerful and headstrong that He had willed them away in favor of the more obedient creations that would be His messengers.

But the Architects had managed to survive, hiding themselves in the shadows of the new world, continuing the purpose for which they had been made—to create.

That is, until the Metatron appeared, stifling their plans, their creativity. Now the Architects sought someone, or something, to remove this hindrance to their plans.

And Tarshish, still feeling the sting of his brothers' abandonment, was more than happy to oblige.

To help him the Architects gave him a partner of great cunning and power, an associate to share the burden of this monumental task. Tarshish's ally had served as second in command of the Morningstar's legions during the Great War. His name was Mallus.

The disdain these two beings had for humanity was their only bond, fueling their drive to succeed—to remove the Metatron from the world and set humanity upon its downward spiral to failure.

"Did you hear me, Tarshish?" Mallus asked.

Tarshish had not, for the wails of the Metatron echoed inside his mind as he had heard them that fateful day when he and Mallus had carried out the Architects' chore.

"I heard nothing but an echo of the past, Mallus," the old being said, staring at his puzzle.

"I said that I believe there might be a way to undo what we have done," the fallen angel repeated.

Tarshish studied his former partner in crime, looking for signs of madness. It would not be the first time that one of God's messengers, fallen or not, had succumbed to the crippling affliction.

"Why do you say such things?" the last of the Malakim finally asked. "Why do you torture me with redemption that can never be?"

"Listen carefully, Tarshish," Mallus said, reaching across the card table to grasp the Malakim's hand. "There is truth—just a glimmer, I know—in what I am saying to you."

Tarshish pulled his withered hand from the fallen angel's.

"Impossible," he said with finality. "There is no turning back from what we did. The awful act was done, and we have been left to bear witness to the repercussions."

"I agree," Mallus said with a nod. "But what if there is a way to fix things?"

"How is it possible to fix what we did?"

"I didn't think it was possible either," Mallus explained. "But that was before I met them . . . before I met *him*."

"Who?" Tarshish asked, impatience in his tone. "Who did you meet that could make you believe in the impossible?"

As if on cue, there was a sudden commotion from somewhere outside the activity room, the sounds of battle escalating as the stink of burning human flesh permeated the air. Mallus was about to investigate, when a section of wall exploded inward and ancient bodies crackling with arcane energies and burning with divine fire tumbled into the room, collapsing into dust as they struck the floor.

And through the broken hole in the wall, a lone figure appeared. He had wings of black, flesh adorned with the names of warriors who had fallen in the war with Heaven, and in his hand he held a sword of Heaven's fire.

Tarshish had never seen such a sight. He turned to Mallus.

"Speak of the proverbial Devil, and he appears," Mallus said, and shrugged. "Or should I say, 'Speak of the Devil's son.'"

* * *

"I found him, Dusty," Lorelei said, heading down the corridor as fast as her cane would allow her. Milton sank his claws into her shoulder, holding on for dear life.

"But where?" Dusty asked as he hurried along beside her.

"I told you, I don't know, which is why we have to get to the library."

The library had been left to her by one of the original fallen angels who had believed in the prophecy of the Nephilim, believed in Aaron and his destiny. The library existed in its own space, its own universe, and its contents were practically endless. Lorelei knew that if any book existed that could tell her how to find Lucifer, it would be in the library.

She pushed open the door with great ferocity, and lurched inside, her brain afire as she skirted the jagged edges of the enormous hole in the floor where Verchiel had come crashing back into their lives. She made her way to the special alcove reserved for Archon magick. She was sure she'd find the answers with the ancient angel sorcerers.

If only the price weren't so damned high.

"I'm sure you've already been through these books and scrolls," Dusty said, trying to join her but stopping near the hole, afraid to proceed.

Noticing his distress, Lorelei gently moved Milton from her shoulder to the table in the center of the alcove and went to guide Dusty.

"Maybe I missed something," she said, sitting him at the table and scanning the rows of old leather-bound texts.

"Do you even know what you're looking for?" Dusty asked.

She pulled a large book down from a shelf, the weight of it sending her cane clattering to the floor and nearly causing her to lose her balance. She glared at him as she turned and stumbled to the table.

"I know exactly what I'm looking for," she said. "I'm looking for my friend who is in some sort of danger."

She let the heavy volume fall with a thud, which sent Milton scurrying to the other end of the table with an indignant squeak. Using the corner of the table for support, Lorelei bent to pick up her cane.

"Let me try to guide you again," Dusty offered, his voice soft.

"You can't," she answered briskly, not even wanting to look at him, lest she be enticed by his offer.

Tapping into the power of the Instrument had devastating side effects. Dusty was still relatively raw when it came to these kinds of powerful magicks, and she didn't want to risk permanently hurting him. What he had done for Aaron and the others by locating the Fear Engines had been more than enough.

And what she had asked of him after that had totally pushed the boundaries of their friendship, as well as his well-being.

"I'm willing to try again," he said.

She could hear the trepidation in his voice, but also his seriousness. He was willing to do this for her—for them.

Milton crawled onto Dusty's hand, his tiny tongue flicking out to lick the salt from his skin.

"I really think the visions are getting easier to control," Dusty continued, lifting the mouse so the two of them were nose to nose. "I think the Instrument is getting used to me."

Lorelei didn't respond. Instead she continued to leaf through the ancient text before her. The smell of old, musty pages wafted up from the book. She'd always loved that smell, and remembered how Lucifer Morningstar did too.

She missed Lucifer terribly, and wanted him back. She needed him. *They* needed him.

Lorelei looked up to stare at Dusty. He was pale, his skin almost waxy. In spite of herself she wondered if she could lend him some of her strength if they again attempted to reconnect with Lucifer.

"We can't," she said quickly, trying to push away the thoughts. "I'm sure we can find another way."

"It isn't like we've got a ton of time," Dusty said. "You've seen how it is out there, what we're up against. If Lucifer is as powerful as you say he is, we really need him right now."

Every word he spoke was true. Lucifer was one of the strongest of all the angels, and not having him to help the Nephilim during these sinister times was an extreme detriment.

"I'm just afraid of what this is going to do to you," Lorelei finally admitted.

Dusty chuckled. "Don't worry about me," he said. "These

visions are going to kill me eventually anyway. I might as well get the most out of them while I can."

She slowly closed the old tome. She hated herself for what she and Dusty were about to do, but she also knew how much they needed Lucifer back.

"We're going to have to go deep," Lorelei warned Dusty. "Even deeper than last time if we're going to make some sort of contact."

Dusty grew paler as she talked, and she was about to dismiss the whole thing, when he spoke up.

"Let's just do it," he said, setting Milton back on the table. "We can't let Aaron and the gang have all the fun."

"No, we can't," she agreed, Dusty's willingness making her throw all caution to the wind.

CHAPTER SEVENTEEN

The wall of sand suddenly came alive and pulled Melissa inside.

Her curiosity had been piqued by the mural on the chamber's wall, and her guard had been down.

Now Melissa was being drawn deeper and deeper beneath the shifting sand. It took everything she had to keep the desert from forcing itself into her mouth and nose, from crawling inside her and claiming her as it had the others from the archeological dig. As she fought to free herself of the sand's hold, Melissa saw the fates of those who had lost the struggle floating past her in this sea of sand.

Am I strong enough? Melissa asked herself. A memory suddenly flashed in her mind. She saw herself not too long after she had first arrived at Saint Athanasius. She hadn't been adjusting well to her angelic powers and had told Aaron that she didn't think she was going to make it through the transition. She'd told him that he had wasted his time finding her and bringing her there.

Melissa remembered the concern on his face as Aaron had asked what made her believe such a thing. Melissa had told him of watching her mother murdered by the Powers, and how the only thing she'd been able to do was run. She hadn't even lifted a finger to help her mother; she had been too afraid.

"I'm not strong enough," she had told Aaron then.

Writhing in the hold of the living sands, the corpses of those who had given in to its course touch floating past her, she recalled the intensity of that fear.

The fear had been stronger than she was.

Or so she had believed.

Aaron had looked at her, with his dark and piercing eyes, and had said simply, "I don't believe you."

She had argued, telling him how weak and cowardly she was. He had listened and nodded.

And when she had finished her rant, he had looked at her and said with all seriousness, "Melissa wasn't strong enough."

She had been startled by his statement, not really expecting him to agree with her. But then he had said the most startling thing.

"Melissa wasn't strong enough, but *you* are not Melissa anymore."

She had looked at him as if he were crazy, but her gaze had

begged him for some sort of additional explanation.

"The old Melissa died with her mother, so the new Melissa could live."

Melissa had wanted to tell Aaron so many things in that moment, like that he was mistaken, that she was still the same awful person who had let her own mother be taken by vengeful angels.

But before she'd been able to get the words out, Aaron had reached out to her with a hand that had started to glow. For a second she'd thought he might burn her.

And maybe in a way he had.

Aaron had touched her with his angelic power, and the thing inside her—the Nephilim—had come fully awake. She remembered crying out, and a feeling like she was on fire from the inside.

It was her fear that had burned away.

Still beneath the sand, her oxygen waned. Melissa tapped into the power at her core, calling it to the surface.

She felt her wings emerge and her body begin to glow with divine fire.

Once again it was the fear that died.

Because she was now, as she'd been then, strong enough.

The prophet had returned to gloat.

As the cobra of sand struck, sending Verchiel to the ground and into darkness, the fallen angel heard the ancient one's voice.

"It is happening as I saw."

Disoriented, Verchiel spun, awash in a sea of shadow. He called forth a blade of flame, illuminating the space so he might find and dispose of his enemy. But the sword barely touched the inky gloom, showing him only the back of an old man as he worked upon his mural.

"What is this?" Verchiel demanded. "Where am I?"

The prophet touched up some details in his portentous art, before he turned to address the angel.

"A frozen moment," the prophet said. "When Heaven showed me a glimpse of what was yet to come." He went back to his painting, recording the images that were inside his head.

"I killed you," Verchiel growled, stepping closer. "I brought the fires of Heaven down upon your head, and destroyed the city that tried to protect you."

"Yes," the prophet agreed. "You did, but not yet."

"Not . . . yet?" Verchiel repeated, still confused.

"A frozen moment," the prophet said. "A frozen moment in time."

"A frozen moment in *your* time," Verchiel said as he finally began to understand.

The prophet smiled and nodded as he continued to paint. "You've got it," he said.

"But I wasn't here for this," Verchiel started. "How . . . ?"

"Because I've brought you," the old man said. "To show you." He reached out, grabbed hold of Verchiel's wrist, and dragged him and his burning blade toward the wall to illuminate his artwork.

In the light of his sword, Verchiel squinted. "What are you showing me?" He leaned closer.

"That you have a part still to play," the prophet explained, "but it has yet to be determined."

"I see something," Verchiel said, trying to decipher the images upon the wall.

"A choice," the prophet spoke. "You have a choice to make."

Verchiel tried desperately to see—to understand—his place in the picture. But the prophet's grip held the light steady so that Verchiel couldn't illuminate his part of the story.

"I cannot see it," Verchiel said. "Let me bring the fire closer so that I . . ."

The flame of his sword began to die.

"A choice not yet made," the prophet said as the light dwindled. "But one that will soon be expressed."

Verchiel's sword disappeared with a hiss. He tried to call forth another, but the darkness bore down upon him, attempting to crush him.

The darkness had become sand, which surged around him, trying to scour the flesh from his form and crush the life from his body under its oppressive weight. Verchiel fought back, but it was as if he were an insect frozen in amber.

Blocking out the pain, the angel closed his eyes and called upon the fire that seethed at the core of his being. But before he could bring it forward, there was a terrific flash. The sand that held him in its stony grip was suddenly pulverized, and Verchiel's body was tossed backward on a shock wave of incredible force.

Verchiel was momentarily dazed, then lifted his head to see that he was still within the excavated chamber, but its dirt and sand ceiling had now been blown away to reveal the twinkling nighttime sky.

"How?" Verchiel rose to his feet as his wings sprang forth.

And then he witnessed the most surprising of sights, for he would have figured her for dead.

The Nephilim Melissa stood across the way in a crater of her own. The sand beneath her feet had turned to an opaque glass, which still steamed in the cool desert air. Here was the force that had set him free. She had her back to Verchiel, facing something that rose up from the sand, unearthed by that release of her preternatural fury.

Verchiel joined Melissa for a closer look at what she had uncovered. At first glance it appeared to be some sort of machine, pulsing as if alive, but closer inspection revealed that its mass was covered in a sickly, gray flesh.

They had found their Fear Engine.

"What do we do?" Melissa asked, not taking her eyes from the loathsome sight.

"Isn't it obvious, girl?" Verchiel asked as he stretched his wings and leaped into the air, a sword appearing in his hand. "We kill it."

* * *

Cameron remembered the squeaking sound Ryan's sneakers had made on the church's hardwood floor behind him. He remembered slowly turning to see what the unpleasant kid was doing, just as the hammer connected with the side of his head.

He hadn't even had a chance to recover before the kid had hit him again, knocking him out cold.

But now Cameron was coming around. His head pounded so badly that he was afraid to open his eyes, positive that the top of his skull had been ripped away and someone had shoved knives into his exposed brain.

Always the glutton for punishment, Cameron opened his eyes anyway. He couldn't comprehend what he saw. Everything was upside down.

In a panic Cameron tried to move, but found that his hands and feet were bound. Remembering that he wasn't alone, he turned his head despite the nearly blinding pain, to find Vilma hanging upside down beside him from an inverted wooden cross. She appeared to be unconscious.

"The poop head's awake," Ryan's unmistakable voice said.

Cameron turned his head toward the sound, still trying to make sense of things.

The church parishioners stood in the pews as if waiting for the ritual of mass to begin. Jinny and Ryan had the best seats in the house, in the front row.

Suddenly a face appeared before Cameron. It was the old

priest. Donnally leaned in close to examine him.

"As a matter of fact he is," Donnally said, smiling cheerily before moving on to peer at Vilma. "Let's see if we can wake your little lady friend too so that we can get started."

Cameron watched the old man gently tap Vilma's cheek. She let out a moan, her face twisting in pain as she moved her head. Cameron guessed that her head probably felt as good as his did.

"There she is," the old priest said, throwing his hands into the air with delight. The parishioners in the pews laughed politely, some clapping softly as the priest strode to the pulpit. Gripping the sides of the lectern, the elderly man readied to address his flock.

"It is a special day, brothers and sisters," he began.

While his captor was otherwise occupied, Cameron strained against his bonds, and found that his wrists had been wrapped with strips of heavy electrical tape.

Glancing over to Vilma, Cameron saw that she had a weird *What the hell is going on* expression upon her face.

He knew exactly how she felt.

"Our god has seen fit to bless two of our youngest with exceptional luck this day," Donnally announced, pausing as Jinny and Ryan stood up from their pew to turn toward the congregation. Everyone applauded while the two children soaked up the adoration.

"They were sent out to the streets to bring us back supplies so that we could continue our worship, and they have returned with the greatest gifts we could imagine . . . sacrifices to the power that has kept us safe during these dark, changing times."

Cameron felt his blood run cold, as Donnally left the lectern and approached them.

"You two have been delivered to us, to continue to keep us safe," he declared, arms spread before them. "Know that your sacrifice will not be in vain, and that you died so that others could live."

Cameron's eyes followed the priest as he walked back across the altar, toward something in the far corner covered with a white sheet of silk. Cameron strained his neck to watch the old man, whose hands were clasped before him. The priest bowed and muttered beneath his breath before the covered object.

Was this the holy object that they prayed to? The god that they were willing to sacrifice innocent lives to?

Finished with his prayers, the old man reached for the white cloth with both hands.

"Behold our god," he proclaimed at the top of his lungs.

"Behold our god!" the parishioners repeated as Donnally tore away the covering.

Cameron didn't really know what he was looking at. At first he thought it was some kind of boxy machine, but then he saw that parts of it seemed to be made of pale, wet skin. The form expanded and contracted, as if breathing, as it squatted in the shadow of the altar.

"Vilma, do you see this?" Cameron whispered. He quickly

glanced over to see that she too was craning her neck to catch a peek.

"I see it," she answered. "Is that what I think it is?"

"If you're thinking 'Fear Engine,' I'd say you're probably right," he commented.

Donnally turned from the throbbing mechanism, hate filling his eyes.

"Silence!" he screamed, his words echoing through the hall. "Show some respect to the holy god that you're about to give up your lives to."

And with those words Cameron heard movement in the church. The wooden pews squeaked as the parishioners left their seats. They had formed a line and were approaching the steps to the altar, all carrying knives.

"Come forth, brothers and sisters," Father Donnally urged. He, too, produced a knife from within the folds of his robes. "Partake of the sacrifice, and we shall all reap the benefit of our god's thanks."

Cameron looked to Vilma.

"I think I've seen enough," he said to her.

"More than enough," she agreed.

That was all he needed to hear. Cameron summoned the power of the Nephilim. His mighty wings exploded from his back, flexing against his bonds and the inverted cross to which he was tied. The wood groaned and snapped into pieces, and Cameron fell to the floor.

Vilma did the same, her own wings making short work of her restraints.

"You're good?" Cameron asked, ripping the tape from his wrists and ankles.

"Good," Vilma said, doing the same. "But we might want to move quickly," she said, eyeing the crowd that had frozen at the sight of what they had revealed themselves to be.

"Oh, these are special sacrifices, indeed!" the priest cheered as the hideous device pulsed and writhed behind him. "Praise be!" He rushed at Cameron, knife poised to strike.

"Praise be!" the parishioners echoed, brandishing their daggers, eager to sacrifice the Nephilim to their terrible god.

Gabriel leaped away as the fist composed of the compacted bodies of birds, rabbits, rats, and raccoons shattered the concrete floor before him.

"Protect the machine!" the animal voices all said in unison.

The monster was on the move again, its misshapen head covered in multiple sets of different-size eyes searching for Gabriel.

Gabriel circled the horrible creature, wanting to get to the Fear Engine but knowing he couldn't until he dealt with this monstrosity.

The terror struck at him again, wielding the sledgehammer-like force of its fist and nearly making contact. A piece of concrete flew up from the floor and hit Gabriel's face, and he yelped.

Gabriel's sudden cry of pain brought forth a weird high-pitched sound that must have been a twisted kind of laughter.

Gabriel wasn't in the least bit amused.

"Protect the machine," the monster repeated.

"Yes," Gabriel said, crouching, waiting for the monster's next strike. *"I've heard all about that."*

The monster rushed at him on thick legs composed of cats, dogs, and raccoons. It groped for him, and Gabriel attempted to dart beneath its arm, but he wasn't fast enough. The creature's hand wrapped around his back leg.

The monster made that obscene amused sound again, as Gabriel was yanked up into the air. The Labrador angled his body toward the disgusting hand that held him and bit down upon one of its thick fingers with all his might.

The power of the Nephilim coursed through the dog, his yellow fur throwing sparks, his very bite filled with the fire of the divine. Gabriel felt the energy of Heaven rush through him. There was an awful shriek, and suddenly he was falling to the concrete floor.

Gabriel recovered himself almost immediately and watched the scene before him with a curious eye. The monster's hand smoldered with divine fire, and the animals that composed it broke apart and fell to the floor.

"Where is the machine?" Gabriel barked. He bared his fangs, which crackled with preternatural fire. *"You know I can hurt you. I won't ask a second time."*

The monster considered this threat, still gazing with many eyes at where its hand had once been.

"Protect," the animal voices grumbled. *"Protect the machine."*

And with the last pronouncement the great beast turned upon its stocky legs and began to run away.

Gabriel yelped in surprise but quickly recovered his wits and chased the abomination across the empty space.

The monster stopped in front of a crumbling wall, and as Gabriel watched, its body dissolved into the multiple animals that constituted it. The Lab reached the wall just as the last of the animals, a mangy raccoon, escaped. Frustrated, Gabriel lunged forward and snatched the fleeing animal by the scruff of its neck. It screeched and hissed as Gabriel pulled it from its freedom, and shook it, savagely snapping its neck. He dropped the dead animal to the floor, watching it twitch before it finally succumbed to death.

Gabriel stuck his snout through a crack in the wall and took in the scents behind it. He could smell the animals that had formed the body of the monster. But there was something else too, something that he couldn't identify. Presuming that it was the engine, he did not hesitate. Gabriel squirmed through the opening, feeling the ground beneath his paws suddenly arc downward.

Into the hungry darkness of the earth.

CHAPTER EIGHTEEN

Aaron stepped over the debris as he approached Mallus and an older man in a wheelchair.

"Who were those people out there?" he asked, ruffling his ebony wings angrily, a sword burning in his hand.

"Old friends that left me a long time ago," the old man spoke. "Didn't have the heart to let them lie down, I guess."

Aaron wasn't sure he'd heard right. "So they're dead, but...," he began.

"I kept them around to watch the place," the old man said. "Like guard dogs, only older."

Aaron looked at Mallus, shocked by the man's words.

"This is Tarshish, Aaron," Mallus said. "The last of the Malakim."

"A Malakim," Aaron repeated. "But I thought the Powers—"

"Yeah, the Powers," Tarshish said with a snarl. "I saw what

they were up to with my brothers, and I kept out of sight."

"You let the Powers kill your brothers?" Aaron asked him.

"No love lost with my siblings," the Malakim said. "They got what was coming to them."

"Nice," Aaron said with a slight shake of his head. He turned to Mallus. "Is he why we're here?"

"He's part of it," Mallus said.

"What have you been telling him?" the Malakim asked.

"Only that I made a huge mistake and that I'm asking him to help me correct it."

"Correct it?" Tarshish asked, his withered old face twisting in confusion. "How the hell is he going to do that?"

"Look at him," Mallus told the wheelchair-bound angelic being. "The unification of humanity and the angelic . . . of humanity and the Son of the Morning."

Tarshish stared. "Huh," he said.

"Would someone care to tell me what's going on?" Aaron demanded.

Mallus ignored him, speaking only to Tarshish. "We killed the Metatron's human aspect, releasing the power of God into the ether," he said.

"Oh, it went somewhere," the Malakim said knowingly. "Right into the service of the Architects."

"We could get that power back," Mallus continued. "We could place it within a host that could handle all its power."

Tarshish was staring at Aaron again. "Him?"

Mallus nodded. "With a new Metatron—"

"Enough!" Aaron roared, his wings of solid black splaying out behind him. "What are you two talking about?"

Mallus looked to Aaron. "If there was something that you could do to stop all of this evil," the fallen angel said, gesturing with a swirl of his hand to the world outside, "would you do it?"

"What are your feelings about becoming one with God?" Tarshish asked Aaron.

Aaron was shocked, frozen by the proposition.

And then the Malakim began to laugh.

MOUNT EVEREST
A VERY LONG TIME AGO

The frigid winds tore at Tarshish as if to say, *You do not belong in this place*, but Tarshish of the Malakim went wherever he cared to.

Or, as in this case, where he was told.

Hearing of the Architects' existence in the whispers of the angels who'd fallen during the Great War with Heaven, Tarshish had sought out the mysterious group of divine creatures. It was only when he had given up his search for the elusive godly beings that the Architects had sought him out.

They'd taken him to a place they had claimed as their own—a place between here and there—and Tarshish had stood in awe of them, the first to come from the sweat of He Who Is the Creator of All.

At first, in arrogance, Tarshish had viewed the Architects as equals to his own angelic might, but he'd soon come to realize that they were so much more.

So, so much more.

The Architects had a vision for the world God had created, and for the life He had entrusted with His greatest gift. But for the planet and everything that lived upon it to live up to its potential—and the Architects' potential—there would need to be those with like minds.

Agents that would serve them. Agents dedicated to the cause of shaping the world to its fullest possibility.

They had asked Tarshish if he would be one of their Agents, if he would partake of their cause, and he had been alone for so very long before this.

Tarshish had agreed, and the Architects had praised him for his decision, but they'd said that they needed to be certain that he truly belonged with them.

That their vision and his were one and the same.

They'd told him there would be a test, and before he could question what would be asked of him, his mind had been filled with his mission's objective, and he'd been in awe of what was expected.

The Architects had told him how important this undertaking was, for without its completion their true design could never be realized. They'd told him that they had faith in his abilities, and without further discussion, he had been dismissed.

And now he found himself here, in the mountains of the world that, if he performed his duty, would be forever changed by this act, allowing the Architects' vision to march forward.

Tarshish turned his gaze upward, toward his destination. There was a storm upon the mountain, winds so fierce that they might flay the flesh from a lesser being's body, but Tarshish was as far from a lesser being as one could possibly be. He continued his climb into the raging white.

He could sense himself growing closer to his quarry and paused a moment to reconsider what he was doing. *Is it really my place to ignore God's wishes and take action against His vision? Do I dare do such a thing?*

From the corner of his eye Tarshish caught sight of something moving in the snow. Immediately his curiosity was aroused, for nothing that currently lived in the world could survive these conditions.

"Show yourself," the Malakim commanded in a voice that caused the very air to vibrate, and an avalanche to rain down upon him.

The ice and snow came in a furious rush, but it did not touch his form, for he had made his body as hot as a star, and the frozen water hissed and steamed as it tried to pummel him with its volume and weight. But it was unable to touch Tarshish.

As it was unable to touch the other creature on the mountain with him.

Tarshish looked upon the being and knew him as a fallen angel of Heaven.

There was a certain air about fallen angels that was unmistakable.

"What brings you to this cold, misbegotten place, angel?" Tarshish asked as the snow at last settled and the mournful winds quieted.

"I could be asking you the same thing," the fallen stated.

Tarshish chuckled, enjoying the conversation with the once heavenly being. He had spent far too long amongst the hairless monkeys that now dominated this place, and he missed these divine interactions.

"You know what I am, fallen one?" Tarshish asked. "I am Malakim."

The angel bowed his head in reverence to Tarshish's position.

"I go wherever I feel," Tarshish said. "Wherever I might find the most wonderful experiences and sensations this world can provide. That is where I will be, for that is my charge."

"And the murder of one most holy," the fallen angel spoke. "What an experience. The sensations it will provide . . . glorious." He smiled knowingly.

"You know why I am here," Tarshish spoke, already planning how he would destroy the insolent fallen. "Now you will share with me the same."

The fallen moved toward him in the snow. "Isn't it obvious, Malakim?" he asked. "We have a job to do."

"The Architects sent you?"

"As they did you," the fallen angel said.

"They doubted that I would be able to perform my task?" Tarshish asked, incredulous.

The fallen angel smiled. "Let's just say they wanted to be sure it was done properly."

The Malakim scowled, disheartened by his new masters' seeming doubt of his capabilities.

The fallen angel clapped him on the shoulder. "No need to frown, brother," he said.

Tarshish did not care to be touched, and ignited the divine flesh of the fallen angel. The fallen quickly removed his hand and plunged it into the snow to quell the hungry fire.

Tarshish stared down at the lowly being, trying to decide whether or not to extinguish his life.

"We've been given a mission, Malakim," the angel spoke, his dark eyes looking up at Tarshish. "Let's show our new masters that we can work as one."

A thought crossed Tarshish's mind, one he hadn't considered until that moment. Perhaps this was one of the Architects' tests. Maybe they wanted to see if he could work with others of like mind to restore the world to what it should be.

The fallen angel knelt in the snow, ministering to his wound, but Tarshish started back on the path to his destination. The Malakim could feel the wounded angel's eyes upon his back.

"What should I call you, angel?" the Malakim asked without turning.

"Mallus," the angel replied.

"Mallus, I am Tarshish," the Malakim announced. "Tarshish the forgotten." He then turned to look at the fallen one, who had withdrawn his charred appendage from the ice and snow. It was a black, withered thing now, but it would eventually heal.

"Prepare yourself for what we are about to do, Mallus," Tarshish continued. "For we will either be exalted for our actions—"

He turned back toward the mountain.

"—or we will be damned."

On the shore Baby Roger sat in the sand, a chilling wind rustling the downy soft hair atop his rather large head.

They'd wanted him to wear a hat, but he would not hear of it.

Jeremy and the old woman had given him a pail and a shovel, and he had gone to work gouging out shovelfuls of damp sand, and dumping them into his bucket.

There is something mesmerizing about the action, the baby thought. *Putting something inside of something else.*

Something hauntingly familiar.

When the pail was full, Roger immediately tipped it over, emptying its contents and beginning the process all over again.

Fill. Put something inside something else.

There was some deeper meaning, just out of Roger's grasp.

He wanted to cry out in frustration, to scream his rage at the crashing waves and seagull shrieking in the sky above, but it wouldn't help him find the answers he sought.

As he dug, Roger checked to make sure that he hadn't been left. Jeremy and the woman were standing close by, talking amongst themselves. He was sure they were talking about him. *What should we do about little Roger?* He wished he had the answer to give them.

Drawn to his task, he again shoveled sand into the pail, filling it to overflowing.

What does this mean? the babe asked himself as he stared at his bucket. With a shriek he grabbed the pail in his chubby hands and emptied its contents. Unable to control himself, he was about to start filling the pail again, when he glanced up at the white-capped ocean. He studied the birds as they rode the currents, the winds beneath their wings making it seem as if they were defying gravity as they hung there in space.

The wings.

The baby was inexplicably transported to another corner of the world, as if lost in a memory. In this vision he was transformed into something akin to God. Standing atop a mountain peak, his grown-up body adorned in armor made from the rays of the sun, he extended his will upon the world of man. Somehow Roger knew that this had been reality.

This was his true nature, what he had been created to do.

His name was not Roger. He was Enoch. And he was an

emissary of the highest order. God, human, and angel, Enoch was a trinity of the Allfather's most cherished creations. He was to watch over the world and its inhabitants.

He was the Metatron, the voice of God here on earth.

Elation flowed through the child, as tears rolled down his chubby face. Memories of being touched by the Lord of Lords filled his mind.

He'd been human, but he'd been transformed into so much more. He could not remember why he had been chosen, but Enoch had been taken to Heaven and paraded before all the heavenly hosts as the recipient of God's greatest gift.

And Enoch had been transformed before all the angels.

Enoch was the Metatron.

On the beach the seagulls wailed, wings flapping against the winds to remain aloft.

The flapping of wings.

The sound in his ears was suddenly deafening.

In his memory, wings beat the air unmercifully as an angel of Heaven flew about his head. Standing atop the snow-covered mountain, he tried to bat it away, but the attack upon him was relentless.

Attack? Who would dare attack the Metatron?

At first he believed it was only one. He saw the angel, a sword of burning in his grasp, darting and weaving through the snow-filled air, attacking Enoch with such ferocity.

He wanted to understand why this was happening . . . why

the angel would wish to do him harm, but he could no longer allow it to go on.

Summoning the power of God from within, the Metatron readied a strike against his angelic foe, but as the power flowed from within, it was taken by another.

Stolen by a second being of Heaven.

He tried to fight them, but they had taken him by surprise, not allowing him the opportunity to defend himself, to strike back.

The pair had driven him to the floor of the mountain peak, swarming atop his large and powerful armored form. He did not know what they wanted, but something told him that soon it would be revealed.

They did not hesitate in their act of savagery. Powerful magicks were at work then, immobilizing him, cutting off his connection to the Almighty. There was little time wasted as they went to work upon his divine armor, cutting it open to reveal the next layer of the trinity beneath.

The pain was excruciating as they sought out their prize, searching for what lay at the core of his being.

The two heavenly beings were eager to reach his humanity, cutting deeply through the angelic aspect to find the soft human center. He saw them as they peered inside the shell of God, finding what they had been searching for.

"Why?" he wanted to ask as the angel reached in to pull his humanity out into the cold. Enoch squirmed in the cold of

the mountain, the angel holding him tightly by the scruff of the neck as the other—the magick user—conjured a dagger of blinding white light and stepped in close to use it.

It was senseless to struggle, but he did. It was what humanity did in the face of adversity, no matter how hopeless it appeared.

Enoch struggled, even as he died.

The angelic being with his dagger of light sliced Enoch's throat from ear to ear, the cut so deep that it nearly severed his head from his body.

And they let his body drop to the frozen ground, gouts of blood pumping from his wound to stain the virgin snow.

The baby's vision had gone completely red with the passing of the memory, and he began to scream. He knew now what he had been, and what had happened.

And why he had returned.

He continued to scream, rolling around in the sand as the birds cried out, riding the winds above his head, the terror of what he had experienced—and what might be to come—pouring out of him in a fit of cries and tears.

The old woman was suddenly there, retrieving him from the sand and taking him into her comforting arms.

But there could be no comfort for Roger now.

The woman tried to shush him, bouncing him up and down as Jeremy stood nearby, confused by his sudden outburst.

"What's wrong, Roger love?" the woman asked in her gentlest whisper.

"My—my name isn't Roger," the baby said between gulps of air as he struggled to compose himself.

The woman looked into his face as she tried to understand.

"I know who I am now," the baby said. "I know why I am here."

With new composure he declared, "My name is Enoch."

Then he shuddered. Because if he knew who he was, then so did *they*.

"Just so I understand," Aaron said. "You two killed a godlike being, and now you want me to somehow help you make it right?"

Mallus and Tarshish were silent. They all sat at the card table. The old Malakim fiddled with a puzzle piece, and Aaron could just make out the puzzle's picture.

An abandoned factory. What an odd choice for a puzzle image, Aaron thought, before getting back to the point. "Well," he prompted.

"We didn't kill the godlike being, per se," Tarshish explained. "Just its human aspect."

"Okay," Aaron said. "So this being, this Metatron, it's still alive?"

"No, the Metatron is comprised of three aspects, the divine, the human, and the angelic. All must coexist together. By killing its human aspect, we caused the Metatron to unincorporate."

"And the other parts went where?" Aaron asked. "Back to God?"

"They exist in the world," the Malakim said. "We would have to find them, control them, and then bring them back to you."

"And what would I do with them?" Aaron asked.

Tarshish was silent as he picked up another puzzle piece and looked to see where it might fit in the image before him.

"These aspects would be joined to you," Mallus said.

Aaron listened. "And?"

"And you would become the Metatron," Tarshish finished, snapping the puzzle piece into place. "The perfect fusion of God, angel, and man."

Aaron considered what they were saying, looking from Mallus to Tarshish. "Why do I get the sense that this wouldn't be the greatest thing for me?"

"Probably because it isn't," Tarshish replied matter-of-factly.

"Being the Metatron is possibly one of the greatest honors that could be bestowed upon a human," Mallus said.

"Yeah? Then why do I hear a big 'but' coming?" Aaron asked.

"But you would be the Metatron," Tarshish said.

"No more Aaron Corbet, no more leader of the Nephilim," Mallus explained. "You would be the Metatron."

Aaron sat there, soaking it all in. He could feel his anger begin to rise as yet another responsibility was thrust upon him. After already giving up so much, the divine still wanted even more from him.

He wanted to tell the two angelic beings to forget it, to find another host for the godlike power that they had set loose upon the world. But Aaron just wasn't wired that way.

The thought of everything he would lose washed over him in one huge, crashing wave. But if he didn't agree to assume the role of Metatron, Aaron knew the darkness would eventually swallow the world. This Darkstar would win, and the Architects' plans—whatever they might be—would draw that much closer to completion.

Something deep inside Aaron told him that wouldn't be good for humanity, not good at all.

"Don't want to rush you, kid, but—" Tarshish began.

"What do I have to do?" Aaron asked finally, hoping this would be the last sacrifice that he would need to make.

Because he had nothing left to give.

CHAPTER NINETEEN

S atan, the Darkstar, prepared himself for the slaughter he would work.

He forged new armor, cladding his form in the stuff of darkness. Standing before an ancient mirror, he looked at himself, and added special details to the armored segments that adorned his limbs.

He was an impressive sight.

"Spectacular!" he exclaimed, his joyous smile nearly splitting his face. "Do you agree, Scox?" Satan turned from his reflection to eye the imp.

"Impressive, my liege," his red-skinned servant said quickly, rubbing his spindly-fingered hands together. "But are you complete?" he asked.

Satan immediately thought of the Morningstar, still loose somewhere within this body's psyche.

"Do you forget who you are addressing, imp?" Satan growled. He considered slaying the creature and then resurrecting his corpse, just to see if death would extinguish his flame of insolence.

"I mean no disrespect, oh Star of Darkness," Scox groveled, averting his eyes from the Darkstar's glare. "It's only that I've been thinking—"

"Thinking?" Satan questioned. "How dare you question—"

"Thinking about your situation with the Community, and why you might be meeting some resistance," Scox interjected.

The Darkstar decided to give the imp another chance, finding himself somewhat intrigued to hear Scox's observation.

"Entertain me with your thoughts," Satan proclaimed.

"I was thinking," Scox began again, cautiously raising his beady eyes to his master's. "It might be your face." Scox quickly looked away and lowered his head.

"My face?" Satan bellowed. He spun back to the mirror to observe his countenance. "What is wrong with this face?"

The imp did not respond, as he cowered in fear.

"What is wrong with this face?" the Darkstar demanded again, swooping down upon his frightened servant.

"It is *his*," Scox screeched with fear, writhing upon the floor, his eyes tightly closed.

"His?" the Darkstar asked.

"The Morningstar," Scox said in a trembling voice. "You look like Lucifer Morningstar, who slew many of their kind, hoping for redemption."

A sword of the same shadow that formed his armor grew in Satan's hand, and he was about to slay the miscreant, when the strangest thought occurred to him.

What if this loathsome creature is right?

He hovered over the demon, who recoiled from his wrath.

"Could it be something so simple?" Satan asked, almost to himself.

Scox opened first one eye and then the other. "It is entirely possible," he said cautiously. "Your appearance could be what's preventing the Community from fully accepting your omnipotence."

The Darkstar brought a shadow-clad hand to his face and lowered his blade.

"What would you suggest?" He felt foolish asking for suggestions from such a lowly beast, but there it was.

Scox stood slowly. "Seeing your face may be the problem," he began, somewhat hesitantly.

"Go on," Satan urged.

"And you are adorned in the most spectacular armor," the imp continued carefully.

"I grow weary of you, Scox," Satan said as the sword manifested again in his hand.

"A helmet," Scox cried out. "Cover up the face with a helmet!"

"A helmet," Satan repeated thoughtfully, turning back to the mirror. He brought both of his hands up to his face, allowing the shadow to flow from his fingertips over his face and head.

The darkness was made solid with a thought. Satan studied his newly helmeted countenance.

"Is *this* the face of their king?" he asked his reflection, turning to fix Scox with an icy stare.

By the sheer terror that appeared upon the lowly life-form's face, the Darkstar knew that it was.

Lorelei needed to find Lucifer once and for all.

Dusty didn't think that they would be needing the science room globe, or even one made of dirt, for what Lorelei wanted to do, so they decided on doing what they had to in the library.

She wanted to have the power of the Instrument again, to use it to, hopefully this time, find out where Lucifer was and rescue him if possible.

"Are you ready?" she asked Dusty.

Dusty was terrified at the prospect of fully connecting to the divine artifact again, but he didn't want to let on. Lorelei and the others needed to find Lucifer and bring him home. It was that important, and he wasn't about to let his own fear stand in their way.

"Let's do this," he said, taking a deep breath.

She'd brought her copper bowl and two doves from her work space, and began the process of making the sacrifice that would allow her to merge with Dusty's link to the Instrument.

She cut one bird's throat and let its blood drain, then

moved on to the other, reciting a prayer of thanks to the birds for giving up their lives to help them.

"Get ready," she told Dusty as she added more spell-casting ingredients to the bowl. Finally she gently removed the mouse from her shoulder and set him down upon the table as a thick, billowing smoke began to waft up from the bowl. And then she immersed her face within the smoke and took it into her lungs.

Seeing her act, Dusty leaned back in his chair and attempted to relax his mind.

When he first took possession of the Instrument so long ago, it became a part of him, but never more than it had become over the last weeks. There wasn't a moment when he couldn't sense it there, living at the periphery of his mind, desperate to show him how badly the world needed to be destroyed.

He guessed that it was probably disappointed that the Abomination of Desolation had failed in its task to purge the world of the disease of evil, only managing to sever the earth's ties to God and Heaven. But who knew. The way things were going, the Instrument might eventually get its wish.

Dusty visualized going to a closed wooden door, watching as it shook, battered from the other side by something of great strength and power, something demanding to be released.

The Instrument never stopped trying to come out, and it was only with Lorelei's help that he had been able to keep it restrained for this long.

He looked at the door in his mind's eye. There were cracks

in its heavy slats as the power of the Instrument threatened to break through. It wouldn't be long now before it destroyed the door that held it at bay and filled his head with so much that was awful out there in the world.

But wasn't that what he wanted right now . . . what Lorelei needed?

Yes, it was, and he had to oblige.

"Come on, then," he said to the door as it trembled and shook.

Dusty hadn't been raised in any particular religion, but he said a silent prayer to any divine being that might want to give him the strength to survive, as he took the latch in his fingers—amazed at how cold it felt, even though he knew it was only a manifestation of his mind—and pulled.

Allowing what was behind the door to come charging in.

Lorelei hovered close to Dusty, waiting for the right moment to wrest away his control and take the Instrument's reins.

With a sigh he opened his mind to the Instrument, and Lorelei went to work. She used her Archon magick to assume control of the ancient power. The last time she'd attempted this, she'd been pummeled by the Instrument's strength. She hoped that she was strong enough to discern the answers she sought from its seemingly endless flow of information.

Just one answer was all that she needed.

Where is Lucifer?

Once she knew, the others could bring him back home.

And they'd all live happily ever after. Or something like

that. Lorelei knew that wasn't likely to be the case, but she also knew the Nephilim had a better chance of surviving with him than without him.

Lorelei felt the power flow through Dusty into her. A barrage of nightmarish imagery of a world on the verge of horrific change inundated her. She bore witness to countless thousands under assault and could do nothing but turn away, as she continued her search for Lucifer.

One image would not leave her. A building of some kind—a church . . . or temple—rested atop an island of rock. The building exuded a sense of menace the likes of which she had never known, and it totally dominated her thoughts.

Lorelei was pulled to it, as if the magicks were taking her to this place for a reason. Having learned not to ignore hunches, she allowed herself to be pulled along with the flow.

The ancient church was made of stone, which appeared to be marble, stained a sickly olive green, as if covered in a mossy growth. Lorelei got the impression that the building had been hidden beneath the ocean waves for a very long time.

She was inside now; the halls were as dark as the night. A violent chill passed through her as she approached the seemingly endless shadows.

She wondered why she was here, but continued to feel the pull of the place upon her, suspecting it was somehow connected to Lucifer. Somewhere within this ancient edifice she would find him, or at least some clue as to where he was.

Suddenly she sensed that she was no longer alone. Lorelei wanted to call out to Lucifer but feared the attention that might draw. It was as if the darkness had somehow come alive, shaping itself from the gloom, to stand before her. For a brief moment she felt as though she knew this thing of night, but she was mistaken. Then the figure reached out, wrapping a gauntleted hand about her ghostly throat.

"I see you," said a voice that chilled her soul, filling her with a dread from which there was no escape.

The spell was broken as Lorelei screamed and flailed her arms, tipping the copper bowl onto the floor.

She trembled as if she were cold. But it wasn't the cold of a winter's day.

There was nothing natural about this.

She pulled herself together the best she could, knowing the kind of danger she was in.

The danger she had put them all in.

"Dusty," Lorelei said, expecting to see the young man snap from his trance. But he didn't.

Dusty sat, rigid in his chair, every muscle taut, his eyes rolled back in his head as the Instrument deluged him with images.

"Dusty," she urged, kneeling with great difficulty and pain beside his chair. "I need you here with me now. Dusty!"

She considered another spell to give him the strength to

break the Instrument's hold, but she wasn't sure if she could afford to give her strength away.

Something had seen her as she'd searched for Lucifer. Something so evil that Lorelei had felt its touch invade every level of her being. That evil had been searching for her—for the Nephilim, too—and now it knew where to find them.

Dusty thrashed wildly, slipping out of his chair and onto the floor, where he flailed about. Lorelei grabbed hold of his head, trying to keep him from hurting himself. Then, as quickly as the seizure had started, it stopped. Dusty's body went limp.

Lorelei was torn. The school's protective defenses needed to be checked, maybe strengthened, and it had to be done quickly. Dusty seemed to be safe for now. She reached up and grabbed hold of the table's edge to pull herself to her feet.

But, lightning-quick, Dusty's hand shot out, gripped her wrist, and pulled her back down to the floor. She found herself practically on top of him, looking down into his face—into his milky, almost sightless eyes.

"No more hiding," he said, but it was not Dusty's voice that was speaking. "I've found you . . ."

She tried to pull herself from his clutches, but he held her fast.

"Time to die," said the voice from the Instrument's visions. "Time for all of you to die."

A powerful shudder passed through the library. Books toppled from the shelves all around her. Lorelei tore her arm from Dusty's grasp and managed to climb to her feet, shielding herself from falling books. Milton squeaked in panic, and Lorelei stuck out her hand so he could climb to the safety of her shoulder.

"I think we're in trouble, mouse," she said.

The floor beneath her feet bucked, and Lorelei fell, tumbling toward the yawning hole in the library floor. She managed to stop herself just as she reached its edge, and peered down into the yawning abyss.

It was filling up.

Filling up with darkness.

CHAPTER TWENTY

The Fear Engine fought them.

It was just as Mallus had said. These infernal machines would do everything in their power to continue collecting the world's growing fear.

And now it was using that fear against Verchiel and Melissa.

Verchiel had said that they needed to kill it. *Pretty simple,* Melissa thought as she followed the angel's lead, flying into the air with her sword at the ready.

The machine looked to have fleshy parts—areas of its large, quivering mass that were made from pale, slimy-looking skin. She'd decided that would be the place to attack, the place that would feel the bite of her burning blade.

Verchiel reared back with a scream, the weapon in his hand seeming to grow larger and more fearsome as he readied to strike.

Then some invisible force reached out from the engine and

hit Verchiel with enough force to send the angel flying backward, slamming him into the ground. One of Verchiel's wings twisted and bent on impact, and Melissa was certain that it had been broken.

Melissa changed course at once, turning around in midair to go to her teammate's side. She landed beside the angel, who was curled into a tight ball, trembling uncontrollably.

"Verchiel!" she shouted, attempting to turn him over. He fought her briefly, but she rolled him toward her.

"What are you doing?" he screamed, his eyes, as black as marbles, bugging from his skull as he looked at her.

"What's wrong?" she asked him. "Are you all right?"

Then she sensed the raw emotion, permeating the air around the angel, trying to leach its way into her body.

It was fear—pure, undiluted fear.

She had no idea what Verchiel was experiencing, but she had to wonder if this being of Heaven had ever really known the touch of fear.

Melissa looked over to the machine. It radiated terror. If she didn't act, it would certainly overpower them.

Verchiel was useless, nothing more than a quivering mass upon the desert floor. For a moment she hesitated.

But she couldn't let the fear, the doubt, take hold of her. Fear had been Melissa's constant companion as her powers had emerged. She and fear had become quite close, actually.

Melissa spread her wings and pushed off from the petrified ground. Her sword flashed as she soared across the desert toward her target.

It was as if the machine could sense her coming. She wondered if it took in its sensory information through its nasty skin, for it had no eyes or ears, but questions of its biology were quickly cast aside. Her only interest was killing it.

Sand, melted and cooled into shards of glass, whizzed past her at frightening speeds as she edged closer, dodging and weaving in the air as Aaron had taught her. The surface of the engine's flesh suddenly opened and pulsated, and before Melissa could react, she felt as though she had been hit by a freight train. She dropped to the desert floor in a roll.

The fear clung to her body like an oily film as it tried to find its way inside her. She could feel it squirming to get inside her brain, turning the rational to irrational. She almost let it take her.

Almost.

Melissa fought the fear, reminding herself of a fear far greater than any other she could possibly imagine—the fear of failure.

The fear of failing her friends. The fear of failing the world.

Struggling to her feet, she managed to draw another sword from the armory of her mind and force herself forward toward the engine. Once again it had slowly sunk beneath the sand to continue its function.

The device sensed her approach, projecting blasts of concentrated terror at her. This time she knew it was coming and tensed her body against it. It was like fighting a powerful blast of wind. Melissa stumbled backward a few feet, but she recovered quickly, inexorably moving toward her target.

The fear tried to take control of her actions, but she just wouldn't let it. Melissa did not waver. She focused on her task. It was up to her now.

The engine seemed to sense her resolve, lobbing more and more blasts of pure terror at her, but she managed to keep moving forward. Each time she fell, she got up and pushed on.

Melissa was close now. She had never seen anything like this machine, metal and flesh, circuitry and twisted sinew.

It continued to attack, the blasts of fear becoming stronger, more powerful. Melissa fell to her knees, grabbed a large chunk of fused sand, and held it before her like a shield. The glass deflected some of the fear, allowing her to move that much closer.

Then she hurled the glass with all her strength at the engine, cutting into a fleshy area of the machine and causing it to psychically cry out, its scream filling her mind.

Without a moment's hesitation she leaped at the machine and landed atop it. Inside her mind Melissa saw her sword as clear as day, and summoned it to her hand. The divine blade cut into the soft tissue of the strange device, and again she was assailed by its ungodly cries.

But she did not let it deter her. With each new shriek she brought her weapon up, then down, hacking away chunks of slimy flesh and pieces of metal.

And just when Melissa believed her skull would explode

from the intensity of the psychic onslaught, all went deathly quiet. The infernal machine had finally been extinguished.

Melissa stood there, perched atop the bleeding wreck of the engine, feeling the fear leak from her body in waves, like blood seeping from an open wound. Melissa poked the body of the machine with the point of her sword, just to be sure it was finished, before leaping down to the ground, to be met with the sound of applause.

Startled, she looked up to see that Verchiel had recovered— and was clapping for her.

Melissa, feeling suddenly giddy, placed her left forearm across her belly and bent forward in a bow.

"Bravo," Verchiel said over the sound of his applause. "Perhaps Corbet will have a challenge to his leadership someday."

She was about to debate the trash talk with the angel when a voice screamed within her head.

It was Lorelei, and she sounded terrified.

The parishioners flowed up onto the altar with murderous intent in their eyes. They carried knives, ready to strike.

Vilma jumped in front of the swarm as they came.

"Destroy the machine," she ordered Cameron, and then turned back to face the murderous mob. They screamed as if insane, each of them desperate to be the one to spill her blood, but Vilma wasn't having any of that. She was tired of all the craziness, inside the church and out in the world.

Sick and tired.

She spread her wings as far as they would go, and brought them together again and again in rapid succession, the powerful flow of air they caused driving her attackers back, sending dust into their eyes.

Vilma turned from the crowd to see how her friend was doing, and watched in numbing horror as the old priest tossed the silk sheet that had covered the Fear Engine over Cameron's head, causing him to crash awkwardly to the ground.

"Damn it," Vilma growled as the old priest positioned himself to stab his knife into Cameron, who thrashed beneath the cover.

Vilma flew across the altar to slam into the old man, sending them both crashing into the pulsating body of the Fear Engine.

Cameron was cutting his way free of the sheet, but he wasn't quite fast enough. The crowd surged forward, attempting to kill him where he lay. Vilma tried to go to his aid, but an iron grip wrapped around her leg and dragged her back to the floor.

"Not so fast, my dear," the old priest said, blood streaming from his broken nose. "Where do you think you're going?" he asked with a crimson-stained grin. "You have yet to pay your proper respects to my god."

Vilma kicked out with her foot, connecting with the old man's face and snapping his head back violently. She rushed to her friend, who was struggling against the crush of parishioners.

"Praise god!" a woman exclaimed as she drove her blade into Cameron's arm.

Cameron screamed, and the power of his thrashing wings tossed the maddened congregation away like leaves in the wind. But they immediately got back to their feet and came after Cameron again.

Vilma called upon a sword of fire. She hadn't wanted to resort to this, believing that the parishioners were somehow being influenced by the monstrous machine, but she was left with little choice. Leaping amongst their attackers, she swung the sword in a burning arc in order to drive them back. Then she reached down to help up the bleeding Cameron.

"A sword might do you good," she said, and Cameron agreed, creating his own weapon of holy fire. They stood back-to-back, keeping the advancing parishioners at bay on one side, and the bloody-faced priest on the other.

"Accept your fate," Donnally urged through a split and swollen lip as he waved his sacrificial dagger. "Feed the god that has protected us from the nightmares outside."

They needed to take out that Fear Engine, and do it quickly, but Vilma saw with horror that the machine was now being shielded by the two children who had brought her and Cameron here, Ryan and Jinny. The two kids were holding hands, their backs pressed to the machine.

One of the parishioners had built himself into a frenzy and threw himself at Cameron, even though the Nephilim screamed for him to stay back. The madman ignored the warning, rushing at him with his blade raised, and Cameron had no choice but to strike the man down. There was a flash of heavenly fire, and the man slumped loosely to the floor, his body billowing a thick, oily smoke. The parishioners were deterred for only an instant as they stared at what could be their own fates, but the religious fervor that drove them was back in no time, and they again advanced as one.

"We have to get to that machine," Vilma said.

"You know the only way to do that, right?" Cameron said, slashing his sword across the face of an older woman, who narrowly missed him with a jab of her knife. The woman cried out, dropping her weapon and stumbling backward, her flailing limbs pushing the crowd back temporarily.

"We have to let it out," he added, waiting for her to respond.

The Nephilim had been training for desperate times. Vilma hated the idea of resorting to that level of violence, but they hadn't been left with many options. The parishioners acted as if they were mindless robots programmed for violence, continually rushing them, without regard to consequence, only to be savagely cut down.

"Do it," Vilma said finally, a sense of dread taking hold of her heart.

"Are you sure?" Cameron asked, swinging his sword and severing a man's hand from his wrist. The air was filled with the sweet stink of cooking meat.

"Do it, before I change my mind," she said.

They were going to let the full power of the Nephilim loose. It wasn't something that was to be done lightly, but in times such as this . . .

There was no holding back now. Cameron tapped into the fury of the Nephilim, and his body began to glow with an unnatural fire. Vilma did the same, feeling a strangely pleasurable sensation as the power that she usually spent so much energy holding back flowed freely through her.

The temperature of the room grew hotter, but that did little to keep their attackers at bay. The parishioners threw themselves at the Nephilim, and Vilma was sickened by the sight of them. Even as their clothes began to burn and their skin blistered, the parishioners struggled to attack them.

And using the full power coursing through their veins, Vilma and Cameron cut them down.

Donnally ran for the engine and the children who still protected it, his white robes beginning to char with the intensity of the Nephilim's heat.

"Defend yourselves!" the old priest wailed, and the two children cried, hugging the body of the obscene mechanism.

Vilma and Cameron stood back-to-back. Cameron faced the engine.

"What's it doing now?" Vilma heard Cameron mutter.

She flapped her wings, and fire spread out into the pews. Then she quickly turned to look at the machine. Through the smoke she could see that something was happening between Donnally, the two children, and the machine itself.

It looked as if the machine were eating them—absorbing them into its pulsating mass.

Vilma had seen enough. She leaped into the air and flew toward the Fear Engine, watching in horror as Ryan's smiling face was slowly pulled beneath the pale, sweating skin of the living machine. One moment the boy was there, and the next he was gone, his hammer the only trace that he had ever been there.

Jinny laughed as she accepted her horrible fate.

"I've always dreamed of becoming one with my . . . ," Donnally began, but then he, too, was drawn into the undulating mass.

The Fear Engine's body throbbed and roiled like the ocean waves.

"Be careful," Vilma yelled to Cameron as he flew past her.

He stood in front of the machine and raised his sword over his shoulder to cleave the unholy mechanism down the middle, but then the engine fought back.

It emitted a nearly invisible wave of power that caused the air around it to shimmer like the blazing heat of August. It struck the Nephilim, throwing him across the altar and into the burning church beyond.

It was Vilma's turn. She rushed the engine with a birdlike cry. The Fear Engine pulled itself from where it had been rooted, and shifted its throbbing mass toward her advance, emitting another mysterious wave of whatever had taken out Cameron.

Vilma saw what was coming. The machine's skin shivered and tightened, and she flew up above the blast. Though it did not strike her directly, Vilma could feel the intensity of its force.

Fear. The engine was using the fear that it had collected from this region of the world to defend itself. She could feel the fear lingering in the air, seeping through her clothes and into her flesh.

Fear. She could feel it rushing through her veins, making her heart hammer and her skin tingle and sweat—and the images, the images that were now flooding her mind . . .

She was afraid for Cameron, for Aaron . . . and for Jeremy. *Jeremy.*

Anger blossomed in a rush of heat, providing her with enough adrenaline to temporarily get hold of her emotions.

Vilma wasted no more time, lunging at the mechanical life-form and plunging her sword deep into the core of the engine.

There was an explosion of force and a psychic cry that tried to rip her brain into tiny pieces as she was thrown back upon the burning altar. Recovering as quickly as she was able, and bracing for whatever was coming, she squinted through the heavy smoke. The engine had collapsed upon itself like a deflated balloon.

Turning to face the church, eyes finding the bodies of those parishioners who had fallen during their battle and the hungry fire that consumed them, Vilma called out, "Cameron!"

She found him huddled upon the floor, rocking back and forth as his body shook from fright.

"Are you all right?" she asked, reaching out to gently touch his shoulder.

"Afraid," he managed, his eyes haunted.

She had gotten only a small taste of the emotion that the engine had used to defend itself, so could only imagine what her friend was experiencing.

"It'll pass."

Cameron allowed her to help him stand, and at the same moment a section of burning roof caved in upon the altar.

"We should get out of here," Vilma said, and the weakened structure groaned under the strain of the fire.

She was about to take them both into her wings, when she was blindsided by an explosion of desperation inside her brain.

A scream for help.

"It's Lorelei," Cameron said as his body shook, feeling the same panicked cry.

Vilma was stunned by the intensity of Lorelei's message, her hand reflexively wiping away the warm trickle of blood dripping from her nose.

What is it now?

Gabriel could smell the stink of the multitude of creatures that had burrowed the tunnel he was now crawling through. He imagined them all digging and chewing their way through the layers of rock and dirt on their way to . . .

Where?

He figured he would eventually find out.

The loose stones beneath his feet suddenly gave way as the decline increased, and he found himself sliding down the tunnel, spilling out onto the rocky floor of an underground chamber.

Getting his feet beneath him, the dog was assailed by the smell of death . . . lots and lots of death.

Gabriel quickly called upon his angelic side, making his fur glow as if he'd been set afire. The warm and comforting light from his body illuminated the grisly findings in the chamber. Animals in various stages of decay lay everywhere; bones and tufts of hair stuck up from the rock and dirt of the floor, and he couldn't imagine stepping anywhere where he wasn't walking upon something that had once been alive.

He imagined these poor, manipulated creatures, controlled by the Fear Engine and carelessly discarded when no longer of use.

There was movement in the shadows. Another chamber was to the right. Gabriel immediately started forward, quelling the glow from his body so as not to alert his prey. He reached the opening and peered inside, his eyes quickly adjusting to the gloom.

The animals that had made up the twisted mass of the monster created to protect the engine had merged once more. The monster squeaked, growled, and chirped in multiple animal tongues as it worked to lift something buried deep within the corner of the chamber.

Gabriel couldn't see what it was within the loose dirt and rock. It could have been a machine, he guessed, but if so, why did it look to be made of skin and metal? The dog was confused, but then again, what should he have expected from a mechanism crafted by the forces that wanted to plunge the world into total darkness?

Gabriel slunk further into the chamber and began to growl.

The monster stopped what it was doing and spun around with multiple emanations of displeasure from its body mass.

"Must protect the machine," the creature said in various animal languages.

"I can't allow you to do that," Gabriel spoke, hoping that whatever was functioning as its brain would understand. *"The machine is dangerous and must be destroyed."*

The creature's body tensed as it prepared to defend its charge, but Gabriel was ready as well.

The Fear Engine began to throb and pulse, a beat passing through its pale wet skin. The monster responded to that, casually glancing over to the machine, as if communicating with it, before coming at Gabriel.

Gabriel thought he was prepared, but as the beast of beasts lunged toward him, its body broke apart into the multiple lifeforms that gave it shape, and he knew how wrong he'd been. The dog didn't know what to attack first as the mass of snarling teeth and claws swarmed at him. Summoning his newfound angelic power once more, Gabriel did his best, snatching up the attacking beasts in his fiery jaws, setting them alight in his fury, before attacking the next.

But there were just too many, and it seemed that even more beasts were being summoned by the monstrous engine, as wave after wave of animals flowed upon him, weighing him down with their filthy mass. But they did not bite him, or rip at his flesh. All they did was pin him down. Gabriel had no idea what they were doing, until he felt the tickling sensation of something unearthly attempting to burrow its way inside his brain.

To convince him to become part of the monstrous mass that was the engine's protector.

Gabriel tried to fight it, but found himself swept up in the flow of bodies as they again took on a humanoid shape. The animals around him bit into Gabriel, attaching themselves to his body, like tendons to muscles, as he was made part of the obscenity's lower body. It was amazing, yet terrifying, being connected to all the different forms of life that made up this mockery of a human body. Gabriel's thoughts were no longer his own. The Fear Engine and the other animals chattered in a cacophony of sound inside his skull.

Gabriel felt that he was drowning. He was losing himself to the Fear Engine. He tried everything in his power to remain an individual, but the engine's power and all the voices exploding inside his skull were far too much for him. He was becoming part of the monstrous servant.

And he felt himself begin to slip farther and farther away.

"I need you here. . . . I need you back here this instant!"

Just as he thought he was lost forever, another voice forced its way into Gabriel's mind. It was strong, desperate, and demanded that it be heard.

It was all that Gabriel needed to regain some semblance of control.

He knew the voice belonged to his friend Lorelei, and he had never heard her filled with such panic . . . with such fear.

The engine attempted to make him part of the body again, but Gabriel remained free—and intended to stay that way.

He started to thrash within the confines of the body. The animals fought, biting down even harder into his flesh, into his tail. Holding on to him.

The pain helped Gabriel to think more clearly, and he was able to call upon the power that was now a part of him. And as the Engine fought to keep him within its clutches, Gabriel released his angelic fury in an explosion of ravenous fire.

The animals squealed and shrieked as their bodies were incinerated, the entity that they had been part of crumbling to fiery pieces. Gabriel landed upon the floor, surrounded by burning animals, some running about frantically before eventually succumbing to death.

The engine continued to thrum with life, but its control over the animals was lost. They ran, afire with the flames of the divine, to what they believed would be their savior. The Fear Engine was quickly covered in burning animals, the fires from their bodies igniting the soft, fleshy parts of the living machine.

Gabriel listened to it scream as the machine's psychic claws attempted to reach into his brain, trying to coerce him to come to its aid.

But Gabriel managed to resist, watching as the fires of divinity ravaged the evil contraption until its plaintive cries were silenced.

Quickly approaching the burning remains, Gabriel checked to be sure that the engine was no longer alive, before calling upon the power of the angels, yet again, to transport him back to the school, and to the aid of a desperate friend.

CHAPTER TWENTY-ONE

Kraus stood before the flat-screen television, flipping past channel after channel of hissing static before finally finding one that was still broadcasting.

Something bad was going on out there, something even worse than before.

The newscasters appeared terrified as they relayed their stories of cities all over the globe experiencing attacks by monsters that seemed to appear from nowhere.

The way the word seemed to roll from their lips—"monsters"—made him briefly consider his sanity. But then he thought of the world he'd lived in before the darkness had fallen, a world where he'd served the needs of Heaven's angels.

Kraus could barely remember a time when the world had seemed at all normal.

The TV showed some grainy footage of a city. Was it

Chicago? He couldn't understand what the broadcasters were saying in the live signal. He wanted to turn off the sound so he wouldn't hear the screams that drowned out the broadcasters, but he couldn't figure out what button to push on the remote.

Buildings were burning and the streets were filled with armored things that seemed to attack with abandon, and it didn't appear that there was much anybody could do to keep the monsters back.

This is what the Nephilim are for, he thought, feeling sick to his stomach as the scene went to static. The program returned to the studio with the two anchors, who looked as though they wanted to burst into tears.

Kraus began to wonder if something had happened to his friends. He knew that they had gone off on a mission of great importance. Had they failed somehow?

Panic set in, and he wished with all his heart that there was something—anything—he could do to help them. But he knew his function was to wait for their return and be ready to heal them so that they might continue the fight against—

Kraus felt it through the floor, and in the very air itself—a strange disturbance that rattled the school property, and him, to the very core.

The television went black, as did the lights. Something had happened to their generator. Kraus looked about the darkened room. For the briefest of moments he considered that Aaron and the others might have returned from their mission, but he knew better.

Something was very wrong.

Kraus left the room, maneuvering through the darkness in search of Lorelei and Dusty, senses finely tuned by his former years of blindness.

But first a quick stop at the maintenance closet where the Nephilim stored many of the swords, knives, and axes that they had collected from the dead beasts who had invaded the school grounds when the last of the Powers angels and the Abomination of Desolation had attacked.

Kraus thought he might be needing a weapon.

Just in case.

Aaron watched as an old woman shambled over to the card table with a tray of three steaming coffee mugs.

"It's instant," Tarshish said, helping himself to a mug. "Hope you don't mind."

Aaron didn't really want any coffee right then, but it seemed like the polite thing to do. "Thanks," he told the old woman, but she didn't respond.

"What's up with them?" Aaron asked in a whisper as the woman walked off with the empty tray.

Tarshish shrugged before taking a sip of his steaming drink.

"That one's Betty," he said. "She's been gone the longest of all of them."

"Gone?" Aaron asked.

"Dead."

"She's dead?" Aaron questioned incredulously, turning in his chair to look at the others, who sat in front of the blank television screen. "They're all dead?"

"Yeah," Tarshish answered, setting his mug down. "I didn't have the heart to let them go. It's amazing how attached I've gotten to them."

Aaron was horrified.

"The power of God released from the Metatron," Mallus interjected, quickly changing the subject. "We need to find it."

"Finding it will be the easy part," Tarshish added.

Aaron took a sip of the instant coffee and made a face. It was horrible. Making good coffee wasn't the dead old lady's strongest skill. Imagine that.

"Why?" Aaron asked, pushing his mug closer to the puzzle border.

"The power of the Metatron couldn't exist alone in the world," Mallus explained, his own steaming mug in hand. "It had to find a host."

"Hosts," Tarshish corrected.

Mallus nodded, taking a slug of the coffee before speaking again. "That power remembered what it had been . . . what it had been part of," he explained. "Part of a special trinity that had composed the Metatron."

"So it found three hosts?" Aaron asked.

"It certainly did," Tarshish answered. "And it was corrupted in the process."

Mallus sighed as he set his mug down. "The power of God, meant to help humanity, has been used for less than righteous purposes all these years."

Tarshish's old eyes fixed Aaron and Mallus in a serious stare. "This isn't going to be easy," he warned. "We're all going to need to be at the top of our game if we're even going to come close to taking back the power of the Metatron."

Aaron understood the gravity of the situation, but could not help but stare at the sickeningly skinny Tarshish, sitting in his wheelchair.

"What?" the Malakim asked.

"Are *you* up to the task?" Aaron questioned, scrutinizing the Malakim.

Tarshish laughed, a short bark that sounded loose and wet. "Don't you worry about me," he said, reaching up and pulling down the lower lid of his left eye. A blinding ray of light sneaked out from beneath the weathered skin. "This is just a suit I wear when I'm taking it easy."

"Cool," Aaron said, satisfied with the Malakim's answer.

Mallus had begun to speak again, when the Nephilim suddenly experienced a sensation akin to somebody setting off a bomb of pure sound inside his skull.

"I need you here. . . . I need you back here this instant!"

It caught Aaron off guard, and he startled, his sudden

movement flipping his chair over and landing him unceremo-
niously on the floor.

"What is it?" Mallus asked urgently.

Aaron scrambled to his feet, too stunned to be embar-
rassed. "It's Lorelei. She's back at the school," he explained.
He could feel his nose bleeding, and wiped the blood from his
nostrils with the back of his hand. "I've got to get back."

Mallus and Tarshish shared a look.

"Aaron, time is of the essence. If we—"

"I know," Aaron interrupted, still feeling his friend's lingering terror. "But this is an emergency."

"The whole freakin' planet is experiencing an emergency,"
Tarshish exclaimed.

"I'm sorry," Aaron said, flexing the muscles in his back and
calling forth his wings. "I'll be back as soon as I can."

Mallus protested, but Aaron wasn't listening. He wrapped
his wings about himself and pictured the school. His friend
needed him. . . . His friend was in danger.

And nothing was going to keep him away.

"Well, I guess that's that," Tarshish said, leaning forward to
pick up another piece to his puzzle.

Mallus noticed that the puzzle's picture had changed again,
this time showing what appeared to be some sort of ancient
temple sitting atop a stony mountain that jutted from a bluish-
green ocean.

"We can't wait for him," Mallus said. "Things are moving too fast."

"So what do you want to do?" Tarshish asked, finding a home for the piece and snapping it into place.

"We go and take God's power back," Mallus said matter-of-factly. "That's the key to stopping the Architects."

Tarshish looked up from his puzzle. "What about a host?" he asked. "Without the boy . . ."

"We'll worry about that after we get the power back from the unholy trinity," Mallus replied.

Tarshish pushed his wheelchair back from the card table. "Let's do this, then," he said, standing stiffly from the chair. He glanced over to the group of elderly men and women sitting before the television. "It's been fun, gang," he said, his words followed by a flash of brilliance.

Mallus watched as the residents of the nursing home all went limp, collapsing in upon themselves and turning to dust before his eyes.

Tarshish, on the other hand, looked stronger as he stared with golden flecked eyes at the place where his friends had once sat.

"I'm really going to miss Wednesday nights," he said sadly.

"Why is that?" Mallus asked, mildly curious as to what might cause a being like the Malakim to experience the emotion of loss.

"Wednesday was bingo night," Tarshish said.

"Bingo?" Mallus repeated.

Tarshish nodded. "I love playing bingo."

The child thrashed so violently that Jeremy was afraid he would drop the little bugger.

"Stop the nonsense!" Jeremy barked as he carried Roger up the walkway to their rented cottage.

"It is not nonsense!" Roger screeched, his arms and legs flailing. "We need to leave this place at once!"

"There, there," Jeremy's mother said, cupping the baby's angry face in her hand as Jeremy stopped in front of the door and dug in his pocket for the key. "Roger's just knackered is all, a little lie-down, and he'll—"

"Enoch!" the baby wailed. "My name isn't Roger; it's Enoch!"

"That's right, Enoch," she cooed, following the two of them into the cottage.

"We're not going anywhere, Enoch," Jeremy said, ready to hand the raving child off to his mother. "You're going to have a bit of rest, and then, when you wake up refreshed, we're all gonna have a nice sit-down and discuss—"

He was handing the child to his mother when Jeremy noticed the point of a knife protruding from her chest.

"Mum?" Jeremy said, feeling the air suddenly punched from his lungs. "Mum, what . . . ?"

Her mouth was moving as she deflated before his eyes, falling to the floor of the entryway.

"It's too late!" Enoch screeched. "They've already found us!"

Jeremy sensed movement from behind him, and he tossed baby Enoch onto the couch as he spun to meet his attacker.

It took a moment for his brain to register, because his attacker was practically invisible. Whatever it was wearing blended in with the colors of the cottage. The chameleon drove a knife blade deep into Jeremy's upper chest. It would have been his heart, but he'd had the instincts to move as his attacker—his mother's murderer—had come in close for the kill.

Too close.

Jeremy screamed, and lashed out with all his might. His fist connected with something that felt very much like a face. His attacker stumbled back, pulling the knife from the Nephilim's chest as the chameleon fell.

Jeremy spread his wings and beat the air, causing powerful gusts of wind that drove his attacker away, and bought him time to collect himself. A lamp clattered from a side table, and sand blown in from the still-open door created a kind of smoky haze in the air, temporarily allowing him to see his assailant.

Jeremy didn't wait for an invitation. He dove across the room with the help of his wings and connected with the figure, driving it to the floor. His assailant was slimmer and smaller than he, but its strength was undeniable, and whatever it was that the attacker wore made it as slippery as hell.

An elbow slammed into Jeremy's face, driving his head back. Then a foot planted upon his chest and kicked him across the living room to slam against the couch.

For a second Jeremy worried about Roger—Enoch—but, chancing a quick scan of the area, he saw that the baby was nowhere to be found, which, given the circumstances, was probably a good thing.

His attacker landed upon him, and instinctively Jeremy threw his arm up to block a punch, feeling the bite of the knife. Growling like something wild, Jeremy tapped into his fear and fury, bringing forward the power of the Nephilim and creating a battle mace of fire, which he swung wildly, hoping to connect with his foe.

The attacker leaped back and away from the flaming weapon, and Jeremy got to his feet, his eyes furiously attempting to keep track of the mysterious assassin that seemed to disappear in the blink of an eye.

Which is exactly what it did.

"Bugger," Jeremy spat, readying himself for the inevitable attack. Continuing to flap his wings, he spun, searching the room for a sign—any sign.

Jeremy's foot landed upon one of Roger's—Enoch's—toy lories, and he lost his balance for a moment before regaining his footing.

But a moment was all the assassin needed.

He dove to the left, Jeremy smelled his own blood and saw the stained knife blade appearing out of thin air and slipping dangerously past his throat.

Knowing that he couldn't keep this up forever, Jeremy reached out to grab his assailant. His hands landed upon something solid, and Jeremy closed his fingers about his prey. It was like trying to hold on to an eel, but he sank his fingernails in as deep as possible.

Instead of using a weapon, Jeremy sent the divine fire directly to his hands. There was a whoosh as the flames came, and then the stink of something burning as the flesh within his hands began to burn.

The fires of Heaven were voracious.

Jeremy was thrown back and away, but this time he didn't lose sight of his attacker. The assassin was burning.

The figure was in a panic, attempting to stamp out the fire creeping up its arm, but this only served to ignite its other hand. Jeremy was already on the move before the murderer could flee. His battle mace formed again in his hand as he lunged at the masked figure, and he smashed the assailant across the face with all his might, sending him crashing and burning to the cottage floor.

Jeremy was stunned to see that his attacker was already attempting to get back up, glaring at him as he rose. The black leatherlike material of its mask had been partially torn with the mace's blow, and Jeremy gaped in awe at what he saw.

"Bloody hell," Jeremy said. "What are you supposed to be?"

It's like looking at a bloody ape, he thought as the murderer, its body still afire, made another attempt to take him down.

Jeremy didn't hesitate, smashing the mace down upon the creature's arm that held the knife, shattering its bones to powder.

The figure did not cry, but it knelt there momentarily before finding its knife with its other hand, ready to go at Jeremy again.

Jeremy had had enough. "This is for Mum, ya bastard," he growled, bringing the ball of fire down upon the attacker's skull.

The would-be assassin slumped to the floor, body twitching.

Jeremy needed to hold back, deciding that perhaps something might be learned if he let the assassin live.

A voice that he could not locate at first screamed out. "Don't even hesitate," Enoch said from hiding. "End its miserable life now, before others can home in upon its location."

Enoch didn't have to tell him twice. Jeremy brought the mace down again, shattering their attacker's skull all over the carpet.

From the corner of his eye, Jeremy saw movement beneath the sofa, and watched as the baby squirmed out from his hiding place. Knowing that Enoch was safe, Jeremy let his mace disappear and went to his mother.

She lay on her back in the entryway, still clinging to life.

"Oh," was all Jeremy could manage as he hovered above her, not really knowing what he should do.

She looked as though she were trying to speak, and he dropped to his knees and gently pulled her into his arms.

"Hang on, luv. We'll get you to hospital," he told her softly, but the look in her eyes told him otherwise.

She'd never make the ride, even if they flew.

Her bloodstained lips moved as she tried to talk to him.

"What is it, Mum?" he asked her. "What can I do? Please, tell me what I can do?"

"Protect," she whispered. Her eyes shifted, searching the room. She was looking for the baby.

"Enoch?" he asked her. "You want me to protect Enoch?"

She didn't answer, but he knew that was what she wanted, as he watched the life drain from her eyes.

"Of course she meant me," the baby's overly intelligent voice said.

He had crawled over and sat beside them.

"I'm the last hope of humanity," Enoch said, staring at the woman's corpse. "If I don't make it, none of us will."

CHAPTER TWENTY-TWO

The darkness was as vast as the ocean and as limitless in its depths.

Every patch of shadow, no matter how small, connected to a greater whole that now embraced a world in its gradually constricting grip.

And the Darkstar used this flow of shadow, swimming through the inky currents like some great prehistoric predator on the hunt.

The scent of those who would oppose him was like blood in the water, and he followed it.

Though he would be loath to admit it, the Three Sisters of Umbra had shown him the way to supremacy. By slaying those who had been deemed the saviors of the world, protectors of humanity, he would prove to his detractors that he was all-powerful, and to worship him would be most wise, for he intended to have this world as his own—to flaunt before a helpless God—for a very long time.

And then there was the Morningstar, still managing to hold on somewhere deep inside the Darkstar's psyche, holding out hope that somehow he might regain control.

Satan would see that hope forever vanquished with the murders of the half-breed Nephilim, crushing it beneath his heel, grinding it to nothing until all that remained of the Son of the Morning was a fading memory.

The stench of angel magick grew stronger, and Satan flapped his wings, surging with speed toward what would be his greatest victory.

Using sinister magicks, the Sisters had linked him to the Community of monsters and beasts around the world. They now knew of his plans to eliminate the last true threats to their evil dominion.

And with just a thought Satan called to them, to the trolls, dragons, goblins, and wraiths. He called to each and every nightmare made flesh, inviting them to participate in a victory that would give them a kingdom.

A world under the Darkstar's unholy reign.

Satan turned his face to the point of light punctuating the darkness ahead of him, his mighty wings pushing off from the stuff of shadow, propelling his armored form ever closer to the obstacles impeding his rise to supremacy.

He could not wait to wrap his fingers about the throat

of hope and squeeze what little life remained from the world, which was about to be forever claimed by night.

Lorelei looked down into the churning pool of shadow. Something was coming up from its depths.

"We need to get out of here!" she yelled, backing up from the edge of the hole. "Dusty, can you hear me? We need to—"

Nightmare incarnate exploded from the library floor. It rose up on wings formed from the stuff of night, its body adorned in armor as black and reflective as a pool of oil. Its wings beat the air with a rhythmic thrum, like the pulse of a mighty heart.

Its face was covered, and it looked at her through slits in a helmet made from shadows.

She knew that this was the one that had touched her, that had followed the residual trace of her magickal connection to the Instrument. And now it had come for her.

It had come for them all.

The armored figure stared at her, and she remained perfectly still; even though the muscles in her aching legs were screaming for relief, she dared not move a muscle.

A moan from Dusty distracted the winged nightmare, its eyes, devoid of any humanity, shifting from her to the source of the sound.

It was the moment she had been waiting for.

"Dusty, run for the door!" Lorelei screamed, summoning

a magickal blast and hurling it at the chest of the invader. The roiling light struck the thing, knocking it back against a floor-to-ceiling bookcase filled with ancient volumes, causing a chain reaction as row upon row of the shelves noisily tumbled.

Lorelei grabbed for Dusty, and they raced for the door.

"What's going on?" he demanded. "Who is that?"

"It's death, Dusty," she said in all seriousness. "That's all you need to know."

The door was right before them, but time seemed to have slowed. Lorelei watched as Dusty reached for the knob, but it was still so far away.

The air in front of them exploded in a blast of black fire.

Dusty screamed as he was blown back and away from the door, colliding with her. They both tumbled to the floor. Lorelei's every joint was screaming, the side effects of using Archon magick again rearing their ugly heads.

Why now? Lorelei thought, when she and her friends' very lives were at stake. She could barely move to crawl out from beneath Dusty's weight.

There were more things . . . monsters . . . hauling themselves out of the hole in the floor. She knew they should have fixed that hole sooner, but that was neither here nor there.

The armored entity had recovered from her attack and was watching from its perch atop the pile of toppled bookcases, appearing to be enjoying her struggle—her panic.

Beasts—trolls and goblins—advanced across the library

toward Lorelei and Dusty, swords and daggers in misshapen hands.

She couldn't bear the thought of them in her library, and used that rage to fuel her magick. Blasts of enhanced angelic fire exploded from her outstretched hands, obliterating the advancing horde, but more were just as quickly emerging behind the ones she had slain.

And the armored figure continued to watch, his gauntleted hands crackling with cold, black fire.

She sensed that he could kill them with ease but chose not to, enjoying their struggle.

That just made her all the more furious, and she continued to kill the advancing invaders, feeling her life force dwindling, her body being eaten up by the use of such powerful magick.

Milton squeaked pathetically in her ear, as if sensing the damage she was doing to herself, but there was no other way. She ordered the mouse to go, to run someplace and hide, so she would hear none of the rodent's primitive arguments.

She felt the loss of the tiny weight from her shoulder as crackling bolts of magick streamed from her outstretched hands. Her magick was getting weaker, and she attempted to rouse Dusty from where he'd fallen.

"Get up, Dusty," she said, her latest volley of defensive magick only serving to momentarily dissuade the advancing legions of monsters, before they were stomping toward them again.

She feared that this might be the beginning of the end for her.

Pushing Dusty toward the burning opening where the door to the science building had been, Lorelei chanced a look at their armored foe.

He tilted his helmeted head and began to raise a hand, and she practically threw Dusty out into the hall.

"Go! Go! Go!" she screamed as she turned to confront her fate.

There were monsters before her, grinning around their jagged teeth as they prepared to take her life. But Lorelei wouldn't go down without a fight.

"All right, then, you sons of bitches," she said, reaching down into the core of her being to find some manner of reserve. Her hands sparked to life as her Archon magick mingled with the power of the Nephilim for one final strike against the invaders. "Let's see how many of you I can take with me."

A troll with a single bulging eye and an empty socket was the first to attack. Licking his cracked and swollen lips as if in hunger, he lurched to cut her down.

Lorelei was ready to let loose with the last of her magick, when the troll's hand was severed. It flew through the air trailing a scarlet tendril of blood and landed upon the floor with a wet slap.

If she hadn't been so close to dying, she would have laughed at the monster's shocked expression as it brought its squirting stump to its face to stare at what was missing. Its head was next to leave its awful body, a blade of cold steel passing through leathery skin and muscle as a geyser of deep red blood fountained into the air.

Lorelei felt a hand grab her roughly by the arm and yanked her from the path of the horde.

It took her a moment to realize who had rescued her.

"Leave," Kraus said, already swinging his sword at the next attacker. "They cannot afford to lose you."

Lorelei stumbled toward the exit, but then stopped. She realized that she couldn't leave Kraus to face his death.

She turned away from freedom and took in the scene before her. Kraus fought bravely, his sword cutting a bloody swathe through the advancing monster hordes, but there were too many. And as their horrible numbers grew, they swarmed upon him, taking him down.

Lorelei knew what she must do as she watched her friend die, amazed that he did not scream or cry out as he was dragged toward the gaping hole in the floor, and over the edge, into oblivion.

"Did you enjoy that?" she screamed at the black-armored specter that watched.

It actually had the audacity to nod its head.

She knew this would be the last bit of magick that she would be capable of casting. The library—her beloved library—was a universe unto itself, a pocket reality that existed within the confines of an impossible space.

An enormous bubble of magick.

A bubble of magick that she was about to burst.

First Lorelei created a wall of corrosive magick to keep the beasties from getting too close while she worked.

The armored specter of death watched her with curious eyes.

Keep watching, you monstrous son of a bitch, she thought as, with a heavy heart, she began to shut down the spells that allowed the library to exist. Without them the library would simply implode, collapsing in upon itself as the reality around it rushed in to fill the void.

What's that old saying? Nature abhors a vacuum?

The library trembled, and the reverberations captured the attention of the monstrous marauders as well as their armored leader.

Stick around a moment longer, and I'll really give you something to take notice of, Lorelei thought as she continued her work.

An increasing rumble began somewhere far back in the library, like the growing roar of a stormy surf. *It's happening*, she thought sadly, taking it all in as she slowly backed toward the exit.

She uttered the final phrase of the special Archon spells, and had just turned to flee when the nightmare visage struck. He extended his arm, the movement a blur, and savagely struck her down in a biting blast of black fire.

Her breath was punched from her body as she crumpled, wheezing feebly, to the ground. It felt as though she had been encased in ice, every ounce of warmth stolen from her being.

It was there that she decided to accept her fate. Lorelei

managed to roll onto her back, watching as the armored leader flew down from his perch to join his nightmarish legion.

The vibrations beneath her body were intensifying, and she knew it would only be a matter of time before it all came crashing down as the library's reality ceased to be.

The armored leader strode toward her, and she smiled in the face of him. She wished he would remove that awful helmet so she could see the sick expression of shock on his face as he finally realized that he and his horde were about to die.

Hands suddenly appeared beneath her arms, and she found herself being dragged through the opening blown in the library wall.

She bent back her head and saw that it was Dusty.

"You might want to think about speeding things up," she suggested as the vibrations through the building intensified tenfold and the lighting fixtures crashed upon the hallway floor outside.

Dusty changed tactics, hauling her to her feet and throwing her arm around his neck before rushing them down the smoke-filled hallway of the science building.

"We need to get outside," she said as they stumbled along.

"Working on it," Dusty replied, his face twisted in exertion as he pushed open the door before them.

Lorelei chanced a quick look over her shoulder, watching as the armored monster emerged into the corridor with his nightmare troops.

Just as the library's reality collapsed in upon itself.

There was no time for warning, not a chance to speak, as the implosion of air pulled Lorelei and Dusty viciously back toward where they had come. Then a magick-fueled explosion threw them through the doors, and outside.

And into the arms of oblivion.

She didn't know how long she had lain there, twisted upon the grass. Minutes? Hours? Lorelei couldn't be sure.

And where is Dusty? She tried to call out to him.

All that came out was a pathetic squawk. She began to cough, choking on the dusty air. She rolled onto her side and took in slow, ragged breaths, watching as the explosions of color before her eyes started to fade.

Confident that she would no longer choke to death, she attempted to rise, pushing herself up on one trembling arm. The pain that shot through her body was incredible, but she endured it. Owned it. There hadn't been many days of late when she hadn't had to deal with some form of discomfort. This was just more of the same, only much, much worse.

Through bleary eyes she looked into a thick, roiling haze of heavy dust and dirt. The library had imploded and the old science building had collapsed. It was deathly quiet on the campus, and she wondered if her plan to trap their attackers had actually been successful. Had the Nephilim managed to dodge yet another bullet?

She cleared her throat, and again called out for Dusty. Her voice sounded frighteningly weak, and she considered the damage done to her health by her extensive expenditure of Archon magick.

Lorelei had a sense that it wasn't good.

Looking to where the science building had been, she caught sight of some movement within the smoky haze, and immediately felt a sense of relief.

"Dusty," she called out, pushing herself into a sitting position. It was going to take a little more time for her to get to her feet. "Hey, Dusty. Over here."

That awful tickle was in her throat again, and she started to cough. The sight of blood speckling her hand was both terrifying and relieving. She'd been expecting something bad like this for quite some time, and now here it was. She wiped the blood on the leg of her pants, her attention returning to the shape that approached.

As it grew closer, she realized that it wasn't Dusty. Whoever it was had wings.

Terrible black wings.

A spell of defense sprang quickly to mind, but as she attempted to call upon it, her body was racked with incredible agony. It just didn't have anything left to give the magick; she was spent.

Defenseless.

But then Lorelei's fear turned to surprise, then to absolute joy.

Lucifer Morningstar stood before her, and he was smiling.

"It's you," she said, starting to laugh, tears of happiness running from her eyes. "You had us—me—worried sick."

Lucifer did not answer but knelt upon the grass beside her.

"Where have you . . . ?"

And then, with a sick feeling twisting in her belly, Lorelei realized that the armor that adorned his body was not only filthy with dust and dirt, but it was totally black.

The realization was an awful thing as she remembered her horrible foe from inside the library.

"You're not him, are you?" she said, looking into the eyes of her dearest friend, and seeing nothing there but darkness.

Leaning in close, the imposter put his arm around her back and pulled her fragile form to his chest. She tried to struggle, but his touch . . . It was as if all the fight had been taken from her.

In his free hand a knife of black fire formed, and he seemed to take great pleasure in showing this to her.

"What have you done to Lucifer?" Lorelei implored with desperation.

"Shhhhhhhhhhhhhhhhhhhhhhh," the imposter whispered as he leaned in close to her ear.

Before plunging the dagger of shadow straight into her heart.

Satan looked deeply into the magick user's eyes as the blade went into her chest.

He wanted to watch her die, to watch the light go out.

But most especially he wanted the Morningstar—wherever he might be lurking inside his skull—to see.

"You are only the first of your kind to die," he whispered, watching as the woman's face grew slack, the color gently leaving her skin.

How fragile and weak these Nephilim are, he thought as he let her body slump to the ground. The air around the location felt suddenly different, barriers of magick crashing down now that the caster of the spells was no more. Satan was gleeful. Now others who had decided to recognize his dark divinity could follow him here.

It was madness to think that the Nephilim actually stood a chance.

Satan rose to his feet, wishing away his knife before reshaping the stuff of darkness into his foreboding helmet. Placing the helmet over his head, he turned to the beasts gathered around him. They were waiting for his commands.

"Take them down," he said, gesturing to the other buildings. "And if you find anyone alive, bring them to me."

Dusty hadn't even been conscious, but the Instrument had managed to take hold of a part of his brain, and stir it to action. He came awake as he lurched across the school property, moving toward the sword. His mind was filled with chaos, and he wished that he could be knocked out again, the chaos was so painful to endure.

What happened? Where's Lorelei? he wondered, and tried to stop to find her, but the Instrument would not let him deviate from his task.

The Instrument was in complete control of his actions, and there wasn't a thing that he could do to stop it. Dusty wasn't strong enough. He had always suspected that, but was too stubborn to admit it, even now.

He tried again to stop, to search for his friend, but the Instrument screamed inside his head, telling him that there wasn't time for that, that Lorelei had met her fate and—

Wait. Met her fate?

Dusty fought the pull of the holy weapon.

What do you mean, 'met her fate'?

The giant sword thrummed in the ground before him, vibrating so quickly that the sight of it was nothing more than a blur. The Instrument willed him closer, and he could not fight it, or the multitude of images that flooded his mind— amongst them, Lorelei's fate.

"No," Dusty whispered, not wanting to see it. He felt his strength leave him as he witnessed her murder at the hands of their armored foe. Legs moving entirely under the sword's control, he continued to shamble, zombielike, toward the vibrating weapon. Dusty wasn't even aware of the danger he was in, until it was too late.

The shadow flowed across the grass toward him and the weapon like an oil slick. Dusty had just enough time to turn his eyes to the sky to see what had passed overhead, before the gout of flame poured down from above.

It was a dragon.

As crazy as it sounded, a dragon flew in the sky above Dusty, and it spit fire at the sword.

Instinctively his arms went up, shielding his face as the blast of fire hit the weapon, engulfing it, and causing it to explode.

The Instrument exploded into millions of flying pieces, the force of it hurling Dusty backward across the property as shrapnel rained down all around him.

Lying there upon the ground, Dusty was shocked to be still alive, never mind conscious, and felt his body begin to violently shake, mirroring the Instrument.

He raised his arms. His clothes were shredded, and his skin was slick with blood. With growing horror Dusty looked at the pieces of the Instrument that were now protruding from his body.

And each and every piece was vibrating.

CHAPTER TWENTY-THREE

Aaron returned to the Saint Athanasius School and Orphanage, the stink of death heavy in his nostrils.

He hadn't been back more than seconds when the explosion occurred, clouds of thick, noxious smoke mixed with dust forming a mushroom cloud in the air.

Aaron flew toward the explosion with all the speed that he could, a fist of dread gripping his heart.

Whatever had happened, it had happened at the science building.

Vilma hoped the sound had been thunder, but quickly came to realize that it was not as her eyes fell upon the roiling cloud of smoke.

Cameron appeared beside her, a sword already in hand.

"Are we under attack again?" he asked, eyes fixed upon the black smoke in the distance.

Vilma was about to answer, when Melissa appeared in a flutter of wings and the heavy smell of divine fire.

"What's happening?" she asked, fear and urgency in her voice.

"I think we've been attacked," Cameron answered.

Vilma realized something at once. "Where's Verchiel?" she asked.

Melissa looked around. "He isn't here?"

There was another flash close by, and Melissa tensed as she summoned her own blade, but it was Gabriel, his fur flecked with golden fire.

"Lorelei?" he asked in his doggy grumble.

"We were just about to go and look for her," Vilma answered, just as something enormous appeared in the sky, flying overhead.

"Get down," she ordered, and they crouched low, using the dormitory building as cover.

"How did a dragon get in here?" Melissa asked.

It was worse than Vilma had thought.

They all recoiled in horror as the great dragon opened its mouth and began to belch gouts of fire.

Gabriel growled, staring intensely into the sky at the great beast.

He then turned his gaze to Vilma's.

"I'll check that out," he volunteered, and before she could even answer him, the dog was gone in a flash of holy fire.

"He's changed," Melissa said, staring worriedly at the spot where the dog had been.

Vilma was going to agree with her, before telling them that they were heading over to the science building, when they heard the scream.

It was as if somebody were having their very soul torn from their body.

And she knew that the scream had come from Aaron.

The first thing Aaron saw was the smoldering pile of rubble where the science building used to be. Concrete, wood, and metal beams condensed into one intensely concentrated pile, as if it had all been pulled toward the center where the building had once stood.

The air was still thick with particulate, but his keen eyes scanned the area for any signs of life. And in an area of grass, just beyond where the concrete walkway to the building would have been, he found her body.

Pulling his wings tight to his body, Aaron dropped from the air to the ground in a run.

"Lorelei," he called out, watching for any sign of movement, but she lay there incredibly still. "Lorelei, please . . ."

He knew that she was gone before he even reached her. Any hint of her life force—that which made her Nephilim— was completely absent from her body.

"No," he said, falling to his knees by her side. He didn't know what to do, repeating "no" over and over again. Without thinking he reached down and took her into his arms, hoping that somehow he was wrong.

But he wasn't.

Lorelei was dead.

"Oh, God," he said, his voice shaking with emotion, and he meant it. *Oh, God, how could You let this happen to her?* Aaron held his dearest friend tightly in his arms, rocking back and forth as he buried his face in the crook of her neck and screamed his anguish.

He sensed them even though they hadn't made a sound. Their very presence was like a blight, a black stain upon the very fabric of life.

Aaron lifted his face from his dead friend's neck to see that he was surrounded. He knew most by species: trolls, goblins, demons, and wraiths, for he had ended many of their kind's lives. And some he knew simply as monsters, one-of-a-kind aberrations that sprang from the darkness during these turbulent times.

But it didn't really matter what they were called, only that they were here and were responsible for the death of someone that he'd cared about very deeply.

Someone who had been helping him save the world . . . someone who was now gone.

They knew that he saw them, but there was no fear, their

courage bolstered by the fact that they had killed one of his number.

Aaron was gently placing Lorelei's body back down upon the ground, when they attacked as one. There was actually very little thought on Aaron's part, a sword of fire—quite possibly the largest and most severe blade he had ever manifested—was there for him as he leaped to his feet, wings lifting him just high enough so that he might dispatch the monsters with ease.

It was almost too easy. Their movements seemed to be in slow motion. They struck at him in places where he had been but wasn't anymore. Aaron showed no mercy, taking their heads and their limbs, making their deaths as excruciating as possible before allowing them the mercy of oblivion.

They were all dead even before he realized. He actually felt a certain level of disappointment that there weren't more of them, for he still had so, so much more anger left.

For a moment he was able to step outside his rage, and he saw that the bodies of the monsters had fallen upon his deceased friend. He quickly jumped to remedy the situation. He was dragging the bodies, and pieces of bodies from atop and near Lorelei, when the sky above him grew inexplicably dark.

Aaron raised his gaze skyward, to see that there was a dragon now above him, its serpentine neck rearing back—its awful mouth agape—as it prepared to vomit flaming death upon him.

His first instinct was to protect his friend, to lift Lorelei's body, to move it somewhere safe before . . .

But there wasn't enough time, and the dragon released a blast of its flaming venom. The unnatural fire engulfed Aaron and the grounds around him. The pain was excruciating, and he felt his friend's body disintegrate within his grasp, his impressive wingspan barely providing him with enough protection to survive the burning onslaught.

Lorelei's ashen remains slipped through his fingers as Aaron opened his wings to face this latest horror. The dragon had dropped to the ground, its yellow eyes fixed upon him as it readied to unleash another blast of its incendiary breath.

Aaron tensed, bringing his wings about him, not sure if he could survive another blast, but he was ready to fight nonetheless.

The dragon's mouth had opened to spew its fiery poison, when deliverance came from the sky.

Vilma was the first to attack, swooping hawklike upon her reptilian prey, her divine blade slashing across its face.

What a sight she is, Aaron thought. But also a force to be reckoned with.

A force to fear, especially for those who served the darkness.

Melissa and Cameron joined the fray, flying about the dragon's head, distracting it.

Aaron was about to help them, when he was overcome with an odd sensation. Turning from the dragon battle, he saw an armored figure watching him.

"Hello, Aaron," the figure said, his voice muffled by the helmet he wore. "It's about time that we met."

Somehow Aaron knew that this was the one that the goblin had praised, the one who the goblins thought would lead their filthy kind to victory over the forces of light.

This was the Darkstar. And, yes, it was time that they met.

Gabriel appeared not far from where the Instrument had originally pierced the ground, the blackened earth still burning from the dragon's attack.

Turning his nose to the air, the dog sniffed, but he couldn't find a trace of the giant weapon.

The dog was confused. *Where could something that big have possibly gone?*

He could not locate the sword, but he did smell something else—blood. And he knew that it belonged to Dusty.

Gabriel launched into action, barking wildly, hoping that Dusty would be able to respond. He placed his nose to the charred surface of the ground, to track the scent to his friend.

There. The metallic smell filled his senses, and he was off, following the trail into a more heavily wooded area.

Gabriel was growing concerned. He could no longer sense the magickal barriers that had protected the school, and he became all the more worried for Lorelei's safety.

But that concern was quickly replaced by another. He saw Dusty's limp and bleeding body being dragged through the dirt toward a patch of shadows beneath a thicket of heavy leaves and flowers.

"Stop!" Gabriel barked, allowing his angelic transformation to overtake him.

Whatever had been tugging Dusty's body stopped at his command. Gabriel waited to see what would emerge from the gloom.

He wasn't sure exactly what they were, but he had seen pictures of something similar in one of Lorelei's many books. Gabriel believed they were called wood sprites, small creatures with spindly limbs that appeared to be made from tree branches.

The sprites circled Dusty's prone form, their bark-covered faces stained red with blood. It appeared that they were already sampling their prey.

"Will you leave your quarry and go along your way?" Gabriel asked them.

The creatures looked at one another and laughed, high pitched and filled with madness. They charged at Gabriel, baring jagged teeth of petrified wood.

Gabriel had known that would be their response, but he had wanted to give them a chance.

Before having to kill them all.

CHAPTER TWENTY-FOUR

Y ou're the Darkstar," Aaron said, creating a weapon in his hand.

"My reputation precedes me," the armored figure answered, a blade manifesting within his grasp as well.

They faced each other, no more than six or seven feet apart. Behind him Aaron could hear the battle between the Nephilim and the dragon, but he dared not take his eyes from the armored figure. There was something about this one, this Darkstar, that warned him to be at his best, and his most deadly.

"Black fire," Aaron said, staring at his opponent's crackling ebony blade.

"Do you like it?" the armored one asked. "I could give it to you." He held the blade aloft. "Through the heart . . . just like the lovely Lorelei."

Aaron flinched at the mention of his friend's name, his divine sword sparking noisily in his grasp.

"That's right," the Darkstar said. "I was the one to snuff out the light in her eyes. I watched it go, so bright and filled with hope one moment, then so dark as she realized the truth about it all."

Aaron knew what his foe was doing, pushing his buttons to get him to act recklessly, but he managed to hold himself together.

Barely.

"All this fighting . . . it was for nothing," the Darkstar continued.

Aaron simmered with fury, but he needed to stay calm, focused. To go off half-cocked now wasn't going to do anyone any good.

"Did I mention that she cried out your name as I slid the knife blade up under her ribs and into her beating heart?"

It was like somebody had set a bomb off inside Aaron's head, obliterating his rational self. He sprang into the air, powerful flaps of his wings sending him colliding into his enemy.

"I guess I didn't," the Darkstar said, and laughed, a throaty, cheerful sound that just inflamed Aaron's rage all the more.

Aaron swung his sword, aiming to sever his adversary's helmeted head from his shoulders, but the Darkstar was incredibly fast, taking to the air carried by wings as black as Aaron's own.

Fueled by fury, Aaron pursued his foe into the sky above

the school. The Darkstar turned, maneuvering with amazing facility, striking out with his blade of dark fire.

Aaron yelled as the sword sliced across the upper part of his arm with an icy numbness.

Through gritted teeth Aaron glanced at the wound, but kept his focus on his opponent as he came round for another pass. The cold sensation was spreading, and Aaron placed his hand over the nasty gash, willing it filled with angel fire to cleanse and cauterize the wound.

Flames filled his palm, and the air stank with the smell of roasting meat. Aaron grimaced with pain, but quickly moved past it to face the Darkstar before him.

The Darkstar was at him again, and Aaron swung his sword. There was a flash as the two blades connected, and the Darkstar reared back, examining a tear in the shoulder of his armor.

"Excellent," he hissed, seeming to enjoy the combat.

Thrusting with his powerful wings, the Darkstar came at Aaron again, but the Nephilim didn't flinch. Instead he began a charge of his own.

Aaron wasn't sure what he expected. One of them to veer off at the last possible second? A game of chicken played by angelic beings? But Aaron had no intention of changing course.

And neither did the Darkstar.

The two struck in midair, the force of their collision creating a sound like a clap of thunder. They grappled, quarters too close for their swords to be effective.

So the weapons of choice became knives.

Aaron was at a disadvantage, his body unarmored. The Darkstar thrust and slashed with blades of black, his moves wild, eager, and Aaron waited for opportunities to present themselves, focusing his attacks upon the joints of his opponent's ebony armor.

Each cut and stab of the Darkstar's black blade stole away more of Aaron's body warmth. He tried to ignore it, tried to wait for that perfect opportunity as he parried and blocked the more deadly of his foe's attempts.

Aaron thrust back and away from his opponent's lunge, bringing one of his wings down upon the Darkstar's arm as he stabbed at Aaron with one of his black daggers. The force of Aaron's blow caused the weapon to fall from his enemy's grasp. Aaron saw the opportunity he'd been waiting for, and he reacted.

With a cry of rage he reached for the Darkstar. The Darkstar tried to evade him, but Aaron was too fast, grabbing hold of the freezing cold metal of the Darkstar's armor, willing the fire of Heaven into his hands.

"Do you feel it?" Aaron asked through gritted teeth.

The Darkstar did not reply, and Aaron held on, letting the fire flow. The fire attacked the armor, the force of Heaven battling its dark opposite.

The Darkstar's armor began to crack, ragged holes appearing in his shell. His struggles intensified, but Aaron held on, tainting the Darkstar's shield with the fires of divinity.

An armored fist savagely struck his face, and Aaron's mouth filled with the metallic taste of blood. Another blow landed on his head, and Aaron himself began to slip from consciousness, but he managed to pull himself from the brink, remembering that this was the one who had killed Lorelei.

Fists engorged with the fire of God, Aaron struck again and again against the black armor. Burning fissures spider-webbed across the ebony surface of his foe's bodily protection.

"Do you feel it now?" Aaron asked the Darkstar, striking wherever the armor appeared weakest.

The Darkstar flapped his black wings wildly in an effort to get away, but Aaron stuck to him like a tick. Aaron knew that this would be his only chance to take his enemy down.

Aaron's eyes locked upon those glaring out at him from behind the black helmet.

Was that fear he saw there?

Aaron experienced a sudden surge of strength, as if somehow feeding upon his enemy's uncertainty, and lashed out with his burning fists, connecting once, twice, three times with the Darkstar's covered face. The helmet cracked and started to smolder in places, and Aaron continued to strike at it, eager to reveal the monster behind it.

The Darkstar grabbed hold of Aaron's throat with sudden, deadly speed and began to squeeze.

"A taste of your own medicine," he growled from behind his broken mask.

Aaron fought to breathe as a cloud of numbing shadow engulfed his face and head. It was like being wrapped in a nightmare. The black fire did not burn as it flowed up into his nose and squirmed between his lips and down his throat. But it stole the heat from his body.

As the fire of Heaven burned away the sin of evil, *this* fire consumed the life-giving warmth of love and hope.

It ate the soul.

Thoughts of the end of all life filled Aaron's mind, and he began to wonder what exactly he was fighting for. It seemed so pointless. The harder he fought—the harder the Nephilim all fought—the further they seemed from victory.

The darkness was winning. Maybe this was the time to finally admit the truth: The Nephilim couldn't fight the coming tide.

Maybe it would be easier to let the darkness win.

Maybe.

Or maybe not.

The darkness inside him squirmed against the divine fire. The black tried to suffocate the glow of Heaven, but the divine fire would not have it.

The darkness tried to show the fire all the death and misery that had come as a result of its struggle, but the holy fire would not be swayed. This was but the price to keep the light of the divine burning.

To keep the forces of darkness at bay.

The darkness surged in a last-ditch effort to envelope the light, but the light of life spurned these advances. It shone brighter and brighter still, burning the creeping shadow from its domain.

Aaron's cold and nearly lifeless body began to glow like the sun. The fire of God rushed through his veins and out his pores, encircling his body in an aura of divine brilliance.

Aaron watched as the Darkstar spiraled from the sky. He could see that his enemy's armor had been practically eaten away. Left behind was a pale, naked man shivering upon the ground.

Descending like an emissary of the sun, Aaron approached his fallen foe, who knelt, face buried in his hands, shivering.

"Please," the Darkstar said softly.

The thought of this thing asking for mercy refueled Aaron's anger. He brought forth a sword.

"Please, Aaron," the Darkstar begged pathetically, and Aaron readied his burning blade to strike.

The Darkstar slowly turned his frightened gaze to him, and Aaron froze as he looked upon his opponent's face, the face of the one who threatened to bring darkness to the world.

The face of the one who had taken his friend's life.

The face of the Morningstar, his father.

Vilma clutched the hilt of her sword of fire and descended toward the fearsome dragon.

This is how it's supposed to be. This is why I'm here, why I'm Nephilim.

The dragon had panic in its large yellow eyes, and looked as though it were going to attempt escape. But Cameron flew down past the spew of burning venom to slice at one of the dragon's leathery wings, taking away its ability to fly.

Melissa targeted the areas underneath its thick armorlike scales, beneath its chin, and around the primordial animal's eyes, where its flesh was unprotected.

In a way Vilma felt sorry for the great beast. It had probably never dealt with Nephilim before.

But then she saw her opportunity. If she remembered Lorelei's lessons correctly, the weakest spot on a dragon was the inside of its cavernous mouth. The flesh was soft, and through it was the best access to the beast's tender brain.

Seemed simple enough.

Yeah, right.

Melissa and Cameron circled the now grounded beast; it fluttered its injured wing, gazing in rage at the rips and tears caused by the Nephilim's weapons. It opened its mouth to spit death at its attackers.

Those two are something to behold, Vilma thought as the two Nephilim flew about the dragon's head, building its anger and causing its caution to slip.

That was what Vilma needed to make her approach. She paced her attack, eyes locked upon her target.

Waiting.

Melissa zipped past the beast's face and sliced one of its eyes.

The dragon tossed back its head in a cry that propelled a plume of fire at least twenty feet into the air.

Vilma drew her wings to her body and dropped like a stone toward the monstrous animal. She knew, through Lorelei's teaching, that the dragon needed some time for the flammable venom to collect within the glands inside its cavernous mouth.

The dragon continued to rage. As the fire began to diminish, Vilma made her move, flying into the dragon's open mouth.

Vilma didn't want to be inside the beast any longer than she needed to be. It stank like death and gasoline within the monster's maw. At the back of its mouth, just behind its rows of yellow, razor-sharp teeth, she watched as two balloons of flesh filled with the volatile poison.

The tongue upon which she stood flexed and writhed beneath her feet as the great reptile registered that something was inside its mouth. A bellow of surprise came flowing up from the back of the dragon's throat, stinking of powerful stomach acids. The scent of its last feast passed across Vilma in a fetid breeze. She knew she needed to act, and get the job done before . . .

The swollen venom sacks began to quiver, preparing to empty. Vilma took her sword of fire, blade pointing toward the roof of the dragon's mouth, and thrust with all her might through the thick cartilage and up into the monster's brain.

Vilma immediately felt the dragon convulse. Its mouth

began to open in a final death scream, and she sprang across the fleshy tongue and flew out from between its wailing jaws, a stream of igniting venom following her out into the open.

Outflying the fire, she spun in the air and watched as the dragon collapsed in a twitching heap upon the school grounds. She heard Melissa's and Cameron's cries of victory, and was giving them the thumbs-up when she caught sight of something not far from where she hovered.

Flying closer, she saw Aaron and what appeared to be Lucifer. Lucifer's arms were outstretched, as if pleading with her boyfriend.

Begging for help.

She watched as Aaron approached, his weapon disappearing.

Then something distracted her, something that chilled her to the very bone. All around the edge of the forest crouched monsters of every conceivable size and shape.

As if waiting for something to happen.

The words were pouring from her mouth before she even realized she was speaking.

"Aaron, watch out—something isn't right!"

No truer words had ever been spoken.

His father was begging him for help. . . . How could Aaron not go to him?

Aaron stepped toward the Morningstar, wishing his sword away as his brain was overrun with a million questions: *Where have you been? What happened to you? Why did you kill Lorelei?*

Lucifer beckoned, and Aaron began to kneel.

"Aaron," his father began, his head bowed weakly. But something in his voice made the hairs on the back of Aaron's neck stand at attention.

The Morningstar raised his face to look at Aaron, and smiled, his eyes filled entirely with darkness. That was when the Nephilim noticed the shadows. They flowed all around them and covered his father's body.

Forming new armor.

Every instinct screamed as Aaron's wings unfurled from his back.

From somewhere above he heard Vilma's cry, and was glad to know that she was safe.

"Aaron, watch out—"

He sprang from the ground as his father—clad again in glistening black armor—came at him, a sword of ebony fire in his hand.

"Something isn't right," was the last thing that Aaron heard as his father's sword struck him. He tried to bring about his own weapon, but he wasn't fast enough.

Aaron watched in horrified fascination as the black blade pierced the flesh of his stomach. The cold was all-encompassing, freezing every aspect of his being as he gazed between the sword protruding from his body and the grinning face of the one who wielded it.

"A savior no more," said a voice that did not belong to his father, and the blade drove deeper.

Aaron could do nothing as the numbness spread through him. He slid from the sword blade to fall upon the ground. In his mind a voice screamed at him to get up—to fight—but no matter how hard he tried, his body would not answer.

Aaron felt himself slipping away, sinking deeper and deeper into the cold darkness, as he realized the truth of what had finally happened.

The battle was over. . . . They had lost.

And darkness took him by the hand and led him down into oblivion.

CHAPTER TWENTY-FIVE

Vilma felt a part of herself die.

She'd yelled to warn Aaron, but Lucifer had been too fast.

All she could do was watch as the blade was thrust into his body. Vilma screamed, hoping that it was all a horrible nightmare and that the louder she screamed, the quicker she would wake up.

But she wasn't asleep. It was all really happening.

And there was nothing that she could do.

"Like hell," she wailed, an anger the likes of which she had never known burning through her body. At that moment her human side completely gave way to the angelic—the warrior inside her.

Empowered by the wrath of God, Vilma descended upon the scene, a spear of divine fire taking shape in her hand.

Below, the armored Lucifer raised his weapon of shadow again, preparing to bring it down upon the helpless Aaron's skull.

Vilma let her spear fly, and the flaming javelin imbedded itself in the ground between Lucifer and Aaron.

Lucifer started to back away just as the spear exploded, setting a line of fire in the earth before him.

Vilma landed in a crouch beside the man she loved.

"Aaron," she called, praying for some kind of response, but he was silent. The blood that stained his lower body made her swoon.

"Oh, my God, Aaron."

"He isn't listening," came a voice from behind the wall of divine fire. Vilma glanced up to see Lucifer's armored figure striding through the lapping flames toward her. "You can call for Him all you want, but He will not answer. God has left this place. He's left this place to me."

Hands beneath Aaron's arms, Vilma attempted to drag him away. This could not be Lucifer but something somehow wearing his form. And he was coming closer, with a legion of monsters at his back.

He stopped, smiling as he looked at the fire that surrounded them, the stink of death hanging heavy in the air.

"Surrender to me now, and I promise to make your end swift," the imposter said.

"You can go to Hell," she spat.

"Too late," he replied. "Already there."

Their adversary spread his wings and flew at her. Vilma barely had enough time to call upon her own weapon as she prepared to defend herself and Aaron.

There suddenly came a spray of foul-smelling liquid, and a thick viscous fluid rained down upon the armored figure and his monstrous soldiers. Vilma jumped back, grabbing Aaron beneath his arms and pulling him away as well. She looked skyward to see Melissa and Cameron flying overhead, dumping liquid from two fleshy sacks onto their foes.

Vilma suspected that she knew what they had done, and that suspicion was verified when the liquid exploded into flames. Melissa and Cameron had removed the dragon's venom sacks and spilled their incendiary contents onto the Nephilim's enemies. Not only did the imposter burn, but so did the monsters that had been awaiting their opportunity to pounce.

Vilma dragged Aaron away from the volatile dragon fire. Melissa was the first to land to help her, followed by Cameron.

"Is he all right?" Melissa desperately wanted to know, bending over beside the unconscious Aaron. "Vilma? He doesn't look so good. We should—"

Vilma had to think quickly. With Aaron incapacitated, she had to take the reins.

"We don't have any time," she interrupted, glancing toward the wall of flames and the silhouettes that thrashed within them. "You need to get out of here."

There was a crackle of energy beside them, and Vilma spun toward it with a knife of fire at the ready. Cameron and Melissa were ready to fight as well.

But it was Gabriel. He held Dusty's bloody hand gently in his mouth, so that they could travel together.

Vilma gasped at Dusty's condition. Everything that they'd worked so tirelessly to achieve was all falling apart.

"Did you find Lorelei?" Vilma asked, forcing aside her escalating panic.

Gabriel did not respond, his dark eyes fixed upon the body of his master.

"Gabriel, listen to me!" Vilma cried.

The dog's eyes shifted to hers.

"No, just Dusty," the Labrador said, his canine voice trembling. His eyes shifted back to Aaron.

Vilma had no idea what had happened to Lorelei, but seeing Dusty, she doubted that it was anything good.

"We have to get out of here," Vilma said, again looking toward the fire. It was only a matter of time before the monsters reassembled.

"Where?" Cameron asked.

"We need to split up," Vilma said. "Make it difficult for them to follow us."

"But where should we go?" Melissa asked, nearly in a panic.

"Someplace safe," Vilma said. "Dig deep into your memories. There has to be a place from sometime in your life, before all of this, where you felt absolutely safe, where nobody could touch you."

She looked at them all, making sure that they truly heard her.

"That's where you need to go."

"What about you? What about Aaron?" Gabriel asked.

"Don't worry about us," she said, scanning the fire. The armored figure who had wounded Aaron had manage to douse most of the flames on his armored body, and was rising to come at them.

"You need to go," she said.

Cameron started to protest.

"Now!" she screamed.

From the look on Cameron's face, he didn't like it. None of them did, but they didn't argue. Cameron wrapped his wings about himself and disappeared.

Melissa prepared to do the same. It looked as though she wanted to say something, but words seemed too hard at that moment, and instead she blinked out of sight after Cameron.

"I'll see you again," Gabriel growled, leaning his mouth down toward Dusty's hand. *"Promise me you'll do everything you can to keep Aaron alive."*

"I promise," Vilma said.

With that the Labrador took Dusty's hand in his mouth. His body at once began to glow, sparks of fire flying from his yellow fur, and then they too were gone.

Vilma watched the armored figure clomp across the scorched earth, beckoning to her with an outstretched hand. Lucifer's face had been severely burned, but she could see that it was already healing.

"This is done, Nephilim," the imposter said in a wheezing voice, vocal cords raw from the heat of dragon's fire. "Surrender your life to me and know peace."

Peace, Vilma thought, taking Aaron's body in her arms. She needed to go someplace where she had known peace. Someplace where she had been loved. Somewhere she'd felt safe, before the darkness had fallen and nightmares had become reality.

Vilma flexed her wings, bringing them around to take her and her love into their embrace. Vilma wondered if that place could still exist.

She hoped with all her heart that it did.

Lucifer was falling.

Deep within his psyche the Son of the Morning felt all the misery that the Darkstar had inflicted.

Lucifer had managed to hold on until now. Bombarded with memories of his past, the enormity of his failures, he'd been buoyed by the belief that there was the slight chance at redemption.

He needed to find a way to survive and reclaim his body.

But Satan had other plans. The Darkstar wanted Lucifer gone, wanted to leave behind only the memories of Lucifer's terrible acts.

Satan wanted to leave behind what Lucifer had been, not what he had been in the process of becoming.

Satan had made Lucifer watch what he was doing. The Morningstar had felt the murder of Lorelei—*poor, sweet Lorelei.* Lucifer had tried to fight Satan, but it had all been for naught.

It had almost been cause for him to let go, to drift down into the darkness of his psyche until he ceased to be.

But the Morningstar had been determined to remain strong and avenge Lorelei against the dark creature that had taken up residence in his body.

The Morningstar had had hope.

And that's exactly what Satan fed upon.

When Aaron had arrived, Lucifer had thought that was the tipping point he'd been waiting for. His son, their savior and Redeemer, would triumph.

Darkness now closed in tightly around Lucifer, and he fell deeper into its cold embrace. He did not want to remember what Satan had done to his son.

Aaron had been going to save them all. He and his Nephilim had been set to rid the world of darkness.

But the Darkstar had had other plans.

Lucifer pulled the black of oblivion about him like a shroud, not wanting to see—not wanting to remember.

Shuddering in the grip of shadow, he recalled what had been shown to him. What he had been forced to experience.

Lucifer had felt every blow, every searing blast of divine fire, and wished that it had ended the threat of Satan—that it had ended him.

But the creature had lured the boy in close, using the face of the boy's father.

My face.

Lucifer had experienced the horrific sensation of his blade being plunged deeply into the stomach of his son, murdering Aaron Corbet—as if by his hands.

My hands.

It was more than Lucifer could stand, and he retreated deeper into the darkness of his being.

So deep that all would be lost.

As if he'd never existed at all.

The Darkstar closed his eyes and sighed with pleasure as the being once called the Son of the Morning surrendered. *What a glorious sensation it is,* he thought, that much closer to totally possessing the body he had grown so fond of.

It wouldn't be long now.

He felt their eyes upon him, and turned to see the gathering of monsters that had answered his summons and were eager to expunge the last threat to their supremacy.

They had come and born witness to his capability.

Satan felt their beady eyes upon his personage. A part of him still didn't trust these creatures and was waiting for another attack, but there was something in the air of this place, something that told him that things had changed.

The armor of darkness had reformed upon his body, and before his audience's watchful gaze Satan placed the helmet upon his venom-scarred head and gazed at the nefarious multitude. Then he forged a sword as black as pitch and raised it high above his head.

"Hail Satan!" The chant spread through the gathering of beasts.

"Hail Satan!"

At last they recognized their savior.

"Hail Satan!"

He who would give them the world that had once belonged to God's chosen.

"Hail Satan!"

The Darkstar walked amongst them, still holding his blade of night high above his head. As he passed them—the trolls, goblins, wraiths, and demons—they lowered their heads in reverence, dropping to their knees as they were touched by his passing shadow.

He soaked in his conquest. The property that had once belonged to their divine nemeses had been reduced to nothing more than rubble and ash.

This was what he would do to all who opposed him, to all who would try to keep him from making this world his own, from making this world *his* Heaven.

His attention was caught by something near the skeletal remains of a greenhouse. He could not say if it was a scent or something more, but he was drawn to the broad patch of open ground. He knelt. The glove of shadow receded from his hands so that he might touch the dirt with bare fingertips.

He sank his fingers into the cool earth, and was filled with joy that everything was progressing as it was supposed to. There, buried beneath the ground, was a new treasure for his kingdom.

Satan turned to address his minions.

"There are bodies buried here," he announced. "The bodies of our enemies who fell in battle against our forces of darkness."

He turned his gaze back to the flat piece of land. Someone had left mementos to remember those who had been slain.

How touching.

"I want these bodies exhumed," the Darkstar told his followers.

The monsters immediately went to work, the trolls digging with their shovel-like hands, while the others used any makeshift tool that they could find to move the dirt away from the prizes their leader sought.

If this was to be his kingdom, then the Darkstar would need special beings to serve him. Messengers for his most holy word.

Satan watched as the shroud-covered bodies were unearthed from their final resting places.

The Darkstar needed angels of his own.

And now he would have them.

EPILOGUE

Verchiel had no idea where he was.

He'd heard the psychic cry of the Nephilim magick user, and had started back to the school.

But he had ended up here . . . wherever that was.

He was in a place of total darkness, and his divine fire did little to illuminate the thick shadow of his foreign surroundings.

The angel's mind raced. *Can this be some sort of trap generated by the Fear Engine?*

He began to make his way through the stygian gloom, in search of answers.

Or at least something that he could fight.

There wasn't a noise to be heard or a scent to be smelled in this place.

A shudder—*could it be fear?*—raced down his spine as he

recalled the nothingness after his defeat at the hands of the Nephilim Redeemer.

Was he somehow back in that oblivion?

Verchiel continued to move forward, his every sense on full alert.

The sudden sound of voices in the oppressive silence was deafening.

"What if he does not find us?" one of them questioned.

"Then it was not meant to be," answered another.

"The darkness is long and deep," said a third. "Give him time, and he will find us."

Verchiel moved eagerly in the direction of the conversation.

"This one, he knows the darkness?"

"Yes, he knows it."

"And the darkness knows him."

The voices cackled with laughter.

Verchiel had had enough. He willed his body to glow with the power of his inner fire. "Show yourselves!" he commanded.

And the shadows parted, like curtains on a stage, to reveal three hunched and hooded figures.

"You have found us," croaked one.

"As I knew he would," declared another.

"What a beautiful sight to behold," exclaimed the third, extending a clawed hand, but stopping short of the circle of light. "The masters have chosen wisely with this one."

Verchiel bore down upon them, his body still throwing off its awesome radiance.

The three retreated into the shadows.

"Who are you? Who are these masters of which you speak?" Verchiel demanded.

"We? We are nobody," said one.

"Humble servants of a greater power," said another.

"A power that wishes to change the world," said the third as the others nodded their hooded visages in agreement.

Verchiel stepped closer to the odd women. "This power—" he began.

"Your light," interrupted one of them. "Dim your glow, for it blinds those who spend most of their days in shadow."

"Light so bright is not known by eyes such as these."

"It is no wonder that our masters have sought you out."

Verchiel pulled back upon his glow, and watched as the three old crones ambled closer.

"Much better," said one as they all wrung their clawed hands in anticipation.

"You speak of your masters," Verchiel repeated. "Who are they, and why have they brought me here?"

"They designed this world," said one.

"They manipulate the events that will shape the future," said another.

"They are the Architects," revealed the third. "And they wish for you to serve their cause."

Vilma stood in the tiny side yard of her aunt and uncle's home on Belvidere Place in Lynn, Massachusetts, watching the sun disappear from the sky, and the night emerge. She had been here with Aaron for a few days.

There was barely any daylight now.

She thought of all that the Nephilim had been through, and wondered if they'd had any real effect at all. The night was still on the march. She guessed that it wouldn't be long before it was dark all the time.

Her angelic nature stirred, and she realized that she was no longer alone in the yard. Standing on the step leading into the house, her seven-year-old cousin Nicole was watching her.

"Hey, you," Vilma said. "Watcha doin'?"

"Better come inside," the child said, eyes wide and serious. "Before the monsters come and take you."

This was the kind of world that her aunt and uncle and cousins were forced to inhabit. A world that she, and others like her, had tried to make better.

They had failed.

"No monsters will take me," Vilma said, shaking her head. "Or you, if they know what's good for them."

She wanted Nicole to believe that she was safe, but Vilma had seen some of the other houses on the dead-end court, and they were boarded up, some nothing more than burned-out shells. Her aunt had said that things had come when it was fully dark, things that had taken away some of the neighbors, and set fire to their homes.

"You'll punch them?" Nicole asked.

"I'll do worse than that," Vilma said, feeling a sudden over-whelming urge to hug Nicole tightly and never let her go.

The child smiled, and Vilma hoped that the little girl felt safe in her presence.

"Why don't you go inside," Vilma suggested. "I'll be just a minute. I want to check on something."

Vilma turned to the back of the tiny yard as the screen door slammed behind Nicole. Vilma wanted to see how her scarecrows were holding up. Two armored bodies hung from fence posts, flies buzzing around their horrible faces. When she'd first arrived with Aaron, Vilma had found these things very much alive and sniffing around the house, looking for a way to get in. She hadn't been in any mood to deal with their filthy likes, so she'd killed them.

The way the trolls were mounted on the fence, it looked as though they were just hanging out in the yard. It was enough to convince any lesser beastie that this house belonged to the trolls, and to stay away.

Vilma walked the perimeter to make sure that the house was still secure. Most of the windows had been boarded up, and things still looked pretty sturdy. She arrived back at the screen door and tried to turn the knob, but it was locked.

"Good girl," she muttered to herself before knocking.

She had drilled this—and many other precautions—into the minds of her cousins.

The door opened quickly.

"Hurry up inside," Aunt Edna commanded. "It's nearly dark enough for trouble to come around."

Vilma did as she was told, and the older woman closed the door behind her, making sure that all the locks were in place.

Edna turned, and the two women said nothing as they looked at one another, but Vilma could see a discomfort in her aunt's eyes. Edna was like a mother to her, and Vilma's heart ached at the thought that the woman might now be afraid of her.

"Everything all right outside?" Edna asked.

"Yeah," Vilma said. "Everything's fine."

After killing the trolls when she'd first arrived, Vilma had then gathered Aaron in her arms, only to find her aunt standing in the doorway.

Vilma had still been wearing her Nephilim appearance, wings and sword of fire in hand. She had actually considered sending the wings and weapon away, to try to convince the woman that it had all been a trick of the darkness.

But she just hadn't had the strength of mind to do it. Instead Vilma had hoped that she had been right to come to this place, and that her family would keep her safe.

She had been right.

Edna had set up the guest room for the injured Aaron and had helped to clean and bandage his horrible wound. It wasn't till things had settled—as much as that was even possible these days—that Aunt Edna had asked for some kind of explanation.

Considering what she'd had to say, Aunt Edna and Uncle Frank had taken the news quite well. But they were very religious, and saw what was happening in the world as God's way of demonstrating that He wasn't the least bit happy by human behavior.

The concept of the Nephilim didn't seem all that far-fetched to them, especially given that trolls now prowled their backyard.

Vilma hadn't gone into detail but had explained that she and Aaron and their friends were trying to protect humanity from the darkness. Her aunt and uncle had seemed to accept all this, but then Edna had asked Vilma to show Frank her angelic guise.

That had been the first time Vilma had seen this look of apprehension in her aunt's eyes.

"Are you . . ." Vilma hesitated now. "Are you afraid of me?"

Aunt Edna didn't answer, going to the sink and washing her hands. She turned off the water, took a hand towel from the front of the stove, and started to dry her hands. It was if she hadn't heard the question.

"Aunt Edna?" Vilma asked again.

The woman went to the freezer and removed a bag of coffee.

"I'm going to make a pot," she said. "Want some?"

Vilma felt her heart begin to crumble. Was the question so hard to answer? The longer it took for her aunt to reply, the more obvious the answer was.

Edna placed the bag of coffee on the counter and turned to face her niece.

"What do you want me to say?" she asked. "That you terrify us? You don't. But the idea of what you represent, of what that means in regard to God, and what's happening in the world—that scares us quite a bit," she admitted.

Aunt Edna silently cried as she began to make the coffee.

Vilma didn't know how to respond.

"I'm trying to make the world right again," Vilma started to explain. "This is why I'm here—why God put us here. Aaron and I—"

"Aaron is very sick," her aunt interrupted, scooping coffee from the bag. "I'm not even sure if he's going to—"

"He'll be all right," Vilma said, mustering her confidence. "He just needs to rest and heal."

"I changed his bandage not too long ago," Edna said, filling the carafe with water and then carefully pouring it into the machine. "The wound is infected."

"We'll just keep it clean and hope for the best," Vilma said.

"And what if things don't work out?" Edna asked as she flipped the switch on the coffeemaker. "What if he dies?"

Vilma had never let her mind go there. When it started

to, she quickly pushed the bad thoughts away and focused on some other responsibility.

"He won't."

"But what if he does? What about your plans then?" Edna asked.

Vilma did not want to think about a world without Aaron, but she had to consider it.

"We'll go on without him," Vilma said, realizing that there was no choice. "We were put here to save the world, and with or without Aaron, the Nephilim will get the job done."

The coffee machine hissed and gurgled as it brewed.

Aunt Edna looked across the kitchen to the boarded-up window over the sink. "I keep thinking that maybe this is just a horrible nightmare, and that I'll be waking up soon." She looked to Vilma. "Do you ever think like that?"

"I used to," Vilma said. "But then I came to terms with the fact that I had changed, and that the whole world had changed too."

"I don't know if I'll ever get used to it," Aunt Edna said, going to the drying rack by the sink and taking a mug from it. "Or if I want to, really."

She paused, pouring herself a steaming cup of coffee and blowing on the scalding fluid before taking a sip.

"Do you think you can change the world?" Aunt Edna asked as she sat down at the kitchen table. "Do you and your angel friends, your Nephilim, really think you're strong enough to do that?"

Vilma came to the table and sat next to her aunt. "We may be down," she said, taking her aunt's hand in hers, "but we're far from out."

Her aunt squeezed back lovingly. "I could never be afraid of someone who I love so much," Edna said.

Later that night the family spent some time together, playing a game of Clue by lantern light. The electricity had gone out again. It seemed to be happening more frequently, and lasting longer each time. Vilma knew that there was going to be a time in the very near future when the power, like the sun, would be out for good.

Even as they played their game, enjoying each other's company, Vilma listened to the night outside for any signs of danger. But it seemed the scarecrows were doing their job.

After Uncle Frank solved the crime, Vilma's cousins wanted a second game, but Edna proclaimed that it was time for sleep. Vilma helped Nicole and Michael get ready for bed, tucked them in, and went over the plans in case something should get into the house during the night.

They knew to go down to the cellar and hide until it was safe.

With the house quiet Vilma went to sit with Aaron. She had set up an air mattress in the guest room, on the floor beside where Aaron lay.

Sitting by his side, she watched him breathe. His skin

was still deathly pale, and her aunt had been right about the wound. It looked an angry red and was seeping a thick green-tinged fluid. Vilma again considered bringing him to a hospital, but she didn't want to risk exposure.

And besides, what doctors would know how to care for an injured Nephilim?

No, she decided. For now Aaron was fine here, with her and her family. They would take care of him, and if there came a time when they couldn't anymore . . .

She would cross that bridge when she came to it.

Vilma wrapped her fingers around his hand and gave it a loving squeeze.

"Hey," she said to him. "How are you doing?"

She waited a moment for a response. Every night she talked to him, hoping for some sort of reaction, but she had yet to get one.

"Things here are as good as can be expected," she said, running her thumb along the knuckles of his limp hand. "It's still pretty bad out there, and it seems to be getting worse. No pressure, but I sure hope that you're planning on waking up soon. I'd hate to be facing off against this business without you."

Those last words hit her hard, and she felt a lump form in her throat and her eyes fill with tears. *What if he doesn't get better? What if—Heaven forbid—Aaron were to die?* What would that mean for her, the Nephilim . . . the world?

Not only did it scare her to think that she might be forced

to lead what remained of the Nephilim against the rising tide of evil, but just the idea of being without Aaron shattered her heart into a million jagged pieces.

Vilma leaned forward and brought her lips down to his. *Maybe it will be like Sleeping Beauty*, she thought, kissing him tenderly, but there was no magick, other than the love that she felt for him.

That had to count for something.

She sat back on the bed beside him, watching him sleep and wondering where he might be. Vilma started to dose off, and was considering calling it a night, when she heard something.

The noise came from somewhere outside the room. She listened, craning her head, waiting to hear it again. It was a strange whirring sound, like moving parts of a machine.

Leaving the edge of Aaron's bed, she wondered if one of her cousins was up, playing with one of their toys. It wouldn't be the first time. She peered out into the hall, eyes adjusting to the dark.

She almost screamed as a tall figure darted into Michael's room.

Vilma physically reacted, her Nephilim nature roused by the potential for danger. She sprinted down the hallway, a weapon emerging in her hand.

She flung open the door, the light of her sword illuminating the darkness. Instead of one figure in Michael's room, there were three. And they surrounded the boy, who remained blissfully asleep.

The intruders turned their stares to Vilma as she entered. She was startled by their strange appearance. They wore long trench coats, and their short hair was slicked back. Covering their eyes were odd circular goggles.

Vilma cried out Michael's name to try to wake him, but he remained fast asleep as she rushed with her sword of fire.

One of the three drew a weapon from inside his coat, and Vilma aimed her blade for the weapon holder's wrist, but the mysterious figure seemed to disappear. Her blade passed through the air and bit into the wooden floor.

Her target was suddenly on her other side. Before she could follow through with her weapon, Vilma was struck in the chest by what appeared to be a blue bolt of lightning. It pushed her violently back into her cousin's dresser.

Vilma slumped to the floor, head bobbing as she slipped in and out of consciousness. She painfully fought to lift her head. One of the figures loomed over Michael's bed, shining a strange, pulsing light into his face.

Michael remained fast asleep through it all.

"This is not the one," the invader said flatly, turning his goggled eyes to his associates. "There is no sign of angelic dormancy."

Vilma pulled herself together and surged up from the ground with a roar, her powerful wings propelling her across the room before the intruders had the chance to harm the boy.

Her previous attacker attempted to take her out again, but

Vilma was ready and dipped beneath the surge of crackling blue lightning. Vilma summoned another blade of heavenly fire and this time cut her foe's hand from his wrist.

As the hand thumped to the floor, the other two intruders approached from either side of her. Her eye scanned for weapons, but they didn't appear to have any.

Looks could be deceiving.

There was a rapid rush of air as huge wings erupted from their backs. But these weren't wings of bone, flesh, and feathers. These were wings of metal. Vilma heard the click and whir of internal mechanisms as the wings flexed.

It was the sound that had originally brought her out into the hall.

"What are you?" she asked.

Neither answered her question. Instead one of the invaders extended his metal wings with a loud snap, and metal feathers flew toward her like throwing knives.

Vilma reacted quickly, knocking many of the feathers from their targeted path, but she wasn't fast enough to catch all of them.

The projectiles whizzed toward her, and their razor-sharp edges sliced through her clothes and flesh. One buried itself in the meat of her thigh.

Vilma hissed in pain and ripped the metal feather from her leg. The injured intruder had risen from where he'd knelt, clutching his wrist, and the three invaders now encircled her, their wings of metal forming a kind of cage.

"Stand down," one commanded in a voice as mechanical as his wings, but Vilma would hear none of it. She had a household to protect. Twin swords appeared in her grasp and she roared as loudly as she could, taking to the air in the confined space to try to escape the invaders.

One of Vilma's swords sliced across a metallic wing. Sparks flew as she dove above their heads. She landed just before the doorway, but suddenly her eyesight blurred and she could hardly stand. Even flapping her wings had become difficult, and she leaned heavily upon the door frame, and then stumbled backward with a pathetic moan.

Were the feathers coated in poison?

Vilma could hear the mechanized whir as her attackers drew closer. She had to do something, anything, but it was getting harder and harder to remain on her feet.

On all fours she crawled across the hall, horrified as more of the mechanical angels emerged from the kitchen and Nicole's room.

"No," Vilma tried to scream. A sword . . . she needed a sword, but the thought wouldn't come. The fire just fizzled in her grasp.

The sounds of mechanics and heavy footsteps on the wooden floor grew louder behind her, and she was hauled up from the floor by her arms. Vilma struggled, trying to use her wings to bat away her captors, but the beings did not respond, as if the connection between their bodies and their brains had been cut.

The mechanical angels spun her around and dragged her

toward the guest room, where Aaron lay unconscious. Her heart beat rapidly as they dropped her numb body to the floor before his bed.

Vilma managed to lift her head, even though it felt like it weighed two hundred pounds. An older woman, her long raven-black hair streaked with white, sat on the corner of Aaron's bed. Trench-coated, goggle-wearing mechanical angels bustled around Aaron and the woman. The angels shone strange devices that hummed and crackled with unearthly lights upon Aaron's pale body.

"Get away from him!" Vilma cried, fighting to crawl to her feet, but it was a futile battle, and she fell onto her side in a heap.

The woman looked away from Aaron and fixed Vilma in her gaze.

"Calm yourself, Ms. Santiago," the woman said. "I'm not going to hurt Aaron." She looked back at the unconscious young man, taking his hand in hers.

"Who are—?" Vilma began, but she felt the rest of the question slip away before it could leave her mouth.

"What kind of mother would I be to hurt my son?"

Vilma was drifting off, no longer able to fight the drug that coursed through her body.

"Mother?" Vilma slurred, her eyelids so very heavy.

"Yes, dear. I'm his mother," the woman said. "I'm Taylor Corbet, and I've come to save my son."

THE BATTLE LINES HAVE BEEN DRAWN.

ARMAGEDDON IS HERE.

LOOK FOR THE DRAMATIC CONCLUSION TO
THE FALLEN SERIES.

FROM SIMON PULSE • PUBLISHED BY SIMON & SCHUSTER
EBOOK EDITION ALSO AVAILABLE

ABOUT THE AUTHOR

THOMAS E. SNIEGOSKI is the author of more than two dozen novels for adults, teens, and children. His books for teens include *Legacy*, *Sleeper Code*, *Sleeper Agenda*, and *Force Majeure*, as well as the series The Brimstone Network.

As a comic book writer, Sniegoski's work includes *Stupid, Stupid Rat-Tails*, a prequel miniseries to the international hit *Bone*. Sniegoski collaborated with *Bone* creator Jeff Smith on the project, making him the only writer Smith has ever asked to work on those characters.

Sniegoski was born and raised in Massachusetts, where he still lives with his wife, LeeAnne, and their French bulldog, Kirby. Visit him on the Web at www.sniegoski.com.

Don't miss this sneak peek of

THE DARK LIGHT

BY SARA WALSH

There have been strange lights in Crownsville for as long as I've lived here. Lights on the Ridge; lights on the river; lights that seep from the ground and then float to the sky in clouds of colored mist. No one really talked about them. No one really cared.

Until now.

The patrol cars parked on the corner of Birch and Main were the first thing I noticed when I left work that night. After what had happened in the neighboring town of Onaly that morning, I wasn't surprised. But seeing the cops in Crownsville still gave me the creeps.

The second thing I noticed was Rusty, my car, parked with his headlights glaring. I groaned.

"Mia . . . Why did you do that?"

I tried to remember even switching them on, but came up blank. That pretty much summed up my day. It was nine o'clock, which meant Rusty's crappy battery had been draining for three solid hours while I'd waited tables at Mickey's. Having only just liberated him from Reggie West's Motor Repair and Salvage—Rusty's second home—a dead battery was the last thing I needed. Now I would probably be stuck here while Jay waited for me at the Bakers'. Pete, as usual, was nowhere to be found.

I heard the door to Mickey's open and close behind me. As I rummaged through my bag for my keys, Greg, the night manager, stepped onto the sidewalk.

"You left Rusty's lights on," he said, stating the obvious.

"Yeah." I continued digging. Some of the stuff had been in my bag for months: spare socks; a million tissues (mostly used); a cigarette lighter, though I didn't even smoke. I swore to clear the purse out as soon as I got home. I mean, how much crap does a seventeen-year-old really need to carry around?

"And you forgot this," said Greg, passing me my jacket.

"Thanks, Greg." I took it from him with one hand as I pulled out my keys with the other.

"Something on your mind, Mia? You've been twitchy all evening."

I glanced at the cops, parked on the side of the road. "It's the Onaly thing," I said. "Have you heard of anything like this happening before?"

"In these parts? Can't say I have. But someone's taking those kids." He shook his head. "Five gone in six months and all within fifty miles of here."

I didn't need reminding.

The media called them the *Crownsville Kidnappings*, but only one of the boys who'd vanished, seven-year-old Simon Wilkins, had actually lived in town. Crownsville was a hub for the small towns and farms that surrounded it. This was the reason there were more than fifteen hundred students enrolled at school. Occasionally, kids went missing, but everyone knew where they were—Omaha, Kansas City, Sioux Falls. They bailed when they'd had their fill of rural Nebraska. But this wasn't the same thing. The boy who'd vanished from Onaly Crossing this morning was ten years old, the same age as my half brother, Jay, so don't tell me he'd gone looking for a new life in the city.

"I've got jumper cables in the truck if you need them," said Greg.

Which I invariably would. I had no one to blame but myself.

He walked me to the car. I slipped into the driver's seat, patted Rusty's dash—a sacred ritual—and turned the key. The engine wheezed, then roared. It was the best news I'd had all day.

"These old homegrown beauties last a lifetime," said Greg. He slapped Rusty's hood. "See you tomorrow night, Mia."

Dark had fallen thick and fast. By the time I turned off Main Street, I'd switched on my high beams. It was a couple of miles to the Bakers' on rural roads that had seen better days. Having once mangled a rim in a pothole down here, I kept to the speed limit.

I'd gone about a mile when my phone burst into "The Star-Spangled Banner." That meant one thing—my best friend, Miss Willie Burkett. I pulled over to take the call.

"How was work?" she asked. Willie never wasted time with "hello."

"Usual crowd," I replied. "I swear the place is some kind of alternate dimension."

She laughed. "Have you spoken to Pete about this weekend at the lake?"

I cringed. "Haven't seen him yet," I said. In truth, I had no idea where he was. "Wills, I promise I'll talk to him. Just don't expect miracles."

"You *have* to be there, Mia. Andy is definitely coming. This is a chance for you guys to finally get together."

I wasn't so sure. Andy Monaghan was a drop-dead gorgeous senior who drove a black Corvette that came straight from the showroom of his father's dealership. We'd come pretty close to dating a couple of times, but each time something had gotten in the way: Andy's broken leg, his ex-girlfriend moving back into town, me and Seamus McEvoy—a month-long fling I'd rather forget. But now Andy had broken up with his girlfriend, and Willie said he'd been asking about me around school. . . .

"I'll ask Pete as soon as I see him," I said. I picked imaginary lint off my jeans. "But I'm warning you, Wills; he hasn't been around much lately, and I can't leave Jay with this psycho loose on the streets."

"Pete needs to sort his sorry ass out," Willie muttered.

True, but I didn't see that happening any time soon.

I slumped in my seat and turned my head to the window. The lights on Rowe Boulevard were faint in the distance. Across the open fields, the trees that bordered the elementary school were silhouetted against the night sky. I watched their outlines swaying in the breeze, resigned to the fact that I was always the one who had to back out of our plans.

". . . and if he doesn't shape up, I'm gonna speak to Dad about it again."

I realized Willie was still talking.

"Don't you dare," I said, catching the tail end of her threat. A genuine threat. Willie's dad was Crownsville's sheriff.

"It's neglect."

"It's Pete being useless. Totally different."

"I guess." She sighed. "Come over and we can figure something out."

"I can't," I replied. "I've still got to pick up Jay."

Silence followed and I knew we'd strayed into difficult territory. Somewhere along the line, Willie had decided that I had the world's most horrendous life. You couldn't blame her; my dad had abandoned me at birth and my mom was in prison. I'd lived with my grandmother in Des Moines until I was eight. When she died, I was shipped here, to Crownsville, Nebraska, to live with Uncle Pete, my mother's brother. Pete wasn't the most attentive guardian, but things weren't that bad. I pretty much did what I wanted. But it also meant that Jay, who'd lived with us for the past six years, had no one to worry about him but me. I wasn't afraid to step up to the plate and take care of Jay. I was an honors student, had a 4.3 GPA, played volleyball and soccer, and still waitressed three shifts a week. I was doing fine.

Resigned to Willie's lecture, I stared out of the window.

And then the light caught my eye.

At first, I dismissed it, thought maybe it was the beam from a flashlight. I was parked on Route 6, and the light was far out, somewhere on the open land between me and Rowe. It was hazy in the faint glow of Rowe's streetlights, but definitely there.

I rolled down the window for a closer look, squinting through the darkness. The beam had widened, and I was sure I saw pastel shades in the light.

"You there, Mia?"

"Yeah," I said, though, of course, I wasn't. Whatever was out there had my full attention. It was like a reflection in one of those crazy mirrors at the State Fair—you expect to see reality, but what you get is indistinct and unreal. "Willie, I'll call you back."

"You're pissed at me."

"Course not." I watched, mesmerized. "I'll call you back."

Hanging up the phone, I stepped out of the car. The light danced in the breeze, the colors deepening. Red and blue and gold, the shades were vibrant against the surrounding silvery mist.

As I tried to rationalize what I was seeing, maybe fireworks or marsh gas, my peripheral vision caught a shadow low to the ground. A *moving* shadow, close to the light. It drifted to the left and, suddenly free of the light's glare, took form. It was a figure, hooded and cloaked, though I knew it must be a trick of the eye; there had been nothing but the light a second ago. Alone on a deserted road, with who knew what out there in the fields, I backed up to Rusty.

The moon broke free of the drifting clouds.

And then they were gone.

The light. The shape. They both vanished.

Mildly spooked, I climbed back into the car. Whatever had been out there wasn't there now. It was just the same old fields. The same old lights on Rowe. Still, I locked the door behind me.

By the time I reached the Bakers' to pick up Jay, I'd banished the incident into the "crazy story to tell Willie" category. Mrs. Baker answered the door with the widest smile I'd seen in days. She always made me feel welcome. Shrieks and screams came from somewhere inside the house.

"They're slaughtering orcs in the living room," she said. "Come on through."

I headed in to find Jay and his best friend, Stacey Ann, sprawled on the rug, Wii control pads clutched in their hands. Both turned when I entered, Stacey staring through those horrific glasses that magnified her eyes to twice their natural size, Jay brushing his wild mop of curly hair from his face. Picture any painting of a cherub. That's Jay Stone. Right down to the chubby baby cheeks and wide puppy-dog eyes. It's clear we only shared a father; my hair was chocolate brown, Jay's was more creamy caramel.

I got a chirpy "Hi, Mia," from Stacey Ann and a long groan from Jay.

"I love you, too," I said. "Time to lock and load."

As Jay packed up his Wii, Mrs. Baker saw me back to the door. "Thanks again for watching him," I said. "Pete . . ."

I paused. What could I say? That Pete was probably off drinking again, infecting the world with his soul-sapping outlook on life, when he'd known I'd had to work? Or that I'd arrived home from school to find Jay alone again at the house with the door unlocked? And Onaly Crossing less than a ten-minute drive on the highway . . .

"I just don't like leaving him alone with—"

Mrs. Baker put her hand to my arm. "He's welcome here, Mia. Anything you need. Any time. Just call."

I offered her a relieved smile. "Thanks."

Jay burst into the hallway with Stacey Ann glued to his side. "Ready," he said.

I grabbed him in a headlock, then marched him through the yard to the car. Rusty started on the first turn.

"That isn't why it starts, you know," said Jay, his feet up against the dashboard.

"I don't know what you mean," I replied, innocently.

"That stupid tapping thing you do. It's just a *car*."

I revved the engine, grinning ear to ear. "Hasn't failed me yet."

"Yet," said Jay. He waved to Stacey Ann as we pulled away.

By the time we arrived home, I was ready to call it quits. Only homework waited on my desk. Jay had other plans. We'd no sooner entered the kitchen than the Wii was out of his pack.

"Hold on one minute," I said. "Homework."

"Did it at Stacey Ann's."

I'd heard that one before.

He tossed a piece of paper onto the kitchen table. It was a detailed pencil sketch of our house. Memories flashed as soon as I saw it. It was the same assignment I'd had when I first moved to Crownsville. I remembered it clearly.

My art teacher, Mrs. Shankles—Cankle Shankles—had

instructed us to draw our homes. I'd sat in the yard with my sketch pad. A few lines here, a few lines there. Porch. Windows. A couple of bushes, a couple trees. How easy was that?

But Cankles had been far from impressed. "You haven't tried, Mia," she'd said. "There's no detail. No *life*. I know you have more in you."

I don't think she ever realized how deeply I took those words.

I'd hid my grade from Pete, not that he'd been remotely interested. Then I'd taken my sketch pad back to the yard. I'd sat. I'd looked. I'd tried to *feel* the house and its land. Over the next two hours, I'd drawn it again. And Mrs. Shankles had been right; there was so much more to see. The wraparound porch sank to the right. The warped white siding had faded to gray. The green paint on the shutters was chipped. The walnut tree. The gravel driveway. I'd never noticed how much detail there was here. But from then on, I saw it. From then on, I stopped thinking about Grandma and Des Moines and started living in Crownsville.

I looked at Jay's drawing. He'd already noticed what had taken me so long to see.

"That's awesome, Jay," I said proudly, but tactfully. Jay wasn't big on fuss. "You should go to art camp this summer."

Jay was rifling through the snack drawer, completely unimpressed. "Art camp?" he blurted. "Too busy with baseball, Mia."

I laughed. Jay was a kid who knew exactly where he was going in life. I often wished I was more like him.

I waited at the kitchen table, the picture in my hand as Jay headed up to his room. There was a lot I didn't get about the world, but nothing shocked me more than what had happened to Jay. Jay's mom was my dad's second wife, and Jay had lived with them until Dad bailed again and the wife took revenge on him by dumping her four-year-old son with Pete! I mean, where do these people come from? At least Jay had our dad for a time, I guess. I wouldn't have known the guy if he'd hit me over the head with a mallet.

So, though Jay was my dad's kid and, therefore, not actually Pete's blood, Pete had taken him in too, and I'd gained the brother I'd always wanted. Don't get me wrong. Pete was pretty much useless. But he had saved Jay from a life without family, and he'd given me a family in the process.

I placed Jay's picture on the table, then headed for the shower to wash the scent of Mickey's fried chicken out of my hair. I'd barely settled in to study when the sound of Pete's truck brought me to my bedroom window.

Pete stood in the driveway, takeout bag in one hand, six-pack in the other. He looked out over the moonlit cornfields that bordered our land. His shoulders were back, his chin was up, and though I couldn't see his face, I knew his gaze swept those fields.

I frowned. It was so unlike Pete, who invariably stumbled when he arrived home this late. I quickly scanned the cornfield. There was nothing there. Yet Pete remained fixated on the horizon. I remembered the light and the shadow in front of Rowe.

"Maybe we're both cracking up," I said to myself. But I wondered if I wasn't the only one to have seen something strange that night.